His breath caught in his throat. She was beyond compare, from the silken ribbon of black hair that flew from her head in the unexpected evening breeze, to the rising arches of her naked, dusty feet.

Finally, he found his voice to ask her name.

*'Aapka kya naam hai?'*

She was suddenly timid, unsure of herself, and looked to the old woman fleetingly for instructions. All she received was a sharp nod. She turned back to James, all shyness.

'Chinthimani,' she said in her sweet voice, scented with the innocence of youth. *'Mera naam* Chinthimani *hai.'*

James flinched, the wind ripped from his stomach, his feet unwilling or unable to take him a step further. He opened his mouth again, as if to breathe her in, never taking his eyes from hers; then, like a thousand suns breaking through a monsoon cloud, her red-painted rosebud lips parted, and she smiled at him. James handed a pouch of money to the old woman without giving her another glance.

WITHDRAWN

KILKENNY COUNTY LIBRARY

KK443141

Born to an Indian mother and an English jazz musician father, Alison McQueen grew up in London. After a convent education, Alison worked in advertising for twenty years before retiring to write full time. Her family story is one of the inspirations behind *The Secret Children*. Alison lives in Northamptonshire with her husband and two daughters. To find out more visit her website at www.alisonmcqueen.com.

WITHDRAWN

# The Secret Children

## ALISON McQUEEN

An Orion paperback

First published in Great Britain in 2012
by Orion
This paperback edition published in 2012
by Orion Books Ltd,
Orion House, 5 Upper Saint Martin's Lane
London WC2H 9EA

An Hachette UK Company

1 3 5 7 9 10 8 6 4 2

Copyright © Alison McQueen 2012

The moral right of Alison McQueen to be identified as the author
of this work has been asserted by her in accordance with
the Copyright, Designs and Patents Act 1988.

All rights reserved. No part of this publication may be
reproduced, stored in a retrieval system, or transmitted
in any form or by any means, electronic, mechanical,
photocopying, recording, or otherwise, without the
prior permission of the copyright owner.

All the characters in this book are fictitious,
and any resemblance to actual persons, living
or dead, is purely coincidental.

A CIP catalogue record for this book
is available from the British Library.

ISBN 978-1-4091-3551-7

Typeset by Deltatype Ltd, Birkenhead, Merseyside

Printed and bound in Great Britain by
CPI Group (UK) Ltd, Croydon CR0 4YY

The Orion Publishing Group's policy is to use papers
that are natural, renewable and recyclable products and
made from wood grown in sustainable forests. The logging
and manufacturing processes are expected to conform to
the environmental regulations of the country of origin.

www.orionbooks.co.uk

# For Mary

*Tell me the stories about India. The names of all the places you have told me of so many times that I have forgotten. Tell me about being taken by bearers to see the circus, carried high above their heads with the way lit by lanterns. Tell me about the man who would come to the gates with his dancing bear. And the woman with her baskets of coloured glass bangles, and how they would always be broken, eventually. Tell me about your mother. Sad and silent with silver bells on her ankles, and how she used to cry. Tell me about the nights you would get into bed with your sister when the two of you were sent away, and how you would stay there during the holidays as the other children left for home, one by one. Tell me the stories that were told to you. The brothers who eat their sister after discovering the sweetness of her blood, the reeds that whisper her name, and the sadness of the song from those which are cut to play. Tell me the stories again. I promise I will remember.*

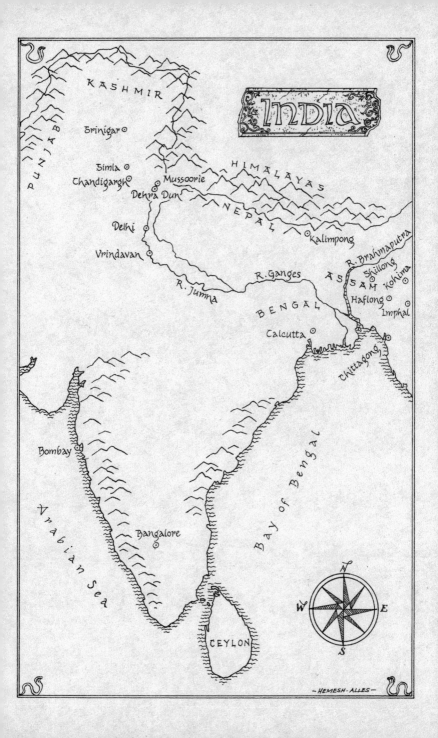

# Prologue

*Oxfordshire, England, 2006*

The cold, persistent drizzle of the early English summer seemed fitting for such a tiny cloud of mourners. Silently they stood, not even a half-dozen in their numbers, waiting for the remains of the day. Caitlin, sombre black coat drawn high around pale cheeks to shield swollen eyes, helped her ageing relative along the uneven path that wound its way between the gravestones set uniformly along this green hillside so far away from home. Slowly they walked, surveying the curtained silence of the recently dead, Caitlin's reluctant whisper hanging heavy on the damp air.

'I'm sorry about the phone call, Aunty. I should never have asked.'

'It's all right. You have nothing to apologise for. You can ask me anything you want to, although I am not sure whether I shall have the answers.'

Caitlin fell silent for a moment, then could no longer help herself. 'She never told us anything. Never spoke of her life. It was as though she never existed before Daddy came along.' Her head dropped. 'I had so many questions, so many things I wanted to know. Ever since Daddy died, all she did was cry all the time and blame everyone around her. There was no comforting her, no matter how I tried. Then she got sick. And now it's too late.'

The old woman halted and looked Caitlin directly in the eye. 'You have to understand how difficult it was for her.'

Although her sight was failing her, there was not a single moment of almost four score years that Mary did not remember with perfect clarity; even those parts she might have wished to forget. Carefully she regarded Caitlin, almost middle-aged now, bereft in her loss. She wished that she could ease her niece's suffering. It was a child's right to know their heritage. Yet there was nothing to be done.

'You mustn't be cross with her.' Mary forced a tender smile. 'Try to think of your mother kindly. For her, it was the only way.'

'I don't understand.' Caitlin shook her head.

'We can only do the best we can,' her aunt said softly. 'And life is not always easy.'

Caitlin sensed that she had said enough. With a resigned squeeze of her hand, they continued slowly along the wet path, a carpet of smooth pebbles shining beneath their feet, finally coming to rest beside the few floral offerings laid out beneath a small plaque carrying the name *Serafina Carlisle*. They paused to look at the wind-chilled blooms, delicate and vulnerable heads nodding rhythmically against the spattering raindrops.

Caitlin bent down to read aloud one of the tribute cards, a bland sentence from some distant friend of her father whose name she had not heard for many years, but the words caught in her throat and were lost to the biting wind. She cried small tears that fell freely like pearls, accepting frail comfort from her only aunt. Mary took Caitlin's arm and led her gently towards the lone bench set into the path beside an ancient yew, a single low bough spreading its shelter above them. Ignoring the small pools of water gathered on the drenched slats, she bade her niece to sit before taking the place beside her. With tiny brown hands flecked with the hallmarks of old age, she took a handkerchief from her handbag, and remembered a promise she had made a long time ago.

*Not for as long as we both shall live.*

*Part One*

# ASSAM
# 1925

The colours that fall across the landscape of this remote north-eastern corner of India are hewn from a different light. Go there and you will see. The eternal blue of the verdant hills sweeps up to meet mountains afloat on a sea of clouds, skimming the edges of the deep valley clefts, their gorges thick with wild green jungle.

The early mists linger across the highest peaks, where, for a while, it is impossible to tell where the land ends and the sky begins. An eerie silence settles in with the heavy moistness that hangs on the air, dampening the skin, raising the hairs on the arms. The sun is slow to rise and cast its unhurried warmth upon the ground, sweeping away the fragile dew, revealing the colourful saris that pick their way along the high terraces, filling the baskets slung behind their heads with the leaves once prized for their healing properties, now cultivated for the silver-lined caddies of the white man.

As far as the eye can see, emerald tea gardens cling to the hillsides, mile upon mile of undulating curves, hugging the steep slopes like moss on an aged stone, paths zigzagging through the low-slung shrubs, cushioning the landscape in miniature green clouds, arid silver trunks reaching gnarled tentacles down into the hardened ground. Perhaps, had it not been for the indigenous *Camellia sinensis assamica* discovered growing in its hidden hills a century before, the British might have left it well alone, this unforgiving, ungovernable place of ancient dynasties and tribal feuds where rulers come and go. There is no place like it on God's earth.

Some took these distant lands to their hearts and made them their own, their families becoming inextricably entwined with the jewel in their king's crown. This is the way it had been for James Macdonald, son of the most eminent surgeon in India's Doon valley, born of these lands, thousands of miles from the Scottish shores that had spawned his father. A tall, thickset man with jet-black hair slicked into daily submission with a curt application of brilliantine, James Macdonald was among the first generation of Britishers delivered on India's burning soil. Every shred of his fabric had invisibly absorbed the intricacies of the British stronghold coiled around India's throat. Raised as a son of the Empire, justly moulded to take up his mantle as colonial overlord, his tongue moved easily between the language of the kings and the song of the natives. His skin, where exposed, had been baked by the sun into a permanent olive hue, deepening his robust features, lending his heavy brow a guarded impression of intensity. There was never any question that he would stay, and never any sense that he belonged either here or anywhere else. Any number of men would have given their eye teeth for such a birthright, to be able to stake their claim and rule their own fate with only the barest minimum of interference. For James, it was just the way things were, his prescribed destiny.

The remote solitude of the plantation pleased James well enough, his temperament neither fire nor water, his predisposition towards introversion perfectly matched to the harmonious ebb and flow of the passing seasons, his sense of detachment somehow less ill-suited to this secluded region far from the bustle of the overrun conurbations. It had been a relief to loosen the ties to his family's influence and to shift

8

eastwards, away from the tiresome expectations, away from the dull, predictable introductions to the well-bred young women who came to the dances at the clubhouses, dispatched to the colonies like brood mares to provide wifely stock for those men who had not the time nor the inclination to return to England in search of a suitable match.

That James's family had wished him to take a wife before he broke away from the fold could not have been made more plain, but his heart had not been in it, his mind cast firmly on the plans and ambitions of every young man who had yet to make his mark, to find his own place in the grand order of things, to savour the freedoms for which every son yearns before being enveloped by the burden of anticipation bestowed upon him by hopeful parents.

James had had no need of a wife, his vitality in no rush to see itself extinguished by an early marriage to a wide-eyed English girl who would serve only to remind him of the rigidities of his upbringing before producing a litter of children, the new generation under whom India would serve. Still two years from his thirtieth birthday, he entertained that he had plenty of time to consider his future. Yet the gradual insistence of his stirring loneliness drew sighs from the emptiness when he least expected it, riding out to survey the high terraces, inspecting the yields, overseeing the tree clearance for the planned expansion to the south, his thoughts all the while nudging him inexorably towards the deep cravings that plagued his every hour.

There were places a man could go to when his yearnings became too much. Remote shacks where women waited with painted faces and beckoning smiles. James had availed himself of such pleasures before, certainly, but he had been younger and more foolish then, and had quickly found that there was no companionship to be had in the brief embrace of a sacrificial lamb.

That a man must have a woman is as basic as his need for water or air, and there were no laws in this lonely province to rub against nature's grain. Here was a place where a man could satisfy his every desire without question or consequence.

Of those precious commodities that the white man came to steal away, among the tea, the oil, the rich seams of coal and the rubies that lay hidden deep within the dry red earth, were other prizes, far away from the prying eyes of convention, of which few spoke except in hushed whispers. It would be an honour for any woman to be so chosen, to be permitted to serve her purpose unto one man and one man only. She must be grateful, for she had been born female, to live a hapless, passive life, and would never amount to anything until she became a man's possession.

The arrangement had been made at his own request, when the long nights began to stretch too far ahead, that a girl be found to satisfy his restlessness, that she be clean and pure, fair of face, and untroublesome of nature.

He was not the first to have done so, and, most certainly, he would not be the last.

'Perhaps Sahib should take an orphan girl,' advised the old, bone-dry widow who lived on the outskirts of the ramshackle village nearby, spinning marriages for anyone who could afford her services, acting as an unofficial go-between for those who did not have the required connections. Her age and position excused her from the usual proprieties that prevented open talk from a woman on such matters.

The old woman eyed the man sitting in front of her, cross-legged on the floor, the small stone slab between them providing a low table on which their cups were set. Of course, she realised exactly who he was. She knew everything that happened here, and the whereabouts of every man not yet married.

She watched the steam rise from his tea, curling in front of her intriguing new customer's face, and smiled a shrewd smile.

'For an orphan girl will be most honoured by your master's attentions and is bound to show her gratitude, and there can be no complications from her family if she has none. Yes,' she nodded in firm agreement with herself, 'I think this would be a good match indeed. Just leave it to me.'

Shiva was not to be fooled and sat calmly, his slender face set with the same expressionless pose he had seen his master adopt when dealing with an adversary. For the past three years and two months, Shiva had attended to James's every daily need, from his morning tea to the turning-down of his bed at night. The Sahib had arrived from the new plantations in the north-west, bringing no wife with him. It was only natural that he should wish for companionship, and Shiva was determined to serve his master well. Shiva was comfortably settled, white cotton lungi tucked beneath him. This was a delicate transaction that would require great patience, and he had arrived at the matchmaker's decrepit house well prepared for the long, tedious negotiations that would be an inevitable part of the deal. He had not liked the woman from the first moment he stepped over the threshold into her grubby home. She was ugly, both of face and of manner, and her house carried the foul smell of must and stale bread. He looked around at the crumbling walls, bare bricks of red earth baked into hard loaves by the sun. His voice, steady and melodious, betrayed nothing of his sentiments.

'And see my master fobbed off with a filthy street urchin you picked up from the gutter for nothing? Would a wise man buy a cow without knowing the stock from which it had come, only to watch it die of disease and then wonder why?' Shiva set his pale hazel eyes upon her. 'You must think me no better than an idiot. Perhaps we should not do business today. I had

KK443141

heard that you were a reliable matchmaker. Now I see that you are just a sly old crone looking to take advantage of a man you must consider a fool.'

'Of course not.' She bowed to him. 'I merely raise the suggestion so that your master may consider all the options. This is not an easy matter. It will take great skill to find the right girl. Then, of course, there will be the delicate issue of dealing with the family. They will expect to be properly compensated, and not everyone is in such a hurry to rid themselves of their daughters, you know.' She took a noisy gulp from her tea and allowed him a little time to properly absorb the difficulties facing her. Shiva took no notice, knowing very well that this was just another one of her tricks to raise her price. 'If your master can afford to be so choosy, then of course he will have to pay a little more. You are an educated man.' He ignored the smile that crept across her face, her words lying somewhere between a compliment and a slight. 'You must know that there are stories that travel among the people far out into the fields and villages. Even the poorest family may think twice before sending their daughter into the clutches of a white planter.'

'I doubt that very much,' said Shiva curtly, sniffing his disdain as the murky aroma of filth reached his nostrils again.

'Then you do not know?' The old woman's eyes sparkled. 'They are frightened to death of them! I will have to use all my powers of persuasion to tempt the girl away from the simple life that she knows.' She drew a protracted breath and shook her head with amusement. 'Ah, perhaps you are right. We should not do business today. I think that this will be far more effort to me than it is worth. I should not be worrying about such things at my age.' She dropped her eyes from Shiva, as though having lost interest. 'I will stick to my usual village customers, and you may take my compliments and apologies to your master.'

Shiva did not move from his place, refusing to rise to her

mischief, knowing that it was merely a matter of money.

'The Sahib is a good man,' he reminded her, although he knew very well that this would be of no concern to her at all. 'The girl will be well looked after and she will have nothing to fear from him. You will find a suitable choice, but not from the hill tribes. That will only cause trouble.' The old woman nodded in small agreement. 'And she must have a fine nose, not a great hook like a fish eagle, and her eyes must not be too slanted.' Shiva imagined that he knew the Sahib well enough to gauge his preferences in matters of beauty. He had seen, on rare occasion, the type of face or figure that might catch his master's attentions for a few fleeting moments. The Sahib did not even glance at any woman who held a hint of Tibetan appearance. Nor did he care for those with overly large features, or the field workers with their ripe hips and rough hands. 'And my master will have to see and approve her before the transaction is completed.'

'What? You ask too much!' The old widow yanked the short woollen shawl around her shoulders in irritation. 'Am I expected to search miles of jungle for this wretch, bargain with her family, feed her, clean her and bring her all the way back for nothing? And what am I to do with her if your master says no?'

'Of course, you will have expenses.' Shiva placed a cloth pouch tied with a reed on the table between them. She took it, peered inside, raised her eyebrows momentarily and settled with a small gesture of her hand. 'But choose carefully, old woman. You are dealing with a man who will not accept anything less than perfection, so you can forget your usual notions of a quick sale and an easy meal. Be very particular, and you will be well rewarded.' Shiva left the tea untouched. 'And one final condition. This is a private transaction. Is that understood? You are not to go gossiping with the village hags, and no one is to see her. This is nobody else's business.'

The old woman smiled slightly, hiding her few teeth behind a wrinkled hand, and slid the pouch into the front of her *choli*. 'I think we understand one another very well,' she said.

Shiva bade the old woman goodbye and felt grateful for the fresh air outside.

The old woman rose from her seat, her movements surprisingly nimble, and watched Shiva through the crack in the wooden door, waiting until he had disappeared along the rough track that cut through the thicket of trees before sliding into the shadows and taking the purse from her breast. She tipped its contents into her hand and smiled to herself, spreading the money over her palms. Returning one third of the coins to the pouch, she took the rest and buried them deep in the hard ground in the corner of her hovel, stabbing at the dirt with a kukri and covering the freshly dug grave with a grimy cooking pot. She would have no need for it now that she had enough money to buy her fill from the street traders for a very long time, and she congratulated herself for striking such a good bargain. Men were fools and made easy prey in matters of love. Had she been bargaining with a woman in need of a wife for her son, she would have been lucky to receive a tenth of the price. The old woman rewarded herself with a self-satisfied yawn, tucked the pouch back into her *choli* and settled herself on the floor to rest through the heat of the afternoon. After all, there was no need for her to rush. She already knew where the girl was to be found.

## 2

A handful of languid blue days passed before the old woman chose to make the journey to the homestead of her cousin – a rough shack set precariously on the ridge between the paddy fields his family tended some miles to the east. She rented a pair of donkeys, and one youth to tend them, from the donkey-keeper in the village, and set out shortly after sunrise to arrive in good time before the light seeped from the day.

The communities around the paddy fields were not like those of the other villages, the houses spread far and wide, perched here and there on the rises of earth that delineated the flooded fields. She was greeted with suspicious courtesy by her poor cousin, until she handed him two shining coins, a large bag containing dried red lentils, and a small parcel filled with fresh spices, the cotton stained turmeric-yellow on one torn corner.

'You need not worry yourself that I have come to ask for your charity,' the old woman said, accepting a small bowl of rice with a thin spoonful of yesterday's dhal from her cousin's wife. 'I am here to pay my respects to you and to see your thriving sons. You can see that I am getting old now, so I must pay my visits while I still can.' She smiled reassuringly and made much fuss of her cousin's wife, the poor woman's pinched face weary from the effort of daily life and much older than her years.

'I have never seen two finer young men! How proud you

must be, knowing that they will bring you such happiness and good fortune. You must tell me when they are ready to take wives and I will choose for you the finest girls in all Assam. But before then,' she came to her point, turning her eyes to her cousin, 'I want you to take me back to the family you presented to me last time I visited.'

Four winters had passed since the old woman had come to her cousin's district in search of a wife for the son of a woman in the village whose husband lay dying. The dying man's wife had a second son too, but he was thought to be an idiot, and the whole family had been tainted by reputation. Without at least one daughter-in-law in her household, the woman might find herself cast out into the street the moment her husband stopped breathing. The old woman had accepted the commission easily and had made her way to her cousin's house, knowing that for a few annas her cousin would be only too happy to do the work she was disinclined to undertake, paying visits to the scattered homesteads and bringing her detailed information about the occupants of each one, while she sat at his house being fed and waited upon by his scrawny wife. When he returned one afternoon and reported to her news of one family, saying that they would be certain to offer any of their daughters, she had thought that her job was as good as done. After walking for almost two miles the following morning, the old woman quickly discovered that the family's daughters were far too young to be of any earthly use in her customer's household and berated her cousin for wasting her time. Yet there was one child among them, a slight girl who had stared at her with black eyes from an unlit corner, burning an indelible image on to the old woman's memory. She had never seen such beauty.

With the purpose of her visit declared, the old woman demanded that they make the short journey before her cousin's wife had lit their supper fire.

'Let us leave now,' she said.

'But we have not yet eaten!' complained her cousin.

'And nor has anyone else,' she replied. 'We are bound to find the family together at this time of day, and manners dictate that they will have to invite us to sit with them when they know the trouble we have gone to and see that we are hungry.'

'We cannot go uninvited and take a poor family's food!'

'Nonsense,' said the old woman. 'In a few hours, they will have more than enough money to fill their larder, and one less mouth to feed.'

The old woman insisted that her cousin lead the way as she rode on one of the two donkeys to save her aching limbs and display her wealth and authority. The second donkey followed behind on a short tether, flanked by the youth, who hung his head and grumbled about his hunger.

'Sing!' the old woman commanded him, but he looked up at her and felt self-conscious. 'Surely you must know a song? Or have your parents taught you nothing? I want everyone nearby to know we are coming, so raise your voice and sing, unless you would rather have them hear the sound of your yelps?' She raised her stick towards him. The boy opened his mouth and began to sing the only song that he knew, learned from the donkey-keeper, even though he didn't really understand it.

Upon seeing their distant approach, the mother of the family recognised the far-off silhouette of the old marriage-maker. She leaped up from her supper fire and began to shout at her husband, for there was no other house nearby and the travellers could not have been on their way anywhere else. The husband shouted back at his wife crossly, telling her to prepare more bread and to summon her daughters.

The youth was given a piece of *roti* to stave off his hunger and told to tend the donkeys and wait. Just as she had predicted, the old woman was welcomed with every courtesy and begged by the mother to share the family's meagre supper. They sat together cross-legged on the swept patch of ground to the front of the tiny dwelling, set before the flooded paddy where the family had spent another long day thinning out the infant shoots and moving them to the half-empty nursery in the neighbouring waterlogged field. The far corner was flecked with the pale blue flowers of the hyacinths they had yet to clear, the yellow sun throwing bright diamond patterns that danced across the patches of water between them.

'Do forgive me.' The old woman pretended to admire the view. 'My eyes are not what they used to be, so I must take in this wonderful sight and ask it to last me a very long while.'

'Please, take your time,' urged the mother, pressing upon her another piece of dry bread. 'We are honoured that you have come to visit us again.'

'I have come to pay a great compliment to one of your daughters,' smiled the old woman. The mother glanced towards her husband, who immediately shouted towards the open doorway of their hut. Juvenile voices escaped from the hidden room before a girl appeared, moving mawkishly towards them, freshly washed hair hanging in damp strands that clung to her bare arms.

'Stand up properly,' her father said firmly, nodding his approval. 'She is strong.' He took her by the arm, showing her to the old woman. 'And a good worker.'

'Yes.' The old woman pressed her palms together and bowed her respects to the girl, then passed on her immediately due to her pockmarked skin and bad teeth. 'She is a fine young woman, but it is not this one that I have come to honour. Where is your second daughter?'

The girl rushed back inside, flushed with shame, and began shouting at her laughing siblings, berating her next sister for refusing to stand in the paddy fields all day long with the rest of them, pointing to her untarnished feet in damning evidence, complaining about the cracked and swollen state of her own. The father leaped up from his place and went after her, threatening to beat his daughters into silence. The old woman was unsurprised. She had already seen the marks of jealousy in the elder sister the first time she visited. The father reappeared in a moment, pushing his second daughter out into the light, where she squinted through the sudden glare of the low sun slicing through the trees before settling her black eyes on the strangers, refusing to smile. The old woman heard her cousin take a sharp inward breath and stole a glance towards him. His face had reddened in an instant. She smiled to herself and knew that her memory of the girl had not been mistaken.

Negotiations were opened with the merest nod of the old woman's head, and a deliberate glimpse of the pouch she adjusted at her waist.

'Who would want to take a bride with no dowry?' demanded the mother, suddenly suspicious.

'What do you care?' said the father. 'Besides, our guest is not a stranger. She is the cousin of one of our neighbours and has made many successful marriages in the village where she lives.'

'And what is the name of the man she will marry?' the mother asked.

'Ah,' said the old woman. 'That I cannot tell you just yet, for his family wish to keep the arrangement secret until the very last moment and I have been asked to remain silent on that matter. All I can tell you is that the family is very well-to-do. They have been in search of a suitable wife for quite some time, but he has insisted that he wishes to marry a simple girl from your district, much to the delight of his mother.' The old woman smiled sweetly. 'Let your daughter come with me now, and you will soon receive the glad news of her marriage.'

Despite the girl's sullen manner, the father agreed to part with her without any further detail and did so quickly and cheaply, happy to be free at last of at least one of his dishonourable burdens. The mother was not so sure, and whispered protests and questions, only to be hushed crossly by her impatient husband.

'Go and prepare your daughter's belongings,' he said to her. 'And tell your other daughters to be quiet. I am tired of their arguing voices.'

The elder girl could be heard wailing, complaining crossly that her sister was disobedient and shamed her parents with her idleness and did nothing but daydream all day and watch her own reflection crouched by the water's edge. The old woman acted as if she was a little deaf and could not hear. It was a pity that the others were ugly. Any poor family cursed with four daughters and not a single son would be only too willing to lighten their load, and she might have been tempted to bear them in mind for future customers had they been less so. The father implored her to take another of them, but the old woman lost interest the moment she had secured her prize, and made ready to leave.

'You keep your other daughters here,' she said in a kindly voice, pleased as she was with herself. 'Perhaps I will return one day and do you another great service.'

The girl came without protest, her mother having quickly scratched around to bundle together what little she could offer – two threadbare saris, one blue, one yellow, and a small, old hair comb made from sandalwood that had long since lost its essence. The old woman allowed the girl to ride on the second donkey, and remarked that she had been smiled upon by the gods that day.

'I will pierce your nose when we return to my village,' she

said. 'Then we shall see about adding some decoration to that pretty face of yours.' The girl did not reply. 'Just because you are poor doesn't mean you have to look like a beggar. I expect I could make you look quite the maharani if I had half a mind to. A man will trade a great deal for beauty, and you shall be my fortune.' The girl remained stony-faced. 'And why do you look so miserable, you ungrateful wretch? You are soon to enter the household of a very rich man. A white man.'

The donkey took fright beneath the sudden jolting grip of the girl, braying and throwing her from her seat.

'Catch it!' the old woman shouted at the boy. The animal reared away as he grasped hold of its loose tether, the boy digging his heels into the earth, gritting his teeth as the rope burned at his hands. The girl pulled herself to her feet, her eyes searching for an escape made impossible by the breath knocked from her body.

'Do not run,' the old woman said, her voice all at once both gentle and commanding. 'You have been chosen to live a charmed life of great riches and comfort that you cannot possibly imagine, being of such low birth. Your sisters can only dream of being as fortunate as you. Your parents would weep with happiness if they knew what blessings await you.' The girl stood, catching her breath in shallow gulps. 'But I see that I may have made a mistake. Perhaps you are not suitable after all. Perhaps you are too backwards to have servants of your own and to spend your days at leisure, preserving your beauty for a man of great status and importance while all around you there are people ready to do your every bidding.' She eyed the girl's threadbare sari, the slender beginnings of womanhood beneath it. 'Anyone can see that you are ready to accept a man. Indeed, to possess him if you knew how, looking the way you do. So what would you rather? To return to your parents' hovel and wait until they pass you into the hands of a rough peasant who will work you like a dog and breed you till you look like your poor worn-out mother? Or are you clever enough to accept this great gift of fate with a smile?'

The youth managed to calm the donkey and brought it to the old woman. The girl looked at it unsurely. 'Go home if you want to,' the old woman said sternly. 'Let your father return my money, and you can rejoin your sisters. I am sure they will be very happy to have you back.' Her cold smile told otherwise.

Although shaken, the girl knew this to be the truth of it, reluctantly accepting the youth's helping hand to resume her mount.

'You have made a wise choice,' said the old woman as they continued on their way. 'All that you have known before will cease to exist. Your childhood is over now. You will have no more of that life. Do you understand?' The girl nodded obediently. 'But you will have to throw off that veil of innocence and wipe that sullen scowl from your mouth. You must learn how to be charming, how to master the art of love and enrapture the man you have been chosen to serve.'

'When will we be married?' Her small voice, artlessly sweet, pleased the old woman, being as fair as her face.

'You will be taken to him when I deem you ready. The ceremony will already have been conducted. White people do not marry in the same way as we do. The bride does not need to be present, and you must not question any of these differences, as they are none of your business.'

The girl frowned her confusion.

'I will not have a wedding?'

'Such ignorance!' the old woman laughed. 'Forget the things you have been taught! Everybody knows that the Britishers have their own strange ways. You will soon get used to them.'

'Is he a kind man?'

'Of course.' The old woman neither knew nor cared.

That the girl would now come willingly was her only concern.

Sixteen days later, on a cool summer evening under a rose-pink sky, the old woman made her way to the gates of the private estate road leading up to the big white house with draping green gables and wide verandas overlooking the sprawling tea gardens. She had seen the house many times before, but only from a great distance. This was a rich man's house, and she had been promised a generous pay-off. The old woman smiled behind her veil. She could easily have fulfilled her task within a week, but had chosen to take her time so that her efforts would appear all the more taxing and therefore worthy of greater reward. She made herself known to the gatekeeper and took great pleasure in the way he stared at the girl standing nervously beside her.

'There is a visitor to see you, Sahib.' Shiva bowed respectfully, interrupting James's evening routine, sitting out in the cool, relaxing with his sundowner, reading the week-old newspaper. Shiva remained at a respectable distance and spoke without glancing up from the teakwood floor, not wishing to catch his master's eye. 'An old woman from the village has a relative she wishes to introduce you to, Sahib. She is in need of somewhere to settle and the old woman wondered if you could take her in.'

After the briefest moment of confusion, James suddenly realised exactly what Shiva meant, but knew it would have been discourteous for his servant to voice it in any other way. His pulse quickened, a sudden hollowness opening up in his chest, his servant's averted gaze telling nothing more.

He tried to recall the exact detail of the brief instructions he had issued to Shiva while bolstered by three glasses of whisky, speaking as if he were ordering a yearling to bring on and break just for the sport of it as he had done last spring. He had subsequently put the conversation out of his mind, wiping it from his conscience, satisfied that he was doing no more and no less than was expected of a man in his position.

'I see,' he said, the pit in his stomach beginning to cast a pall of doubt. He could always change his mind if he did not find her attractive, say that his servant had misunderstood him entirely and send the girl away with a few coins by way of compensation. 'And where is she?'

'They have been sent to wait at the summer house on the viewing point, Sahib.'

'Good.' James rose from his seat, found that he was still clutching his newspaper and dropped it to his empty chair. 'I will go and greet them myself.' Shiva kept his eyes downcast, sparing his master the sight of the embarrassment flushing to his face. 'Is everything ready should she wish to stay?'

'Yes, Sahib.'

'I see.' James paused by the low table, his heavy brow suddenly clouded. 'You had better come and meet us at the viewing point with a bullock cart. It is too far to walk at this time of day, and I expect she will be tired.'

'Yes, Sahib.'

The summer house, a small, open-fronted wooden affair, painted cornflower blue, with seating enough for perhaps six familiar people, lay a short walk from the house, set well behind it where the hill began to rise and the valley fall, taking in the best of the views to the east where the moon first showed itself each night. The old woman sat, leaning forward on her stick, milky eyes squinting towards the pathway that led to the grand house, now fading with the disappearing light. Her bones were complaining, having been jarred by the donkey ride from the village and tested even further by the steep walk to bring her here. She saw a shape approach; the hazy khaki image soon cleared sufficiently to tell her that the planter had come himself – a tall, dark-haired man with broad shoulders and a purposeful stride, gathering pace as he moved towards them. She lifted her stick and prodded the girl sharply to stand up straight and mind herself, telling her that she would be sent back to the fields and her parents made to give back the money if he didn't like what he saw, warning her of the beatings she would receive.

The old woman watched James carefully, eyes shielded behind the thin fabric of her black veil. She would be able to tell in a moment whether or not her merchandise was acceptable. There was no uncertainty about the girl's chastity. The old woman had checked that for herself. Yet although she was undoubtedly beautiful, the old woman feared that she might prove too highly spirited to make a suitable concubine. There was something about the way she held her head and stared without fear, just as boys did. The old woman put it down to her isolated upbringing and ignorant parenting. The girl would just have to learn to take her place and forget her insolent pride.

James slowed as he reached the pair of them, hardly glancing at the old hag as he began to fully take in the shock of the girl who stood before him. He had not expected her to be so young, juvenile in her awkwardness, yet with the unmistakable promise of the woman within, the soft outline of her breasts pressing through the thin fabric of her cotton *choli*. Her unsmiling eyes, black as the midnight sky, seemed to gaze right through him.

His breath caught in his throat. She was beyond compare, from the silken ribbon of black hair that flew from her head in the unexpected evening breeze, to the rising arches of her naked, dusty feet.

Finally, he found his voice to ask her name.

'*Aapka kya naam hai?*'

She was suddenly timid, unsure of herself, and looked to the old woman fleetingly for instructions. All she received was a sharp nod. She turned back to James, all shyness.

'Chinthimani,' she said in her sweet voice, scented with the innocence of youth. '*Mera naam* Chinthimani *hai.*'

James flinched, the wind ripped from his stomach, his feet unwilling or unable to take him a step further. He opened his mouth again, as if to breathe her in, never taking his eyes from hers; then, like a thousand suns breaking through a monsoon cloud, her red-painted rosebud lips parted, and she smiled at him. James handed a pouch of money to the old woman without giving her another glance.

Despite Shiva's warnings, such was the sight of the girl that word had spread quickly. There were already those in the village who said that she would bewitch him, that she had been found in the hills and that no one knew where she came from. That perhaps she was not human at all, but a daughter of one of the gods, sent to do their bidding. They said that she was a vision, and that she would be his downfall.

## 3

On a generous plot sitting just past the western estate road at the edge of the plantation, beyond the reach of the diminutive tea trees and the fleeting hands that attended them, stood a little enclave of simple whitewashed buildings, set about a dusty courtyard nestling within high, whispering trees. Beyond the trees lay the homestead's lands. Paddy fields stretching all the way down to the river, where water buffaloes wandered unhindered, white paddy birds riding gracefully on their backs.

Shurika was happy to be here, having roamed for many weeks through the previous season's monsoon with her younger brother after their father had died from the fever and left them without a roof over their heads or a grain of rice, as she always knew he would. Theirs had been a small family, her father being a rare only child, averse to the notion of hard work, with parents long perished. He indulged his preference for idleness and big talk, charming his wife with flowers picked from the forest, keeping her awake long into the night with his affections. The illness had come upon him all at once, his faculties waning by the end of the first day, before the dreadful convulsions wrenched at his body as he slipped into a terrible sleep that finally stopped his heart. At the moment of his passing, Shurika's mother had clawed at her clothes and ripped her hair out by the roots, screaming her curses at the gods. His remains were taken to the village funeral pyre to be cleansed by the eternal flames. Broken and defeated by the loss of her beloved husband, Shurika's mother had stood bereft as he burned, spent in her grief, weeping at the sight of her destitute children, bending as though her every bone had been removed.

This was the last memory that Shurika chose to carry of her mother, a kind and gentle woman who had sung and smiled and shared ancient stories of love and wisdom with her, who had wanted nothing from her life other than to serve the ones she loved. This was how Shurika would remember her mother, not the wailing woman who had thrown herself upon the licking flames of her husband's engulfed body, nor the terrible screams that had torn the sky in two until, finally, the fire silenced her.

In the ramshackle house that she and her brother had returned to, there was not even a piece of stale bread for them to eat. Shurika had searched in vain for some small mercy, a few hidden coins, a bag of rice, but had come to find nothing other than a handful of worn clothes and a string of empty promises left to the many people from whom her father had borrowed. There was little charity to be had from their neighbours either. In her sixteenth year, Shurika should have been married off long ago, having been vaguely promised in her infancy to an eleven-year-old boy whose mother had subsequently changed her mind when it became apparent that there would be no dowry, no matter how long they waited. Shurika's father did little to remedy the absence of a match for his daughter. She was a good worker in a home of idle hands, and there was always something to be done.

The man who came for the goat before the ashes of her parents had cooled and blown to the wind told Shurika that he would take her and her brother in, out of the goodness of his heart. At his request, she had followed him inside to show him the exact spot where her father had ailed and died. He had then smothered her mouth with his hand and told her to keep still while he did what he had come to do.

Blinded by the sudden, searing pain, Shurika had sunk her teeth deep into the man's fleshy fingers, biting down until she tasted his blood, but still he would not let her go. The air around her became thick with the sickly-sweet scent of her fear, and she had felt her own living death come upon her.

When night fell and all became quiet, Shurika had washed her weeping, bloodied body, searching for the courage to do as her mother had done. She prayed to the gods all night that they might give her the strength to put an end to her life, but they had forsaken her, whispering that she must now take care of her mother's precious son. At first light, she had gathered together what few scraps they had, woken her brother, and told him that they must leave that place and make a new life for themselves elsewhere. He had complained bitterly, yet had followed her as she slipped away in the half-light.

Shunned in the remote villages, they had wandered for many miles on their way to their new life, the brother unwilling to work, Shurika reduced to begging for bread and gleaning what food she could from the land. She had once been caught trying to steal eggs and had been beaten black and blue while her brother concealed himself in the trees and watched on, then berated her for making too much noise and failing to bring the eggs. How she had mourned, feeling the guilt of her mother's shame as, with hands outstretched to strangers, she was looked down upon like a stray dog. This would be her punishment for having lacked the fortitude to drive the knife home and be reunited with her mother's spirit, no matter how briefly, before their rebirth. This would be her curse – that she would wander the earth, a spoiled woman, with each new day a terrible trial.

Shurika had come across the estate quite by accident, just when she thought her weary legs would not be able to take one more step. It was she who had insisted they go up to the house and ask for work, but her brother had shrunk from her suggestion, having never lifted a finger in his idle life, so Shurika had left him by the gates and gone by herself, driven by hunger and desperation. She found the cookhouse easily, the aroma of frying spices having beckoned her for hundreds of yards, and threw herself to the ground outside the door, begging the mercy of the cook, explaining that she and her brother had no food and nowhere to go. The cook was a jovial man with a sympathetic heart. He gave her a bowl of boiled rice and vegetables and told her to sit in the shade of the peepul tree and wait.

Shurika sat for hours, watching the sun arc steadily across the afternoon sky, worrying about her brother and wondering how long he would wait before coming in search of her, or whether he would simply take off on his own and abandon her to her fate, as he had threatened to do every day. Their one remaining piece of bread was in his bundle, so he would not starve, and she had been sure to leave him near the silver stream that she had noticed on the way, so that he might have fresh water fallen from the mountains if he became thirsty. Her own thirst she quenched with a few handfuls of bitter water from the small trough meant for the kitchen animals.

Towards the end of the afternoon, the cook emerged from his kitchen to wash the sweat from his face and torso in the water trough, and told Shurika to go fetch her brother. She ran the whole distance and found him sleeping in the long grass, his arms raised lazily to guard his head from the sun. She shook him awake. He sat up and rubbed the sleep from his eyes.

'Where have you been for all this time? Did you find food?' he asked.

'No!' she said with an elated smile. 'But perhaps I have found something better. Come, quickly.' She pulled at him. 'I think they have work for us.'

'What sort of work?' the brother said.

'I don't know. What does it matter?'

'I'm not going to work in the tea fields,' he snorted. 'That's women's work.'

'Then I will do the work,' Shurika said. 'Now get up and hurry, before they change their minds.'

The pair of them returned to the cookhouse, from where they were taken on a bullock cart to a small enclave of buildings on the edge of the plantation. The gates were hanging loosely, broken on both hinges, and the courtyard around which the buildings sat lay unkempt and overgrown. Shiva eyed the sullen youth as he jumped down from the cart and chose to address the young woman instead.

'There is plenty of work here and a home for you if you want it,' he told her. 'The Sahib wants this place to be cleaned up and made ready for habitation again. If you do a good job, you may stay and continue to work for the new mistress who will come to live here soon. You will have to clear the plot over there and make a new vegetable garden, repair the buildings and put up fences for the animals. There are paddy fields beyond those trees that have gone to rack and ruin. Have you worked paddies before?'

'No, sir.' Shurika glanced towards her brother pleadingly, in the hope that he would speak up and claim to be a good worker, but he just stood there and said nothing.

'It doesn't matter,' Shiva said. 'I can send someone to show you. It's easy enough. The irrigation gates are already there somewhere. Just overgrown like the rest of the place.' He looked around the ramshackle homestead and sighed at its state of disrepair. Perhaps it was not as bad as it looked. 'The Sahib has hundreds of workers. If there is anything you need to make the repairs, go to the gatehouse and tell the gatekeeper to send a message. You can go to the cookhouse and ask for some basic provisions.' Shiva noticed that the brother had no intention of walking back the way they had come. He had sat down on the ground instead, picking at the loose stones. 'I would hurry.' Shiva looked up at the sky. 'It will be getting dark soon.'

Shurika was unable to hide her joy. She sank to her knees, pressing her face into her skeletal hands, and wept with gratitude, promising that she and her brother would work their every waking hour.

Since that first day, Shurika had offered *puja* to the gods, morning and night, for safely guiding her and her brother here. Before beginning the work that had been asked of them, she built a small shrine at the edge of the trees and laid gifts of food and flowers at sunrise and sunset.

The work progressed slowly, for her brother was lazy and had to be nagged and cajoled constantly. When he did attend to a job, he would do it badly and the repair would quickly fall apart. Shiva visited every week, to check on their progress, but never on the same day. Whenever he arrived, he would find Shurika hard at work and the brother either sleeping in the shade of the silver oaks or nowhere to be found. Shurika made excuses for him, saying that he was sick that day, or that he had gone to fetch reeds from the river bank to make a new roof. Shiva made a point of visiting two days in a row and, upon finding Shurika gone and the brother sleeping, he gently kicked him awake.

'Where is your sister?' he asked as the youth scrambled reluctantly to his feet.

'She has gone to find dung to dry out for the fire. Why do you want her?'

'I don't,' Shiva replied. 'I have come to tell you to pack your things and be gone by sundown.'

'What?' cried the brother. 'You said we could stay for as long as we wanted the work!'

'Ah yes,' said Shiva. 'But you do not want the work, so you will have to go. Your sister is a good worker, so she can stay, but you are a good-for-nothing layabout, so you must be on your way. Remember that there are many hundreds of men who work here. Your idleness has not gone unnoticed, and the Sahib does not care to be taken for a fool.'

When Shurika returned with the dung, she was surprised to find her brother busily pulling the overgrowth from the sides of the buildings. Naked down to his lungi, he had already cleared one wall completely, and his body shone with perspiration.

Shurika crouched in the vegetable garden, tending the plants that had begun to show themselves two weeks ago. She had gone to the gatekeeper when the beds were ready to ask for seeds and the next day had been sent a handful of tiny paper packages, each one a neatly folded sheath in which the seeds lay, some big fat pods, others just a few tiny specks scattered at the bottom. On the front of each package, a small picture had been drawn in simple pencil line to identify the plant that would grow from the seed. Shurika guarded them like buried treasure, and tied rags, dyed red from crushed areca, on a row of sticks to keep the birds away. When the first shoots appeared – a few fine, pale green threads where she had placed the onion seeds – she shouted her excitement to the crows and rushed to fetch her brother, but he had shown no interest. Shurika picked the weeds from around each precious shoot and hummed to herself, making up a song in her head about harvesting the toil of her labours.

The distant sound of voices and distinctive clatter of rough wooden wheels creaking against the hard ground travelled to her sharp ears. Shurika was not expecting a delivery today. She

33

stood up, arching the ache from her back, shielding her eyes from the low sun, and peered into the near distance. Shiva, driving a bullock cart laden with furniture, called encouragement to the struggling beast as it staggered over the pitted track. Riding up on the front of the cart with him was a girl. Shurika's eyes widened, the weeds dropping from her hands. She pulled up the hem of her sari and rushed to the furthest of the buildings, shouting for her brother, telling him that he must hurry. The cart pulled up by the wrought-iron gates, now hanging securely on their hinges and painted with the same thick black paint used on the main estate gates. Shurika ran and pulled them open, bowing her greeting to Shiva.

'This is your new mistress,' Shiva said, and stood down to help Chinthimani from the bullock cart. 'You are to take good care of her and help her to settle in.' Shurika kept her eyes downcast. As her new mistress stepped to the ground, she could not help but notice her feet. They were small and fine. Perfect, like a painting she had once seen beside a shrine at a holy place. And above them, resting around her ankles, were silver chains hung with tiny bells. When her mistress finally took a step, the bells tinkled, a fragile sound like shards of glass falling.

'*Namaste*,' said Shurika, palms pressed together, head bowed respectfully.

'*Namaste*,' replied Chinthimani.

At the sound of the soft, youthful voice, Shurika looked up so see her mistress's face, and her mouth fell open. From beneath the shade of the pale yellow sari draped across her head, worn thin from years of use, peered out the darkest eyes beneath perfectly arched brows that twitched with curiosity. Chinthimani let her veil drop, revealing a fine nose hung with an ornate golden ring and a full blood-red mouth with rosebud lips. There was not one blemish on her heart-shaped face. Not

34

a single fault to corrupt the perfection of her beauty. Shurika quickly dropped her eyes to the ground again, wondering what age her mistress might be. She was perhaps a little younger or a little older than herself, but certainly no more or no less. In a family from another life, they might easily have been sisters.

'You will be maid and servant to your new mistress,' said Shiva. 'This is her household now. She will decide who stays and who goes, so serve her well. And know that the Sahib will be visiting, so you must keep the place clean and tidy.'

As Shurika nodded her understanding, she heard running footsteps behind her. Her brother slowed to a halt and began to stare, showing no shame for his open interest.

'You!' snapped Shiva. 'What are you looking at? You do not stare at your mistress, is that understood?' The brother mumbled his apology and looked away. 'Now get all this un-loaded and see to it that your mistress is made comfortable as quickly as possible. There will be more deliveries tomorrow, but for now she is tired and must rest.' Shiva waited until the brother, bent double beneath a large bundle of linen and a chair in each hand, had gone into the house, then addressed the two women. 'You must prepare for the Sahib,' he said. 'He will be here soon.'

# 4

It was an hour before sundown the next day before the heavy sound of cantering hooves slowed at the gates.

'*Koi hai!*' shouted James. 'Is anybody there?' He threw himself out of the saddle, boots grinding grit against dust as he pushed open the gate and handed his horse to the sullen-looking boy who appeared from nowhere. 'Where is your mistress?'

Shurika's brother pointed towards the unpainted door at the far end of the courtyard. James crossed the short distance in confident strides, pulling the kerchief from his neck. He stood at the door for a moment, then knocked gently before entering without waiting for an answer.

Chinthimani sat on the single chair, facing a small table with a dressing mirror into which she gazed, transfixed by her own reflection in the magical glass. Shurika stood behind her, drying her mistress's hair with a small cotton cloth, untangling the knots with patient fingers. Both turned at the sudden intrusion and stared at James. His broad frame filled the doorway, his height requiring that he dip his head slightly to step inside, where he paused and looked down upon the two of them. Shurika felt herself begin to tremble, the wet cloth falling limp in her hands. It was the Sahib, that much she knew, for she had heard from the gatekeeper and from the boys who made deliveries that he was a powerful man with a dark, fearless expression. She could feel him in the room immediately, his life force crowding in and pressing against the cinnamon rust petals of the flower-painted walls, the soft flood of evening light behind him shadowing his features into a watery cast. The opening at his collar glistened with pearls of perspiration that rose and fell against the hollow of this throat with every laboured breath.

Shurika knew why he was here. She clutched the damp cloth to her chest, her eyes rushing to her mistress's reflection in the looking glass, but, to her amazement, she saw not a trace of apprehension on the perfect face. Chinthimani stared back at him boldly, her mouth curved into a small smile. She lifted her head, just a little, and allowed the sari to slip from her shoulder. Shurika dared not look up to see the Sahib's face and felt colour climbing to her burning cheeks.

Shurika waited outside her mistress's quarters, squatting against the ground, hiding in the shadows and covering her ears, terrified of what she imagined to be happening behind the closed door, and of what she might find when she returned there. Try as she might, she could not shut out the jagged remnants of memory that still pressed like splinters into her wounds — the stench, the pain, the blinding fear. Calming herself with a whispered prayer, her eyes soon grew heavy, and when the Sahib came quietly from the room, he found her dozing, her head nodding gently against the thin arms folded on top of her knees. He leaned down to touch her shoulder, causing her to wake with a start and tumble from her haunches.

'What is your name?' he asked.

'My name is Shurika, Sahib,' she replied, standing immediately and bowing to him, embarrassed to have been caught napping when she should have been alert.

'Go and tend to your mistress, Shurika.' He smiled at her. 'She is asking for you.'

Shurika rushed into the room, her face etched with worry,

stomach wrenching as her eyes fell upon the petal-red bloodstains blooming against the sheet laid upon the bed. Chinthimani stood naked beside the small window set high up in the wall, her outline glowing in the lamplight.

'Mistress?' Shurika whispered, her throat rasping dry, the violence of the bloodstained sheet pulping her insides. 'Are you hurt?'

Chinthimani shook her head slightly, and smiled into the darkness.

Shurika soon learned what was expected of her. She stayed close by while Chinthimani spent her days resting and eating, then walked with her through the paddy fields down to the river to keep guard while she bathed, wading waist-deep into the water, her sari clinging to her curves, leaning her head back until her hair floated out on the surface like a wide black lotus leaf. As Chinthimani washed, she sang, her sweet, tuneful voice carrying across the water, shaming the birds. She held her nostrils closed and submerged her head, sometimes for a whole minute or more, lying beneath the surface, imagining that she could hear the fish, their silver scales shimmering just the way her own skin did at the feel of her lover's touch. When her face finally broke through the surface, searching for a gasp of air, she would be smiling to herself, resplendent in her happiness and good fortune. This was her river, where she bathed under the watchful eye of her servant. How her sisters would howl with envy! How her mother would reach for a stick to beat her with, convinced that it was just another of her fanciful stories.

'You are afraid of the Sahib,' Chinthimani said.

'No, mistress.' Shurika smiled at her mistress's gentle chide, having quickly forgotten the fear that had engulfed her upon first sight of him.

'Well, you should be,' Chinthimani said proudly, venturing

that she knew something of the man, the picture in her head as clear to her as the waters in which she bathed. 'He is the most important person in the whole region. A nobleman. And I was the one chosen to be his wife. Me! Of all people!' She sat at the table and gazed at her reflection in the mirror for a little while, then tilted her head back, allowing Shurika to thread away the few stray hairs between her eyebrows above the bridge of her fine nose. 'It is a pity that they do not do things as we do. I should like to have had a grand wedding and to make my home in my husband's house instead of having to keep to my own quarters.' Shurika remained quiet, contemplating her dead mother's words. *Daughter of mine, never speak to the white man. They have made us slaves. They are liars. All of them. Thieves who will stop at nothing to get what they want.*

'The old woman told me I would get used to it, but she was wrong about one thing.' Chinthimani smiled as Shurika concentrated on the threading. 'There is no hardship to be found in this charmed existence. None at all. I am not even expected to have children in case it should spoil my body. Imagine that! I wonder what my mother would say if she could see me now, being waited upon by servants of my own. My sisters would die of jealousy.'

'Yes, mistress.'

'None of them shall ever have a proper bed like mine. It is like sleeping on a cloud. I could never go back to the old ways. It wouldn't suit me now that I have become a rich man's wife.'

'Does he call you wife, mistress?' Shurika did not seek Chinthimani's eyes in the mirror. She had heard in the village the word used to describe her mistress's position, and it was not wife.

'He does not use words like that,' Chinthimani said. 'He calls me by my name. Sometimes he even calls me "little woman". He doesn't like to talk much. It makes him tired.'

\*

Each day, after bathing in the river, Chinthimani called for Shurika to comb her hair, and urged her to rub harder with handfuls of oil, perfumed with jasmine and the soft scent of cloves, massaging until her skin tingled and glowed before helping her into a clean sari. Shurika would light dozens of oil lamps, small clay pots with tied cotton tapers, and set them near to her mistress's door, laying a night moth's trail, then together they would sit and wait peacefully, indulging in a little small talk of the day's events, but never for very long. The Sahib would hurry to her when his day was done, striding into her cocooned world and leaving his own far behind. Shurika knew his urgency from the slant of his body, the pull of his breath, and she saw plainly that there was nothing more intoxicating to her mistress than the scent of her impassioned lover.

Shurika would leave them in peace, settling herself on the reed mat she had placed on the ground near to the doorway of her own quarters, allowing herself to rest awhile, her mind wandering freely as the day's fatigue left her body, sometimes pondering the work that needed to be done the next day, the growing vegetables, the roof for the cowshed, sometimes drifting towards the man and woman who lay together a few yards away. She had caught her brother spying on them one night, alerted by the rustle of his feet against the dry grass, and had beaten him away quickly, but not before she stole a glimpse for herself. Entwined in Chinthimani's arms, James whispered to her, gazing in awe at her nakedness, her smiling, moonlit face.

'*Aap khubsoorat hain.*' You are beautiful, he said.

'*Mujhe tumse bohat pyar hai.*' She softly returned that she loved him with all her heart.

Shurika slipped from the window, humming the words of a song she half-knew ... that a man's appreciation of beauty is not the same as love ... that one passionate act is not the same as a lifetime of devotion. She crouched to the floor and mourned that she would never have a husband of her own, her body ruined, its honour stolen by a stranger who had cared nothing for a worthless orphan, leaving her to drown slowly in the endless abyss of her shame. She grieved for the feelings that rose inside her while she yearned to find sleep, and turned her back on them.

Hours later, when the Sahib was long gone, Shurika would rise from her mat and attend to her mistress once more. Chinthimani washed again, this time from the bowl of fresh water Shurika brought from the well, squatting over it to remove the seed while Shurika turned away. The old woman had shown Chinthimani how to preserve herself, having bathed her roughly and demonstrated with her own hand what must be done. Her mistress would not lie down to rest again until the stars had moved the width of the twin peaks. Shurika would wait with her and listen to Chinthimani's tales of her lustful husband, sparing her none of the details. While she listened, she prepared two spoonfuls of false pepper and long pepper, crushed to a fine powder and mixed together in equal quantity with a little warm water, and gave it to her mistress to eat with bread and honey to sweeten the bitter herbs.

Yet despite the ritual washing and the spices that she brought to her mistress every evening to ward off her fertility, Shurika knew that there would be no stopping what the gods intended, and no changing the laws of human nature. Chinthimani followed the old woman's instructions to the letter, and everything was fine for four whole seasons, then she missed her moon cycle, and another, and then a third.

'What is this?' The Sahib reached his hand down, passing it across the swelling of her belly. Chinthimani pulled away from him, quickly reaching for a sari to cover herself.

'It is nothing,' she said, the chill in the night air suddenly around her.

'Do not think me entirely ignorant, woman.' He spoke softly, a taut strangeness in his voice. 'Did you think you would be able to conceal this from me?' Chinthimani fell at his feet.

'Oh, Sahib!' she cried. 'I did everything I could to stop it! I have drunk bitter herbs and wished it away! Forgive me for my stupidity! I would kill it if I knew how!'

James lifted her from the floor, taking the fabric from her to see for himself what could no longer be hidden. His heart came into his mouth. 'I think it is too late for that,' he said, pressing the soft mound of her abdomen, the skin on his face tightening with the stark realisation of the fruit that lay within. A child, of his making, having silently taken form while he took his pleasure. He cursed himself under his breath. He should have been more careful. He should have heeded his own warnings and controlled his urges, no matter how strong the temptation. The blood raced through his veins, his stomach tensing against the clamour of voices that rose in his head.

'Sahib!' Her voice seemed to dim in the room around him. 'Sahib! Will you not lie with me?' James found himself staring at the wall, the rust-coloured painted petals, the washstand with its white marble top set with the deep enamel basin, the bed, so out of place, its coverlet pulled aside. 'Sahib!' she implored him.

'You should rest,' he said grimly. 'And there will be no more talk of you doing yourself any harm, is that understood? We wouldn't want you to go and kill yourself by accident, would we?' The heavy brow settled into a resigned frown. That she was now carrying his child was a complication he had not bargained for, but to have her death on his conscience would be intolerable. 'You will be well taken care of.' Lifting the sari from her hands, he opened its folds and wrapped it around her protectively, covering her nakedness. 'It is high time you had your own cook anyway, so I can be sure that you are eating properly.' His arms remained around her. 'And you are to send word to me if there is anything else you need.'

Chinthimani cried her relief, and promised to bear him a strong, healthy son.

# 5

Chinthimani's firstborn had not come easily. She had fought against the pain and torn at the bedclothes laid down for her comfort, refusing to give passage to the child that had clung to her womb for too long, fearful that the blight on her flesh would herald the death of her husband's cooled affections, feeling her body's destruction as the baby demanded to be released, ripping through her. When the agony had become too much for her to bear, she had cried out and reached for Shurika's hands, crushing her fingers until she too wept with pain. Then, finally, in the still of the night, the cry of a new life carried up into a stargazer's sky.

Word had been sent to the Sahib that his child had arrived, the message laced with undertones of the troubled birth in the hope that it would bring him to her, but James had not come. Instead, he had sent Shiva with the bullock cart laden with rich provisions, and a name for the child. A name that meant 'burning fire'.

Now, once again, Shurika prepared as she had done before to welcome Chinthimani's child into the world. Chinthimani had said nothing of her baby's coming, but Shurika had known the moment she saw her mistress's face that morning. She was unsettled and snapped ungratefully that her tea was too bitter and the bread too hard. Shurika recognised the signs at once – the tightness in her mouth as she pushed the tea away, the uncomfortable stretch of her hips as she rose from her bed. This was just the way it had been two years ago when the first baby came, although they had been younger then, Shurika unsure of what to do, Chinthimani more frightened than angry.

Shurika watched over her mistress like a hawk as she laboured quietly all day, pacing her quarters, barely speaking at all, except to emit a low moan and to bend to the wall when her breath came sharply. But this time would not be as difficult as the first. Shurika could tell that this baby was smaller and would cause her mistress less distress. The cook made sweets to tempt her appetite, but she hardly touched a thing.

When darkness drew in, the time came close and the baby let it be known that it was ready to be born. Chinthimani sank to the floor, leaned against Shurika and asked her to sing her a song. Shurika rocked her from side to side, humming softly, while her mistress lay quietly for an hour or more, breathing deeply, slipping in and out of a restless slumber. Then the pain came over her again, this time in great waves, tossing her hopelessly from sea to sea before she succumbed to the final moments. She roared, and with all her remaining strength expelled her second child from the depths of her body into Shurika's waiting arms. Shurika set her gaze upon the mother's joy, blinked the tears from her eyes and blessed the child with a softly voiced prayer song.

'Tell me.' Chinthimani's voice rose meekly from her exhausted body. 'Do I have a son?'

'No, mistress.' Shurika looked down and exhaled. 'It is another girl. A sister for a sister.'

Chinthimani turned her head away in shame.

'I am cursed,' she said. 'My mother has set the evil eye upon me so that I may suffer the same humiliation as she did.'

'You must not say such things,' Shurika said. 'It is our own sorrow to wish for a male child, but this is not the way of the

Sahib, mistress. I hear that in some places, a daughter is worth two sons.'

'And where did you hear this?'

'From my mother.'

'Then she must have been a very ignorant woman.'

Shurika bathed the infant and wrapped her in clean linen before giving her into the mother's arms, watching the tiny hand reach up to clasp the tip of Chinthimani's little finger, yearning to know the feeling for herself.

'She is perfect,' Shurika whispered. 'The Sahib will be pleased.'

Chinthimani leaned to her baby's head, taking in her scent, and allowed Shurika to rearrange the pillows around her and to take away the soiled sheets that she had birthed upon. Rolling the cottons into a small bundle, Shurika squeezed it to her waist and felt its warmth, pressing it tightly against her emptiness.

The dim golden light thrown from the kerosene lamp cast a glow across the open doorway upon a small child, black eyes burning into the darkened chamber. Shurika had thought her asleep and hesitated at her presence, then smiled tenderly, rising to bring her into the room, leading her gently by her small hand, encouraging her to peer within the bundle cradled to her mother's breast. Serafina looked on silently at the squalling newborn with the squinting face and rooting mouth. It was of no interest to her, this thing that came in the night and caused the terrible, piercing noises that struck fear into her insides. She stared down at it and refused to smile.

'Come,' Shurika said, leaning in close to the child's ear. 'Kiss your sister, then we must take you back to your bed and let your mother rest. She has worked hard and now she is tired. Tomorrow we will bring her sweets to eat and buttermilk to drink. It will make her strong again.'

Serafina did as she was bid and kissed the baby, holding her breath to close out the sickly strange smells that cloyed at her pulsing throat. Before she could stand and flee the room, her mother reached a hand to caress the waves of her soft black hair.

'For you,' she smiled. 'So you may never be alone.'

# 6

The morning rounds were over, and James had been sent for by one of the boys, who ran all the way from the house without pausing for breath. There was a visitor, the white man with the pale hair on his face, and he was in no mood to be kept waiting. The boy urged the Sahib to hurry, fearful of the punishment the man had threatened to mete out if he did not run like the wind and come straight back. James told the stricken youth not to concern himself unduly, and sent him off to the cookhouse instead with a message of no importance. That the news should have spread so quickly came as no surprise. There was always somebody in the village willing to impart a man's business for the price of a handful of grain.

James paused a while, removed the kerchief from his throat and doused it in water from his canteen, wiping his face cool. Felix could wait. Let him take a drink or two before testing their friendship again.

'You know I don't like to interfere, James.'

James watched Felix pacing the wide veranda, worrying at his extinguished pipe, his linen suit partially sweat-damp from the heat he still found intolerable after five long years.

'There's not a tea planter in the land with your competence. You have a way with these people, no question about that. If only every one of the company's managers were more like you, we'd have a lot less trouble. This place is quite the model of modernity. Excellent yields. Top-quality leaves.'

James studied Felix's awkward manner, calculating when the reprimand would come, a perverse sense of amusement touching him, just briefly, as he waited for the inevitable.

Shiva appeared from the house, set the silver tray down on the low table and served his master and his guest without so much as a murmur before retreating inside, the wood-framed insect screen flapping lightly against the open door.

'I'm guessing you didn't come all this way to congratulate me on my management skills,' James said with a wry smile. 'Or the quality of my tea.'

Felix picked up his drink stiffly and made some pretence of looking out across the plantation. 'I hear you've gone and got yourself another problem.' He rocked on his heels and failed in his attempt to veil the disapproval in his voice. James turned away in irritation. 'For God's sake, man, say something! I hardly recognise you these days! It's this bloody place, if you ask me. Stuck out in the middle of nowhere.' He fixed his eyes on James. 'You know very well that my high regard for you makes these matters all the more complicated. You want to be careful, James. Family like yours. We expect that kind of thing from men like Hutchinson who can't keep their hands off their own servants, but you?' Felix pursed his lips, embarrassed by the ridiculous comparison.

'I'm flattered that you should think me so honourable.' James caught Felix's eye. 'But, alas, it would seem that I have disappointed you, my friend.'

It was a trite remark, James knew. To mix the heritage of his bloodline in this undisciplined manner would bring untold shame on his father's unblemished name. After two generations, the Macdonald title commanded the very highest respect in Dehradun. In James's early years, there had always been much high-minded talk of morals and the effects of one culture upon another, the adults declaring that the British must lead by example. His parents had agreed wholeheartedly with the ancient wisdom of the caste system and opined, pointedly, that people should stick to their own kind.

Felix composed himself and lowered his tone. 'People will talk, you know. And it won't be doing your career any good, let me tell you. It's just as well that it's fallen to me to have a word with you about it before it went higher up the chain. There are others who would be a lot less tactful.'

'I stopped worrying about such idle tittle-tattle long ago.' James, his demeanour cool in the face of the implied threat, did not move from his seat. 'And what should they care anyway? As you yourself said, I'm running the most profitable estate in the region. How I choose to conduct my private life is my own business.'

'Private? I wouldn't be so sure about that. These trees whisper, you know.'

'Then let the truth be known and be damned.'

'James.' Felix gave out a huge sigh. 'Don't you think this has all gone too far?' James's subtle composure issued no denial, no excuse, no justification. 'It could ruin you. You have to put an end to it. Get your affairs in order and sweep this whole unfortunate business under the rug before it can do you any more damage.'

'And what do you suggest I should have done? Drowned them in the nearest well?' James threw back his whisky. 'And we have the audacity to call *them* savages. You might not like it, Felix, but what's done is done. Now go back and tell them whatever you want, and let me get on with my job.'

Felix shook his head in defeat and relaxed his shoulders a little. 'I suppose it will do no good to rake over the same old coals again. I've made my point, and that will just have to do.'

'Yes, I'm afraid it will.'

Felix took a large swig and stared into his glass. 'Why don't you get yourself married and put all this nonsense behind you, eh? They like that kind of thing at the London office. I suspect it's the only obstacle holding you back from greater things. Quite the popular one back there, from what I hear. Your pedigree doesn't go unnoticed, James, and I imagine they have plans in store for you that neither you nor I know about. I wish I could say the same for myself. I expect they'll have me pushing pointless bits of paper around and chasing all over this God-awful country until my hair turns white.' A small smile rose on James's lips. 'I know it might sound like a daft sugges-tion given your current circumstances, but a wife makes a man complete.' James half raised an eyebrow, causing Felix to clear his throat uncomfortably and acknowledge his own unmarried position. 'Or so I'm told. You know, poor old Cruikshank's been trying his damnedest to get out of that bloody Calcutta commission since Christmas, and Penderghast won't even hear his petition. Now he's got himself lined up with a nice girl from home apparently and is planning to ship her over and march her up the aisle within the month. Poor girl! Bound to be half-sharp.' He snorted, then corrected himself quickly. 'If he turns up with a wife, they won't dare send him back. Bloody awful place. You should count yourself lucky.' Felix trailed off, his friend appearing to have drifted, eyes wandering towards the wide path leading to the western estate road. He cleared his throat again to mask his discomfort. It was a habit of his. 'Don't worry. All these things can be taken care of. Christ. It's not as though there aren't a thousand of these little bastards—'

Suddenly James reached to the table and rang the small silver bell, silencing Felix. Shiva appeared immediately, step-ping silently from the shadows where he constantly watched and waited.

'Yes, Sahib?'

James nodded towards Felix's empty glass.

'What? Oh yes. Splendid idea.' Felix thrust it at Shiva. 'And put some bloody whisky in it this time, eh?'

Shiva's eyes remained downcast. 'Yes, Sahib.'

Felix had tired of the cat-and-mouse game and resolved instead to lighten the heavy mood.

'Look, there's a little group of us going off to Simla at the weekend.' He stretched his shoulders uncomfortably. 'Thought we might see what's going on at the theatre up there. There's always a few interesting characters hanging around at this time of year. Why don't you come along?' He forced a smile, but James appeared not to be listening, his thoughts elsewhere. 'Make a bit of a party of it, hmm? Get you out of this bloody jungle for a while and see if we can't find you a decent girl who can speak a bit of English for a change.'

Felix slapped a mosquito on the back of his neck and reached tetchily for a handkerchief to dab the perspiration from his ruddy face. God knows, this was no place for a man with the fair complexion of his Irish mother. His beard, strictly against company regulations, had only been permitted when the chief medical officer wrote in the strongest possible terms that the man's face would not tolerate a razor for much longer under such conditions.

James sat unhearing, consumed by a sudden urge to ride out to the homestead and check on the well-being of the new infant. His first brief glimpse of the bundle in Shurika's arms had brought his heart to a standstill. She was tiny, smaller than he imagined any life could be, the clasp of her hand barely covering the tip of his little finger. The sight of her vulnerability had left him unexpectedly moved, and he had bestowed upon her the most blessed of names, as if to capture her innocence.

Prompted by Felix's persistent throat-clearing, James finally seemed aware that he was being asked a direct question, of which he had no recollection. 'I'm sorry, Felix, I'm afraid I ...'

'What do you say, old boy?'

There was nothing to say, of course, so the world stayed as it was, and the years rolled by.

## 7

One of the houseboys picked his way cautiously a few yards ahead of the party, beating at the ground with a stick and poking at the parched long grass. A baby cobra is born every ounce as poisonous as its mother, and much, much harder to see. To step on one would bring the day's outing to an abrupt halt. Better that everyone took the time to tread carefully.

Shurika had nothing to burden her today, the Sahib's bearers from the big house having taken charge of the fetching and carrying, and she took pleasure in swinging her arms freely as she followed the troop down to the river, keeping a watchful eye on her two young charges pulling at their father, demanding his attentions.

'Is it not a perfect day for a picnic?' Chinthimani appeared by Shurika's side, smiling proudly and bucking her head towards her master and children.

'Yes, mistress,' Shurika replied, lifting her face to the sun. 'It is a perfect day.'

The warm air circled a gentle breeze, the sounds of Mary and Serafina's delighted squeals spreading toothy smiles across sun-drenched faces. The Sahib's servants trailed like a line of soldier ants, carrying furniture, baskets, tiffin boxes, richly patterned rugs, and games to play with the children after lunch.

'Do you ever wish for a husband?' Chinthimani asked.

'No, mistress.' Shurika turned her face away, hiding its sudden colour.

'No? But surely you must have wished for it sometimes?'

'My place is here with you, mistress, and with your children.'

Shurika followed Chinthimani's gaze towards James, now quite far ahead, his younger daughter perched on his shoulders, the elder carried in the same manner by Shiva. Every now and then, James jolted the child and danced on his feet, shouting, '*Snake!*' before pretending to drop the squealing child to the ground then swooping her back up to his neck. Shiva copied his master, the two men laughing with the children as they played.

'Did you leave everything prepared in my quarters?' Chinthimani asked.

'Yes, mistress.'

'I am certain that my husband will want to stay with me tonight.'

'Yes, mistress.'

Shurika knew better than to give voice to her own misgivings. It was wiser to smile and nod and play along with her mistress's pretence. It seemed to calm her beneath the brittle veneer that had settled upon her once perfect face as the Sahib's visits became shorter, more sporadic, gradually petering out altogether save these occasional, stolen days when he would arrive bringing half his household with him, obliterating all traces of the intimacy they had once shared. Whenever he came, Shurika would obediently prepare her mistress's quarters, collecting fallen blooms from the trees to float upon dishes of crystal-clear water, twisting tapers of cotton for the tiny red clay oil lamps, burning sweet-smelling herbs while Chinthimani made the *burra-peg* as Shiva had once shown her.

But the Sahib did not stay. He had not done so in three years.

And Chinthimani no longer poured the drink away.

Shurika smiled and nodded, sensitive to the strain in her mistress's voice.

'He has been spending too much time working and travelling. I have told him that he must not neglect his family. I think he knows that we have been missing him. Perhaps that is why he has gone to so much trouble today.'

'Yes, mistress.'

Shurika was pained at the sight of Chinthimani's brief happiness. The smile that once lit up her face from morning until night had become rarer. There were some days when she would do nothing but pace the courtyard, up and down, up and down, stopping only at the gates to stare out towards the western estate road. As the babies came, so the Sahib had stayed away. And as the babies grew older, so her mistress had grown restless. Shurika had seen the change in many women from the village once their life purpose was fulfilled. A girl could not remain so for ever. Once she had crossed that divide into motherhood, she could never return to her former self, and no man would ever look at her again with the same eyes.

The sound of the children's screams brought the party to a sudden halt. This time, the snake was as real as could be. The two houseboys thrashed at the ground, beating with their sticks and jabbering wildly to each other until, finally satisfied, one bent down, then stood triumphantly, dangling the corpse of the dead cobra high in the air for everyone to see.

Reaching the riverside, the servants began to unpack their loads, laying down the rugs and setting out the table and chairs. Mary refused to get down from her father's shoulders and clung to his head with her tiny hands, staring down as the cook threw a big white cloth over the table and set out dish after dish, each one covered with a tin plate and tied with a welt of dry grass. The cook looked up at her and raised his eyebrows mischievously, holding his finger in front of his lips and tormenting her with hints of what might lie within.

The river ran low at this time of year, the water flowing in gentle currents that swirled in the shallows and lulled calmly where the pools became deep in the shade of the trees. Shurika sat at the water's edge and slipped her feet into the stream to cool her blood. She would not be missed, for the children were fully occupied and the servants far too busy setting up the sun canopies and searching for the missing cricket stump to notice her gone.

Chinthimani moved to oversee the servants, but they, perfectly practised in their roles, took little notice of her. Her eyes travelled to James constantly, but his were always elsewhere, following his children, delighting in their joy. When she did manage to meet his gaze, he would look straight through her, or offer her only the smallest of smiles before turning away. It emptied her, slicing through her skin and sapping the few shreds of hope she so desperately clung to, forcing in their place instead a bitter, insidious sense of envy for her daughters' higher position in his affections.

Shurika moved her feet in the cool stream, forcing tiny eddies to form around her ankles, and looked out towards the dark depths where her mistress once loved to bathe. Now she preferred to have her water drawn from the wells, and only ventured down to the river when her melancholy mood could not be lifted.

The cook's loud sing-song voice was quickly followed by the crash of his picnic dinner gong: a pair of tin plates banged together with enough vigour to wake the dead. Mary, still too small to clamber on to the chair herself, reached her hands up. The cook lifted her with ease, swung her around his head for a moment, then landed her softly in the seat piled high with extra cushions.

'Hungry?' James spoke in her native tongue. She nodded. 'Good. Now let's see what we have here.' He lifted the first lid. 'Ah! Roast chicken.' He handed a piece to each of his children before passing the dish to Chinthimani. Mary had the chicken in her mouth before anyone could stop her. James laughed good-humouredly. 'You're supposed to wait until everyone has been served before starting, young lady.' She stared at him, mouth full, unable to understand this last sentence, spoken in strange words. Instead, she concentrated on the plate in front of her being gradually loaded with spoon after spoon: potato salad with mint and onions, rice with fried brinjals, spiced fritters that she had smelled from the cookhouse yesterday evening while she lay in bed, now all the better for being cold and covered with sweet chutney.

'Eat slowly,' Chinthimani scolded her. 'You look like you're going to choke.'

'She's hungry,' said James.

'That one is always hungry.'

'Then perhaps you are not feeding her enough.' James did not look up from his plate.

'Of course I am! She is never out of the cookhouse!'

James winked at his daughters. 'Would you like me to take you for a dip in the river after lunch?' They both nodded eagerly. 'Then eat carefully. We wouldn't want the pair of you to sink, now, would we?'

The servants sat on the ground to eat their simple lunch of rice and vegetables in the shade of the nearby trees. One of the houseboys had brought with him a drum, and began to form a steady rhythm with his fingers before lifting his voice to sing a popular song. The servants clapped along happily and joined in with the choruses, humming the melody of the parts for which they did not know the words, and breaking into laughter when the boy made a mistake and had to start again.

Chinthimani sang for a little while in her sweet voice, hoping to catch James's attention.

'You know,' he settled a small reprimanding glance upon her, 'we British consider it rude to sing at the table.'

Chinthimani silenced herself immediately, mortified by her mistake.

All the way home, the drummer kept up his steady, hypnotic beat. The party, pleasantly tired from the day, were glad of the song to encourage their weary legs over the rough terrain, the children's small, sleeping bodies slumped against strong shoulders.

'I will see them straight to their beds,' Shurika said, taking her leave of her mistress before she could answer.

James supervised the loading of the furniture back on to the bullock cart, which they had left at the homestead that morning, while the two houseboys went in search of the ox they had tethered by the gates, supposedly in the care of Shurika's brother. Chinthimani watched James from afar, impatient for his company.

'Let the servants do that,' she approached him gently. 'Come inside and rest with me a while. I can make you a *burra-peg*, just the way Shiva does. I have a bottle of your favourite whisky. I sent for it from the house and I know how to mix it the way you like it.'

'You know that I cannot,' James replied. 'It is already getting late and I have a great deal of work to attend to in the morning.'

'You never used to mind that it was late,' she tested him. 'And your children have been wondering what could be so important as to keep you away from us.'

'They had a wonderful day today, didn't they?'

'Yes.' Chinthimani lowered her eyes. 'I wish that I were one of them sometimes. Then perhaps you would spare me more than the few words you have exchanged with me today.'

'Now, now. Don't be like that.' James smiled at her. 'Or you will spoil the end of a lovely day.'

'Then stay with me for a little while.' Chinthimani opened her arms to him.

Shurika waited outside, resting on the mat near to her mistress's door, but she must have fallen fast asleep, for when she awakened, the pitch black of the night sky had lifted, bringing with it the first lilac hues of morning. Perhaps the Sahib had stayed, for she had not heard him leave and had not been called to attend to her mistress afterwards. She crept inside the children's room and found them as she had left them, curled into their charpoys. She lay down on the floor between them. As she began to drift off, she heard the small sounds from her mistress's quarters – the low, soft moan of her grief. Quietly Shurika slipped out to go to her, then stopped, pausing her hand on the door. There was nothing that she could do for her, and if the children woke to find that she was not beside them, they would become upset and cry for her. Shurika returned to the children, slid back on to the floor and closed her eyes.

## 8

With the tireless passage of one year upon another, life in the courtyard remained steady and constant, cradled as it was within its own tiny world. The main house, the mill for milling corn, the open-sided wooden barn that housed the big machine for winnowing rice, the cookhouse, the cowshed, the chicken run. There was space for other animals too – the goats, two fat pigs and the humped Brahmin cows that ambled wherever they cared to wander. Chinthimani's children would never hunger for bread. They grew stronger with each passing day, their paler skins and strange names marking them out from the village children they were permitted neither to befriend nor to play with. Instead, they ran through the courtyard and pestered Shurika to ask the cook to make sweets and sugar syrup, Serafina a proud and handsome child of seven summers, freckles powdering her nose.

'We want to go and see Papa.'

Shurika was used to Serafina's demanding ways and stood her ground in front of the petulant face. At the mention of their father's name, Mary skipped to her sister's side and began to jump up and down. 'Papa! Papa!' She unclasped her hands and reached up as Shurika scooped her to a slender, cottoned hip.

'He's away on a big hunting trip,' Shurika smiled, rearranging Mary's slight weight and dangling legs. 'You will see him soon enough. Be patient.'

Serafina's eyes burned. 'It's not fair. Mother said that he would come to see us. She said she went up to the big house herself and she promised us that he was coming.'

'If that is what your mother said, then you can be sure that it is true.'

Mary bounced in Shurika's arms, but was no burden, delicate like a doll.

'Papa soon! Papa soon!'

'Why does he have to go hunting? Why can't we go too?'

Shurika was careful not to laugh at the girl's indignation. Serafina's waters ran deep and dark. She was not a child to be toyed with.

'You can't go hunting! The tigers will eat you up like a little rabbit!'

'No they wouldn't. I would kill them with Papa's gun.' Serafina lifted an invisible rifle in her arms, took aim and shouted *bang*.

'You have the heart of a lion.' Shurika smoothed her hand against Serafina's neck, felt it stiffen and raised her eyes to follow the girl's gaze. Their mother appeared silently from the door to her quarters, set at the far corner of the courtyard where the main house abutted the outer wall, her white sari fluttering a soft reflection of leaf-dappled sunshine under the afternoon sky. She walked towards them, her slow progress told by the sound of the silver bells that jingled around her fine ankles.

'*Maa! Maa!*' Mary clapped and smiled. Her mother reached them, kissed her younger daughter and stretched out a hand to place on Serafina's shoulder.

'The courage of your father.' Chinthimani smiled thinly. 'But the beauty of your mother.'

'Did you see him?' Serafina carried her father's strong features and sensed the power they held over her mother. The urgency in her voice rang clearly around the courtyard. 'Did you ask him if he was coming to visit? When will he—'

'Quiet, child.' Shurika raised a hand to silence her. 'Let your mother speak.'

'Soon. He will be here soon. So you must be sure that you are washed and looking your very best. You want him to be proud, don't you? And what do you think he would say if he arrived to find you looking like a ragamuffin with your hair hanging in strands like that? Go and get ready. Go now!'

Their squeals of excitement sent the chickens scattering and the geese honking. Mary struggled from Shurika's arms and the two girls ran off into the house. Shurika waited until their voices were far away before asking their mother herself.

'Did you see him?'

Chinthimani shook her head quietly and looked down at the dusty ground. Before she could stop herself, Shurika's hands flew to her cheeks in despair.

'Why did you not tell them? Oh, mistress, I beg of you not to do this again! Do you not remember how upset they were last time? And the time before that?' Tears sprang to her eyes. 'They are happy when they forget. And it is cruel of you to torment them like this. You cannot let the children think that he is coming when he is not!'

Chinthimani's anger flashed a stinging slap across Shurika's face. 'Who are you to tell me what I can and cannot let my children think? Are you their mother? No! You are just the *ayah* and you will do as you are told.' Her agitated hands wrung anxious folds through the unseated shoulder of her sari. 'He will be here. He always comes eventually. His manservant said that he would be back today and I told him that he must visit us as soon as he returns. Now go and help the children wash and dress.'

\*

63

Shurika finished brushing the girls' hair, her long, steady strokes pressing against their shining curls, then tied the satin sashes around their white cotton dresses. They were a perfect copy of the creased picture torn from the British periodical that had found its way to them, brought down from the big house by one of the boys at Chinthimani's instruction. The *darzee* had at first scratched his head and frowned at the illustration, before nodding his understanding, showing Shurika his finest cottons and agreeing his price. Serafina fussed that her sash wasn't tied right, undid it and began again, refusing any assistance. Mary giggled and found it all rather funny.

'Hold still,' Shurika scolded her, struggling to steady the child's constant fidgeting. 'Or you will look like the cook's apron on a Sunday and you won't have any sweets for a month.' Mary squirmed but tried her best to stand still while Shurika settled the pink bow, her eyes wandering through to the next room. She could see her mistress, standing listlessly by the door, taking in the coolness of the late breeze, looking out into the fading courtyard, drinking from the whisky glass she had once kept only for the Sahib but now nursed by herself, as though it brought her closer to him.

'Let me clean that for you, mistress.' Shurika attempted to take the glass from Chinthimani's hand, but she snatched it away and glared at her.

'Huh!' she said. 'Do you think I don't know what you're up to?' The rosebud lips fell into a sneer. 'If you want some, why don't you just ask me for it?'

'Please, mistress. You do not want the Sahib to find you like this when he arrives.'

'Oh, that!' Chinthimani laughed bitterly. 'He won't come. You and I both know it. He has far more important things to do than to worry about his whore and his bastard children.' She reached to the table and uncorked the bottle that stood there, pouring more. She offered the glass to Shurika, who shook her head solemnly, her eyes pleading with her mistress not to drink it. 'You should have thrown them into the river when they were born. Why did you let them live? What am I to do with two daughters that nobody wants? It is the disgrace of my family. No sons. What good is a woman without a husband or a son? I am cursed.'

'Please, mistress. Do not upset yourself again. Let me bring you something to eat. You should rest.'

'Rest? What for? I have no reason to rest.' Her words were muffled, each one colliding with the next. 'I am nothing, a no-body, and my miserable children are merely an accident of one man's waste. A punishment sent by the gods because I served as a white man's harlot.' She drank from the glass again, deeply this time, her face grimacing against the burning sensation tearing into her chest. Shurika began to cry.

'Stop. I beg of you, please stop.'

'Fetch a knife from the cookhouse.' Chinthimani smiled at her, a cold smile with no mercy. 'Then cut my throat, and those of my unwanted children. When you are done, you can cut your own throat too if you want to, if you have the courage. Maybe you will rebirth as a white man and I will come back as the snake that bites you. Now go away.'

Shurika went back to the children and found Mary where she had left her, swinging her legs on the chair and trying to make a bow with the ends of her sash.

'Here,' said Shurika. 'I will show you how to do it, but you must be patient.' Her eyes flicked around the room in sudden concern. 'Where has your sister gone?'

Mary pointed to the darkest corner of the room, where Serafina hid, crouched beneath the table under the window, hugging her arms around herself. The expression on her face halted Shurika's breath.

'Serafina?' She left Mary's side and crept slowly towards the shape in the shadows. 'What is the matter?' Serafina shook her head violently and refused to answer. 'Have you been listening to things that you should not listen to?' Serafina turned her head away, her breathing heavy. 'Answer me!' Shurika reached for Serafina's arm, but she ducked away and hid herself deeper under the table.

'I heard you!' Serafina shouted. 'I heard what you said!'

Shurika got down on her knees and craned her head to find Serafina's face. 'You mustn't listen to things that you don't understand. Your mother is upset. She doesn't know what she is saying. She has not been well.'

Serafina glared back at her. 'I heard everything.'

The night-time sounds of the jungle make a music all of their own. Insects sing. Frogs chirrup. Animals stir, rustling the broad leaves that grow wide and low to the ground. Darkness had fallen hours ago. Mary lay sleeping on the bed in her crumpled white dress, the pink satin sash crushed and tangled around her tiny middle. Shurika left her in peace. The dress was of no importance. She helped Serafina out of her clothes. The girl was crying. Bitter, angry tears that stung at her eyes and spilled endlessly down her reddened cheeks despite her strong will and vehement dislike for showing her feelings. Shurika comforted her, as best she could, stroking her hair and humming gently to quieten her shaking frame.

'Hush,' she said. 'Hush now. Do not upset yourself. Go to sleep and you will wake up to a new day when all will be well. And if your dreams are not sweet, wake me in the night and I will sing to you.'

Shurika remained beside her, humming a soft lullaby until Serafina's breathing fell slow and regular, before taking her place on the floor between the girls. In the semi-darkness, she settled herself, her half-dreams wandering to the time when the Sahib would come every day, throwing the household into an excitable burst of chaos each evening as they prepared for his arrival. Now there was nothing. Just the endless darkness, and the empty sighs of her pining mistress.

Chinthimani sat in sickly silence on the stoop, her white sari heavily tarnished by the loose dirt beneath her, staring out listlessly towards the moonlit courtyard where all was still, save the song of the night-time. Tomorrow would be another day. She would take the children up to the white man's club, where they would be permitted treats, and Mary would fill her pockets freely and forget her disappointment. Her head began to spin. She leaned it against the cool stone of the wall beside her, closed her eyes and felt the breeze caress the damp of her fevered brow. It was like a deep sickness, this reeling feeling inside. It did not comfort her as it should. The glass slipped from her hand and rolled into the dirt. She must wait here awhile rather than try to stand. Shurika would come and help her soon, when the children were finally asleep.

## 9

The plantation house sat in an enviable position, occupying a spot midway between the lower gardens and the high terraces, taking in the very best of the heavenly views and displaying its glorious wealth for all to see, its green-tiled roof generously shading the open veranda surrounding the bungalow in grand surveillance. One would have thought that such opulence had no earthly place in such a simple land, yet the temptation of the Empire to display its superiority remained strong. The heat left the day the moment the sun dipped behind the highest hill to the west, taking the light with it, urging the birds all at once towards their roosts. Suddenly from all over they appeared, heading towards the same thicket of trees, heaving with flapping white wings all arguing and vying for a perch. The branches quietened as soon as dusk drew in. Night fell quickly here.

Shiva cleared away the remnants of his master's sundowners from the low table on the veranda, listening intently to the jazz floating through the open windows from the big brass-horned gramophone that graced the mahogany dresser in the far corner of the drawing room. The rug had been rolled aside, and Felix was clumsily leading the new girl arrived just three weeks ago who hadn't yet learned that lipstick did not behave quite as it should in this climate. Her aunt, Mrs Gardner, chose to stay on in India despite being widowed more than three years ago, and was pleased to have her niece's company regardless of her oversight.

'A supper invitation to the Macdonald house is always a welcome distraction,' Mrs Gardner whispered behind her hand to Mrs Edwards. 'Even if I did have to pass a poorly disguised hint on more than one occasion to get it.'

'It doesn't do any good for a man like that to spend so much time alone,' Mrs Edwards replied discreetly. 'I've heard a reliable rumour from Felix that he may well be getting ready to settle down.'

'Really? Now that would be a turn-up for the books.'

'Not before time, if you ask me. Handsome fellow like that? I would have thought he'd have been snapped up long ago, were he not so interested in his precious tea leaves.'

'I don't mind telling you,' Mrs Gardner confided, 'I've had my eye on our James for quite some time.' She nudged Mrs Edwards's arm and nodded towards the dancing couple. 'Lucy is quite adamant that she expects to meet her future husband while she's in India, and I know that's exactly why her parents sent her out here. I'm rather hoping that she might catch James's attention.'

'I shall watch with interest.' Mrs Edwards's tone became playful. 'He doesn't strike me as the sort of man who'd be bothered with the usual inconveniences of courtship. It's all work, work, work with these types.'

'But of course he is! A man of his background is bound to be on the lookout for a wife. It's all a matter of timing, dear. I realise that Lucy's rather flighty.' She eyed her niece dancing boisterously with Felix. 'But she's terribly pretty and is bound to grow out of her nonsensical manner in another year or so. I think they would make a perfect match.'

Mrs Edwards nodded politely, but she had already seen that despite Mrs Gardner's effusive introduction of her niece, James had offered Lucy little more than a polite handshake.

'And how is your timid little house guest getting along?' Mrs Gardner indicated with her glass towards the young woman sitting on her own in the corner of the room, looking rather uncomfortable.

'Who, Dorothy? Still quite overwhelmed, I'm afraid. I've told her that she can stay with us for as long as she likes, but I'm beginning to wonder if she'll ever venture out of the door without me to guide her. I thought she might have made a few more friends by now.' She sighed her disappointment. 'You know these bookish types.'

'She does seem something of a wallflower,' Mrs Gardner observed with obvious relief. 'In fact, were it not for Felix, I expect that this would have turned out to be a very dull evening indeed!'

'I really don't know why these girls insist on coming out to India,' Mrs Edwards said. 'They would be just as well served to find themselves a nice young man back in England. Poor Dorothy has had all sorts of problems with her constitution, although I do think that she's beginning to get used to it. When her parents wrote and asked if they could send her out for a while, we could hardly say no, could we? Her mother is quite at a loss to know what to do with her. She point-blank refused to settle in England. Said she'd rather take her chances with malaria than succumb to the humiliation of trying to make her mark in a profession where she's clearly not welcome. A relative is a relative, no matter how distant. Geoffrey and I thought she'd be begging to be sent back to her family by now, but, credit to her I suppose, she appears quite determined to stick it out.'

James stood by the open window looking away towards the hills, their hazy blue outline becoming fainter against the dusk, forgetting his duties as a gracious host, allowing his mind to wander. The conversation among his half-dozen guests was tiresome anyway. He raised his face slightly to the breeze, the cool of the evening refreshing his clean-shaven skin. The rains would be here soon. He could feel it in the air.

Dorothy watched him quietly from the corner where she sat fidgeting, her eyes darting this way and that, flicking back to him whenever she thought his gaze elsewhere. A slight, fair-faced young woman of sufficient years to know her own mind, she had yet to meet a man who could hold her interest for more than a few minutes, and had resigned herself to the prospect of a long, happy spinsterhood. She had been asked up to the big house only once before and had found herself strangely drawn to the quietly brooding man who spoke so politely yet seemed so very distant. He had scarcely noticed her at all, so she had taken extra care with her appearance this evening. Not one to put herself forward, Dorothy had to steel herself before rising from her seat to approach him. She crossed the room in silent steps hidden beneath the music, then, reaching his side, became immediately conscious of his preference for solitude. Her tongue tied in a moment and she found herself saying lamely, 'Penny for your thoughts?'

James, rudely roused from his deep trance, adjusted his manner immediately and smiled, noticing her discomfiture. Perhaps it was the way she held her drink with both hands, or found it hard to look him in the eye without blushing. He straightened himself towards her and looked around the room with an air of semi-surprise, as though his guests had just appeared out of nowhere.

'I'm afraid I was miles away. Really. Quite unforgivable.' Dorothy smiled and hoped that the flush she felt rising to her cheeks was not noticeable. James spared her. 'It's Dorothy, isn't it?'

'Yes.' She reddened further.

'Thank goodness for that.' James exaggerated his relief and decided to enjoy the offer of her company, if only for a little while. It might turn out to be a pleasant diversion. She seemed charming enough, if a little plain. He lowered his voice. 'I'm usually hopeless when it comes to remembering names.'

'I expect you must meet lots of new people all the time.'

'No.' James sipped his drink and eyed her carefully. 'Not really. I find that the trick is to avoid meeting new people as one might avoid the plague.' He seemed quite serious. Dorothy laughed nervously. 'Then I don't have to worry about remembering who anyone is, and nor do I have to sit at a dinner table with a group of strangers and pretend to be interested in their small talk.'

'Oh!' Dorothy wasn't sure whether or not he was teasing her and wished that she had remained in her seat. James smiled at her mischievously.

'Why so shocked? You don't strike me as the sort of young woman who's interested in small talk, or are you just like all the others?'

'Others?'

'The ones who come out here to hunt among the unsuspecting for a husband.'

'No! I ...' Dorothy floundered.

'It's all right.' James raised a hand in apology. 'You must excuse me. I'm just terribly out of practice with my social graces. Felix says that I've been stuck in the jungle for far too long, and he's probably right. You'll find me nothing but a terrible bore, I'm afraid. I'd ask you to dance were it not that I have two left feet.'

'Nonsense!' Dorothy, suddenly seized by courage, took James's drink and put it down on the table with her own before leading him boldly into the middle of the room. 'There's nothing to it, is there, Felix?'

Burning cigarette hanging loosely from his lips, Felix spoke through the side of his mouth while dropping Lucy into an unexpected dip. 'Absolutely, old girl. Any chap can dance if he has half the brains he was born with.' He winked at James, who smiled back at him and took a firm hold of the surprised Dorothy. James could dance perfectly well, and set them both into a light foxtrot, much to the combined shock of his guests. Suddenly the room filled with laughter. The lights seemed brighter. The music louder. Dorothy did her best to keep up, and remembered the way her younger brother used to sweep her around the bare floorboards in their drawing room before he was sent up to Oxford to read history.

Felix eyed his old friend. 'Quite a beast you took down there yesterday, James.' James refused to acknowledge the compliment and concentrated instead on Dorothy's flushed, smiling face. With his attempt to engage with James rudely cast aside, Felix demanded the attention of Lucy instead. 'One clean shot. Took it down in an instant! You don't see that very often, let me tell you. It'll make a fine rug.'

'Send it back to England!' called Mrs Gardner from her perched position on the settee. 'They're ten a penny here.'

'I've never been on a hunt before,' sighed Lucy. 'Take me with you next time? I promise I won't get in the way. My aunt says that if a girl is to get along in these parts, she must learn to live like a queen and hunt like a man.'

Felix raised a mocking eyebrow at her breathless zeal.

'Have you any idea what it's like to ride out on the elephants at first light and be stuck out in the heat all day?'

'Not yet.'

'Then I suggest you keep it that way. There are some things that simply aren't meant for the fairer sex. The last thing we

73

need is to be held up by fainting women just when the bag starts picking up, eh, James?'

'Quite,' replied James, without taking his eyes from Dorothy's. 'It wouldn't do to spoil a sweet nature like yours with a gruesome passion for bloodlust.' Colour rushed to her face again.

The music came to an abrupt halt and Shiva quickly changed the record, holding it gingerly by the edges and returning it to its paper sheath before placing the next one carefully on the turntable, winding the gramophone the way he had done so often and setting the needle back down with a crackle. Such a marvellous invention. The Sahib had brought it with him when he first arrived, and had demonstrated its wizardry to the curious staff, who had laughed and chattered excitedly when the dizzying music burst from its shining trumpet.

'Shall we catch our breath for a few minutes?' James steered Dorothy towards the carved wooden seat beneath the window, the remnants of light from the flickering storm lanterns outside passing through the lattice to pattern the floor in a fretwork of gold. The breeze played with Dorothy's hair, prickling at the skin on her bare arms. To her alarm, she discovered herself lost for words, unable to muster so much as a sentence, and looked very ill at ease. Trying desperately to think of something conversational to say, she was thankful when suddenly the room filled with music again.

'Oh! I love this!' squealed Lucy, the two whisky sodas quite apparent in her enthusiastic assault on the now ruddy-faced Felix. 'There's a new dance! It's all the rage in London. You absolutely must let me show you!' She pulled at his arm while he tried to bat her away.

'Enough of this nonsense!'

Felix, while good-humoured, was not a particularly physical kind of man. A dance or two was all very well, but his limbs complained quickly and he was soon looking for a seat.

'Oh, come on, Felix!' she persisted, much to the subtle annoyance of her aunt, who had noticed clearly enough that her niece might well have missed her chance to dine beside James this evening.

Felix ignored her and looked around instead for Shiva, who was standing, as always, near to the door waiting to be of service to anyone's whim. As the only one of James's household to speak and understand English well, it was generally left to Shiva to relay instructions to the house servants, even though James spoke three dialects with unshakeable fluency. Felix snapped his fingers at him. 'Bring out some more soda water, will you? And make sure that it's properly chilled.'

'Yes, Sahib.'

Felix grunted and dropped himself into an armchair. 'And when's bloody dinner? I'm starving.'

An hour later, Felix was once again content, his claret glass full and his plate heavy with roast beef with no thought given to the politics of slaying a cow. He leaned drunkenly towards Lucy, seated hopefully to his right.

'Give me a good old waltz any day.'

'To jazz?' Lucy widened her eyes in warning. 'You'd never get away with it at the club. You might as well let me teach you or you'll look a complete fool when the next big dance comes around!'

Geoffrey Edwards laughed at her enthusiasm and patted his wife's hand. 'We really must do something about the servants, darling,' he addressed her. 'James handles his household so much better than—'

'That's because he's a bachelor, dear. They really don't like taking orders from a woman, you know.' Mrs Edwards looked up and engaged the whole table in her usual authoritative way. 'That's why I'm firm. It's the only language these people understand.' A formidable woman, Mrs Edwards was of the no-nonsense type who had toughened up and stayed the course, unlike so many of the other women of her generation who found themselves to be of too weak a disposition to make a go of it and so returned to England to live a quiet life and share their stories of Imperial India over high tea in a well-tempered garden.

Dorothy whispered conversation to James seated beside her, occupying the head of the table.

'I always knew what I wanted to be,' she said quietly. 'My mother was completely against it. Said it was no life for a woman of my upbringing. But what else was I to do?' She played with her beef, her appetite having deserted her. 'I was bored silly in England. Once Bertie had gone up to Oxford, I got the distinct impression that I was to be married off as quickly as possible. My father understood how I felt about that. He got around my mother by telling her I'd be better off getting it out of my system. I don't suppose either of them expected me to stick it out for a minute, but the moment I started, I knew I'd never turn back. Those early years in medical school were the happiest days of my life.' She cleared the memory with a sip of wine. 'And the toughest. My goodness. I'm sure I was made to work twice as hard as the men. And I was always the one expected to make the tea!'

'So what brings you to this far-flung corner of the earth?' James said.

'Ah.' She shrugged. 'Once I'd qualified, I found myself running the gauntlet of the old school tie so decided my services would be put to far better use elsewhere. Mother was horrified, of course, but that's nothing new.'

James smiled towards his plate. 'And how are you finding the jewel in his majesty's crown?'

Dorothy tipped her head in a so-so fashion. James sipped his wine and watched her with interest. 'It takes a bit of getting used to. This heat!' She fanned herself mockingly with her napkin, although the evening air was cool enough. 'I haven't decided whether I want to stay yet. I'm just waiting to see how things work out. There's so much to take in. And you? Geoffrey tells me that you've been here all your life.' She stopped herself short, aware that she had accidentally disclosed suggestion of her discreet enquiries after him following their first brief meeting. James twisted the stem of his glass and pursed his lips.

'Yes,' he said, pondering her question more deeply than she could possibly imagine. 'I suppose you could say that India is my lifelong love affair.' The words hung there for a while, out in the open, so easy to say. A small shiver passed over him. 'Or perhaps it was being shipped off to a freezing English boarding school with an enormous trunk filled with thick grey socks that sealed my fate for good.' He offered her an explanatory laugh, pushing his demons aside. 'I think they must have been knitted from elephant hair.'

'I've heard a great deal about your father.' Dorothy became sheepish for a moment and blushed again. 'I've read a lot of his papers, too. Between you and me, I think I had a bit of a crush on him in a silly kind of way, especially during my training. I do feel rather ridiculous about that now. Does he still practise?'

'Yes, indeed. Very much so. I hear he's been involved in pioneering some new procedure or other. I'm afraid I don't remember the details of it. There's a letter about it here somewhere. I expect you would have a far better understanding of what it entails than I do.' He frowned at his forgetfulness. 'He stayed up in Dehradun. I have to confess that it's been some years since I've visited.'

'So you didn't want to follow in his footsteps?'

'Good heavens, no. With hands like these?'

James held up a pair of handsomely manicured hands with

strong, delicate fingers that would have done a surgeon's job perfectly well. Dorothy laughed and, before she realised what she had done, daringly took one of them in her own. The move did not go unnoticed. Mrs Edwards, with her famously voracious appetite for a generous supper, paused her cutlery and stole a furtive glance in James's direction before smiling to the frustrated Mrs Gardner. For one tiny moment, Dorothy thought to shy away, to apologise and let go. But she did not. She was glad of her bold move and took a deep breath.

'I'd love to meet him one day. Do you think he would approve?'

James smiled back at her and wondered.

## 10

'We shouldn't be here.' Shurika's voice trembled with warning. She watched on nervously as the girls ran excitedly ahead, sensing that her mistress's proud defiance was terribly out of place. 'The Sahib has said—'

'Said what? That we are to remain within the confines of that prison while he ignores us for year after year?'

'We want for nothing, mistress.'

'What I want is for my husband to treat me with the honour I deserve.'

'Mistress.' Shurika bowed her head. 'He is not your husband. You must not speak of him as such. We must be careful. There is nothing here for us except trouble.'

'Of course he is.' Chinthimani's voice hardened. 'Whether he likes it or not. I refuse to be silenced, to pace around and wait for his permission to take a glass of water from my own well.'

'The children should be at home, mistress.'

'Why? Because anyone with a pair of eyes can see whose children they are? Because their skin is too pale and their hair does not lie straight? Good. Let him be shamed into the truth of his family.'

'But mistress,' Shurika implored her.

'Don't tell me what to do! Who do you think you are? It is me who tells *you* what to do. Don't you forget that, or you'll be turfed out on the street with that no-good brother of yours. Do you hear me?'

They passed the ancient peepul tree where a holy man sat in the shade of its heart-shaped leaves, cross-legged in unblinking contemplation, hair matted, body daubed in the white ash of the village funeral pyres. Chinthimani dropped two annas into his begging bowl.

'Let the children have their treats, then we must take them home.' Shurika pulled her sari over her head, mindful of her mistress's ill-judgement, and quickened her pace.

'Be quiet,' Chinthimani hissed at her, smiling a greeting to the surly watchmen on the gate, ignoring her companion's nerves. 'We will do no such thing. My children have every right to be here, and then we will go and visit my friend Athira up in the village.' Shurika gasped her involuntary disapproval, then immediately quietened herself before she could be punished. 'We will pay our respects and congratulate her on her daughter's forthcoming wedding. They have made her a very good match with the son of a cloth merchant. I hear that he has the face of a pig, but a girl with such a modest dowry should be grateful to be taken at all.'

Shurika shook her head gravely. 'I don't know where you hear of these things, mistress.'

'I hear everything,' answered Chinthimani with a wry smile. 'And much more besides. There is always somebody calling at my gate looking for a bowl of lentils in exchange for the village gossip.' Her laugh, now so seldom heard, remained as infectious at it had always been. Shurika could not help but smirk. 'The stupid girl refused to eat for three whole days and said that she would rather scorch her skin out in the fields with the tea pickers for the rest of her life than be married off to a man who she could not bear to lay eyes on. Her mother beat her black and blue and threatened to push the rice into her mouth herself. Imagine that!' The women exchanged a familiar glance and chuckled knowingly. 'Her fair face is a curse and has given her ideas above her station and foolish notions of love.'

The two girls reappeared from the back of the clubhouse, Mary's cheeks flushed and pockets bulging with biscuits. Serafina trailed behind her sister, solemnly picking at a piece of cake. She had barely uttered two words all morning and dragged her feet moodily. Shurika had tried to stay close to her from the moment they left home, but Serafina had walked away each time, rejecting Shurika's hand, yet constantly checking her surroundings as though deeply self-conscious, harried by her own thoughts. Shurika could not prevent her aching heart from returning to the words that had spilled from her mistress's slurring mouth the previous night. Yet this morning, Chinthimani had shown no recollection of the way she had sneered and spat her children's names.

'I think Serafina is unwell,' Shurika said quietly. 'Let us go back now and I will see that she takes some herbal tea and does not get any worse.'

'Unwell? There is nothing wrong with her. She is just temperamental today. She gets that from her father. Let her sulk all she wants to. It makes no difference to me. She'll soon become bored with it.'

'But mistress, she has not been herself all morning. Please, let me take them home now. You can go to the village if you want to. I can send for someone to go with you, or ask the cook to watch over the children and I will walk back with you myself.'

Shurika regarded Serafina anxiously. The child was seemingly miles away, lost in a daydream that creased deep worry lines into her face. A lone crow swooped down, landing by her feet to take the cake crumbs falling from her hands, shrieking its sudden melancholy caw and sending Serafina rushing into

Shurika's swiftly opened arms. Shurika held her tightly, feeling her small heart fluttering through her back.

'Still afraid of the crows?' Her mother smiled. Serafina did not answer, humiliated by her spontaneous display of weakness. Eyes tightly closed, she buried her face into Shurika's body, enraged by her mother's mocking smile. 'You should be grateful for them, for without the crows, we would have no sun.' Chinthimani began to walk. 'The crows were once great enemies of the owls, you know. The owls had said to them, "We don't want the sun as you do; we can see without him, for we can see in the dark," to which the crows replied, "We don't believe you can see in the dark; those who cannot see in the day can much less see at night." So the owls said to them, "You don't see in the night because you are a part of it; how else would you be so black?" The crows took this as a great compliment and returned it to the owls, saying, "You cannot see during the day because your eyes are a part of the sun; how else would they be so brilliant and round?" So the sun was saved, and the owls and the crows became great friends.'

The gatehouse was suddenly before them. Serafina did not want to leave, to go home, to the place where she was not wanted. She held back, pulling lightly on Shurika's arm.

'Shall we be staying for some tea?' she asked.

'No,' replied her mother. 'You have your biscuits?'

'Yes.'

'Then come along.'

Serafina dropped Shurika's arm and hung back, dawdling several paces behind, drawing tracks in the dust with her feet, glad to be left behind. She could slip into the trees and disappear in just a few moments. Nobody would miss her, and by the time they realised she was gone, she would be far away if she ran fast enough. She could find her way to her father's house from here. He would take her in and dry her tears and make her feel safe again. He would be pleased to see her and would pick her up and tell her how much he had missed her and apologise that he had not come to visit for so long. But in her heart she was uncertain, otherwise she would have run all the way there last night, when everyone else had fallen asleep. She would have told him everything that she had heard, and he would have laughed at her kindly and told her that it wasn't true, that she must have imagined it. Serafina stared at the thicket of trees above the small grassy bank and her courage deserted her.

The two guards on the gate smiled and waved her mother on, then whispered to each other and laughed as only men do. The taller of the two noticed Serafina watching them from lowered eyes and nudged his accomplice.

'Look at that one,' he sniggered, pulling a knife from his belt. He unsheathed the curved blade, tipped it towards the sun and fired the blinding rays directly at her eyes. Serafina was trapped in the sudden glare, rooted to the spot, no longer able to see her small family. She lifted her hands to shield her eyes and found herself gripped by a terrible fear. The guards took pleasure in her discomfort.

'I didn't think they allowed dogs in the club.'

'Or common prostitutes.'

The man with the knife took a pouch from his pocket and cut a piece of paan for each of them. Serafina wanted to run, but her legs failed, the air sucked from her body.

'Has she no shame? Parading her filthy bastard halflings and dropping us an anna or two as though we're beneath her? She should stay in her master's kennel and eat off the floor.'

'She should be beaten,' laughed the other. 'Made to recognise her place as a whore whose face is not fit to be seen by decent people. My brother found a dog stealing a juicy bone from the plate by his wife's supper fire. She was going to use it to make a broth. He beat the dog to death with a stick, then he beat his wife and told her to pay more attention next time.' They spoke loudly enough for Serafina to hear every word.

'When I take a wife, I shall beat her every day.'

'Then she will honour you for sure!'

'And if she does not give me sons, I will drown her useless offspring and beat her to death just like that thieving dog.'

'What are you looking at?' one of the men called quietly to Serafina, his voice menacing. 'You are not worthy to breathe the same air as us, or are you a prostitute too, like your sluttish mother? Come over here. We will show you what we do with such low life forms.'

Shards of bright colour kaleidoscoped in front of Serafina's eyes, her sight still scarred by the flash of the blade. A slight shape appeared somewhere before her in the distance, moving hazily towards the gatehouse, then Shurika called her name.

'Serafina! Where did you get to?' she said. 'I turned around and you were gone!' The gatekeepers quietened, smiling and eyeing them both with disdain. Serafina clutched at Shurika's hand, holding tightly, gratefully, as she was led away. 'It's all right,' Shurika whispered. 'Do not look at them.' She heard a snort from the guard as they passed by, then the distinctive sound of his filthy habit as he sniffed and drew. His red spittle flew through the air, spattering to the ground at Serafina's feet and catching the hem of her dress, staining it dark like old blood. Serafina did not dare look up. As they passed through the gate, she heard the same word that she had heard her mother use the night before, muttered clearly enough for them both to hear. Shurika ignored them, gripped Serafina's hand and walked quickly on.

'Come,' she said when they were far enough from the threat of the men. 'Your mother wants to walk into the village and see what is happening there today.'

'Really? But you said that we were not allowed.' Serafina brightened a little.

The village. That forbidden place filled with vibrant colours and foreign sounds and the delicious aromas of food, where the traders called news of their wares in sing-song voices, and the street cooks fried spicy treats in hot oil and served them straight into your hands on a shining salver of banana leaf with soft milk curds spooned over to calm the fiery chillies. They were supposedly not permitted these things, but children have a habit of getting their way. Serafina pulled at Shurika's hand, and the two of them took the old road that led through the trees on the far left to the village beyond, bravely dismissing the eyes that watched them.

Mary was afraid of the threshing machine. She knew from the cook's stories that her father had built it for her mother the season she was born six years ago, so that she might profit from the paddies. There was none other like it for miles around, so come harvest time, a steady stream of people would arrive bearing their crops, hoping to take advantage of the ingenious labour-saving device. Mary liked to hide behind the corn sacks when the villagers brought their rice for husking, and watched the cook's helper reach up and start the machine with the big handle. It made a ferocious noise, its deep first groan shuddering across the ground, travelling up her little legs and releasing a thousand butterflies in her stomach. She covered her mouth to stop herself screaming and wondered what would happen to any child who should fall into its jaws. They would be threshed to death, torn into a thousand little pieces and scattered all around. The men stood back once it was running, wiping their hands on a soft cloth with a sense of satisfaction and watching awhile, transfixed by the rhythmic motion of the machine. It made Mary feel sleepy if she looked at it for long enough, its sound deepening into a swishing mechanical song, leaving her eyelids heavy. She was not supposed to be there, but Mary was always to be found in the places that she should not be.

The three deep water wells on the homestead all followed the same line at equal intervals. Mary ran between them and leaned far over, waiting for her eyes to adjust to the darkness, to watch the frogs glistening at the bottom with no thought of what would happen to her should she tumble over the side. The field intended for vegetables lay fallow again this year. A flat-backed truck, broken down some time ago, sat there in place of the crops and provided a playground attraction for the children instead.

It was Wednesday. Provisions day. Cook had left for market soon after first light this morning, while the black-faced langurs still lolled around the misty courtyard, picking at each other's parasites before loping away at a reluctant canter to warm themselves in the early pools of sunlight. Mary's only occupation today was to wonder what sweets the cook would bring back for her. He always brought them something. She had hinted yesterday that she had been suffering a hankering for laddus, deliciously sweet balls of coconut and til, saying that they tasted different from the market. Her mouth watered at the thought of them, freshly fried and piled into pyramids by the smiling street trader. For their mother, the cook would fetch the speckled black and white seed crackers she was so fond of. She would break a piece off and give it to Mary if she stood nearby looking hungry, but Mary found them bland in her mouth and didn't care for the seeds that stuck in her teeth.

The hours stretched out, the sun gaining height and beating down upon her. Mary didn't mind waiting. She liked the cook and would go with him to the gate later when the man came with his big dish of milk curds. Cook would bring a pot from the kitchen and cut huge swathes out of the white curds with the flat wooden spatula, pulling faces at Mary, pretending that he was lifting a great weight with each scoop and delighting in her giddy laughter. Mary liked to sit at the gates. There were other traders who came too, although less frequently. The toothless man with his dancing bear, the cheerful lady with her basket of glass bangles who called her song from the gates. Their mother always bought bangles from her, filling her wrists and those of her delighted daughters with the bright jewel colours. Their arms jingle-jangled with every small movement, but the joy was soon over, the spun glass far too delicate to withstand the curiosity of an inquisitive child for any length of time.

Mary sat and waited patiently for the cook to return. She had a chicken settled in her lap. She thought it might be about to lay an egg, but she wasn't sure, so she hummed to it softly and kept it close by just in case.

'Come into the shade, little one,' Shurika said, one hand reaching for Mary, the other curved above her head to steady the bundle of clean linens she carried. Mary shook her head and concentrated on the chicken.

'Want Sera,' she mumbled.

'She will come and play with you soon.' Shurika put the bundle down and sat beside Mary. 'Maybe tomorrow, or the day after.'

'Want Sera to get up,' Mary said, her mouth pursed into a pout.

'Be patient, little one. You want your sister to get better, don't you?' Mary nodded at the ground. 'And what would happen to her if we made her get up and run around?' Mary shrugged. 'In that case, I will tell you exactly what would happen. She would feel much worse, then she would have to stay in her bed again, but this time it would be for much, much longer.'

The chicken gave small, contented grumbling noises under Mary's practised hands.

'Why?'

'Because she is not yet ready to play with you. You must remember that she is older.' Shurika reached out to Mary and pulled her into her lap. 'So she has to grow up first, and it is not always easy.'

The chicken began to struggle, unsettled at having been moved. Mary threw it high into the air and squealed as it flapped to the ground indignantly and scurried away.

'Come on.' Shurika stood up, balancing Mary awkwardly on her hip, and bent down to take up the laundry bundle again. 'Let us go and see if she would like to hear a story, shall we? But you must promise not to pester her.'

Serafina lay in her bed, eyes closed against her mother's cajoling voice. She wished more than anything to feel herself sliding back into the dreams where she felt safe from harm, to sleep until her spirit left her body and lifted her into the cool mountain streams that flowed down in clear, rushing torrents into the valleys and far away. Her mother's pitiful pleading filled her with fury, her murmured words of persuasion ringing hollow in the terrible new world in which she found herself. Serafina silenced her breath and kept rigid beneath the covers, the constant shape of her body set into stone. It was because of their mother that their father no longer came. Because of her shrill manner, her angry glances, her refusal to please him. Serafina felt her mother's hand on her hair. Her skin shuddered. She wished that she would go away.

'What is the matter with her?' Chinthimani demanded from Shurika the moment she came into the room. Shurika startled, surprised to see her mistress there. 'She has no fever. She should get up and enjoy the sunshine before the rains come.'

'I will look after her, mistress.'

'The doctor said there is nothing wrong with her.' Chinthimani's eyebrows twitched in irritation. 'Why does she pretend to be asleep like this?'

'Please, mistress. The child will be better in a few days. We must not force the sickness to let go of her. It will be gone in its own time.'

Mary slipped out of Shurika's arms and crept quietly to Serafina's bed. She leaned down close to her sister's face and watched intently as Serafina's eyes flickered against the wisp of her breath.

'Sera sick,' Mary said, placing a childish hand of concern on the bed. 'Poor Sera.'

'I will see to them.' Shurika examined Chinthimani's manner closely, aware of the barb of aggression placed in her voice by the whisky she smelled in the stillness of the room. 'It is a beautiful day, mistress. Will you not go outside and admire the flowers growing in the garden? I will cut some and bring them to your room if you tell me which ones you like best.'

'Hmph.' Chinthimani dismissed her, then reconsidered. 'Perhaps I will.'

The gentle tinkling of the bells on her ankles grew fainter and disappeared as she crossed the courtyard.

Shurika crouched to the floor beside Serafina's bed and whispered to her.

'I will save the most beautiful flower in the garden for you,' she sang quietly into her ear. 'Although the gods never made a flower more beautiful than you, nor a bird that could sing more sweetly, nor a jewel that could shine more brightly.' A small smile began at the corners of Serafina's mouth, lifting her cheeks into soft, pale mounds. Shurika reached out a tentative hand and pulled lightly at the velvet lobe of Serafina's ear, encouraging her into play, lifting her voice a little so the tune carried to fill the room. 'And the flowers will sigh, and the birds will fall silent, and all the jewels in the world shall be yours!' Serafina opened her eyes. 'Ah!' Shurika said. 'There you are!' Serafina pushed her covers down and stretched her arms around Shurika's neck. 'The flowers and the birds have been wondering when you will come outside to see them. We are all bored without you.'

'Sera awake!' clapped Mary. 'Sera play!'

'No.' Shurika smiled at her. 'Sera will not play today, but she will sit up and let me brush her hair, and then I will tell you both a very special story about the golden fishes who swim in the enchanted river. I have not told it to you before.' She hushed her voice to a whisper, drawing them both in, glazing Mary's eyes. 'Because it is full of a rare magic that few people can understand.'

The sudden sound of the heavy gates squealing on their hinges snapped Mary out of her daydream. She gave a yelp of delight and ran from the room.

'Careful!' Shurika shouted after her, before returning her full attention to Serafina, still so quiet, leaning into her lap. 'There, now,' she said. 'Isn't it better to open your eyes and smile?' She felt Serafina's head nod slightly. 'It sounds like Cook is back, and I know that he will have brought you something special from the market. He was most unhappy that you wouldn't eat his cake yesterday, so he gave your pieces to Mary. She almost made herself ill!'

Serafina pulled herself up, slowly bringing her legs around to sit on the edge of her bed. There was hardly anything of her.

'Is he cross with me?'

'No! Of course not.'

'Is Mother cross with me?'

'No!' Shurika hugged her tightly. 'Why would you think that?'

'She doesn't want us. She lies and pretends. You all do.'

Shurika sat on the floor and took up Serafina's hands.

'Serafina, look at me.' Serafina's eyes wandered this way and that, uncomfortable with the sudden intensity of Shurika's expression. 'Listen. Listen to me closely.' She squeezed Serafina's hands hard. 'You must forget what you heard, child. You must put it out of your mind and never think of it again, do you hear me? You are not like other children, you and your sister. You must prepare yourselves to be strong for each other, and make ready to live your life when it comes to you, which it will.'

Serafina felt the urgency in Shurika's tight grip. It frightened her, deep down inside where no one could see it, but she knew from Shurika's voice that she must listen, for here lay trust, and in that moment, she believed with all her heart that there was no one who loved her more.

Shurika settled her eyes deeply on Serafina's own, and with a voice filled with knowing said to her, 'You must not be afraid. The gods look after their own, Serafina. They will look after you as surely as they have looked after me.'

The rains came less than three weeks later, the skies darkening with the unimaginable weight of the clouds that gathered in great heavy blankets above. Serafina felt them moving near before the first drop of water fell. She could sense it in the thickened air, in the nature of the breeze that filled the silver oaks, their leaves shimmering with anticipation, aching for the downpour. She yearned for the rains to break, watching the animals moving anxiously outside as they tensed against the building pressure. The goats became skittish, unnerved by the crackling skies. The chickens refused to lay. The cook peered out from the cook-house, surveying the heavens with a wary eye. And so it came. The first thick, fat droplets hitting the dust, spattering one, two, three on the thirsty ground. Then, as though the skies had burst open, a mighty deluge cast down colossal sheets of water, silver curtains falling one after the other, setting the courtyard awash in a shallow lake, rich with the scent of the freshly bathed earth. Unable to see her hands in front of her face, Serafina stepped out into the rain. The might of the monsoon swallowed her up, drenching her in a moment, pouring in rivers down her outstretched arms, washing her troubles away.

## 12

Come September, the clouds parted and released infinite skies of iris blue. The sweetness of the rains left its peppery taste on the landscape, groaning with lush new growth, the rivers running high and filled with plump fishes that almost threw themselves into the fishermen's nets. After three months of rain, the air was fresh and new, the people smiling and happy, their lands habitable once more.

Felix liked nothing better than to make a show of things, and went to great lengths to parade his sophistications and pursue his passion for frivolities. It was folly to keep a motor car in an area almost devoid of the fuel on which to run it, or indeed the parts should anything break – an all too common occurrence given the non-existent state of the roads, yet Felix had insisted on bringing the Riley to drive them all to the clubhouse. He held the door wide open, helping Dorothy into the back seat before settling himself behind the wheel again.

'Well don't just stand there!' he shouted at James. 'We haven't got all day, you know!'

James hung back, absently pulling at his chin and looking out across the tea gardens. 'Just give me a minute, would you?'

'James?' Dorothy, aware of his sombre mood since they arrived an hour ago, knew that to enquire would be fruitless. 'James? Is something the matter?'

He didn't answer. Just ran his hand through his thick, dark

hair as though contemplating a weighty issue.

'Come on!' Felix huffed his impatience, starting the motor and revving thick fumes into the grass-scented air. 'Whatever it is, surely it can wait until later?'

James hesitated a moment before approaching the car window. 'It's no good,' he said. 'We've been having a few problems on the high terraces. One of the bull elephants ran amok last week, killing his mahout and injuring three of the coolies. We had to shoot it, and now the rest of the working herd is unsettled. If I don't go and check, I'll only worry about it. Why don't you two get going and I'll follow on a little later?'

Unable to mask her disappointment, Dorothy leaned her hand on the open window and frowned at him. 'Oh, really, James. Can't you send one of the boys to deal with it?'

A ridiculous urge to laugh overcame him. *Send one of the boys to deal with it.* Send one of the boys to deal with the consequences of his foolishness. To deal with the growing rumblings from a discontented mother and her two conspicuous children. He looked at Dorothy, her quietly pretty face, her disappointed smile. If only she knew, he thought. What would she think of him then? A man who feigned such high respectability, yet had set aside all laws of common decency so that he might have the convenience of a willing pair of lips to quiver beneath his own whenever he took the fancy? *Send one of the boys to deal with it.* He had sent one of the boys to deal with it every day, from sunrise to sunset, year in, year out. Why should today be any different? No. Today he would not send one of the boys to deal with it. Today he would deal with it himself. If thine eye offends thee, pluck it out.

'Don't worry.' James smiled briefly. 'It really shouldn't take long. Then we can relax and forget all about it.'

'Dorothy,' Felix barked. 'Talk some sense into this man of yours, will you? He certainly won't listen to a word I say.'

James had already turned away, calling instructions to Shiva in his servant's tongue. The words rolled from him with a careful softness. It was his way of closing any further conversation with Felix, who never learned a word outside of the daily commands necessary to direct his staff and to deal sternly with the pestilence of street children.

'I gave up on that long ago,' she said.

'Oh well.' Felix leaned his arm on the back of his seat and sympathised with her. 'It looks like you're going to be stuck with me again, I'm afraid. Want to come up here and join me?'

Dorothy slipped into the front seat beside him, clutching the hem of her skirt to preserve her modesty. 'I've spent enough time in his company these last few months to know when I'm fighting a losing battle.' She smiled dejectedly. 'There really is no arguing with James when his mind is made up. He's best left alone when he's like this. I really don't know what the matter with him is lately. I've not had so much as an ounce of conversation from him. Perhaps he's sickening for something.'

Felix concealed his concern, patting her hand, shouting merrily from the window, 'You're ruddy impossible, man! It would serve you bloody well right if I stole Dorothy from under your nose and made her fall in love with me instead.' He winked at Dorothy. 'I'd give him his marching orders if I were you. You're far too good for him.'

Felix pressed his foot to the accelerator and the car lurched away uncomfortably, kicking up a savage storm of red dust.

James watched the car turn and head towards the south gate, Dorothy's expression tugging at his conscience. He had seen that face many times before. Her expectation, her gentle manner, the way that she would not ask what it was in his heart that made him so withdrawn. He stood there long after the car had disappeared, pressing his chin into his palm, pursing his lips.

Shiva waited, out of sight behind the insect screen, watching

95

his master's indecision, the sun beating down on his bare head. He should not stand out in it for too long. The minutes passed before Shiva finally showed himself, carrying James's hat.

'Can I bring you something, Sahib?'

James forced his attentions to Shiva. 'Hmm? No. No thank you, Shiva.' He frowned at the ground, then suddenly changed his mind. 'Yes. Bring Titan. Quick as you can. And ask one of the boys to fetch my boots.'

'Yes, Sahib.'

The children played barefoot in the courtyard, running in between the cottons drying on the line and reaching for each other's hair, their untidy dresses smeared with the grubby marks of childhood freedom. Serafina ran to chase the waddling geese, sending them hissing angrily with outstretched wings while the cook shouted at her to leave them alone. Mary seemed unaware of the straw stuck to her clothes and bothered the chickens, picking each of them up in turn, looking for eggs. The white sun shone high in a cloudless sky, casting no shadow from the tall trees. An earthy rhythm rolled in on the warm air, gathering pace like small thunder against the ground, unnerving the goat, who began to pull at her tether, upsetting the tin bucket. Birds took fright and flew from their branches, scattering into the sky. The sound grew steadily until a powerful horse, flanks frothing, slowed and cantered heavy hooves into the courtyard. The children looked up and ran towards the open gates, shrieking with excitement.

'Papa! Papa!'

'Whoa! Careful there!' James brought his mount to a halt, jumped down and lifted Mary with ease, swinging her around and kissing her smiling cheeks. She laughed and flung her arms around his neck, snuffling into his shoulder. Serafina broke pace and suddenly stopped short, her smile fading as the nightmarish feelings of anxiety that had held her to her bed for six days rose in her again. She hung back, eyes downcast, waiting her turn, her mouth fixed into a serious repose. James noticed the rapid change in her demeanour and gently returned Mary to the ground. He looked down at Serafina and mimicked her doleful face.

'Oh,' he said solemnly. 'I see that I have come at a bad time.' He raised his hand to his chin and rubbed it thoughtfully, furrowing his brow. 'Perhaps you are so busy being serious that you do not have a kiss for your papa?'

Serafina could not help but break into a beaming smile. She rushed at him and threw her arms around his waist, holding on so tightly that he was for a moment left breathless. He pulled her arms away, lifted her with a kiss and put her into the saddle. In that fleeting moment, Serafina felt a hundred feet tall. Taller than her father. Taller than the silver oaks.

'Hold on tightly there.' James patted the front of the saddle, picked Mary up again and led the shining animal towards the stand by the cowshed, shaded beneath a curved roof of dampened reeds. The cook emerged from the cookhouse and saw the three of them, the big pan of water falling from his hands and crashing to the ground, spilling the rice everywhere.

He threw his arms in the air, shouting, 'The Sahib is here! The Sahib is here!'

Shurika came running from the house, almost tripping on the sari tucked so carelessly into the front of her waist.

'Sahib!' she cried. 'Oh, Sahib!' and rushed across the courtyard.

'Shurika.' James girded himself, the smile he readied for her overshadowed by the burden of his motive. 'And how are my girls?'

He put Mary down, threw the lead rein over the crossbar between the wooden struts and reached up for Serafina. She slid from the saddle into his arms and he returned her to the ground. Shurika, suddenly aware of her untidy hair, wished that he could have sent word of his arrival. Of all the days to have allowed the children to wear old, worn clothes and to let their hair fly loose. Chinthimani had refused to get up that morning, so groggy had she felt, so Shurika had left her to sleep and had allowed the children to play in the vegetable patch. Her hands rose to her face in shame.

'Oh, Sahib! Can you not see for yourself? Are they not growing into the most beautiful daughters any Sahib could wish for?'

James forced a laugh and regarded his children with mock judgement, these creatures who had never asked to be born, who carried his resemblance and called him Papa, tugging at his heart with their guileless ways.

'Mmm.' He squinted down at the pair of them. 'Let's see now.' He looked at Mary. 'This one is a little skinny around the legs.' He leaned down and tweaked her knee. She laughed wildly, spinning in circles. James turned to face her elder sister. 'And this one is too serious. What do you think we should do with her?' Serafina blushed and smiled, glad of his sudden attention, but her smile disappeared as quickly as it came.

'Why have you not come for so long, Papa?' She peered up into his face, searching for the truth. 'You used to come and stay here with us and take us on picnics together. Now we never see you. Are you angry with us? Have I done something wrong? We once put on special dresses and waited for you until it got dark. I didn't eat any supper in case it spoiled my clothes.' She lowered her eyes to the ground, hiding their sadness.

James's expression became pained. He looked at Shurika, but she was unable to offer him anything other than a sympathetic shrug. He paused while he tried to think of an answer, then, instead of speaking, he wrapped his arms around Serafina's shoulders, bringing her close to him.

'Serafina, Serafina,' he whispered. 'Such a sensible head on such tender shoulders.' He pulled away and took her hands before speaking to her in the grown-up manner that she demanded. 'And where is your mother?' Serafina pointed towards the door leading to their mother's quarters. 'Let me go and speak to her for a little while. Then I'll come back and take you both for a big long ride on Titan. We'll see if we can find you a tiger or two hiding in the trees, shall we?' He nodded at Shurika. She bowed her head respectfully and pressed her palms together.

Watching James walk to the house and disappear inside, Shurika and the girls fell silent. The cook stood motionless outside the cookhouse and took everything in. It was as though none of them dared to breathe. A few moments passed, then came a sudden shout from Chinthimani, the violent crash of objects being broken, a momentary raised voice from James. Then deathly quiet. Shurika took the girls' hands and led them away.

'Come,' she said. 'Let your mother and father talk. We'll go and ask Cook if he has a nice apple and a bucket of water for Titan. He must be hot.'

Chinthimani's parlour held an air of peculiarity about it, the furnishings in the simple room sparse but handsome, having been carried down to her from the big house along with anything else she wished for, the richly patterned rugs on the floor a luxury that few of her kind would ever know. Soft, spiced colours warmed the walls with naïve flowers, the paint peeling here and there, the motifs worn thin and faded. Dust sparkled in the shaft of sunlight streaming through the single window cut into the thick, earthy wall. Chinthimani sat weeping in a chair, fragments of broken clay scattered on the floor around her. James paced the length of the room, up and down, up and down, exasperated, sighing, and firmly resigned to his decision.

'You're letting them run wild! What have I told you?' He stared down at her. Chithimani cried and murmured prayers, rocking gently in her seat. 'Mary in with the chickens? Serafina chasing geese in her bare feet like a savage? What did you think was going to happen? This cannot go on any longer.'

'I don't understand!' she wailed. 'What is it that you wish me to do? Just tell me and I will do it! Have I not existed just for you? Have I not pleased you? Yet you cast me aside like yesterday's sour milk. And what am I to do? I am here all day long, trying to manage the homestead with no husband. You cannot imagine how I suffer or what it is like for me to be all alone in the robes of a widow. Do you think I do not know what is in your heart? Do you think I have not noticed that you cannot bear to look at me any more? You don't want me, that is clear. And now I have nothing. Why do you not just kill me and release me from this evil life?'

'This was not supposed to happen.' James spoke as if to himself, hiding behind the English words that passed unheard. 'None of this was supposed to happen. I would have cut out my own heart had I known.'

Chinthimani got up as if to leave, then threw herself at his feet in a wave of contrition, grasping hopelessly at his boots, crying and begging. James remained resolute in his determination to stand strong, his heart heavy with the finality of his judgement, this tiny hidden world, once seeming so peaceful, so perfect, now disintegrating before his very eyes and running through his fingers like a thousand grains of sand.

'There is nothing more I can do,' he said stiffly, taking a folded piece of paper from his inside pocket and holding it towards her in a futile bid to make her understand. 'I have received a letter. You were seen in the village again with the children. What have I told you? Why did you not leave them here if you wanted to go and see that woman? Did you think you could get away with it again and again? There are eyes everywhere.' How he wished that it were not so. That he could find another way. Any way except this. 'We spoke of this a long time ago. Do you remember?' He shook his head in fury. 'My God, it was such a simple instruction. So long as they were kept hidden, there would be no one who could object and I would be able to protect you. But would you listen? No. And now look where your defiance has led them.' She refused to answer. Refused to look up at him. Just cried and held on to the floor. 'What on earth were you thinking of? Do you have any idea of the trouble you have caused?' He sighed and lowered himself to his haunches beside her, softening his voice. 'The time has come. You always knew.' He thought for a moment, and corrected himself. '*We* always knew.'

'What will become of us?' she wailed. 'Where shall we go?'

James reached down for her hands and brought her to her feet. He could not bear to see the ruin on her face, so he put his arms around her and closed his eyes to the sea of human wreckage that drifted hopelessly in his wake.

The sun sank slowly behind the furthest peaks. The light dimmed, casting a lavender haze before the sky burst into a sea of pink and blue then began to ebb before the eyes could fully take it in. Such a vast sky. Heavenly scent hung from the garlands of orange blossom strung in readiness to offer their fleeting beauty to the deities at first light. The children lay in their beds, web-strung charpoys dressed comfortably with cotton sheets and blankets pulled high around their faces. Shurika hummed to them gently. Serafina turned to her, propping herself up on one elbow.

'What would happen to us if Mother died?' she asked, her voice barely more than a whisper.

Shurika stopped humming, and seemed both startled and puzzled by Serafina's question. 'You must not say things like that, child.' She stole a glance towards Mary, concerned that she should not hear them, but saw that she was quite happy, burrowing into her bed.

'But what would happen if she did?' Shurika did not respond and busied herself with the blankets. 'Would we go and live with Father? Or would we stay here on our own with you?'

'Shhh.' Shurika urged Serafina to lie down. 'We'll have no more of this talk. It doesn't do to tempt the gods with idle chatter about something that will never happen. Now go to sleep.'

'Tell us a story,' Serafina asked. Mary peeped her head out of the covers.

'Which one would you like to hear? Perhaps the one about the fat maharaja who cut off his servant's head?' Mary's eyes widened and she shook her head. 'Or shall I tell you the tale of the white monkeys who steal babies in the night?'

Serafina leaned back on her pillow. 'Tell us about the brothers who lived in the forest.'

Shurika turned down the hurricane lamp and settled on the floor between them, crossing her legs beneath herself.

'There were once four brothers who lived in the forest with their sister. Their parents were dead. The sister did all the work while the brothers lay idle. She sang and hummed with the voice of an angel while she cooked their meals and cleaned the house and never complained. One day, while she was preparing the stew, she accidentally cut her finger and a droplet of her blood fell into the cooking pot. At supper that night, all the brothers said how tasty the stew was, and asked her what she had done differently to make it so much more delicious. She told them that she had cut her finger, and that a droplet of her blood had fallen into the pot. After she had gone to bed that night, the brothers began to talk. They said, "If the stew tastes so delicious with just a single droplet of her blood, imagine how good she must be to eat." So they killed her and cooked her flesh, then sat and feasted upon their sister. Only the youngest brother was so upset that he could not eat. He pretended to put the meat into his mouth and chew, when really he was hiding it in his clothing. When his brothers had eaten their fill and gone to bed, he crept away and buried his share in the tall reeds that grew by the river. The next morning, he heard his sister's voice, a distant singing and humming coming from the river bank. Overjoyed, he rushed to find her, only to discover that it was the song of the wind as it passed through the reeds by the water's edge.'

The children were fast asleep.

## 13

'Get rid of the lot of them,' Felix concluded sternly with a flick of his cigar. 'Unless you want to see your entire life blighted and your name dragged through the mud. God knows, nobody could count the number of men who have humiliated themselves by going public. They're nothing but a laughing stock. Remember that Sheridan fellow?' Felix's distaste rang a sour note. 'The next thing we knew, he was walking around in a tartan frock, wearing curly shoes and declaring himself an honorary Indian! Christ only knows where he is now. Probably living like a savage somewhere in the back of beyond and eating curry and rice with his fingers.' James laughed to himself softly. 'What? It's not bloody funny, James. It's this sun, you know. Goes straight to the head and sends some men quite mad. That and the women, of course, cunning little devils. I suppose she must have thought it was Christmas come early when he declared his undying love and married her. Damn fool.'

'He seemed happy enough.' James remembered the small, much-copied photograph that had done the rounds in the clubhouses for months after the event, amid great ridicule.

'You're not thinking of—' James quickly assuaged Felix's alarm with a sharp shake of his head. 'Thank God for that. I wouldn't let you do it to yourself. Best that you get it over and done with. Send them off and get on with your life. It's the only answer. You know damn well that I'm right.'

'That's easier said than done,' James replied evenly. 'Like it or not, these are my children, for Christ's sake.'

'Only if you choose to acknowledge them.'

'Acknowledge? Is that what we're calling it?'

'Call it what you like. You know what I'm saying.'

'I don't have to put an announcement in *The Times* to meet my obligations, but I'll be damned if I'm going to turn my back on them. God knows their lives will be hard enough as it is. What chance will they have unless I take the matter in hand myself?' An involuntary sigh escaped his weary lips.

'Well I don't see what's so bloody difficult about it.' Felix puffed on his cigar. 'Money, James, that's all it takes. Just give her a hefty whack and tell her to be on her way. What she chooses to do after that is her own affair. They'll soon forget all about you. Let them go back to their own people and live a normal life.' He took a swig from his glass. 'Whatever that is.'

'A normal life? With two half-caste children? They wouldn't last five minutes, and I have no intention of spending the rest of my life wondering what became of them. That would be more punishment than even I deserve. It's out of the question.'

'All I know is that you can't keep stringing Dorothy along like this. You're starting to make the girl look like a fool. Anyone can see that she's potty about you.'

'And you'd be the expert on that subject, I suppose?'

'She's a wonderful woman, James. You'd be mad not to marry her. And if you won't, I will.' James smiled into his brandy. 'I'm serious!' Felix said. 'I can't think of anything more splendid than being married to a lady doctor. Better that than to be stuck with a woman whose only interest is the latest fashion in hats, eh?' Felix's left eye became lazy, drooping under the weight of the claret at dinner and the half-empty decanter. He warmed to his own suggestion. 'You need never call for a witch doctor again. God knows, most men would give their right arm to have a wife and physician all rolled into one. Old Mrs Edwards keeps telling me what a marvel she is. And let's face it, the only reason Dorothy has stayed with them for so long is because she's hanging around waiting for you to make up your mind. Do you know, she's been offered a place at the Royal Free?'

'Has she?' The hairs on James's neck stood to attention. 'She hasn't mentioned anything to me.'

'I'm not bloody surprised. It seems that there's no talking to you about anything these days. If you weren't so wrapped up in yourself, you might even have bothered to ask her. No doubt she'll turn them down on the off-chance that you might actually make an honest woman of her. A woman can't have a career and a husband, and right now poor Dorothy has neither.'

'I should never have taken up with her in the first place, sweet girl like that. God knows, it was the furthest thing from my mind.' James shook his head in confusion, burdened again by the weight of this all-consuming worry. 'Oh, what a bloody mess.'

'You're damn right.' Felix stared at the glowing end of his cigar.

'I've tried to broach the subject once or twice, but where the hell to start?'

'What? Don't be an idiot! Keep your mouth firmly shut. What could you possibly gain? If you're hoping to absolve yourself of the guilt you so obviously feel, you're very much mistaken. This will be nothing but a whole heap of trouble, James, just you mark my words.'

An awkward pause fell between them for a while, souring the friendship that had grown through a thousand evenings like this. Felix had become used to his friend's long silences. They spoke more clearly than any protracted discussion.

'There are places, you know,' Felix said quietly. 'Good

places, where you could be sure of their safety if you are so determined to salve your conscience.' He stepped carefully, mindful of James's ill-hidden distress. 'If there is anything I can do to help, anything at all, James, you have only to say the word. But please, for the love of God, you have to spare Dorothy this humiliation. It'll be the end of it for both of you.'

'You're a good friend.' James smiled, a tired smile that had known too many lies. 'But that would be unconscionable. I've already ruined one woman's life.'

Felix tossed his head in exasperation. 'Don't be ridiculous. We all make mistakes. No one will think any the less of you for it, not that it's likely that the news will get out if you're careful about it. Nobody will ever hear it from my lips, that you can be sure of.' He reached for the brandy and refilled their glasses. 'If you're worried about anyone in the household, just buy their silence with a few rupees, or give them the sack and send them back to the jungle. You'll soon see where their allegiance lies if you threaten to take the food out of their mouths.'

'I shall have to tell her.'

'What? Have you not listened to a word I've said? I'd bet you a pound to a penny that she'd be on the first boat home.'

'There's no other way, Felix. She deserves to know, then she can make up her mind for herself.'

'You're drunk,' Felix snapped. 'Don't be a fool.'

'It's too late for that. A fool I have already been.' James swirled the brandy in his glass, watching the rich, viscous liquid cling to the sides. 'I should have taken my chances with a wife long ago. God only knows what was going through my head.'

'You're making a very big mistake, James, but far be it from me to tell you what to do.'

'Time will tell.' James drained his glass, then pushed it at Felix to fill up again.

'Well, if that's the way you want it, so be it.' Felix rose

unsteadily from his seat and slapped James heftily on the back. 'But whatever you do, for heaven's sake hurry up and do it soon, James, before you go and make yourself ill.'

## 14

James eyed the dust on his shoes and cursed himself for agreeing to the trip, before returning his gaze to the passing scenery. Dorothy had gone to such trouble to surprise him, revealing with uncontainable delight at the eleventh hour that they were not going to Simla at all, but were instead heading many miles west to Mussoorie, perched in blessed splendour on a natural ridge in the Garhwal Himalayas overlooking the Doon valley and the city of Dehradun. His father's city. She had seemed so pleased with herself that he had not the heart to tell her that he had kept his distance for good reason.

So sure was she that he would be thrilled at the prospect of seeing the family he had not visited for so many years that Dorothy had taken the brave step of writing ahead in the hope that they would be able to meet up and enjoy a grand reunion among the quiet charms of Mussoorie's spectacular setting. James sat quietly in the carriage and remembered it well. The clear and sunny days when the snow-peaked Himalayas seemed close enough to touch with outstretched hand, the sacred Ganga visible from one end of the saddle ridge, the Jamuna from the other, and endless views that stretched effortlessly from Cloud's End in the west to Jabarkhet in the east.

Over the years, the distance between James and his family had widened into a gaping chasm filled with far too many unanswered questions and uncomfortable hints about his future plans for a family. If only they had known, he thought to himself as the train heaved its great length along, what a conversation that would have been. With each passing mile, his thoughts returned to his last visit, soon before the birth of his second child. Edith, his elder sister, had taken him aside and casually mentioned that there were some men, of course, who did not care for the company of women at all. Her raised eyebrow had added a clear subtext, to which he had mockingly pretended to choke on his *burra-peg* and assured her that she need not worry herself on that count. What he could not have done, however, was to admit to her the family that had grown illegitimately through the seed of his desire.

He now knew that that had been a grave mistake, that he should have confided in Edith right there and then and told her of the mess he had made. Perhaps then he might have been spared this terrible journey and the torture of writing the impossibly brief letter that sat burning in his breast pocket, waiting to be handed to an express messenger the moment they arrived. Edith would know what to do, even if he did not.

The weight of his deeds bore down upon him, the dilemma almost too much to endure. It was as though his life was stuck in a no-man's-land, his yearning to take up his future now rendered quite impossible by the choices he had once made. Dorothy looked across at him staring out of the window. She reached out and touched his hand.

'Penny for your thoughts?' She smiled at him. James covered her hand with his own.

'So many memories,' he said. 'It will be good to see the place again. Would you like me to call for some tea?'

'No,' she said. 'I'm still sleepy from lunch.'

'Then why don't you close your eyes for a while? We still have hours to go. I'll wake you up when there's something to see.'

Dorothy settled a small cushion beside her head, leaning into the side of the carriage wall, and allowed herself to drift with the lapping motion of the gently lilting train.

The journey was every ounce as arduous as James had anticipated, the final twenty miles from the railway station to the hotel an interminable, jolting ride on sickening winding roads. Yet the magnificent views that extended without interruption as they reached the hill resort swiftly erased all memory of the discomfort.

Dorothy emerged well rested from an afternoon locked away in her rooms, dressed for dinner in the new sage-green silk gown she had ordered from Mrs Edwards's tailor. The *darzee* had made a splendid job of it, the shoulders sitting just right, the fabric belt exactly where it should fall, the soft hem skimming her ankles precisely as she had asked him. Around her throat she wore her mother's pearls. The single string that her father had given her the day Dorothy was born. Her mother had passed them on to Dorothy just before she left for India, so that she might have something 'quintessentially English and equally appropriate for an intimate lunch with friends or dinner with a maharaja. They say the Maharani of Jaipur has one the size of a thrush's egg!' Dorothy heard her mother's excitable voice, ghostly in her head, as she fastened the clasp. Checking her rosy reflection in the hallway mirror, she decided that her extravagance with the tailor had been worth every penny, and could not help but feel that there was something special in the air tonight, her sense of premonition so strong that she was unable to settle herself. James had been unusually reserved on the journey, a sure sign that he had something important on his mind, and she had speculated wildly while resting in her room before convincing herself that she was getting all worked up over nothing.

The cool of the evening air reached Dorothy's skin immediately she stepped out on to the terrace, and she wondered whether to return for her shawl before dismissing the thought, not wanting to conceal her dress too quickly. English voices chattered amiably over drinks above the dramatic panoramic view, the Doon valley glittering lantern jewels far below. Dorothy found herself unable to prevent her pulse from racing just a little, and began fussing unnecessarily with a lace handkerchief.

'Well! Don't you look a picture!'

Dorothy jolted, startled by James's voice, much to her disappointment. She had wanted him to catch her just so, standing on the terrace perhaps, looking wistfully out towards the twinkling lights, the moonlight settling a soft glow across her small features.

'Oh!' She blushed and accepted the kiss he offered her cheek. 'You caught me by surprise! I was just admiring the view. Isn't it magnificent?'

'Mmm,' he agreed. 'There's none other like it. If you have a fancy to get up early one morning, it looks completely different, and changes every few minutes as the light comes up. We could ask to take early morning tea out here.'

'That would be lovely.'

'It's almost as though the high peaks have been cut off and left to wait on a cushion of cloud before being set down again.' He smiled at a distant memory. 'I always thought it was like sitting on top of the world, although when the fog rolls in, there's not much of anything to see at all, I'm afraid.'

'It's just wonderful,' Dorothy sighed.

'I should take you to Kempty Falls while we are here. They're a little way off, but the journey is well worth it when you get there. We could have the hotel pack us a picnic. Shall we sit?' He motioned her towards the vacant table behind them.

'Yes, thank you.'

'Is that a new dress you're wearing?'

'What? Oh, this!' Dorothy, suddenly terribly self-conscious, became aware of the extra little pad of rouge, the deeper shade of lipstick she had tried this evening. Perhaps it was too much and he did not approve. She had never known him to notice her appearance like this before, and sometimes wondered if he would give her a second glance if she were to turn up dressed in a sackcloth.

'It's quite lovely. You should wear that colour more often. It suits you well.'

'Thank you.'

James ordered a pair of gimlets from the boy and settled his full attention on Dorothy, touching her hand, admiring her modestly styled hair. Her heart thrilled.

'There is someone I'd very much like you to meet,' he said.

'Oh?' Dorothy's veins pounded.

'If you think you're ready to run the gauntlet of my family?'

'Of course! Oh my goodness, I had no idea!' Dorothy's face flushed with excitement. 'I thought we weren't seeing them for a couple of days! I've heard so much about your father that I'll probably babble on like an idiot. You must promise to nudge me if I start gushing or dash headlong into a silly conversation that loses its way after two sentences. Think first, speak later!'

'Ah,' James said with some embarrassment. 'I'm afraid it's just my sister for now. I didn't think it would be a good idea to overwhelm you with the whole clan at once. Edith's quite a girl, you know. One of those no-nonsense types who won't be forced to settle no matter what anyone says, much to everyone's chagrin. I expect the two of you will have quite a lot in common.'

'Oh.' Dorothy's disappointment shamed her.

'It's all right!' James said reassuringly. 'It was quite proper for you to write ahead, and I have no intention of interfering with your plans, whatever they may be.' His attempt to add a little mischief to his voice did nothing to relieve the knot in his chest.

'I'll have to be on my best behaviour while she gives me the once-over. From what you've told me, she does sound awfully ferocious.'

'Edith? Nonsense. I sent a message as soon as we arrived. She'd never forgive me if I didn't. She'll be travelling to London in a couple of months, so heaven only knows when we shall next see each other.' James tutted softly and shook his head, suddenly aware of the passing years. 'We were always close as children. She used to complain constantly about having been born female. Said that she would much rather have been a man so that she could live the high life without being remarked upon. I think she's had quite enough of this place and is looking forward to getting away from it all and kicking her heels up with the smart set.'

Dorothy, still lost in the romance of the moment, gazed out at the view and sighed. 'I don't think I could ever tire of it.'

'Fed up with being under the constant scrutiny of the family, I expect. She knows all about you, and I think the two of you will get along very well indeed.' Dorothy blushed with pleasure. 'I asked her to come along and join us for drinks this evening.' He glanced restlessly at his watch. 'I would imagine she will be here any time. You don't mind, do you?'

'No! No, of course not.'

'Are you sure?' James frowned. 'You must be tired from the journey. How thoughtless of me. I should have discussed it with you first.'

Dorothy smiled at him. 'Don't be silly! It's just that there's so much to take in. Perhaps I'm a little more nervous than I thought. She's bound to be protective of her brother and probably thinks that you're after a second opinion. I'm simply dying to meet her.'

'Here.' James passed Dorothy her gimlet with a sly wink. 'Better see this off then, and we'll order another one at the double.'

They quietened and sat together, sipping their drinks and taking in the vast ink-blue horizon, peppered with pin-sharp stars. James reached discreetly for Dorothy's hand, squeezed it affectionately, then placed his glass noiselessly on the table and moved his chair a little closer to hers. She almost dared not look at him, feeling so happy at that moment that she might spill over and cry like an overwrought child. She was so certain that she could make him happy, if only he would let her. Mrs Edwards had insisted on sharing her uninvited views over tiffin last Tuesday and told her that it was only a matter of time before he made his move. 'He is of that age, my dear,' she had said. 'You must be patient, and on no account must you try to force the issue. James is not a man to hurry into a decision so important. Men like that are like thoroughbred horses. Spook them and they bolt, and you'll be left standing in the middle of the field with a bridle and no groom!' Dorothy had flushed scarlet, causing Mrs Edwards to howl with laughter.

James's face took on a new solemnity, the squeeze of his hand urging her to lean closer to him. 'My dearest Dorothy,' he said softly. Dorothy raised her eyes to his and forgot to exhale. 'You do know how much you mean to me, don't you?'

'Do I?' she said shyly.

'You must realise that this has all been leading somewhere? All this wonderful time we have been spending together?'

'I suppose.' She tried to laugh a little, but could hardly think for the rushing in her head.

'Although I have to say, I have asked myself a hundred times over what on earth you must see in me.' He stopped her with a squeeze of his hand before she could respond. 'Heaven knows, you have shown the patience of a saint. I realise I'm not the easiest of people to be around. I can be a bit, well …' he thought, 'distant, I suppose.'

'Yes.' She smiled, touched by his admission. 'Sometimes it's as though your head is way up in the clouds somewhere, just like the way you described the mountains. I don't mind. Really I don't.' However distant he might be, she knew she could bear the loneliness, the silences, as long as they were together. She could never hope to love another man the way she loved him. There was nothing she could do about it, and had she not felt it for herself, she would never have believed such devotion could have existed. 'In fact, I happen to like it that you're not one of those bullish sorts. I've heard all kinds of stories about their terrible antics in the clubhouses. Those are exactly the kind of men I have spent most of my adult life trying to avoid. You're different from other men, James. Everyone can see that. Even Felix says so. I know that we might seem like a terrible mismatch to some people.' She realised that she was beginning to ramble so held herself in check, taking a moment to consider what he was really saying to her. 'It's true,' she surrendered. 'I often wonder where your mind wanders off to. It looks like a peaceful place. Perhaps you could take me there with you one of these days.'

'Well.' James straightened himself a little, picked up both her hands and kissed them. 'That, my darling, is exactly what I want to talk to you about now.'

As the words fell from his lips, Dorothy's whole world and every shred of hope that she had ever held for herself came crashing down around her, the future she had secretly imagined that very afternoon disappearing instantly in a tiny vaporous wisp.

'No,' was all she could say, whispering it over and over. No, no, no. The walls began to close in around her, the magnificent view stretching beneath them blurred by the tears that ran helplessly down her face as she felt the dagger twist inside. 'I won't believe it. You wouldn't.'

'Dorothy. I ... I'm so sorry.'

She began to feel sick, then faint, finding herself unable to stand, as though swept away by an avalanche. 'It's not true.' She shook her head at him in disbelief, eyes wide with shock. 'Tell me it's not true.'

Amid the words, other noises escaped from her mouth – unrecognisable, pitiful yelps that rose like bile. The once laughing guests seated at the tables around them quietened, craning their necks to peer at the distraught woman, then accusingly towards James. At that very instant, Edith appeared. James stood the moment he saw her, left the table and rushed to her.

'James!' She threw her arms wide open to greet him, then, taking in the scene, her smile disappeared, her face flushed with concern. 'James? What on earth ...'

'Thank God you're here.' James moved to kiss her cheek. Edith could feel the heat in his face. 'I've been a damned fool, Edith. Poor Dorothy's in a terrible state. I've ...'

Dorothy's eyes widened.

'You haven't gone and ...'

'Yes. Yes, I'm afraid I ...'

'What, here? *Now?*'

'Yes, I ...'

'Oh, for God's sake, James!' Edith glared at him, her eyes filled with pity. 'Why can't you men stop to *think*?' She shook her head and stared towards Dorothy, wilted in the seat, head in her hands.

'I'm sorry, I thought ...'

'No, James, you didn't,' Edith hissed. 'Just look at the poor girl! I suggest you just stay out of the way and leave us alone for a while. Go on.' She pushed him away. 'I think you've done quite enough damage for one evening.'

'Dorothy?' Edith bent over her, sliding a supportive arm around her shoulders and picking up the small jet-beaded evening bag from the table with her free hand. 'Come on now. See if you can stand up.' Her usually sharp voice became soft. 'I'm Edith, but I think you probably already knew that. I've sent James away. You won't have to see him.' She helped Dorothy to her feet, pressing a clean handkerchief into her trembling fingers, and steered her past the curious onlookers, through the silenced hotel lobby and upstairs to the small suite of rooms James had taken for her.

Behind the closed door, Dorothy stood and stared at her puffy reflection in the mirror. Her make-up had run terribly, smearing her cheeks, dropping tear-sized stains all down the front of her new dress. Still weeping, she began to dab at them, then rubbed at them violently with a towel, spreading the marks.

'Leave the dress.' Edith urged her towards a chair, but Dorothy refused and began to sob. Her temper fraying, she tore at the dress, ripping it from her shoulder, buttons flying. 'Dorothy, my dear, please don't upset yourself!'

'Upset myself?' Dorothy shouted. She wrenched the dress from her body, splitting the green silk like paper, flinging it to the floor and kicking it away. 'How could he!' she wailed.

Edith quickly went to the door and shouted for a houseboy, before barking her order at him.

'Please, Dorothy. Sit down and try to calm yourself. You've had a terrible shock.'

'Shock? Is that what you call it? And I suppose you've known about this all along?' Edith sighed and sat heavily on the edge of the armchair. Dorothy's rage spilled over. 'I want to leave this very instant. I shall not stay another moment in this godforsaken place. I must insist that a car be found for me at once. And you can tell your brother to go to hell!' She began lurching around the room, pulling at the case she had unpacked so carefully just that afternoon, indiscriminately throwing her belongings into it, hurling one thing after another across the room to where it lay open. Her precious cut-glass powder dish bounced from the case and crashed to the floor, smashing into a thousand shards. 'Oh!' Dorothy cried. 'Oh no!' She dropped to her knees and stared at the pieces. 'It was my grandmother's!' She pressed her face into her open palms and gave in to the racking sobs that enveloped her.

Edith rushed to her and held her closely. 'I'm so, so sorry,' she said.

There came a small knock on the door. Edith answered it to take the tray she had ordered. She mixed the hot milk and brandy herself, adding a spoonful of honey and holding the warmth of the cup against Dorothy's hands. She was shivering in her petticoat, seemingly unaware of her undressed state. 'It's far too late for you to leave tonight,' Edith told her. 'And besides, you're in no fit state to travel.' She sat Dorothy on the bed and slipped a shawl around her bare shoulders. 'Drink it.' She pushed the cup towards Dorothy's lips. 'It will help you to sleep.'

'I don't want to sleep,' Dorothy said. 'I feel like I've been asleep for months. How could I not have known?'

'As far as I'm aware, nobody knows. Today was the first I'd heard of it, and I must say, I can scarcely believe it myself.'

'How could I have been so blind?'

Everything began to drop into place. His brooding silences. The long unexplained absences.

'Don't,' Edith said. 'Don't blame yourself. I expect James

has been worried sick about telling you. The longer these things are left, the harder they become.'

'Well I hope he's satisfied. I shall never see him or speak to him again.' Dorothy began to cry once more.

'Sshh,' Edith said. 'You need time to think. You must stay here for a few days and gather yourself.'

'No. I want to go home.'

'All right. But don't force yourself into any decisions right now. If you feel the same way in the morning, send word to me and I will come back and escort you myself to anywhere you wish to go.' Edith placed a silk eiderdown across Dorothy's exposed legs. 'I really am truly sorry, Dorothy. If only I had arrived a little earlier.' She sighed heavily. 'Men can be such idiots. I don't know what must have been going on in that head of his. And I'm certain that he would rather have stuck a knife in his own heart than hurt you like this. He really is terribly fond of you, you know.'

Dorothy buried her face in her hands and succumbed to the waves of grief that overwhelmed her.

'Well,' Edith said to James, finding him alone in the bar nursing a large whisky. 'I don't think I've ever seen a woman so upset in my whole life. Get me one of those, would you?' James nodded to the boy. 'You have no idea of the pain and misery you've inflicted on that poor girl this evening, James. I hope you're proud of yourself.'

'That's unfair, Edith.'

'Unfair? Hmph. You bloody men are all the same. You, of all people. You should have known, and that letter of yours would have been better addressed to your conscience.' Edith took up her whisky glass and swallowed half the contents without flinching. 'I burned it, you know. Before anyone else found it. Thought it was some kind of bad joke at first. My own brother, taking up like that with some ...' She quietened herself quickly, glancing around, lowering her voice to a whisper. 'What the devil were you thinking of?'

'I have no excuse,' James admitted lamely. 'I was lonely. I wanted companionship.'

'Companionship, indeed.' Edith raised her eyes to the ceiling fan moving in slow, stealthy circles above their heads. 'You can save your euphemisms for the jury, James. Everyone knows what you wanted, and it wasn't fine conversation over a cup of tea, was it?' James bowed his head to his lap. 'Oh well. No point in crying over spilled milk.' Edith pursed her lips. 'Tell me about the children.'

'Two girls.'

'Girls?' Edith raised a distinguished eyebrow, just the way James did sometimes. 'Isn't that funny? I somehow imagined they'd be boys.'

'No.' James smiled, his face pitiful. 'They're girls. The eldest, Serafina, is eight. The little one is six. Her name's Mary.'

'Serafina and Mary,' Edith repeated to herself quietly, as if to embed them in her memory.

'I suppose I somehow just thought it would all go away. I know it sounds ridiculous.'

'What about the mother?'

'I don't know.'

'What do you mean, you don't know?'

'She's ...' James struggled to find the words. 'I never thought about what this would do to her. I thought it would be a neat arrangement that would eventually run its course with no one any the worse off.'

'Idiot.'

'They've been well looked after.'

'Really? That's what you think, is it?'

'And I am quite resolved to see that they should be properly provided for.'

'I can't even begin to imagine what our parents would say if they knew about this. As far as they're concerned, their darling, precious son has finally found himself a nice young woman to settle down with. Not that they're likely to so much as clap eyes on Dorothy after your little performance this evening. I'd like to be a fly on the wall when you explain to them her sudden departure.'

'Dorothy,' James said ruefully. 'Dearest Dorothy. What have I done?'

'Not only were your actions unforgivable, your timing was rotten. Can you imagine how she must have felt? My God, you'd hardly been here five minutes.'

'I thought it best to get it out of the way.'

'Oh, did you now?' Edith laughed sarcastically. 'And I suppose you thought it would be a good idea to drop a bombshell on her in front of the whole hotel too?'

'No.' James hung his head in submission.

'No, I thought not. You should be thoroughly ashamed of yourself.'

They sat without speaking for a little while, James's indefensible position silencing him into quiet contemplation, unable to tear his thoughts from Dorothy.

'Is she all right?'

'No, of course she isn't! She wanted to leave immediately, but naturally that's out of the question now. I promised to come back and escort her home tomorrow if she still wants to go, although I did try to persuade her to stay here for a little while, just long enough to gather herself.'

'Thank you, Edith.'

'Don't thank me. I did it for her. Heaven knows she's in no fit state to go anywhere right now. I've promised her that you will stay well out of her way. She doesn't want to see you or speak to you, and I can't say that I blame her one little bit.'

'No,' said James. 'I suppose not.'

'If I were you, I'd just keep my fingers crossed and hope that she comes round, but I think you've really done it this time.' She watched the distress distorting her brother's face and smiled at him sympathetically. 'Oh, James. It really is wonderful to see you again. How long has it been?'

'Seven years.'

'Really? My, my. It's no wonder I've become so crotchety. I must have got older than I'm admitting to. I wish you luck with Dorothy. If only we could have met under more enjoyable circumstances, I expect things would have gone quite differently this evening. Call me when you know what's happening.' She leaned over and kissed him on the cheek.

Dorothy remained in her rooms for two days. The more she thought about it, the more she cried. Then she began to wonder, the seeds of doubt sown, whether the arrangement had remained in place while their own subtle courtship was gradually blossoming. She finally emerged from the solitude of her anguish and sat down to breakfast with James on the third morning.

'Thank you,' James said.

'What for?' Dorothy was unable to look him in the eye for fear of what she might see.

'For agreeing to have breakfast with me this morning. I've been worried about you.'

'I'm fine,' she said emptily. Her tears began to rise again, but she fought them back, determined that her crying was over. When she finally felt that she could trust her voice to serve her without cracking, she asked him outright. 'There is one thing I want to know, James.'

'Yes,' he said, relieved to engage with her at all. 'Of course.'

'And it is the only question I wish to ask of you on the matter.'

'Anything.' For a moment, James wanted to reach for her hand. As if sensing it, she moved hers from the table and placed them in her lap.

'The woman ...' She hesitated, not sure of what she should call her. 'Were you still seeing her while we were ...'

'No!' James was aghast. 'There has been nothing between us for years. Heaven only knows the number of times I have wished to be able to turn back the clock. The children arrived before I could ...'

Dorothy lifted her hand.

'I don't want to know,' she said. 'All I was asking was whether or not you were still carrying on with her.'

'No.' James reached under the table and took her hand firmly, brooking no argument about it. 'I have not so much as looked at another woman,' he said. 'And nor will I. Not for as long as I live to take another breath.'

## 15

Shiva stepped down from the bullock cart, loaded high with the hard leather packing trunks that had been brought down from the big house by three of the servants, now filled with the untouched clothes that had been sent for specially all the way from Hall & Anderson in Calcutta. All around, the seething spectrum of humanity teemed through the railway station, a bustling hub leading to the whole world, from the highest hills to the congested cities to the sea and the ships that sailed.

James was content for Shiva to supervise the children's luggage being transferred to the platform and laid down by the red-shirted coolies. Sleep had eluded him last night. Instead, he had lain awake, hour upon hour, listening to the night sounds and worrying himself in and out of fitful meditations. That morning, as he had washed and dressed himself in the light-brown suit he favoured for travelling, he had been unable to coax his thoughts away from his daughters for more than a few moments. He had told them himself several days earlier, the news disguised as a sweet surprise for two very lucky girls who would soon have more friends to play with than they could imagine. He spoke of another world, full of wonderful new things to discover. He spoke of the future as though it were a place that must be travelled to. Mary, too young to comprehend, had squealed and giggled in her usual way, but Serafina fell silent and ran away before anyone could stop her. She was missing for the whole afternoon. James immediately sent for Shiva and told him to organise a search party, telling him to take the four houseboys, the cook and his helper. Chinthimani threw clay pots, smashing them on the ground outside her quarters, and cursed herself and everyone around her before taking to her bed.

Much later, it was Shiva who discovered Serafina hiding beneath the idle threshing machine, curled up into a ball, exhausted from hours of useless tears. He had reached in and coaxed her out, then slowly, carefully, he had picked the stray pieces of twig and leaf from her dress and hair, tidying her and brushing her down before carrying her back to her mother's house.

James stared towards the parallel tracks and checked the time on his chain watch, tapping the glass for no good reason and forgetting what the dial said the moment he returned it to his pocket. The girls stood self-consciously, dressed awkwardly in their new cotton frocks and wearing the uncomfortable straw hats that felt much too stiff. Mary pulled at the strap beneath her chin, trying to set it in a less uncomfortable position, but it snagged against her ears each time she looked down to the heavy brown shoes on her feet, and felt as if it would tumble from her head. She imagined that her legs ached. She had cried when the shoes were first put on her feet, and kept pulling them off until Cook bribed her with a piece of sweet semolina cake.

Now she gazed down at the ugly lumps beneath her, lifted them up, turn by turn, still unable to comprehend their weight, and wiggled her toes inside, unsure that they were still there because she could neither see nor feel them. The small, experimental steps she had taken the day before felt as though someone had tied two bags of rice to the bottom of her legs. She had walked around the room, awkwardly raising her knees and feeling her feet imprisoned, while Shurika looked on and encouraged her to walk normally.

Chinthimani stood silently, her sari barely moving in the insufficient breeze, its white cotton pulled high above her head to veil her face from the onlooking world and the idle groups of men who stared at her uninhibited. Inside, she was all emptiness, every grain of hope sucked from her. She was unable to feel the breath in her body, the blood in her veins. Just a cold space that felt like death.

Serafina loitered at the grey platform edge, waiting for the train that she knew would change everything. How she wished it would never come. That she could close her eyes and shut out the sounds around her, then wake in a cold sweat and find herself lying in the darkness in the simple room she shared with her sister in their mother's house, Shurika asleep on the floor between them, quick to come to her side when the bad dreams began. She clenched her fists and screwed up her face, willing the tears not to come. She wished that Shurika were here. That she could run and hide in the folds of her sari as she had done so many times when she was small and saw a gecko scurrying up the wall. She was afraid of lizards. Even the tiny tuc-tucs with their translucent bodies. Sometimes they would lose their footing and fall to the floor, landing with a minute slap. She would scream in terror and insist that they be killed in front of her.

But Shurika was not here today. She had not eaten properly for two whole weeks, even though Cook had gone to the market specially and brought back jaggery and semolina and all the things that she loved. He had made more sweets in the last month than they had seen in the past year or more, but Shurika was not to be tempted, her grief refusing to swallow, and instead offered them to the gods with flowers and prayers, day and night, pleading with her head bowed as her already slight body faded before their very eyes. That morning, she had embraced the girls after dressing them and brushing their hair, her eyes red and swollen, her lips dry from fasting. Unable to speak, she had not hummed her tuneful songs to them for days. Mary begged her to sing, but she had said that she could not.

The strange family stood together, waiting and watching, until the huff-puff of the approaching train with its rising clouds of steam and smoke curled into view. Serafina opened her eyes. At that moment, all she wanted to do was turn and run, run as fast as her legs would carry her, and find somewhere else this time, somewhere that nobody would think to look for her. She glared down at her sister, who held on to their mother's hand, squealing at the sight of the enormous engine pulling into the station.

'Train!' shouted Mary, pointing and jumping around. '*Maa*, look! Train! Train!' Serafina envied her the luxury of her infantile ignorance and yearned for the courage to throw herself in front of its wheels.

The arrival of the train brought with it a rush of frenetic activity. People suddenly appeared from all quarters, whistles blowing and bells ringing. Hawkers offered food up to the windows, calling loudly news of their wares, clay cups of sweet steaming chai, small pots of curried chickpeas with flat chapattis, trays piled high with fresh fruit. Passengers crammed on and spilled off amid huge clouds of steam. Tied bundles were thrown down to the platform and others heaved up to waiting outstretched hands. Among such confusion, it was a miracle that anyone ever managed to find their place. James saw that the trunks were loaded into the luggage car, spoke a while to Shiva, then guided his daughters and their mother towards the first-class compartment designated for ladies only. He lifted the girls in, one at a time. Serafina was perfectly capable of managing the big steps without any assistance, but stood and waited patiently to be carried up, wanting to feel the strength of her father's arms.

'What about you, Papa?' she asked.

'I'll be right here in the next carriage.'

'But why can't you travel with us? Why make us go in a carriage on our own?'

'It is the proper way,' he chastised her gently. 'Now you look after your mother and I will come and visit you each time we pull into a station. It will be a great adventure and a good opportunity for you to learn that there is a whole world out there. I want you to tell me everything that you see.' He busied himself, unable to meet their uncertain faces. Chinthimani reached her hand towards him. He looked at her briefly, admonished her with a shake of his head, then moved away to join the next carriage.

The crowds dispersed as quickly as they had arrived, scattering and disappearing in a thousand directions. A whistle blew long and hard and the train began to groan, straining at its couplings, metal squealing against metal, pulling at the impossible weight. With one huge final effort, the engine suddenly belched a bitter cloud of black smoke, wrenched itself towards the landscape, and huffed its way upwards as the hill rose into a burnished evening sky.

*Part Two*

# HAFLONG
## 1940

## 16

The gardens of St Agnes ran all the way around the perched, isolated buildings then fell sharply away, stretching down into the wide valley cleft below, leaving the whitewashed convent peacefully stranded above the deep ravines of thick, mist-bound forest. Within these walls lay a place of sanctuary, far from the prying eyes of the outside world, dedicated to the glory of God.

The music of children's voices carried faintly from the schoolroom across the high lawns, chanting in practised unison a chorused sing-song, *three times three is nine, four times four is sixteen,* floating through the stillness of the morning, drifting through the open windows of the infirmary to Mary's guilty ears as she lay in her bed, willing the thermometer under her tongue to boil the mercury to a temperature of a hundred and one.

Sister Margaret, resplendent in the long grey habit that flew about her, arranged her ample behind on the edge of Mary's bed, a large, comfortable affair more suited to a hospital than a school, with three plump pillows instead of the single, thinner allocation on her usual bunk in the chilly dormitory. Of all the girls in the convent, it was Mary whom Sister Margaret had grown most attached to, Mary who had followed her around like a lost lamb when she and her sister first arrived six years ago, neither of them able to speak a word of English.

'Back in the infirmary again, Mary Macdonald?' Sister Margaret narrowed her eyes. Mary nodded solemnly, trying her best to appear very ill indeed. 'Sister Rosemary tells me that you were feeling sick during the night. Any better this morning?' Mary shook her head. 'I see.' Sister Margaret glanced deliberately at the crucifix bearing down upon them from the wall. 'And this wouldn't have anything to do with the maths lessons today now, would it, child?'

Mary gave her a look of all innocence, hoping to suggest that she had no recollection of the day's curriculum at all. The thermometer protruding from her mouth prevented her from speaking her answer, and she was glad of the excuse to remain honestly silent.

'Well now,' Sister Margaret adjusted the rosary dangling into her lap, 'we can't all be as clever as that Albert Einstein fellow, I'll grant you, but every girl needs to know her times tables by the time she's twelve years old, otherwise the world might stop turning, and that would never do now, would it?' Her pale lavender eyes twinkled kindly, the twitch at the corner of her mouth hinting at a hidden smile.

The infirmary held only two other ailing occupants today, one of whom coughed and spluttered incessantly, the other being hidden in the corner behind carefully arranged screens with a handwritten notice hanging loosely from the frame, marked INFECTIOUS. The five remaining beds lay empty, their bedclothes perfectly arranged, mosquito nets pulled up high and tied into neat cloud-like bundles suspended above each one. A small, welcome breeze drifted in with the chanting through the open windows. Sister Margaret hummed a little, checked that the thermometer was properly placed beneath Mary's tongue and kept half an eye on the clock. From behind the fabric screens, Sister Rosemary appeared, the enamel tray in her hands piled high with cotton swabs sodden with pale pink calamine.

'Dear Father in heaven,' she flustered, replacing the screen behind her. 'I've never seen so many chickenpox land on a single child.'

'Let's just hope she manages to keep them to herself,' Sister Margaret replied, returning her attentions to Mary. 'And you should count yourself lucky that you've had the chickenpox already, young lady, otherwise you'd be looking like a fine currant bun yourself in a day or two.'

'There's nothing wrong with that one.' Sister Rosemary marched past Mary's bed, heading towards the door. 'At least, nothing that a good dose of castor oil won't cure. I'll be back in a minute, then we'll see how ill she is.'

Sister Margaret took the thermometer from Mary's mouth and held it up to the light.

'Mmm,' she said. 'And what do you think this might tell me?' Mary's bottom lip began to quiver, her doe eyes filled with shame. Sister Margaret sighed a small sigh and squeezed her hand. 'Did you ever hear the story about the little boy who cried wolf, Mary?' Mary nodded. 'And you know that it's very wicked to tell lies?' Mary's face reddened. 'Sister Rosemary will have your guts for garters, child, you just see if she doesn't. She was a nurse in the Great War, you know, where thousands of men died for want of a clean hospital bed and a bit of care. She says there's nothing worse than a shammer who lies around pretending to be sick when they're not, and I have to say that I'm inclined to agree with her.' Mary began to snivel, her eyes widening at the sight of Sister Rosemary heading towards her, armed with the dreaded bottle and spoon.

Sister Margaret stood suddenly, shaking down the mercury in the thermometer, clucking to herself thoughtfully.

'Would you just look at that, now?' She waved the thermometer briefly at Sister Rosemary. 'Almost a hundred and one!' She tucked Mary in firmly, pinning her down with the sheets and pressing her hand against her forehead. 'Red as a beetroot a moment ago, she was. I wouldn't go near her if I were you, Sister. The last thing we all need is for you to go down with a fever again, especially if we're on the verge of another outbreak of the chickenpox.'

'Really?' Sister Rosemary frowned. 'She seemed perfectly fine to me an hour ago.'

'I expect she just needs to sweat it out.' Sister Margaret threw an extra blanket across the bed, her broad back to Sister Rosemary, and winked at Mary. 'I wouldn't bother with the castor oil, Sister. She'll only bring it back up again and make a terrible mess. And as for you,' she spoke to Mary sternly, 'I'll come and check on you a little later, if I have the time. You had better keep yourself quiet now and not be any bother to Sister Rosemary. She's very busy, you know.'

'I won't,' said Mary, a little too quickly.

'Let's just get those pillows plumped up for you, then I'll be off. I can't sit around here all day playing nursemaid to you now, can I?'

Sister Margaret rumpled the pillows around Mary's head, shoving her hand beneath the pile momentarily, then mumbled half a prayer, crossed herself and swept out of the infirmary.

Mary closed her eyes and snuggled deep into the crisp, warm covers, feeling comforted by the reassuring smell of disinfectant and the small, pathetic whimpers of the girl hidden behind the screens. Every now and then she contrived to take a peek through the tiniest slits she could make in her eyes, letting in a shadowy image of the clinical white walls, to inform herself of Sister Rosemary's precise whereabouts. After what seemed like a thousand hours, Sister Rosemary finally disappeared behind the cordon to attend to the girl with the chickenpox again. Mary surreptitiously reached her hand up to feel beneath her pillows for the lump left there by Sister Margaret. Sliding out the rolled-up handkerchief with its telltale monogram, a pale-blue M neatly worked by hand, she put it under her nose and sniffed at the sweet, sugary scent, then quietly opened the tiny bundle to reveal two jelly babies hidden within.

'Are you feeling any better, Mary?' Sister Rosemary's sharp voice snapped Mary awake. For a moment, she was not sure where she was, the act of having been fast asleep in the middle of a fine, sunny afternoon having left her deliciously dis-orientated. She blinked against the sudden light, but the nun's hand was upon her small forehead before she could fully rouse herself and employ her most ailing expression. 'Well! Your fever's gone, that's for sure.'

'Yes.' Mary stifled a yawn. 'Thank you, Sister Rosemary. I'm feeling much better now.'

'It's nothing short of a miracle, I'd say.' Sister Rosemary eyed her suspiciously. 'But then again, the good Lord does have a habit of sending miraculous cures for your mystery ill-nesses, doesn't he?'

'Yes, Sister Rosemary.'

'Skinny little scrap like you, it's any wonder you haven't died from your ailments.' Mary blushed and chewed her lip. 'I suppose he's saving you for a good reason, although quite what that could be, heaven only knows. You had better get yourself up and dressed and be off with you.'

'Yes, Sister Rosemary.'

'But before you go, just to make sure ...' Sister Rosemary produced the spoon and bottle from the deep pocket of her long white apron. 'We wouldn't want any of those nasty bugs hanging around inside your tummy now, would we?'

That night, lying in her own flat bunk in the gloomy dormitory, Mary wished that all the beds could be as soft as the ones in the infirmary. She spread her arms out by her sides, feeling the relative narrowness of the thin mattress on which she lay, and wiggled her toes against the rough sheet, comparing its texture with the crisp, stiff cottons on Sister Rosemary's tiny ward. Her tummy rumbled, reminding her of its emptiness. After the unavoidable dose of castor oil that afternoon, she had been unable to face her supper, the foul taste of Sister Rosemary's panacea still coating her hungry mouth an hour or more after she had swallowed the vile spoonful. How she wished that she had saved one of the jelly babies.

Mary lay back quietly and tried to think of anything other than food, her efforts serving only to make matters worse, as vivid images of laden plates danced in front of her tightly closed eyes – spiced sausages with curried lentils, warm chapattis wrapped around tender pieces of chicken dipped in soft milk curds and toasted seeds. Her tummy growled louder. She pulled the thin white sheet high up around her face and chewed on the edge of it, glad of its papery taste.

'Have you heard the news?' Roley whispered, lifting her head a little to peer across from her pillow.

'No?' Mary quickly ejected the sheet from her mouth, eager to hear the gossip.

Amelia sat up from the next bed. 'The Williamson girls are to be sent to Kalimpong.'

The whole dormitory rustled as half a dozen heads appeared beneath the hazy clouds of mosquito nets.

There had been many a night when they had all lain awake quaking at the stories, imagining the orphanage at Kalimpong, a great gruesome building where cruelty reigned and the terrified cries of forsaken children rose from the cold walls unheard.

'It's true.' Roley raised her voice just a little, sharing her news with everyone. 'I heard Sister Rosemary talking to Sister Ann in the chapel. They've been dropped by their father. He stopped paying the bills three months ago and now they don't even know where he is.' An icy chill blew through the dorm. 'That's why we haven't seen them for the past week. It wasn't malaria at all and they're definitely not in the infirmary. Mary was in there this morning and she said the only other girls there were Joanna Stevenson with one of her silly colds and somebody else hidden in the corner with the chickenpox. Isn't that right, Mary?' Mary nodded, sending a small murmur of affirmation from bed to bed. 'It was decided that they shouldn't be allowed to mix with us any more. Not now that they're proper orphans.'

'They've been writing to him like mad ever since they had to stay behind last holidays, and I haven't seen them get a single letter in return, have you?' Nobody answered. 'It always happens like this, just when everything seems so settled. There's no telling who might be next.' Amelia sighed.

'Perhaps he's ill and can't get a message to them,' Mary whispered in disbelief. 'Perhaps he's *dead*.'

'Or he's been kidnapped!' Somebody spoke from the darkness. 'It does happen, you know.'

'I heard Sister Rosemary saying that she never trusted the man and that he should be mighty ashamed of himself,' Roley declared. 'She called him a coward and said that she hopes his conscience eats him alive.'

'They can't be thrown out just like that! For a start, it's unchristian. What's the point of teaching one thing then doing the exact opposite?'

Everyone fell quiet for a while. Mary pushed the corner of the sheet back into her mouth and chewed on it, her heart thumping. Terrible fates were rumoured to befall those unfortunate souls who were abandoned and denied. She fought to expel the nightmarish pictures creeping into her head.

'Why can't they just stay here with the rest of us?' The new

English girl leaned up on her elbows, long plaits dangling back on her pillow. Mary glanced at her sympathetically.

'Don't be so naïve,' Roley said. 'What do you think would happen if everybody's father suddenly stopped paying? You might as well know how it works around here. If you're dropped, you're out. Simple as that. After all, that's what the orphanage is for, isn't it?'

'But we didn't even get to say goodbye!'

'And what would be the point of that?' Serafina's slow, deliberate voice drifted from the far corner, its modulation steady and unwavering. Everyone quietened to listen to her, surprised as they were that she should have lifted her head from her book long enough to take an interest. 'Best to pack their bags and ship them out before they get wind of what's going on and run away. There's no helping them now.'

'That's the most awful thing I've ever heard. My parents would never—'

'Your parents?' Serafina cut her off with a small laugh. 'You need never concern yourself about being dropped, I expect.' She returned to her book, holding it up to the moonlight, deliberately turning the page.

'Serafina, stop it,' hissed Jane. 'You know we're not allowed to discuss—'

'I didn't say a word,' Serafina said. 'I just don't see what she's got to get so upset about.'

'Not allowed to talk about what?' asked the girl.

'Our parents,' whispered Amelia.

'But that's ridiculous!'

'It might be to you,' Serafina said. 'Your parents are British.'

Mary hid her brown arms beneath the sheets and peered up at the picture of Jesus on the wall. Jesus the white man, with blue eyes, pale hair and the gaping hole in his chest right through to his glowing heart, watching over them with a half-raised hand from every wall. He saw everything. Even the things that you were thinking in your head and would never say out loud.

'It's the rules,' said Roley. 'Mother Superior says it's wrong to ask people personal questions and that we should respect each other's privacy about our families.'

'In other words,' Serafina said, 'we're not supposed to talk about girls like the Williamsons.'

'I don't believe it,' whispered the new girl. 'I don't believe that anyone could be so cruel and heartless.' She shook her small head incredulously. 'The only reason I'm here is because my father's taken a posting to Burma to work for one of the big oil companies and my mother refused to go with him. I said that we should all go and take a governess, but Mother insisted that I'd be much better off in a proper school.' She looked around, unconvinced.

'Then you have nothing to worry about,' Serafina said lightly.

The sound of heavy footsteps marching towards the door had the instant effect of flattening everyone to their beds. The door opened, the unforgiving outline of Sister Ann's habit standing for a while, silhouetted against the glow from the single lamp in the corridor, surveying the rows.

'That's quite enough talk from all of you,' she said sternly. 'Good night, girls.'

'Good night, Sister Ann.'

Mary woke with a start in the cold of the night, trembling in her bed, her overactive imagination filled with visions of the Williamson girls. In her dream, she had seen them being thrown from a bullock cart, their belongings violently stripped from them, the two quaking figures thrust in through rusting gates, screaming with terror, before being locked in with the filthy crowds of wretches that nobody wanted. Some said that children were stolen during the night and used as slaves, or sold for the price of a piece of bread. There was much to be feared from a place where life held so little value.

Mary crept out of her bunk, her bare feet recoiling from the cold floor, and made her way to the far end of the dorm. She pulled gently at the edge of Serafina's mosquito net, loosening the tucks beneath the mattress, and carefully lifted the edge of the blankets. The warmth of her sister's sleeping body rose from the bed and she began to stir.

'What are you doing?' Serafina's eyes opened slightly.

'I can't sleep. I had bad dreams. Let me get in with you.'

'No.' Serafina pulled the blanket from Mary's hand. 'There isn't enough room for both of us.'

'Please,' Mary insisted. 'I promise not to disturb you.'

'Oh, for heaven's sake.' Serafina moved over. Mary slid in beside her.

'Do you ever worry about us being dropped?' she whispered.

'No,' Serafina said, swallowing the sour sickness that had burned in her throat all night.

'But what would happen if we were?'

'We'd be packed off, just like the others.'

'I'd kill myself first,' said Mary solemnly. 'I'd find some poison and swallow it.'

'Oh, stop being so dramatic.' Serafina pulled the blanket and turned on her side. 'He won't drop us.'

'How do you know?'

'Because I just do. Now go to sleep.'

Serafina lay still, eyes wide open, and prayed.

## 17

At the far end of the garden, where the grass had been left to grow high just before the small apple orchard began, a handful of girls huddled together under the shade of the old mango tree. Roley came puffing towards them, breathless with excitement.

'Flossie's father has sent a piano!' she blurted. 'I heard the mother superior telling the house servants to make room for it at the end of the refectory.'

Serafina looked at her disparagingly. 'A piano? Whatever for?'

'Everyone knows Flossie's father's some kind of genius,' Amelia said. 'It must have driven him mad to have a deaf mute for a daughter.'

'Beethoven was deaf,' said Rose. 'Maybe he's hoping for a miracle.'

'He might as well have sent her a tree trunk for all the fun she'll get out of it.'

'The poor girl was so upset she ran off to the chapel making her funny noises and shut herself in the confessional.'

'Pipe down!' Roley said. 'The Nagas are dragging it all the way from the station!'

The girls' eyes widened, and they rushed towards the east wall overlooking the furthest paths leading invisibly through the dense forest towards the railway halt at Haflong Hill. The ancient Naga tribespeople, virtually untouched by the outside world, continued to inhabit the remotest hills in ever dwindling numbers, and had forged a reputation as the region's finest bearers. That the girls might catch a rare glimpse of their exoticism was unbearably exciting. Small and strong, with the flattened features of their high mountain ancestry, their near-naked squat bodies were decorated with rows of beads and stiff feathers fixed in their short black hair. The girls kept quiet as they waited and listened out for the first signs of their rhythmic chant; the distinctive *umm … aah* from the deep breaths drawn as they worked together to move impossibly heavy loads.

Serafina took the book from her pinafore pocket, opened it at the page where she had placed the small cross fashioned from a sliver of palm leaf, still pale green, and began to read to herself. Not much happened here. One day segued into another with nothing remarkable to distinguish it from the next, and she had learned to while away the long hours by immersing herself in the foreign worlds of the novels she devoured. The sudden, silent departure of the Williamson girls had been quickly swept under the mat. It would do no good to dwell on their rumoured fate, but each time she thought of them her heart quickened, her breath coming just a little shorter. She could not leave her mind to wander, nor trust her dreams at night. So she read, or studied, or concentrated hard on the small carvings on the walls of the chapel during the services she had memorised over the years, word for word. Anything to keep her thoughts from straying where she knew they must not, for there she would find nothing but sorrow.

'What are you reading?' Jane whispered.

Serafina ignored her.

'She can't hear you,' said Amelia. 'You could fire a gun next to her head and she wouldn't take any notice.'

Then, suddenly, there it was, softly, way off in the distance,

carried in on the stillness of the air. *Umm ... aah. Umm ... aah.*
Amelia scrambled to her feet.

'Quickly! Somebody give me a lift!'

All eyes fell on Roley, who grudgingly obliged by getting
down on her hands and knees.

'Why is it always me?' she grumbled.

'Because you're the biggest. Now hurry up!'

Roley allowed the slight Amelia to stand on her back and
pull herself up to peek over the high wall, careful not to lean
against the whitewash and ruin her pinafore. Pressing the tips
of her toes painfully into Roley's back, she managed to steal a
glance down into the valley below to a great black shape being
heaved and hauled in the middle distance. The sun bounced
shining rays from its polished surfaces, its legs bound in pale
hessian sacking tied with ropes.

'It's huge!' Amelia whispered loudly, her eyes fixed on the
path where the Nagas moved like a line of black ants, precise
in their trajectory, some with enormous tied bundles, others
with packing cases balanced effortlessly on their heads. 'There
must be a hundred of them dragging it along, and a whole lot
of other stuff too!'

'Let me see.' Rose began to clamber on to Roley's back.

'No! Get off!'

'Oh, do be quiet, Roley. And for heaven's sake hold still,
will you!'

Of Portuguese descent, Rose de Souza often waited in the
garden during the early evening, listening out for her father,
who would whistle his signal as he passed over the bridge
crossing the valley before the sharp rise. A train driver on the
Assam Bengal Railway and happy in his work, he called her
a tuneful hello whenever he rolled through Haflong. It took
two engines to manage the soaring hill, one huffing from the
front, the other shunting up the rear, pushing and pulling the

trail of carriages up the steep incline on the racket and pin railway. The curve beyond the halt where the train circled the hill before beginning its graceful descent was the nearest point to the convent, and the engine's whistle could be heard clearly on a still day. Rose pulled herself up and peered over the wall.

'At last!' she bellowed. 'They've brought parcels from home! I can see them!'

'Food parcels!' Amelia gasped with delight and sank dramatically to the grass. 'Thank heavens! I'm so hungry I could just die!'

The pupils sat uniformly in tidy rows at long trestles, perched straight-backed on the hard benches that served their purpose adequately without offering undue comfort. Food was laid out in simple dishes from which they would help themselves, supervised by the sisters, then pass along. By the time the formalities were attended to and they had all said amen and crossed themselves, the potatoes were usually stone cold. Mary didn't mind. She loved potatoes, cold or not, and the sudden clatter of cutlery once grace was over was usually sufficient to cover a whispered conversation with her neighbour. She looked at the pale piece of flaccid meat on her plate, pulled a face and waited until the patrolling nun had walked by before impaling it on her fork and passing it under the table to Roley. Roley took the offering gladly and slipped it on to her own plate, hiding it under her potatoes.

'What did you get in your parcel?' she whispered. 'Did you ask your father to send those big cakes again? I do hope he sent jam. I never get any jam in mine.'

'I don't know,' Mary whispered back.

'Do you think you will get any butter? Will you bring it to the breakfast table and share it? Imagine! Butter and jam in the morning! I won't be able to sleep a wink tonight! My tummy will be rumbling like an earthquake.'

'Leave her alone, Roley,' Amelia said. 'She needs it more than you do. Besides, we never see you sharing anything of yours, do we?'

A sudden, sharp call of *Silence!* rang around the room, and the girls returned to their plates without another word.

Anyone fortunate enough to have heard their name called after lunch gathered in the cramped corridor just inside the pantry house, watching on while the mother superior unlocked the big, heavy doors with the old iron key that she kept tucked somewhere under her habit on a long chain with many others. Sister Rosemary took the parcels out one at a time under the mother superior's direction, reading the name on the tag aloud before handing it down.

'Maria Rowland.' Roley leaped forward and took hers off into a corner.

'Amelia Wilson-Hill.' Amelia stepped up and claimed hers with a wide smile.

'Serafina and Mary—' Serafina was there immediately. Mary stood back and let her sister take charge. She set the package down on the floor between the two of them, tore at the brown wrapping paper and opened the box. Inside were big round cakes bound in greaseproof paper tied with string, Kraft cheese, brown paper bags filled with shining boiled sweets and twists of deep russet barley sugar, Lyle's golden syrup in dark-green cans, two pots of jam, a tin of Staffordshire butter and all manner of other good things to eat. Serafina ignored the food and searched deeper, sifting through the layers of crumpled newspaper, looking for something else. Sister Rosemary hurried the proceedings along.

'Take out what you want, girls. Hurry up about it. We don't

have all day. You'll get them back after lunch tomorrow and then you can choose something else. And if anyone has something they'd like to keep out for breakfast tomorrow morning, let me have it now and I'll label it and give it to Cook for safe keeping in the pantry.'

That evening, Serafina lay on her shallow bed in a white cotton nightdress, a small woollen shawl pulled around her shoulders, the flame of the candle flickering on the table beside her, quietly reading aloud the letter sent from home. Mary knelt on the floor, hanging on her every word.

> *A big cat has been going into the villages and taking pigs, and when it can't find a pig, a tasty little dog will do just as nicely. The villagers have been going out at night with torches, banging pots and pans to scare it away.*
>   *Shurika made you the bookmarks and hopes that you are studying hard. The Staffordshire butter is a gift from your Aunty Dorothy. She has just returned from England and says that the sea passage was rather awful. Enjoy the parcel, my darling girls. The holidays will be here soon and I will come to collect you. Cook has promised to make gulab jamuns for you and says he will prepare an extra special picnic on the first Sunday you are home.*
>   *It won't be long now. All my love, Papa.*

Both girls fell silent, their father's words resonating around the dimly lit dormitory with its austere beds and small windows. The thought of having to wait even another day before travelling home for the annual holiday was just too much to bear, but bear it they must, as they had done each year from the moment of their arrival. Serafina turned over and stared at the wall, hiding her face and tucking the letter inside her shawl, close to her heart. Her body became still, except for the small shudder that passed over her shoulders. Flooded with homesickness, Mary looked down at the big piece of cake in her hands and picked at it half-heartedly, its crumbly sweetness now sitting uncomfortably in her mouth, dry and unwanted.

Nobody ever pretended to be ill on a Sunday, yet Serafina had barely spoken a word since rising, rejecting the rare offer of butter and jam at breakfast, hardly touching her lunch, saying that she was not hungry, before taking herself off to the gardens, book in hand, and hiding herself away. Two white-veiled novices walked by quickly on their way from chapel, where Father Lazarus stood in the shade of the tall agarwood, watching the monkeys throwing themselves from tree to tree, babies carried in sinuous arms. Big, gruff and German, with a long white beard reaching almost down to his midriff, Father Lazarus nursed a huge corporation under his cassock, evidence of his fondness for sugar and sweets. Recognising the figure sitting quietly in the far corner, he wandered in that direction.

'Good afternoon, Serafina.' He smiled down at her. Caught unawares, Serafina quickly slapped her book shut and pulled herself to her feet.

'Good afternoon, Father Lazarus.'

Instead of blessing her and moving off as he usually did, Father Lazarus reached beneath his robe and produced a small leather pouch, then again into his pocket to search for his pipe. Serafina stood before him unsurely, not knowing whether she was expected to stay or go, and watched him as he took a large pinch of tobacco from the pouch and pressed it firmly into the bowl of his pipe, tamping it down with his yellowed thumb. He put the pipe to his mouth, testing its draw for a few moments, then lit a match and held it above the bowl, sucking the flame downwards, puffing until a steady stream of smoke escaped through his nostrils. It smelled sweet, like a mixture between the charred stubble of last year's crops and the incense from a shrine.

'Mother Superior tells me that you've been very quiet lately.' He concentrated on his pipe until it was properly lit, the surface of the tobacco glowing orange with each small draw, then leaned back on his heels and let out a great aromatic cloud from his mouth. He took the pipe from his bearded lips and peered into the bowl. 'Now, I know that quiet can be a good thing, but I also know that it can be a bad thing. Is there anything that I can help you with, Serafina?'

Serafina felt her throat tighten. She shook her head sharply and looked away. Father Lazarus did not press her. Instead he held his place and continued to enjoy his pipe, looking up now and again into the branches of the trees to admire the chattering birds. 'I have seen some weeds growing near my roses,' he said, pointing his pipe towards the priest house. 'And I'm far too old to bend down and pull them out myself.'

Serafina glanced over her shoulder. 'I have to go on the Sunday walk, Father.'

'Ah,' he replied kindly. 'I think you can be spared for one afternoon. Unless you would prefer to go marching around the hills with Sister Margaret? I'm sure if you ran you could catch them up.' At last Serafina smiled. It was no great secret that she found the Sunday walk tedious. 'Come then,' he said, and the two of them strolled comfortably towards his gate.

The garden of the priest house was quite unlike those that surrounded the main convent. A neat picket fence ran around its small perimeter, bordered with deep beds cut into soft curves to suit the unusual plants and shrubs that grew there and nowhere else. Serafina knelt at the edge of the grass and picked at the stray shoots around the plants, her face brushing against the flowers that stretched their colours heavenwards, bursting from the richness of the fertile soil. The sun warmed her upturned features, and she found a certain solace in the monotony of the task she had been set. She wondered why Father Lazarus had not done the weeding himself. Everybody knew that he liked to stroll barefoot in his garden after mass on a Sunday, and that he enjoyed nothing more than to inspect his plants and pluck out any unwelcome visitors.

Father Lazarus emerged from the priest house, his ornate Sunday robes now replaced with his daily blacks, just as Serafina finished taking the last of the weeds from the rose garden. He leaned over her, inspecting her work.

'I have always found there's something very therapeutic about putting your hands into the earth.' He bent down easily and took a handful of dirt, squeezed it in his palm, then let it fall back to the ground in a small clod before lifting his hand to his nose and breathing in its scent. Serafina sat quietly. 'Serafina. If you have things that worry you when you should be happy, you can always come and talk to me if you want to.' He spoke earnestly. 'And you mustn't be afraid to say what is in your heart. Whatever you tell me shall remain between the two of us.'

'Yes, Father.'

An uncomfortable silence stretched between them, Father Lazarus waiting for her to speak, Serafina not knowing what to say, or where to start. With the moment passed, Father Lazarus sighed, leaned down and picked up the pile of weeds gathered at the edge of the lawn.

'Let's go and put these on the compost heap before they can get their roots back into the soil,' he said. 'And after that, I want to show you something. I have a feeling that it may be the answer to your troubles.' Before Serafina could reply, he had headed off towards the gate, calling over his shoulder, 'If we're lucky, we might have a whole hour to ourselves before our noisy womenfolk get back.'

*

The refectory was eerily quiet, the tables bare, the windows locked closed. Father Lazarus went to the far end of the room, pulled the cover from the piano and raised the enormous lid, propping it carefully on the long stick as though opening a huge sarcophagus. He set himself down on the stool, lifted the fall, and then, from those big, gnarled hands perfumed with the soil of the earth, there flowed a few notes, hesitantly at first, as his weed-stained fingers awakened and remembered.

Serafina stood spellbound, watching his hands as they began to glide with effortless grace through the tangle of a thousand notes, the likes of which she had never heard. The claustrophobic walls of the cold refectory seemed to break open under the intensity of the sound.

She had never heard anything so uplifting.

She felt the music flow through her, deepening with every breath she took, lifting her away from the unbearable burden of her sorrow, and stared in amazement as the priest unleashed these few moments of unrestrained passion, daring to tell the whole world of his place here on earth as a man who could be moved. Then, almost as quickly as he had begun, he closed his eyes and stopped, placing his hands in his lap, dropping his head for a moment. Serafina held her breath, barely able to conceive of what she had just witnessed, willing him to forget her presence in the room and continue. He turned his head to her slowly and lifted his finger to his lips with a small smile.

'Father Lazarus!' She shook her head in disbelief.

'Shh. I could not resist it.' He laughed a little. 'Come and sit,' he said, removing himself from the stool and indicating her to take his place.

'But I can't play.' Serafina stared at the seat nervously.

'Not yet.' He smiled at her. 'Not yet.'

## 18

The long stretch of the school year from March to November seemed like an eternity. Night-times echoed with the small sobs of children who still nursed fresh memories of home. It was especially difficult for the little ones, who screamed and wailed, clutching at their thin pillows for comfort when the monkeys clattered across the dormitory rooftops. For five months out of the nine, the days and nights were dominated by the heavy rains that fell relentlessly from May to September, drumming heavy droplets against the thick forests and swelling the gently meandering rivers into raging torrents. The calm surface of Haflong's pale lilac lake, set high up on the plateau reflecting a painterly image of the sky above, became a menacing dark grey, its surface bubbling furiously with the onslaught of the monsoons. But for the occasional lull in the downpour when the sun broke through the clouds and shone for a while, the constant rain might have been enough to send a soul mad. Some seasons were worse than others, the rain never quite falling in the same place, the flooding fast and unpredictable. It was just as well that the deluge would be over and forgotten before the holidays began, mercifully lifting the pressure that had hung so heavily overhead.

During the final month of school, the trunks would be fetched down from the hidden storage spaces in the attics and outhouses, and the packing would begin amid much speculative whispering and excitement, signalling the imminent arrival of the three-month holiday when the girls would leave for their homes, spread far and wide across the state and beyond.

Mary knew the time was coming near when the bright green parrots arrived, flocking to Haflong as they did each year for a little while, circling in the sky like an emerald cloud, taking roost in the trees of the lower hills where they could be heard screeching for a full hour before nightfall. Chinthimani knew the time was coming near when the rice hung heavy in the ear, leaning towards the earth, ready to harvest. Unable to settle herself, she would order the cook to bring in far more supplies than they would ever use, her agitation becoming constant, the bells on her ankles sounding their silvery notes long into the night as she paced the dark courtyard and felt the pull of her daughters' spirits.

The convent gates were opened to welcome the gradual influx of parents and chaperones, the pupils gathering to the east-facing windows of the school house waiting for their escorts, pressed to the panes from where they could see the open road to freedom. Soon the gates would be crowded with the red-shirted porters who had made their way from the railway halt, talking among themselves cheerfully, assured as they were of a busy day with generous payment. Piles of packing trunks lay stacked precariously beside the high perimeter wall, their tags bursting into a flutter of tiny flags with each passing breeze. Amid the excitement in the classroom, embraces were exchanged, whispering earnestly the false promises of childhood.

Sister Margaret burst in, holding her list aloft. 'Serafina and Mary! Your father is here!' She raised her arm in a wide beckon. Mary stared at her friends, then turned and ran as fast as her legs would carry her without stopping to say goodbye.

On sighting his children, James lifted the hat from his head and held it high, waving it towards them, their shouts of joy drowning out his call of hello. He opened his arms as they crashed against him, hugging him tightly, loosening his footing.

'Goodness me!' he laughed, dropping his hat on to Mary's head. 'How much have you grown?'

'My clothes are all too small for me!' Mary pulled the hat lower, covering her eyes.

'Then we shall have to buy you some new ones!'

Serafina did not move, still pressed against his jacket, her face buried into his chest. James tightened his arm around her while he continued to jest with Mary, feeling the small convulsions of Serafina's tears.

'Did Mother come with you?' Mary looked past her father towards the gates.

'She is at the station waiting for you,' James said. 'So we had better hurry along. Your trunks have already been taken down. Shall we go?'

'Yes!' she shouted.

'Then lead the way, young lady!'

Mary danced ahead a few paces, holding his hat proudly on her head, turning constantly to check for his presence. James leaned down and took a handkerchief from his pocket. 'Here,' he whispered to Serafina. 'Dry your tears. There's nothing to cry about. I'm here now.'

Serafina took the handkerchief, laced with his scent, and put it to her face. *Nothing to cry about*. What would he know of her tears? What would he know of her agony? Of the blood she had begun to shed three months ago as she came into womanhood? What would he know of the whispers that passed from bed to bed at night? She dried her eyes and offered them back to him with an empty smile.

The stationmaster at Lower Haflong seemed keen that

everyone should know the importance of his position on this busy day. He shouted crossly at the porters, directing them this way and that for no particular reason, demanding that they place their luggage loads first in one place, then in another, depending on his whim. A loud, angry exchange broke out when he insisted that they must stay with their piles until the train arrived then load them properly before leaving, rather than abandoning the cases where they lay and rushing back to the school to collect another commission and double their wages.

Chinthimani listened to their squabbling while slowly pacing the ladies' waiting room, sari held over her head, obscuring her face, peering out from the small window in the thin fabric at the commotion outside. The sharpness of the sunlight behind the crowd pulled their forms in and out of focus, her head softly buzzing as it had done for so long now, eyes gritty from kohl powder and fatigue. She soon tired and sat, curling like a chrysalis as she leaned into the bench and allowed herself to slacken. Among the softening colours of the watery figures on the platform, the dark shadow of a man appeared. He bent down for a moment, then thrust his arms forwards, releasing the two smaller figures towards her.

'*Maa!*' Mary saw her in an instant and broke into a run. '*Maa! Maa!*'

Chinthimani's hands flew to her face. She stood and became immediately unsteady on her feet, leaning to the arm of the bench for support, then, unable to stop herself, sank back into the seat, opening her arms, the howl from her throat overwhelming her.

'*Maa!*' Mary felt herself swept into the soft cotton of her mother's sweet perfume, its wide white veil lifting up like a cloud and enveloping her completely, vanishing the world around them.

'Mary!' wept Chinthimani. '*Mary, main tumse bohat pyar karti hou! Tum jawan aur balshaali ho!*'

'I love you too!' Mary mumbled into her body, the rich scent of spices diffusing into her dress. 'I have grown, haven't I? Father noticed it too!'

Chinthimani looked into her daughter's face, cupping it in her hands, unable to comprehend these fast foreign words that scattered from her own child's mouth. '*Kion, abghar chalain?*'

'Yes.' Mary nodded. 'I want to go home very much, *Maa*.'

Chinthimani released Mary's face and stood up, wiping the tears from her cheeks, looking around with concern. 'Serafina *kahan hai?*'

'She's here.' Mary turned, expecting to find Serafina directly behind her. Instead she saw her sister walking away, returning to their father. She took his hand and spoke to him. As she did so, James glanced towards the children's mother. He shook his head, and smiled at her sadly.

## 19

Shurika hummed to herself as she tended the vegetable garden, cropping the brinjals she had saved specially and setting them aside in a clay bowl on the ground before spreading mounds of dry grass over the new seedlings to protect them from the birds. The crows had taken all the strawberries, no matter what she did to conceal them, so she had given up on the soft fruits and added them to the cook's market list, if any could be found. From her lowered position, squatting on her haunches close to the earth, she could see Chinthimani pacing the courtyard slowly, one hand worrying at its fingers, the other fussing with the end of her sari. She was talking to herself again, mumbling as she walked, stopping sharply here and there to point at nothing and shake her head, shouting her refusal, arguing her victory over the imaginary opponent. There would be no reasoning with her today. No way to soothe her troubled mind.

Shurika placed the last handfuls of dry grass over the smallest shoots and collected up the bowl of brinjals. She would ask Cook to prepare some now for her mistress, hoping that she could tempt her into eating something before the children returned. The Sahib had sent for them for many days in a row now, each time with the promise of some grand entertainment. Shurika wondered if he knew. She had often caught Shiva glancing at her mistress suspiciously, and there had been times when he had questioned Shurika about the marks that appeared on her face and arms. But Shurika did not betray one word. There was nothing else she could do, except to pray every day for her mistress and her children. It was better that they were not here to see her like this. Each year when they returned home for the holidays, it had become harder for Shurika to conceal their mother's weaknesses. They were growing up, and there comes a time when a child will view the world with unclouded eyes.

They were no longer the barefooted children who once ran through the courtyard, chasing the animals and dodging between the drying sheets, reaching for each other's pigtails. They spoke English now, instruction in their mother's tongue having been deemed unnecessary. It was a miracle that Mary spoke any Hindi at all, and it was only that which she had learned from the cook. She was not supposed to go anywhere near the cookhouse, yet the moment she was home, she spent much of her time there, and was constantly getting into trouble for it. She liked to watch Cook slaughtering poultry, slitting the chicken's throat, releasing it to career around, head severed, splurting warm blood into the dirt until it finally dropped down dead. She had asked him just this morning if he was going to kill any chickens today, but he had said no and sent her away with a piece of sweet sugar cane instead.

Shurika rose from the vegetable patch, stretching the ache from her spine, and made her way to the cookhouse.

Serafina sat, posture-perfect, in a wide wicker chair on the veranda, reading the few carefully selected pages James had given her from his newspaper. Their father encouraged them to practise small talk of current events, although his efforts seemed to be entirely wasted on Mary, for whom any information appeared to go in one ear and straight out of the other. It was probably just as well, James thought, keeping the bulk of the newspapers to himself, their pages filled with bleak reports of historic cities lying in ruins in the wake of German bombs and Allied reprisals. It all seemed so far away, so far removed, the ripples in the pond long dispersed before reaching these hills.

Every now and then, he glanced up from his article to regard his daughter's serious expression with fond amusement. Serafina pretended not to notice him looking at her and concentrated hard on the open page, barely moving a muscle, determined to absorb the complexities of each piece she read. James cleared his throat lightly.

'Have you found anything interesting in your newspaper today, Serafina?'

'Yes, Papa,' she replied without hesitation, delighted that he had at last asked the question that she knew would come eventually. 'There's a new cartoon film in America and nobody likes it.'

'Really?' James nodded his approval. 'What's it called?'

Serafina trawled her memory, knowing that she had read the information somewhere, not wanting to have to glance at her newspaper to remind herself. For a moment she was plunged into self-doubt, frustrated at not being able to summon the answer at once. James sat patiently and gave her an encouraging smile, his head cocked in mock anticipation. She remembered suddenly with a triumphant smile.

'*Fantasia!*'

'Very good indeed.' James raised a distinguished eyebrow at her. 'Heaven knows, right now the world could certainly do with a little light-hearted entertainment.' He tutted and returned to his paper. 'There are evil forces at work, Serafina,' he said quietly, almost without thinking. 'Some men will not rest until they have forced the hand of fate towards catastrophe yet again. We must all pray very hard and hope that good sense will prevail.' Serafina sat to attention, eyes fixed on her father, trying to comprehend his change in demeanour. 'I sometimes wonder what would happen to us if our newspapers did not exist. Whether we would still be carried along with the rest of the world, or if we would continue to go about our daily business, living in ignorant bliss.'

Serafina watched her father's thoughts darken, leaving her far behind, confiscating his warmth. Sensing the distance that suddenly opened between them, she wished that she could bring him back to the moment when he had first smiled at her and asked her about the newspaper.

On the brief lawn set neatly before the veranda, Mary played with her father's dog, a long-legged boxer with a daft temperament, throwing sticks for him then running to hide behind the clipped hibiscus each time he tried to bring them back to her, barking his impatience. Several of the shrubs had been rudely dishevelled where she had deliberately flung the stick to a place she thought he would not find it, only to see him bolt after it and launch himself right into the middle of the rhododendrons.

Shiva appeared from the house carrying a tray of lemonade from the kitchen, where James's cook was busy preparing their favourite sweets.

'Ah, thank you, Shiva.' James shook off the concern that had rumpled his face, set his newspaper down and gratefully accepted a glass from Shiva's silver tray. Serafina observed her father closely, noting his every move in minute detail, and deliberately folded her piece of newspaper in precisely the same way before taking a glass for herself. James drank a little and watched Mary teasing the dog for a while, a slow smile coming over him that quickly stretched into a full, raucous laugh.

'Mary!' he called out to her. 'Let Buster rest for a while before the poor animal dies of exhaustion! It's wearing us all out just to look at you!'

'Papa!' Mary dropped the stick to the ground, ran up the steps to the veranda and leaped to her father's side, causing him to spill his drink, then supped down half her glass in one go. Serafina scowled at her disapprovingly and sipped her own lemonade politely in remonstration. Shiva smilingly handed his master the cloth from his tray to mop the mess from his drenched hand.

'Now look what you've gone and done,' Serafina said crossly. 'Why do you have to be so clumsy?'

'It's all right!' James laughed. 'No harm done. I'll just have to hope that I don't start attracting insects.' Mary watched him dab the lemonade from his lap.

'Why does Mother never come here?'

'Be quiet, Mary!' Serafina snapped.

James nodded at Shiva to refill their glasses, giving himself a moment to consider his response.

'Your mother is a very busy woman. She has many things to attend to. Why? Do you not like spending time up at the big house with me?' Clearly, he was teasing her. Shiva smiled and returned to the house with the empty tray. James sat up straight, pulling Mary into the crook of his arm. 'Besides,' he announced dramatically, 'I have a very big surprise in store for you today.' He picked up his glass and took his time with a deliberately slow sip. 'I was going to keep it a big secret, but judging by the state of your socks, young lady, I suppose I will have to give you a little notice.'

'What is it?' Mary pulled at his shirt. 'Tell us!'

Her head filled with vivid memories of the wonderful surprises he had arranged for them during the school holidays long past, when they had been permitted on rare occasions to come and visit him at the big house. The first time, when she was still smaller than Buster, a travelling theatre had come and put on a show just for them up at the summer house on the viewing point, where they sat together laughing and clapping until her hands stung. The year after that, a famous fortune-teller had travelled all the way from Silchar and pitched a bright red tent in the garden. He wore a jewelled patch over one eye and had told them that they would marry princes, then magically made coins appear from behind their ears which they were allowed to put in their pockets and keep for a rainy day. And last year, their father had thrust upon them the very greatest surprise of all, when, as night fell, they were kept from their beds and taken off to see the circus, carried high by the servants through the dry paddy fields with the way magically lit by a luminous trail of swaying lanterns.

Mary and Serafina exchanged an excited glance and grinned at each other. Unable to contain herself for a moment longer, Mary buried her face in her hands to stifle her squeals. James basked in her delight and gave her knee a tweak.

'We have a very special guest coming to meet you today, so I want you to be on your best behaviour over tiffin, all right?' He wagged a playful finger at her. 'I assume that you're both old enough now to be introduced to polite company? Or do you think I should wait another year or two?'

'Who is it?' demanded Mary, beaming from ear to ear.

Serafina sat patiently and held on to her own curiosity, knowing that her unguarded sister would invariably ask the awkward questions that she herself would not dare to raise. It was sufficient for her that they were permitted to visit the big house more regularly now. The house that she had stolen so many yearning glances at for so long. The house that she had crept through the trees to spy upon ever since she was big enough to get away with a small unwarranted absence from her mother's compound.

'Is it the fortune-teller?' Mary tried.

'No.' James shook his head.

'Is it ...' Mary thought hard, but couldn't suggest anyone else, because there was no one else she knew.

Serafina moved in her seat uneasily, wondering who could be so important that their father would invite them here. They never had visitors, and she was not so ignorant as not to know why. She found her hands clenching.

'Do you give up?' James asked.

'Yes!'

'You know those big cakes that you like so much?' Mary nodded at her father eagerly. 'And the enormous tins of Staffordshire butter?' She nodded again. This time, James turned towards Serafina. 'Well, your Aunty Dorothy is coming to visit this afternoon so that she can see for herself where all those food parcels have been disappearing to.' He gave a little roar and tickled Mary's tummy, Mary squirming in delight. Serafina, suddenly agitated, looked down into her drink, her mouth set into a slight rigidity that gave her away. James squinted at her playfully. 'And may I ask what you are looking so worried about?'

'I don't know.' She shrugged, unable to pinpoint the reason for her anxiety, yet saturated with its charge.

'Good. Now go and tidy your dresses and ask one of the boys to polish your shoes.'

Dorothy's nerves ran away with her as she prepared in her suite of rooms at the clubhouse, her home-from-home for three months every winter. It was now part of her yearly routine, to take her leave of the plantation for the sake of appearances, sometimes travelling to England to remind herself of the reasons she had left, reasons that had worn thinner as her resentment grew. She had not argued with James about the arrangement, hearing his plea that it was the only sensible thing to do. She had not protested at the gathering of her belongings and the erasing of her presence to preserve the carefully orchestrated veneer created for the sake of his children. She had not issued a word of complaint in seven years. Nor had she found herself blessed with a child of her own, her heart heavy with her husband's concealment. She had known it the moment their marriage was consummated, that his love for her was grounded in sedate devotion rather than the passion she had so dreamed of. Melting into his arms, sweet orange blossom still clinging to her hair, she had found his lovemaking perfunctory, his ardour restrained, and the truth of their union came upon her like an unexpected blanket of cloud on a summer day. James had no intention of creating a child with her. He had learned to be cautious, to chasten his desires, and she, in turn, had been forced to learn the lesson of acceptance.

Dorothy dressed carefully, choosing a simple day dress in a deep shade of fawn and a pair of mid-heeled shoes with small buckles on the single strap. Such was her state of unease that her hands trembled as she fumbled with the fastenings. She was ready far too early, and fretfully paced her rooms for half an hour, the gin and tonic in her hand rather stronger than she would usually permit herself. Checking her wristwatch every few moments, she couldn't prevent her thoughts from wandering. Her heart contracted painfully each time she recalled the terrible scene on that mountainside in Mussoorie, and the moment that she had surrendered to her fate, pledging to James that she would share the responsibility he so steadfastly refused to give up. Had she known what she was saying, the sacrifices that would be expected of her, she would have conceded defeat there and then instead of taking his hand.

Little by little, her wounds had slowly healed, but the scars remained indelible. She began to write to the children regularly, cheerful, shallow missives that told nothing of herself, designed merely to fill the gaps left by a father who spent too long meaning to write and not enough time putting his pen against paper, always signing herself Aunty Dorothy, as though it lent some regularity to her life. She asked James if she wouldn't be better suited to pick out the things they needed while they were away at school, particularly the occasional pretties for a growing girl, and busied herself with their requirements. It was, she had felt, the very least she could do, a penance of sorts, for the wrongdoings of the man she had chosen to love. Yet as the years slid by, it became the cruellest torture, the unspoken words wedged uncomfortably between them, the forbidden subject never permitted to surface. His secret children. His secret wife. No matter how she tried to contain her rancour, silencing herself at every turn, her efforts were never enough. She had finally insisted upon meeting them, if only to exorcise the spectres that haunted her every waking moment.

A gentle knock disturbed her faint heart, the voice behind the door imparting that her driver was ready and waiting.

The girls sat awkwardly in the parlour, Serafina concealing her nerves with hands folded neatly in her lap, Mary beside her on the settee, nudging and giggling much to her sister's annoyance. Serafina was determined to make a good impression. Perhaps, if the introductions went well, her aunt would invite her to stay with her in England when school was over. It was common enough for the older girls. She had frequently overheard detailed talk of their plans for finishing, of being sent to live with their most well-connected relatives, learning the finer points of the social graces required to get along. Several of Aunty Dorothy's letters had been postmarked from London, and Serafina imagined that she would like it there very well indeed.

The sound of a car and raised voices outside jolted her to attention. She sat up straight, knees pressed neatly together, and after what seemed like an eternity, the parlour door opened.

'Children?' They stood immediately at the sound of their father's voice. 'Your Aunty Dorothy is here.'

Dorothy stepped into the room, a slight hesitation in her manner, and smiled nervously. Both girls chorused, 'How do you do?' and dipped a small, much-practised curtsey, Mary leaning back rather too far, stealing a furtive glance at Serafina to remind herself of how it should be done.

Without warning, Dorothy felt herself suddenly beset with a shocking surge of emotion. Her hand rose to her mouth to stifle the small sob rising in her throat and she found herself powerless against the unexpected onslaught of tears pricking at her eyes. In that very moment, every poisonous droplet of the hurt and humiliation she had held inside for so long evaporated like beads of water in the midday sun. James moved towards her, then stopped himself. Dorothy looked at him fleetingly, just long enough to see the concern on his face. She had promised him that she could handle it, that she would not react badly or cause a fuss, but nothing had prepared her for this.

Here before her stood the truth of it – two girls, twelve and fourteen years old, innocent and free from sin, dressed in the ribbon-edged yellow smocks that she herself had picked out for them not more than six weeks ago. Even then, they had not existed. They were not real at all, these two ethereal figures who plagued her thoughts and haunted her dreams. She had done her duty and tried to be generous of spirit, all the while wishing them away, swallowing bitter tears when no one was looking. The shame washed over her in great, drowning waves. She removed the gloved hand from her mouth, her stinging eyes darting to James, before taking her ravaged heart in hand and returning their greeting.

'How do *you* do?'

Before Serafina could deliver her rehearsed response, Mary

broke rank and rushed to Dorothy's side, grabbing hold of her hand, her face lit up with a beaming smile. 'We've been dying to meet you! We're having stuffed roasted chicken for lunch! I watched Cook kill it and it ran around for simply ages! There was blood everywhere! Do you like roast chicken?'

'Why, yes!' Dorothy returned Mary's enthusiasm. 'It just so happens that I like roast chicken very much!'

Seated at the dining table she had become so familiar with, Dorothy scarcely knew what to think or what to say. Physically, they were not as she had imagined them at all. The elder of the two bore a striking resemblance to her father, the wave in her hair, the dusting of freckles across the apples of her high cheeks. There was a squareness to her jawline. An elegant symmetry to her shoulders. And she was tall, like him, with the same slightly haughty expression that could not be helped. She could be Italian, Dorothy mused, Spanish perhaps, but not Indian. Definitely not Indian. The nose was all wrong. The bone structure. Almost as though nothing quite went together. Yet among all that, beneath the yellow ribbon-edged dress, her startling aesthetics could not be denied, the first traces of a great beauty waiting to bloom already quite visible. Dorothy tried to wipe from her mind the notion of the mother who could produce such a child. Her eyes wandered to Mary, smaller, darker, with a pretty, doll-like face and rosebud lips, her whole demeanour less angular than her sister, less brooding, with a constant, trusting smile. Dorothy sensed James watching her closely, his sudden vulnerability a new quality that she had not seen before.

'Where do you live?' asked Mary.

'Ah.' Dorothy stalled. 'Well, sometimes I live in—'

'London,' James interjected. 'Your Aunty Dorothy is a lady doctor, and that's where she did her studying.'

'Really?' Serafina said. 'Did it take you a very long time?'

'Yes,' said Dorothy. 'I had to study hard for years before they gave me my white coat, but I loved every moment of it.'

'Do you have one of those tubes?' Mary asked.

'Tubes?'

'Yes, you know.' Mary mimed having her chest listened to.

'Oh! You mean a stethoscope! Yes, as a matter of fact I do.'

'Did you bring it with you?'

'Why, yes, I think it may be—' Dorothy stopped suddenly, struggling to find a reason why her doctor's bag would be in the house. 'Oh, wait. I'm not so sure, come to think of it.'

Serafina stared at Dorothy, sensing her nervousness. 'What's London like?'

'Well,' Dorothy began. 'Let me see now. It's very busy, and jolly cold in the winter, with endless rain, and there are lots of people, and big red buses that drive everybody around.'

'And special trains that go under the ground,' James added.

'Under the ground?' Mary laughed. 'That's impossible!'

'No it isn't,' he assured her. 'Some very clever men built a catacomb of tunnels under the streets and then made little trains to go in them.'

'It's true.' Dorothy smiled.

'That's silly!' Mary, quite unable to comprehend the concept, wrinkled her nose idiotically and concentrated hard on cutting a roast potato.

'I'd love to go to London one day,' Serafina hinted, sitting perfectly straight against her chair. 'Are you going back there soon?'

'Well ...' Dorothy hid her hands beneath the table, conscious that they were fidgeting. Oh, if only they had talked this through properly. 'Yes.' She hesitated. 'I'm planning on staying here for a while, then back to London, then hopefully another visit here.'

'Are you married?' Mary piped up.

Dorothy, unable to remove the glass from her lips quickly enough, choked on her wine, spluttering into her napkin, blanching at James to rescue her.

'Really!' James chided Mary good-naturedly. 'What a very personal question, Mary. Don't they teach you anything at that school of yours?'

'Sorry, Papa.' Mary looked at her plate and went red. 'I didn't mean to be rude.'

'So,' Dorothy recovered and smiled brightly, 'how are you enjoying school?' Serafina opened her mouth to speak, but was cut off instantly.

'I hate it,' complained Mary. 'The food's horrible and there's never enough to eat. We have to go to church all the time and it's freezing at night so I have to wrap myself up in an extra shawl that always gets tangled up in the bed with me. Jane Cavendish snores and wakes everyone up. We're not friends or anything. She's older than me, but even if she wasn't, I wouldn't want to be friends with someone who snores like that.'

Serafina glared at her sister, clearly outraged by her babbling. Dorothy was careful to include them both in the conversation.

'And you, Serafina?'

'It's a very good school, Aunty Dorothy. We realise how lucky we are to be there. Please don't take any notice of Mary. She's always complaining about something. She doesn't mean to sound ungrateful.' Mary scowled into her chicken. 'The parcels are lovely. And thank you for sending the cakes.' Serafina rested down her cutlery noiselessly, demonstrating the benefits of their distant education. 'We always look forward to them very much, and to your letters.'

'And the butter!' Mary interrupted again. 'And the jam! I love jam, although Roley does go on so. She sulks like mad if

I don't take it to the breakfast table, then everyone wants some and it's all gone in just a few days.' She sighed heavily and leaned one elbow on the table in a show of grief. 'But how can you have jam and butter and not share it with your friends? I don't think I'd be able to sit there and eat it in front of everybody else when—'

'Mary!' Serafina kicked her hard beneath the table. 'You're talking too much again. And take your elbow off the table!'

'No I'm not! I'm just saying about—'

'Aunty Dorothy doesn't want to hear about your silly friends!' Serafina snapped.

'Nonsense,' said their father. 'In fact I think I'd quite like to have a few silly friends myself.'

Dorothy flashed her eyes towards James. Her heart went out to him.

Finally, after all these years, she understood.

## 20

'We had fresh lemonade and Cook made roast chicken stuffed with mashed potatoes and mint.' Shurika listened quietly to Mary's excitement over the meeting with her aunt. She held the hairbrush firmly, delivering long, steady strokes, working at each strand of hair until it gleamed. Mary turned suddenly, causing the brush to jump out of Shurika's hands. 'She gave me a book with pictures of birds in it. Look!' She leaped up and rushed to fetch the book she had secreted under her pillow. 'There are more birds in here than you would ever think lived! It tells you the names of all of them and where to find them if you're patient enough. There are some birds that are even bigger than a man!'

Shurika smiled and patted the empty seat. For her to look at the book would be of no use at all. Such things had never been meant for her. 'Come here and let me finish your hair.'

Mary returned the book to its hiding place and sat back on the chair. Shurika began brushing again methodically, the movements quietening her charge just the way they had always done since she was little. She watched on as Mary's eyelids became heavy, the small smile fading as her mouth drooped into irresistible fatigue. Shurika sang to her softly, an ancient song of unrequited love that her mother used to sing, making up the words for the parts she could not remember. She helped Mary into bed, tucking the sheets around her shoulders, gradually reducing her song to a poetic whisper. Before long, Mary was in a deep slumber, her face peaceful, filled with the dreams of a contented child.

Serafina appeared in the doorway and crept in silently to sit on the edge of the chair before releasing the tie from her hair.

'Is Mother ill?' she asked softly, the concern in her voice raising its inflection. Her mother had hardly spoken a word since their return, keeping to her quarters, moving slowly from wall to wall, head bowed as she mumbled, her feet moving the weary walk of the dead. Mary had to be prevented from rushing in with the book of birds and was tempted away with a promise of sweets tomorrow.

Shurika examined Serafina's eyes in the mirror, took up the brush and began, working first at the ends to free the lowest tangles, stroking her hand lightly against Serafina's head with each gentle pull.

'No,' she said. 'She is just tired today.'

'She was crying again. I saw her.'

'You mustn't mind. She has many things to do. Many people who come to ask for her help. One day, when you are a grown woman, you will understand that life is not always easy. You must be grateful for all the things that you have, little one. Most others are not so fortunate.' She watched Serafina's reflection.

'Why can't we live in the big house? We are going back there tomorrow anyway. Why do we have to stay here? And why do we have to go away to that stupid school? I hate it there. I want to be here with Papa and with you.'

'There are no easy answers to your questions, Serafina. There are many things that you do not know.'

'So tell me.'

'No,' Shurika said. 'That is not what I mean. You will understand better when you are older.'

'I understand already.' Serafina stared back at Shurika

defiantly. She turned suddenly and pulled at Shurika's arm, turning it outwards. 'How did you get that?'

Shurika pulled her arm away quickly and covered the bruise with her sari.

'I slipped and fell against a tree.'

'No you didn't. You never slip. You never fall.'

Shurika sighed and rested the brush in her lap. Mary stirred a little. 'Hush, child,' Shurika said. 'Before you go and wake your sister. Come. Put yourself into bed. Time for rest now.'

The room became dark, save for the glow of the full moon through the dusty window and the soft golden blush from the kerosene lamp in the next room. The girls were fast asleep, their breathing reduced to a rhythmic sigh. They did not hear the gentle humming nor the delicate tinkling of the silver bells that graced their mother's bare footsteps. She appeared in the doorway, leaned against the frameless opening and watched on as they slept, sipping from the amber drink in her hands until it was gone. She put down her empty glass on the washstand, padded quietly into the room and attended to each of her daughters in turn, smoothing their bedclothes, whispering to them softly in the language of their childhood. She ran a gentle hand around their heads, making sure that their ears were flat against the pillow so as not to cause them that terrible ache when they had been slept on awkwardly. As she left them in peace, the flicker of light from the distant lamp shone against the stream of tears that rolled down her sorrowful face. Serafina held her breath and stared wide-eyed at the wall.

There was much excitement at the big house the following morning. Two of the working elephants had been brought down from the high drifts of the western gardens, where they had been clearing age-old trees in readiness to plant the new terraces. The infant tea shrubs, propagated and brought on in the nursery, would be spaced a few feet apart and encouraged to spread their dark, pointed leaves for several years before any yield could be expected of them. James had watched the plants' progress carefully for the past three seasons, checking them over for the characteristics he knew would do well, assessing their gradual development, weeding out and discarding the runts. Six years, he thought. Six years before they revealed their bounty and proved him right or wrong. He had left the nursery early that morning after his inspection to select the final plants, wondering if he would be there to witness their debut.

The mahouts waited patiently, murmuring softly in their animals' ears whenever they began to complain in their low rumble, carrying in deep tremors along the ground. Everyone was calling for Mary. Shiva and the two houseboys had been sent to search for her, checking each of the rooms by turn, methodically walking the garden paths in case she had wandered off. Cook sang loudly, chanting the names of her favourite sweets, tapping the side of a glass bowl, teasing that he had dishes of them waiting for her in the kitchen, calling out that he would eat them all by himself if she did not come out and show herself. Serafina stood at the bottom of the wide veranda steps with her father, his sigh suggesting the beginnings of slight agitation.

'Where on earth is she?'

'She'll be hiding somewhere, Papa. She's frightened of the elephants. She says that the hairs scratch her legs but I know it's because she's scared silly.' James was unable to suppress a smile. 'You should have seen her face when she was up close to Dionysus last Christmas. I've never seen anyone so – petrified.' Serafina was pleased that she had at last found an occasion to use the new word she had learned.

'Well, he is a jolly big fellow,' said James. 'And next to him she's not much bigger than a mouse, is she?' The largest of all the working elephants, Dionysus was an enormous bull who had broken his chains and gone wandering two seasons ago, only to reappear some weeks later with one tusk missing. A male elephant, when in musth, was a constant danger.

Inside the house, Mary flattened herself beneath one of the low settees in the parlour, the small space between the tapestried seat and the polished floor barely sufficient for her to squeeze into. She lay there stock-still, staring fearfully at the bared teeth of the tiger-skin rug on the floor. The cook once told her that her father had shot the beast himself years ago, taking it down in one clean hit, and that it was without doubt the finest rug she would ever see. The lifeless, glassy eyes stared at her from a head three times the size of her own. She imagined being eaten alive by such a beast and could not move her quivering legs. Mary knew that everyone was looking for her. She had seen the gathered anklets of Shiva's white cotton pyjamas walk in and out of the parlour three times while they called out for her. Perhaps if she stayed here for long enough, they would give up and leave her behind. Outside, her father's patience was wearing thin.

'Mary! Come out of there this very instant or we'll send the tigers in to find you!' He winked down at Serafina, who gazed back at him adoringly.

'I'm not afraid of the elephants, Papa.'

'You're not afraid of anything, my little lionheart. What I wouldn't give for some of that courage myself.'

Shiva emerged from the house, a sorrowful Mary trailing behind him. She looked quietly ashamed and stared down at the ground. Shiva smiled at his master, and delivered Mary to his side.

'There you are,' James chastised her gently. 'We've been looking all over for you.'

'Sorry,' she mumbled. 'I couldn't find my shoes.'

James bent down and spoke quietly in her ear. 'You must be very careful around the elephants. Very careful indeed. They have come all the way down from the high terraces this morning just to visit you, and if they think that you don't want to see them, they will get upset and cry. They might be big, but they are very, very sensitive.'

Mary frowned at him. 'Elephants don't cry!'

Shiva stepped forward and smiled at her kindly, resting his palms together respectfully and offering her a small bow. 'Yes they do, *missybubba*. Everyone knows that elephants cry. You must understand that they know much more than we do. They know what you are thinking. They are the wisest of all God's creatures.'

Mary's head was quick to turn to the two elephants. She eyed them with a renewed sense of suspicion and wondered if Shiva was telling the truth. The closer of the two rumbled a small murmur and looked at her with a single brown eye lowered beneath long grey lashes. Shiva took a sweet from his pocket and gave it to Mary. Instead of eating it herself, she crept forwards with tentative steps and offered it to the elephant, thinking in her head: sorry for hiding and keeping you waiting. The velvet tip of the trunk reached placidly to her hand, barely touching her skin as it accepted her gift and swept it into its pink mouth.

The mahouts called the enormous animals to command with a *hut! hut! hut!* to lower themselves to the ground. Their youthful apprentices, who would train for many years before being charged with an elephant of their own, helped the children to clamber up across the gigantic legs and on to the back of the animals' necks, urging them to hold on tightly to the wide rush-filled cushion as the elephants rocked suddenly forwards before rising up to their full towering height. Mary felt the swell of the enormous body with every breath. This was the thing that frightened her most. The thought that any creature could breathe that much air in a single gulp. The breath inside her own body felt tiny, like a minuscule puff. The mighty beasts moved away, feet pressing silently into the bare earth, hips swaying, bulk rolling from side to side as they headed slowly towards the gardens. Mary's terrified shrieks faded into the distance as James returned up the veranda steps to the house, leaping them two at a time, laughing and shaking his head.

In accordance with the routine that had formed invisibly over the years, it was Shiva who was charged with the task of returning the children to their mother's house. James would not go there now, the prospect of witnessing such unhappiness too much for him to bear. He had heard the stories of her condition. There were still times when he caught himself standing on the veranda at sundown, staring unthinkingly towards the western estate road, his feelings aroused in one way or another. This evening, he gazed in the same direction, watching his daughters leave under a softly setting sky.

It was quite a distance to the homestead when measured in a child's footsteps, so they rode in a small cart tethered to the mildest of the oxen, an ageing cow who knew the way well and never complained. They took their time in returning, mindful of the few days they had left, Shiva pausing to point out the iridescent flash of a kingfisher, waiting awhile to see if another came along, allowing the ox to dawdle the route at her own pace without a flick of encouragement from his switch.

The cart pulled to a halt shortly before the wild thicket with the spreading banyan tree with its grasping tendrils twisting painfully upwards like a parasite winding itself up the mighty trunk. The track was rough from here, lying pitted and unrepaired since the Sahib had stopped calling years ago. Instead, solemn deliveries were made regularly by one of the runners with messages passed formally from household to household through the layers of protocol set by the servants. Anything Chinthimani needed or wished for was taken to her without question, but little else crossed the impossible distance between one world and the other.

Shiva lifted the girls down from the cart. Better to walk the rest of the way and enjoy the fragrant frangipani flowers that fluttered to the ground each day. As they walked, Mary reached down here and there, gathering the fallen blooms, picking them up carefully, filling her hands with the pale, creamy petals and lifting them to her face to take in their sweet vanilla scent. Shiva watched her, approving of the joy the child found in her surroundings, and remembered the night that she was born. The way the Sahib had paced the veranda and worried so. The moment that one of the boys was sent running all the way to the big house to deliver the news that the child was arrived and well, barely able to pull the words from his smiling mouth. Shiva remembered being told that she was tiny. That the clasp of her hand barely covered the tip of the Sahib's little finger. He watched her skip ahead and wondered what her future would bring.

Still some small distance from the gates, the sounds of Chinthimani's anguish crept towards them. Serafina tensed, her head drooping earthwards, as she felt the gaiety of the day seeping inexorably away. With each step that took her closer to this place they called home, her heart dulled just a little more. It was as though a sinister sense of loss hung over the courtyard, even when she and her sister were there. The cook no longer crashed around, instead silencing his pots to a respectful simmer and dutifully serving his place without disturbing his mistress. Their mother no longer smiled as she used to, the pride in her eyes now shadowed with the tamarind bitterness of her deep sorrow. They turned the final corner, finding the gates left wide open for their return.

Chinthimani stood in the courtyard shouting her suffering at Shurika, her high-pitched voice fuelled by the wrath that lived with her constantly, its fire never far from the surface. Shurika stood meekly, eyes downcast, and did nothing to retaliate. Neither woman noticed the children arriving with their father's faithful manservant. Chinthimani stumbled and raised a hand to hit Shurika, howling painfully about nothing and everything, slurring her words. Shurika bent like a reed, flinching in anticipation and lifting her arms quickly to protect herself from the rain of blows that would certainly follow.

Serafina wrenched her hand from Shiva's immediate grip and ran into the courtyard, swooping down to pick up a small branch fallen from the silver oak. As she flew towards the two women, she flailed the stick above her head defiantly and screamed at her mother.

'If you touch her, I will kill you! Do you hear me? Leave her alone!'

Serafina shook, her whole body caught up in the brutality of this wretched place, shaking from her head down to her feet, her face red with rage. The women, visibly shocked, froze in their positions as they stared at this child of such composure. Serafina's outburst filled the courtyard with a storm of violence, then dreadful silence. Mary stood beside Shiva, wide-eyed and open-mouthed. He squeezed her hand, but said nothing.

## 21

March came and went. School had started weeks ago, but James, weakened by the constant pleading from his children to stay just a little while longer, had not the strength to deny them.

'You can't keep them here for ever, darling.' Dorothy sympathised with him as they strolled the wide manicured lawns together, her voice soft and understanding.

'I know,' he said.

'And I can't stay here at the club indefinitely. People are beginning to talk.'

'They've been doing that for a long time, darling,' James conceded, nodding a brief hello to another couple passing them by. 'I wouldn't take any notice. If they're not talking about me, they'd only find some other poor beggar to persecute.'

'This is different,' Dorothy said. 'People stop speaking when I come into the room, then quickly change the subject. It's so obvious. They smile politely at me as though I'm some kind of fool who doesn't know what's going on. It's humiliating, James. No one wants to be made a laughing stock of. Least of all you and me.'

'Since when did you care what people said?'

'I don't!' The sudden rise in her pitch protested too much. 'But one servant goes talking to another, and the next thing we know, the whole world knows your business, and mine too.'

'I'm sorry, darling.' James's exasperation twitched at his jaw muscles. 'You shouldn't have to put up with that sort of thing. God knows, this has all been hard enough on you as it is.'

'Oh, James.' She touched his hand. 'Don't you have enough to worry about? You know Felix has done everything he can to keep the dogs off, but he's said that even he has his limits.'

'It's just so damned difficult,' James said.

'So you haven't told them yet?'

'How can I? This is the only home they have ever known, no matter how precarious it may seem. Take that away from them and what will they have?'

'They'll have a future, James.'

James peered up at the darkening sky threatening from above. He stopped and paused, glancing back to the clubhouse. 'Come on,' he said casually, as if hoping to change the subject. 'It looks like we could be in for a soaking. I think we had better make our way back.' Dorothy ignored the rumble from above and stood her ground.

'Listen to me, James.' She took both his hands in hers. 'You have to face facts sooner or later. There's trouble brewing everywhere and we both know it, and I'm not just talking about the children. Look at what's happening in Europe, for heaven's sake. The newspapers are full of all kinds of terrible stories. And if what they're saying is true, this war is coming our way, no matter how much we all try to pretend it isn't.'

'The newspapers exaggerate, darling. They always do.'

'Don't treat me like a child.' Dorothy glared at him. 'Any idiot can see that there's just as much trouble in the east, and we're stuck right in the middle of it. It could spill over these borders and into our lives before anyone has a chance to even think about it.' She shuddered involuntarily against the damp, humid air. 'And God only knows what might happen then.'

'No doubt the self-rule revolutionaries will have a heyday,'

James replied. 'At least they ought to, if they had any sense. This is the chance they've been waiting for. We're hardly in a position to argue about it while the Germans are bombing the hell out of us, and there's no more attractive target to a tiger than the sight of weakened prey.'

'The Empire's not what it used to be,' Dorothy sighed.

'Nothing is what it used to be. And I have a feeling that this is just the beginning.'

'Then you know you can't wait indefinitely.' Dorothy linked her arm through his and together they began to walk back towards the clubhouse. 'You have to make proper arrangements. What if something should happen to you?'

A sudden shower fell from the clouds, engulfing the gardens in a curtain of warm water. James quickly pulled off his jacket and threw it across their heads as they rushed for the cover of the nearest tree. Beneath the protection of its branches, he shook the rain from his jacket and placed it around Dorothy's shoulders.

'Thank you,' she said, pulling it close, feeling the remnants of his warmth within its soft lining.

James put his arm around her.

'I'm sorry.'

'What for?'

'For everything. For getting you caught up in this mess. You deserved better.'

'I didn't want better. I wanted you.'

'And children.'

Dorothy averted her face. 'We promised each other we wouldn't talk of that any more.'

'I couldn't,' he said. 'I just—'

'Please.' The old, familiar ache began, just behind her eyes, pulling their lids tight shut. 'Let's not do this. Not now. I don't think I could bear it.' James swallowed, nodding towards the ground. 'Your first responsibility is to those girls. Don't shy away from it, James.'

'You're right,' he said. 'You're always right. I'll take the children back at the end of the week. But don't ask me to tell them before they go. I just can't do it.'

'What about the woman?' Still, after all this time, Dorothy was unable to allow Chinthimani's name to pass her lips.

'That will have to wait too, at least until the children have gone. Who knows what she might go and do? Probably run away into the jungle with them. I wouldn't even put it past her to take a knife to them all. She's losing her mind, you know.' His face clouded. 'Although quite what I expected to happen I don't know. The more I hear, the more I see that there's no other way, but it doesn't make it any easier.'

'Think of the children.' Dorothy pulled at his arm, willing him to make his resolve. 'As hard as it may be, you know it's the right thing to do.'

## 22

The train waited in the station, idling with a lazy hiss from the exhausted engine. The children sat in the carriage beside their father, Mary, mistrustful of the hired chaperone, staring dutifully out of the window at the teeming life on the platform edge. Their mother had stayed behind this time, as she often did, her headaches rendering her unfit for the journey. Serafina had said nothing about it, barely able to give her mother so much as a glance. Mary sulked her disappointment but knew it would do no good to argue. She hated being stuck with a chaperone. They always behaved charmingly enough in front of her father, but the smile usually faded the moment he had retired to the first-class gentlemen's carriage and they rarely offered much in the way of conversation. Mary chattered incessantly to her father, who humoured her kindly and tried to keep their spirits up despite Serafina's glum expression.

'I expect you'll be looking forward to seeing all your friends again.'

'I'd rather stay at home.' Mary pulled her face into a sulk. 'I hate school. The beds are awful and we hardly ever get taken out for treats. Sister Ann doesn't like me because I always mess up on the big sums. She makes me write them out again ten times and it makes my fingers ache.' She stared down at her hand forlornly.

'And what would you learn if you stayed at home all the

time? You would never be able to find your way in this world, and that would be no good at all, would it?'

'You could teach us yourself,' Mary decided. 'Then we could live with you up at the big house. I'd do anything you asked me to. We wouldn't be any trouble.'

At that moment, the train began to pull out.

'Papa!' Serafina shouted. 'We're moving!'

Through Mary's busy conversation they had missed the stationmaster's final whistle. James got up quickly, thought briefly about making a dash for it, but saw that the engine was already picking up speed, the platform edge sliding past, taking the waving spectators with it. He sighed and sat back down.

'Papa! You are in the wrong carriage!' Mary's delighted face lit up with mischief. 'What are you going to do?'

He smiled and put a finger to his lips. 'I won't tell if you won't. Let's just hope that the guard doesn't come along and make a big performance about it. I'll change over at the next stop.'

Mary moved along the seat and snuggled in close beside him, resting her head against his arm, smelling the fabric of his clothes, feeling for the tie tucked in her pocket, a brown silk one with cream polka dots. James had taken her to his dressing room the previous day and had opened his closet doors then told her that she might choose one of his ties to take back to school with her as a reminder of the holiday. A keepsake from him. It was as though she had been invited into the very core of his distant, grown-up world. She had stopped to look at the bed in which he slept, carved from dark teakwood, but was unable to imagine her father at rest, his constant vitality the only picture she could ever conjure. When she asked him why it was so big, he had told her that it was an English custom, and said that he would be more than happy to sleep in a hammock strung up between the trees.

Once in his dressing room, Mary had been overwhelmed by the sudden presence of her father's unmistakable redolence. It was everywhere, on everything she touched. On top of a high chest of drawers with polished brass handles that fell flush into the body of the wood lay his toilet paraphernalia. A razor, sheathed within a slender ivory handle, a small teak box with an ornate silver escutcheon, a pair of hand-held hairbrushes with tortoiseshell backs, a pot of thick white hair cream. She had reached up to dip her finger in, and held it under her nose for a moment before rubbing it on to her bare arm. With his closet thrown wide open, she had slowly felt her way along the rows of her father's things, wanting to lose herself among them, breathing in the intoxicating mixture of camphor and cologne. She had lifted each of the ties to her face, turn by turn, until she found the one that carried the strongest scent.

'This one!' She had smiled triumphantly, pulling it out and holding it high above her head as one might wield a trophy. He had sighed comically and raised an eyebrow, teasing her that she had gone and chosen his most particular favourite, then had rolled it up and given it to her. Mary had slept with it under her pillow last night after stubbornly refusing to have it packed in with the rest of her things.

Serafina remained quiet and stared out of the window at the changing landscape as the carriage rocked along, its soporific tilt lulling her softly, reminiscent of how it had felt to be carried as a small child.

The familiar train journey was long and slow, full of stops and interruptions, with a constantly shifting picture postcard passing the window looking out on to the lush terrain. Rough dwellings sat here and there, dotted along the trackside, simple shacks set in small patches of land, whitewashed or painted in earthy pinks and yellows, roofed with reeds, some with old sacking stretched across fragile wooden frames, shading their entrances from the elements. Women with black-eyed babies balanced on hips stared as the train rolled by. Children appeared from nowhere and ran alongside for a while, laughing and waving cheerfully at the passengers. As the terrain thickened, so the houses became fewer and further between. Steep hillsides rose then cut away sharply into deep gorges with ribbons of sparkling rivers below. The bitter smell from the engine passed down the length of the snaking carriages. Steam. Soot. Sweat. Mary loved the train, the adventure of it all. Serafina detested every long mile of it, reminding her that she belonged nowhere, passed like an unwanted consignment from one place to another.

They settled in and coasted along, swaying with the motion of the journey, silently harbouring their own disappointments. Eventually, James broke the silence.

'I will miss you girls when you are gone,' he said sadly. 'We had a wonderful holiday together this time, didn't we?' Mary and Serafina nodded quietly, heads filling with brief flashes of the days now gone. 'You know,' he seemed suddenly uncomfortable, his face taking on a marked expression, 'whatever happens in the future, you must always remember the good times.'

'Why?' Mary didn't like his tone. It frightened her in ways that she could not understand. 'What's going to happen in the future?'

'Ah.' He smiled at her. 'Now that is something that nobody knows.' He leaned back in his seat. 'All we do know is that things change. Things change for all of us. It is just the way that life is.'

'I don't understand, Papa.' Serafina felt her cheeks beginning to flush.

The chaperone concentrated deliberately on her book, but James knew that she was merely making pretence and listening to his every word. As if a distant memory had tapped him on the shoulder, he heard his sister Edith's words, ringing echoes of her condemnation for the ill-considered way in which he had dropped his bombshell on Dorothy in full view of those strangers' eyes. It brought him up short. This was not the time or place to try to explain the pain of life's futilities to his children.

'It's all right,' he reassured Serafina, opening his arm and inviting her to sit against him. 'It's just my way of telling you that you are growing up now. You have your whole lives ahead of you. I want you both to know that no matter how far apart we are, I will think of you every day. You can always be sure of that.'

There was a certain something about the way he spoke that fell across them all with a sense of finality. The talking ceased, as though there were nothing left to say. Serafina wrapped her arms about herself and allowed her eyes to close.

All at once, there came a terrible commotion. A tremendous sharp noise crashed against the carriage, followed by a quick succession of desperate scrabbling sounds that seemed to scrape against the inside of the walls. The chaperone looked up from her book, her face immediately white with alarm. 'What on earth?'

James became alert in an instant, his whole body tensing as he realised what was happening. Outside, two men had leaped on to the train from their hiding place within the dense trees and now gripped the moving carriage. Crude weapons in hand, they banged menacingly on the roof, then slid down and began wrenching at the door handle, trying to get in. Terrified, the children grasped hold of their father, their screams deafening his senses. James jumped up from his seat, thrusting them roughly towards the shocked figure of the chaperone.

'Don't just sit there, woman!' he shouted at her. 'Take them!'

She immediately encircled them in her arms, hiding their

faces in her chest, telling them to be quiet, drawing them into the seat with her.

James pressed himself against the carriage wall, quickly stole a glance out of the window, then pulled back.

'Bandits!' He shouted a helpless warning to his cowering children, then swore under his breath, wishing more than anything else at that moment that he had with him the small pistol that he kept in the teak case above his dresser. It had never seen the light of day, fool that he was. God knows, Felix had warned him often enough, telling him that this was no time to stick to a matter of principle. In his regimented comfort on the plantation, it was all too easy for James to forget that this was lawless territory and that these incidents had become increasingly commonplace as the world's troubles grew.

His anger at himself – for this and a thousand other things – rose in a sudden storm of fury. He reached quickly for his cane and pushed the window down, thrusting the full armoury of his strapping frame outward and flailing violently at the two men, shouting, *Chale jao! Chale jao!* in the same commanding tone he used when there was trouble afoot in the coolie huts. The robbers, visibly shocked to find a broadly built Englishman in the first-class ladies' carriage, glanced at each other, wide-eyed and bewildered.

Seeing his chance, James pushed himself out as far as he could and thrashed his cane at the leg of the nearest assailant. It hit its mark with savage accuracy, causing the man to cry out in pain and grasp down towards his injured knee. His accomplice, waving a long, broad knife, lurched towards James, screaming a stream of abuse, the confusion of the situation opening before him sending him into a deadly panic. With one hand holding on to the outside rail, the man swung himself out from the moving carriage, using the speed of the train to aid his swift movement, and flew directly towards James, knife outstretched. James ducked back quickly, throwing himself against the inside wall, the blade crashing against the window frame, lodging itself into the wood at the very point where his head had been just seconds before. As the robber tried to recover his balance and retrieve his knife, his face contorted into a mixture of fear and blind rage. James rushed forward once more and slammed his cane into the man's neck. The chaperone screamed in horror as the man seemed to gurgle, eyes bulging, the knife dropping from his hand. James hit him again, this time full on the head, the scalp splitting and spilling crimson blood. The man lost his grip instantly, falling to the moving ground far below. The second assailant howled down at his friend's disappearing body. James, shocked by the brutality of his own actions, lost sight of his concentration for a moment, then, realising his mistake, turned on the injured man still clinging to the train, shouting and hurling his cane against the side of the carriage, inches from the man's remaining good leg. The bandit, face twisted from the agony of his wound, looked back desperately towards the spot at which his accomplice had fallen, released his grip and dropped harmlessly to the ground. James watched helplessly as he rolled down the escarpment, the train quickly distancing the frustrated men from their intended victims.

With pounding temples and trembling hands, James pulled himself back into the compartment, gathering every ounce of his self-control to keep his head and conceal the sickening rush that overwhelmed him. Allowing himself just a fleeting moment to regain his composure before turning to face the chaperone, he calmly replaced his cane beside his seat, drawing a deep breath and skilfully veiling the fit of panic now dispersing through his body, his shirt wet with perspiration.

'It's all right. They've gone,' he said with a hollow smile, smoothing his dishevelled hair, trying to banish the flashing images of his bloody, murdered children from his mind's eye.

'I don't think they'll be back again.' He retook his seat, dabbing the sweat from his brow with a handkerchief. Serafina sat rigid, staring at him as though in a stupor, then threw herself towards him and held on tightly. 'It's all right,' he told her. 'We're all perfectly safe. They would never have managed to get in anyway. These carriages are stronger than the Tower of London.' Mary lifted her head from the chaperone's lap, her eyes agape with fear, cheeks wet with tears. 'Are you all right?' He tried to smile. Mary shook her head and started to cry again.

'Dear Lord.' The chaperone crossed herself, then reached for her handbag and began scrabbling inside for a handkerchief. 'There is no imagining what might have happened had your youngest not driven you mad with her chatter and distracted your attentions. This is the very last time I risk using the train like this. They should have done away with these separate carriages long ago.' Her voice rose as her own panic set in. 'What is a woman supposed to do? They say it is for our own protection, but—'

'That's quite enough.' James silenced her with a ferocious glare. 'You were never in any danger,' he insisted, the sharpness of his tongue declaring her talk to be out of place in front of his children. 'But perhaps I had better stay here with you for the rest of the way.'

James returned home the following evening to find Felix waiting for him, he and Dorothy sitting out on the veranda, watching the storm clouds gathering overhead.

'Good God, James.' Felix took one look at his friend's exhausted face. 'Whatever's the matter? You look as though you've seen a ghost, man.'

Dorothy stood the moment she saw him. 'Are you all right, darling?'

'What?' James seemed unaware of his unusually disordered

appearance, the slight tear in the elbow of his jacket not quite visible from his own viewpoint. 'Yes,' he said. 'Yes, I'm fine.' He accepted Dorothy's kiss. 'Get me a drink, would you, darling?'

'Yes, of course,' she said, skimming Felix a quizzical look before leaving them together.

James dropped himself into her vacant chair.

'What are you doing here?' Fatigued, he reached for a cigarette from the box on the table and struck a Vesta.

'I've been asking myself that very same question for years,' Felix replied. 'You know I've always done my best for you, don't you, James?'

James drew on his cigarette long and hard. 'That I cannot deny,' he said. 'But if you've come here to give me another one of your lectures, you might as well save your breath.'

'I'm afraid not.' Felix spoke levelly. 'It's all a bit late for that now.' Hearing the resignation in his friend's voice, James found himself for the first time genuinely concerned by Felix's disquiet. 'There's been a whole lot of brouhaha at the Calcutta office, James. Penderghast has been under pressure from the bigwigs in London. All this political nonsense going on. Those bastards have a lot to answer for.'

Dorothy stepped out of the door with James's drink and placed it on the low table in front of him. Just as she was about to take a seat, Felix half stood from his own.

'Dorothy? I don't suppose I could ask you to leave us two chaps alone for a few minutes, could I?'

'Well, I ...' Dorothy looked embarrassed. 'Of course.'

'Just the usual dull business talk,' Felix explained diplomatically. 'We wouldn't want to bore you with it.'

She smiled understandingly. 'Come in when you're ready to eat.'

James waited until her footsteps faded before challenging

his friend. 'All right, Felix. What the hell's going on? I leave the place for two days and come back to find you looking like an executioner waiting on my doorstep. Let's have it.'

'It's a mess, James,' Felix said. 'And if it isn't now, it soon will be. The company has demanded detailed inventories from each of the regional managers. They want to know everything about the company's assets, its interests, all the plantations of course, and a complete account of each one.'

'So?' James picked up his drink and took a large swig. 'Sounds like you're going to have to work for your living for a change.'

'I don't think you follow me, James. This isn't just about money; there are all sorts of other rumblings going on. They're not prepared to turn a blind eye any longer.' James felt the whisky burning his dry throat. 'It's not just you. They're making a clean sweep under these ridiculous new rules of con-stitution. If tested by the letter of the law, God only knows how many of these lands will be exposed as having been plundered with no legal claim upon them at all.'

'I still don't see what that's got to do with me.'

'Then you bloody well should, James!' Felix snapped cross-ly. 'It's been decided that there's quite enough trouble for the company to deal with without having the added complication of a load of illegitimate half-castes running around the country-side. It causes a lot of bad feeling, you know.' He leaned back in his chair and released a plume of smoke into the dense air above him. 'They can't allow anything to jeopardise future diplomatic relations. It's all just one headache after another.'

'So,' James said wryly. 'The British are finally discovering that their once faithful and subservient colony has had enough. I wonder what took them so long.'

'Quit India, indeed,' Felix huffed. 'Can you imagine these bloody peasants trying to rule themselves? They mean to take control of everything that we British have toiled so long to achieve and throw us out on our ears.'

'It was only ever a matter of time,' James said.

'Well let them do what they want.' Felix threw back the rest of his whisky. 'Let them have their wish and may the whole bloody lot come tumbling down around their ears. You know, I've had to fight my way through more street demonstrations than I care to recall in recent months. Calcutta's complete chaos, and I'll be damned if they expect me to keep trudging down there just to pay them lip service and kowtow to their ridiculous demands. It's no bloody wonder half the managers want out. This is exactly what happens when you let the wogs start getting ideas above their station.'

'Don't let it get to you, Felix. It'll blow over, you wait and see.'

'Blow over?' Felix banged his fist against the arm of his chair. 'Are you mad? The whole world's in turmoil. First Europe, now north Africa, and it won't stop there either. You just mark my words.'

'In that case, whatever you do, it would be no more effective than placing a matchstick on the line and expecting it to halt an express train, would it?' James sat calmly and allowed his eyes to roam the far terraces, patterning the hillsides in an undulating cushion of jade. 'The writing has been on the wall for a long time, Felix. We were going to have to deal with it at some point, so you might as well get used to it. We'll all have to make adjustments, one way or another.' He waited for Felix to launch into another tirade, but instead of coming back at him with his usual bluster, Felix just sat there in silence. Then he put his empty glass down on the table quietly and sighed.

'You're to be moved on,' he said, without looking up.

The words hit James like iced water.

In that moment, the whole world stood still. He felt his

mouth open and close, his fingers flexing against the cool of his whisky glass. His throat tightened, strangling his reply.

'What?'

'Moved on. Shipped out. Whatever you want to call it. I'm sorry, James. I did everything I could to persuade Penderghast against the decision, but it fell on deaf ears. He knows all about your predicament. For heaven's sake,' Felix let out a small, ridiculous laugh, 'I don't know who doesn't, the way you've carried on.'

'But I've been here for over fifteen years! I can't just—'

'A damned sight longer than you should have been, if you ask me.'

'But what about—' He stopped himself.

'Forget it, James. You should have thought about all that a long time ago.' James sat frozen, speechless. 'I'll take care of the place myself until the new chap arrives.'

'Who are they sending?'

'What does it matter?' Felix said impatiently. 'By the time they get here, I'll see that your tracks are well covered, if that's what you're worried about.'

'You'll let her stay where she is?' James heard the impotence of his words. 'It's out of the way. They wouldn't be in anyone's—'

'Oh, just give it up, will you?' Felix said irritably. 'Haven't you had enough yet?'

A hollow surge rammed through James's stomach. So this was it. The end. The end that he could never envisage, no matter how often he tried to force himself towards it.

'Where will you send her?'

'What the hell do you care?'

'*Care?*' James jerked from his seat, throwing his arms into the air. 'Of course I bloody care! What the hell do you think

I've been doing all these years? Where do you think I've been these last two days?'

'I know,' Felix said, finding his compassion. 'Dorothy told me all about it. You've done the most honourable thing a man in your position could have.'

'Then why do I feel like such a heel?'

'She'll be paid off, just like the others. Where she goes will be up to her, James. There is nothing more that you can do. They're sending you west.'

Deeply shaken, James sank back into his seat. 'Where?'

'That I don't know yet, but your time here is done, my friend.'

'Have you told Dorothy any of this?'

'Of course not. What kind of idiot do you take me for? I'm afraid that will be down to you.'

'I see,' said James.

'I expect she'll be bloody grateful and more than a little relieved if you ask me.' Felix huffed and dropped his eyes from James's unmasked discomfort. 'I don't know how she's put up with your preposterous arrangements for this long. You should count yourself lucky that she hasn't upped and left you. It's probably a blessing in disguise, James. This place must have caused her nothing but heartache.'

It had never occurred to James that this might be the case, and the grim realisation crept upon him like a cold winter wind. Suddenly, the weight of the world seemed to descend upon his shoulders. He leaned forward and dropped his head into his hands, running his fingers through his hair. 'You have no idea,' he whispered.

## 23

Shurika regarded her mistress's wan reflection in the cracked mirror of the dressing table. The once rosebud lips, luscious red, soft as morning dew, had given up their bloom long ago and seemed lost in the grey pallor of her sunken complexion. Teasing the tangles from her hair with slow ritual, Shurika sat behind her, working gently, beginning at the ends of its waist length, moving gradually upwards with practised fingers, massaging her scalp with perfumed oil. To mask the awful silence, she sang to her softly, a poem of the greatest love ever known, between a god and his goddess.

Chinthimani did not move, hearing nothing, feeling nothing, the blood sleeping in her veins, her heart lying still as a dead pool. Setting down the shallow dish of oil, Shurika ran the sandalwood comb through her mistress's glorious mane, the shining ribbon of jet-black hair holding the light and casting it back like polished onyx. She finished the task, set the comb into her lap, dropped her head and wept.

'Weep for us both,' Chinthimani said to the mirror, her voice dull. 'For I have no more tears.'

'I will never leave you, mistress.'

'That is up to you. You have your money. You may do as you please now.' Her eyelids drooped heavily.

'My place is with you. This is my purpose.'

'Your purpose,' Chinthimani said, drawing the words out

in a slow chant. 'My purpose. Your purpose. My curse. Your curse. I want no more from this incarnation. I could wake no more and be content. There is no life inside me now.'

'We must make a new life for ourselves,' Shurika said. 'A new life far away from here.'

Shurika had chosen what to take carefully. Nothing heavy, nothing large, nothing that would draw unwanted attention, instead selecting only small objects of value, some clothes, sufficient food to sustain them on their journey for a while. They would have to manage the bullock cart on their own, the cook and his helper having upped and left almost the instant Shiva took his leave of them. Her brother had gone too, disappearing into the night after promising with empty words that he would stay and protect them. Shurika had heard him moving around when he had thought them asleep, his footsteps creeping in, his hands reaching into the darkness to pick up and take whatever he could find. She had left a few coins and her mistress's gold nose ring on the table deliberately, along with some trinkets that looked more valuable than they were, knowing that he would steal whatever he could and flee, fearing that if he did not find what he was looking for, he might take a dagger to their throats in frustration. She had listened intently as he picked his way around, her heart racing at the thought of the money she had sewn into the folds of the sari wrapped tightly around her middle. The rest of their valuables she had hidden in the earth by the vegetables that grew in her mistress's garden. It was all still there, undisturbed, when the sun rose and her brother was long gone. Shurika had then walked to the gatehouse, to leave one final message, before returning to the courtyard and waiting for a response.

'They have all left us,' she had said. 'What should we do?'

'I cannot help you,' Shiva replied.

'Please, tell me! We cannot stay near here. It will be too dangerous for us.'

'It will be dangerous for you anywhere. Take this.' He had handed her a small, unsealed envelope. 'It is a letter of introduction, vouching for your good character. It is the only protection I can offer you. Do not lose it.' Shiva had taken pity on her. 'Be sure to travel simply. Do not have anything that people will want to steal from you. Take care not to let anyone see that you have some money. Do not speak to anyone unless you have to.'

'Where should we go?'

'I don't know.' He saw hopelessness in her eyes. 'South,' he told her. 'There is talk of much trouble in the north. Go south. Or west. There are more people there. Find somewhere to disappear, where you will not be noticed. Somewhere bigger than a village. A town, or a city where you will become invisible. That is what you must do. You must become invisible, and hope that the gods are kind to you.'

Shurika sat quietly behind her mistress and dried her tears. They had a long day ahead of them, the bundles she had prepared ready and waiting, the mild-mannered ox already tethered to the cart outside. She wiped the oil from the sandalwood comb and rested it in her lap. Chinthimani watched her closely in the mirror, took the drink from the table and swallowed it.

'Now finish the job you started,' she said, holding her head up proudly.

'Yes, mistress,' Shurika said. 'It is my honour to serve you.'

Piece by piece, Chinthimani's hair fell to the ground, its shimmering light dimming as it dropped, disturbing the dust, the floor around them becoming a silken carpet of one woman's life. With the work of her scissors done, Shurika took up the sharpened razor, dipped it into her bowl of oil, and passed it gently across her mistress's head, carving the silhouette of a widow, the outcast of outcasts.

## 24

Six months passed. The Angelus bell rang out from the chapel of St Agnes. Three rings, a pause, another three rings. The sound carried, clear and pure, sailing out and down into the valley. All around, everyone halted, no matter where they were. The cook put down his utensils, slipped the cloth cap from his head and closed his eyes to pray, pans bubbling on the stove beside him. The house servants stopped sweeping and bowed respectfully, brushes silenced behind their backs. The pupils stood and quietened, ready to recite the Angelus so embedded in all of them. It was Mary's favourite. Her head filled with the sound of Father Lazarus singing *Angelus Domini nuntuavit Mariae,* then the momentary silence before the sisters sang their response. She liked that it was a prayer to Mary, and the way her name sounded when sung in Latin. The ritual soon passed, and the small world of the convent reawakened and continued to go about the daily business of life.

The convent gates opened and out filed the girls, in full uniform and straw hats, for their afternoon walk, marching smartly towards the small town spreading in undisciplined fashion on both sides of the single road that passed through it, all the time hurried along and jealously guarded by the sisters.

'I see Serafina's cried off the Sunday frogmarch again,' grumbled Roley, her face flushed from the exercise. 'I hate walking. It makes me feel quite ill.'

'It's good for you.' Mary smiled. 'Take some deep breaths and enjoy it!'

'I can breathe perfectly well without being forced to hike for miles and climb hills the size of Mount Everest. Thank God we're breaking up for the holidays next week. Once I'm on that train, you won't catch me walking more than fifty yards for the whole three months.' Roley stopped for a moment to catch her breath, leaning one hand on Mary's slight shoulder. 'One of these days I'll drop down dead when we're miles away from anywhere and they'll have to drag my body all the way back and bury me in the orchard. Then they'll be sorry.'

Mary pushed Roley's arm playfully, her happy mood irrepressibly lifted by the sight of the green parrots, screeching and wheeling in high circles above their heads. 'What's the first thing you're going to do when you get home?'

'Make a big bonfire and burn my uniform,' Roley said. 'What about you?'

'Oh, I don't know.' Mary clasped her hands together, beaming from ear to ear. 'My father always has lots of surprises for us. You know, special treats that he keeps secret until the last minute. I expect we'll be seeing our aunt too. She's really nice.' Mary nodded approvingly. 'And she's a doctor, so it doesn't matter if we get sick because she can look after us.'

Sister Margaret's voice sang out from the front of the line. 'Come along, girls! Keep up! It's a lovely afternoon, so we'll take the lake route today!'

'Oh, for heaven's sake.' Roley huffed her indignation. 'Why couldn't we have gone for a nice picnic instead of trudging around endlessly for no good reason?' Mary smiled and was glad to have Roley beside her. 'We haven't been on a picnic for simply ages. Great big dishes of cold roast chicken and potato salad, then a gentle wander down the banks to cool our feet off in the water. *That* I can understand. But this? It's just so

202

pointless.' Sister Margaret turned off the main thoroughfare and headed up along the rough road that led to the very edge of the town before coming to an abrupt dead end above a wonderful vista of the lake. Roley groaned at the sight of the incline.

'I love this way,' Mary said, her voice breathless from exertion. 'There is the most beautiful house right up at the end of it.' Roley showed no interest, concentrating instead on putting one foot in front of the other, reluctantly hauling herself along.

Fifteen exhausting minutes later, the road came to a grassy halt at the edge of the steep hill. Set some distance away from it, still in full view, was the house that Mary sometimes dreamed of as her own. It sat perched at the very lip of the land, bathed in golden sunlight, its broad path, neglected and overgrown with a soft carpet of moss upon stone, curling a steep gradient away from the road towards its once grand entrance. The generous white-gabled windows, shuttered tight closed, would gaze westward if thrown open, drinking in the breathtaking scene that stretched achingly across the slate blue of the mountain lake. The ghostly, sloping gardens lay abandoned and untended, the high swaying grass hinting at well-kept lawns in better times. Mary could not imagine the reason why anyone would want to desert such a heavenly place, and had decided that the house must have suffered a terrible tragedy and been left in peace to mourn. It was the name on the decaying gates that captured her imagination most.

'The Limit,' she whispered, eyeing the sign hanging loosely from the broken gate. 'One day I shall have a house called The Limit, and it will make me think of here.'

In the quiet of the empty convent house, Serafina sat calmly in one of the two chairs set before the mother superior's desk. A small fire had been laid in the hearth, the single crackling log sufficient to warm the day's slight chill from the room. Hands folded neatly in her lap, Serafina concentrated on the steady ticking from the long-case clock while the mother superior busied herself, uttering pleasantries about the sunshine outside while returning a leather-bound book to the shelf before taking her seat. She removed her half-moon spectacles and regarded Serafina with compassion.

'Serafina,' she said. 'I expect you will be wondering why I asked you to stay behind this afternoon.'

'Yes, Mother Superior.'

'You know that we can never be sure what the good Lord has in store for us, Serafina. Sometimes we do not understand why certain things happen ...' Serafina felt her blood run cold. The droning, meaningless words faded from her hearing, drowned out by the torrent rushing through her veins, heart pounding in her chest. She stared at the mother superior, empty-eyed, placing an invisible wall of protection between herself and the one piece of news she had always dreaded hearing. 'There is going to be no easy way to explain this to you.' The mother superior indicated a folded letter on the desk in front of her. 'I'm afraid that you and your sister will not be going home for the holidays.'

Serafina looked her straight in the eye and asked her outright. 'Have we been dropped?'

'No! Oh, dear child! Of course not! Your father is devoted to both you and your sister. He made that perfectly clear to us from the very beginning. But he has moved to another job hundreds of miles away, so it just isn't possible for him to have you home for the holidays.'

'What about our mother? Has she moved with him?'

'I ...' The mother superior flushed a little. 'I don't know. But that isn't really the—'

'Then we could go and stay with her as we always do,' Serafina said.

'I'm afraid that won't be possible, Serafina. Your father has left us strict instructions. You are to stay here with your sister.'

'I see.' Serafina showed not a hint of emotion.

'I'm sorry,' the mother superior said. 'It is never easy to be the bearer of difficult news.'

Serafina remained perfectly composed, her eyes coming to rest on the desk. 'May I be permitted to read the letter for myself?'

'It is not addressed to you, child.'

'I'm fifteen. I am not a child any more.' Serafina glared at her. 'And I don't suppose that anyone will tell us the truth about it.' An awkward silence settled between them. 'All this talk about God, and honesty, and being a good Christian.' She hissed the words through her teeth. 'And yet so many lies everywhere.'

The momentary shock that passed across the mother superior's face gave Serafina some small satisfaction. She took up the letter and handed it to her.

'This is much against my better judgement, Serafina.'

With the pale-blue slip of paper in her hand, Serafina sat motionless and made no move to open it. She had no intention of reading the letter in front of her and sat, unmoving. The mother superior rose from her seat with a sigh. She stepped out of the room but remained close by, pacing the corridor slowly. A few moments passed in silence, then came the unmistakable sound of grief seeping through the closed door. Reaching for the handle, the mother superior found the door to be locked from the inside and fought to suppress the wave of panic that descended upon her.

'Serafina?' She pulled at the doorknob, rattling it hard.

Serafina slid down into the chair, turning to liquid, arms curled over her head, suffocating beneath the avalanche of shame that crashed down upon her, her skin crawling with the humiliation of her father's disgrace, the sheer degradation of it all plucking out her insides.

'Serafina! Open this door immediately!' Giving up on the handle, the mother superior rapped on the door, softly at first, then more urgently. 'Serafina! Open up this instant or I shall have someone come and break it down!'

Serafina felt the walls close in around her. That she should have been reduced to this was incomprehensible. Yet as she rocked in the seat, squeezing herself into a tight ball of self-reproach, she knew that she had deceived herself all along, that love had had nothing to do with it, that she had been no more than a burden of duty from the very beginning. Her stomach flinched at the painful memories of her foolishness, her blind adoration of a father who wasn't even fit to show his face in polite company, her shame over the mother she knew to be nothing more than the dirt on his shoes. It was loathsome. Detestable. The nausea came over her in an instant. She closed her eyes and breathed deeply until it passed, shutting it out, renouncing every last shred of their reprehensible behaviour and her own despicable situation. An involuntary chill took hold of her, shuddering her bones, and she hated them all.

It was some minutes before the mother superior heard the release of the lock. She took a deep breath, then entered the room to find Serafina sitting precisely where she had left her, as though she had not moved at all, the only indication of her anguish the rosy flush in her cheeks and the rawness still visible in her eyes. Serafina spoke before the mother superior could seat herself or properly gather her own thoughts.

'Mother Superior, I would like to ask that this news be kept from Mary,' she said dispassionately. 'There's no point in telling her now. It will only upset her.'

'Of course,' the mother superior replied with some relief,

her racing heart finally slowing to a less stressful pace. 'I think that would be sensible.'

Serafina then fixed upon her a gaze of pure rage.

'And this letter is to be destroyed. Mary must never know what was in it, and I don't want anyone else to know either.' Before the mother superior could answer, Serafina held up the fist into which she had crushed the letter. In one swift movement, she threw it into the flames of the open fire, the mother superior watching on, speechless, as the thin blue paper combusted, the licking yellow flames reflected in Serafina's black eyes.

## 25

Serafina sat alone at the piano in the empty refectory, softly playing a simple piece of Chopin from the volume of preludes Father Lazarus had presented to her for her birthday last year. Her heart sagged under the weight of its melancholia. All around her the convent was bustling with activity, the corridors choked with luggage, everyone toing and froing. The trunks had been brought down from storage two weeks ago and were now filled to bursting point, ready to load on to the line of carts waiting impatiently outside the high convent walls. The girls scurried around in readiness for their departure, saying their goodbyes to each other, hugging one another excitedly and talking with great animation about where they were going and who they would see. Rose de Souza rushed around the garden, scarcely aware of the rich notes that carried through the air from the open refectory window.

'Where's Mary got to?'

Roley gave her a fearsome expression. 'She's been sent to the mother superior's office.'

Rose rolled her eyes. 'What's she gone and done this time?' Roley shrugged that she didn't know. 'Probably been in the cookhouse sticking her fingers in the sugar again. You'd have thought she would have learned her lesson by now. It wouldn't be the first time Cook has chased her out of there with a wooden spoon.'

Jane pushed through. 'Has anyone seen Serafina?'

'No.'

'I wanted to give her book back.' Jane held it up in explanation.

'Well don't look at me.' Roley shrugged. 'She's not my friend.'

'Mine neither,' Amelia sniffed.

'I do hope Mary won't be too long.' Roley frowned in frustration. 'We'll be off in a minute and I'm supposed to be on the first cart.'

The door to the refectory opened quietly. Father Lazarus entered the room silently so as not to disturb Serafina's concentration, returning the heavy latch with his fingertips. Serafina stared ahead at the music with fixed determination. She knew that it was the priest from the shadow of his form, but she did not look up and made no attempt to greet him. Father Lazarus said nothing and quietly took a seat beside her, perching his weight unobtrusively on the edge of the black duet stool, watching with an occasional nod of approval before reaching out to turn the page for her. Serafina made no acknowledgement of his presence and continued to play, her mouth set into a hard line across her increasingly beautiful face. Through the open window drifted the shrill noises of excitement, the pupils shouting their final goodbyes and waving to the gathered smiling staff as they left one by one for the holidays. The nuns and servants watched as their charges gradually disappeared before retreating behind the convent walls and closing the heavy gates.

Inside the mother superior's office, Mary sat wailing, great long, angry sobs filling the wood-panelled room, bouncing from the walls and ringing back at her, the mother superior and Sister Margaret trying hopelessly to console her.

'Why can't we go home? I don't see what could be so

important that we should have to stay here for the holidays. It's not fair! I want to go home!'

The nuns looked at each other. They had said that her father had been called away, sent to work on a big plantation in Chandigarh in Himachal Pradesh, and that their mother was unable to take them for the holidays due to some trouble on the homestead. It was thought better than telling her the whole truth: that it had been said that their mother had gone mad and had been sent away, that she was not to be trusted with them, that she was to be turned away should she ever come looking for them, that their father's house was now lived in by another man, that they would never be sent for again.

Sister Margaret leaned over the sobbing Mary and said *there, there, child*, shaking her head sadly and looking to the mother superior for some better word of comfort. She had come to love this immature girl with her silly ways and her ready smile. She prayed for her every night and pleaded with the Lord to keep her and protect her.

In the refectory, Serafina finished the piece and sat paralysed. She waited until the last note died away, then dropped her head into her hands and cried bitterly. Father Lazarus wrapped his huge arms around her and brought her into his chest.

'Shh, my child. Hush now.'

He stroked her head and looked to the open window.

## 26

'Not that one,' Shurika said, eyeing the bruised brinjal. The vegetable seller cast her an irritable frown, muttering under his breath before returning the brinjal to the back of the basket and reluctantly taking up another, this time with taut, shiny skin, from the front of his modest display. It was a meagre specimen, Shurika thought, compared to the plump fruits she had once nurtured in her own garden in another life, long ago, far from here. She inspected the goods and paid the man before tucking the brinjals into her bundle with the rest of her provisions. Drawing the string closed on her coin pouch, she pressed it firmly into her palm, wrapping the thick cord tightly around her wrist lest anyone should try to snatch it from her again.

Shurika held on to her bundle tightly, the jostling crowds in the cramped, noisy street harbouring more than their rightful share of thieves, particularly at this time of year as the population swelled. She had learned this, and much else besides, the hard way, having found her money stolen more often than she cared to recall in the early days before they finally found their feet and learned to live in this suffocating place. In high summer, when the stench of humanity threatened to overwhelm her, Shurika would retreat to the haphazard patch of open woodland on the edge of the town, seeking out one of the ramshackle shelters built beneath the trees for the purpose of meditation and worship, hiding herself away while she offered her devotions. In the cool winter months, she would walk towards the temple of Madan Mohan, overlooking the muddied Jamuna, its sacred waters looping protectively around the promontory, giving most of the town something of an impression of being an island, stranded in the great landscape that stretched far and away.

Moving patiently along the crowded street, Shurika kept her eyes firmly fixed on the ground, threading her way through the narrow thoroughfare, bodies pressing against her as she held her breath, carried along by the tide of humanity until she came to the narrow path that led away from the bazaar. It was no wider than a rough, cramped corridor, flanked on either side by ancient buildings in various stages of decay, each one housing its own populace, spilling out noise and waste in equal measure. Relaxing her grip on the bundle, Shurika drew her breath deeply in relief, glad to be able to move her feet at last without stepping on somebody else's, grateful to be away from the swarming masses. In the last week, it seemed that every person in India, whether able-bodied or not, had chosen to descend upon Vrindavan, filling every available space, choking the streets, the excessive heat and humidity rendering the whole town ripe with the cloying odour of congested living.

Shurika made her way quickly through the winding maze of unmarked alleyways, then disappeared into the narrow, doorless aperture that led to the tightly squeezed dwellings hemmed in behind. She did not stop to speak to her neighbours, and they did not speak to her, merely glancing up from their chores to convey their general disdain. It was bad enough that she should have brought bad luck upon them all by subjecting them to the presence of a widow. Not long after they had arrived, the sour old matriarch who lived in the first of the houses had screamed at Chinthimani, shouting that she had no right to live, no business polluting their air with her deathly breath. She had quickly roused support from her neighbouring cronies, demanding of the landlord that Chinthimani be evicted before she could cast her evil eye upon any of their children. But Shurika had taken care to negotiate at least some degree of security from the man, handing him the slip of paper Shiva had given to her before they had left the homestead. What it said, she did not know, but the man had looked at it, pulling at his bottom lip thoughtfully with his fingers, copied down its contents and returned it to Shurika with another small document that she did not understand. She paid him the money he asked for, being the greater part of all they had, and he told her not to scrimp on the cost of a decent lock for the door. Thereafter, any attempts made to banish them fell on deaf ears.

Ignoring her neighbour's sideways glances, Shurika crept invisibly past the first few shabby houses before slipping unseen through her own door. In a dim corner lay Chinthimani, bound in a shawl, curled up with a blanket wrapped around her feet.

'Where have you been?' she grumbled, her voice still rasping with the sickness that had plagued her chest for months. 'You said you would not be long. I have been lying here suffering for hours. My throat is on fire.'

'I brought you some medicine.' Shurika put the bundle down on the floor by the stove and knelt down beside her, feeling her forehead. The persistent fever seemed to have abated, for now at least.

'I don't want medicine,' Chinthimani mumbled. 'Give me a little whisky. It helps to ease my pain.'

'Mistress, you should not—'

'Don't tell me what to do!' Chinthimani snapped irritably as Shurika helped her into a more comfortable position, folding the mat she had lain upon, fashioning it into a cushion and placing it beneath her bony hips.

'I will give you whisky if you promise to take some medicine and eat a little food.'

'Hmph,' Chinthimani conceded, screwing up her face in distaste as the bitter tincture was forced upon her. Reluctantly, Shurika poured a small measure from the whisky bottle. Without it, her mistress would sicken, as she had done before when Shurika had returned from the back-street liquor seller empty-handed, claiming that she could not find him. Chinthimani had become agitated, clawing at her skin, shaking and descending into fits of anger then confusion. After just one night of watching the demons take hold, Chinthimani lying on the floor, drenched in perspiration, Shurika had abandoned all hope of a cure and gone in search of the merchant. It had become her daily medicine, essential to her existence. Chinthimani took the drink without thanks and tipped it into her mouth as though it were water.

'It is a pleasant day outside if you keep away from the crowds,' Shurika said. 'We should go out for a while. Stretch our legs. I will make us some herbal tea, then we could go down to the river and bathe.'

'I am too weak to bathe.'

'I will help you.'

'There are too many people. How can I bathe when there is barely room to move?'

'Then you can sit on the steps and watch me while I wash our clothes. You have been stuck in here for too long. It is not good for you.'

'I don't want to go out today. Let me have another drink. My hip is paining me.'

'Later.' Shurika smiled at her tenderly. 'And there is nothing wrong with your hip.'

'What would you know?'

Shurika ignored Chinthimani's irascible manner. It was still too early in the day to expect anything else of her. 'Tonight is the night of the full moon,' she said, pouring some water into the small cooking pot and setting it down on the stove, persuading heat from the smouldering clod of solid fuel, fanning it with a piece of palm leaf matting until a waft of smoke appeared. She added a green cardamom pod to the pot, a pinch of sweet herbs and one dried tea leaf, picked carefully from the battered tin. 'The whole place is teeming with pilgrims. I think that more have come this year than ever before. It is no wonder the market traders are demanding too much money for everything today. I'd be surprised if there is enough food to go around.' Chinthimani feigned irritation, but Shurika could tell she was listening. She always listened to Shurika's stories, brought back from the streets, sometimes embellished with a small addition she had made up in her head on the way home, simply for her mistress's amusement. 'The vegetable seller tried to fob me off with a pair of brinjals that looked as if they had been harvested a month ago, so I tipped his basket over in the street to teach him a lesson.' From the corner of her eye, Shurika caught sight of Chinthimani's small, silent chuckle, and felt pleased.

Shurika quietened herself and busied her hands. For four years now she had watched her favourite festival come and go, pretending no interest, insisting that she too preferred to live a quiet life of withdrawal, hidden down a musty alleyway in a tiny house with thick walls and just one small window. This evening she would do what she always did – sit quietly on the floor, listening to the start of the celebrations, wishing she could be a part of it. And tomorrow, tomorrow when every man, woman and child let loose and danced in the streets, she would sit again, imagining the vivid clouds, the palettes of brightest blues and pinks and orange and every hue in between being thrown into the air, picturing herself among the jubilant pilgrims, drenched in coloured water, her smiling, painted features exchanging *bura na maano Hoi hai!* wishing happy Holi to her neighbours while rubbing *gulal* and *abeer* on each other's faces. It was a special time. A time to send blessings to loved and dear ones. A time to breathe in the air, thick with excitement, and to drench one's heart in the joy of love and romance, immersed in the spirit of devotion.

'You should go to the festival,' Chinthimani said with a small, distasteful sniff. 'I've seen you smiling to yourself, watching our neighbours' preparations. Just because I have no joy left does not mean that you have to sit here like a corpse. It is not my fault that you would not go and make a life of your own. I have no reason to keep living,' she repeated matter-of-factly, as she always did. 'So I sit, and I wait.'

'I have no wish to see the festival, mistress. Besides, they will be making a commotion for a week. There will be no avoiding it.'

Suddenly Chinthimani was overcome by another coughing fit, racking her bones, her face streaming with the uncontrollable onslaught. Shurika crouched beside her, rubbing her back, pressing a cloth in her hands into which Chinthimani hacked and spluttered crimson stains. After a while, it subsided, Chinthimani catching her breath and closing her eyes, exhausted by the severity of the attack. She wiped the blood from her mouth with the cloth and gave it back to Shurika.

'Just go out and leave me here.' Chinthimani lowered herself to the floor. 'How can I be expected to die when you are always watching me?'

'You are not dying. Now get up.' Shurika pulled at her. 'Sit up and take some tea. You must eat something too. I have brought some nice vegetables from the market.'

'Vegetables,' Chinthimani muttered. 'What do I want with vegetables?'

216

Taking the pan from the stove, Shurika poured the tea into two small clay cups and, from a small earthenware jar, spooned a little honey into the one for her mistress. 'Drink this,' she said. 'And look,' she reached into the bundle not yet unpacked, 'I found you some seed crackers.' Chinthimani looked at the two pieces in Shurika's hand.

'Hmm,' she said grouchily. 'Perhaps I will try just a little, if only to stop your constant nagging.'

Evening closed in, the acrid smell of bonfires rising and hanging over the town, signalling the ritual burning of the effigy of Holika, the devil-minded sister of the demon King Hiranyakashyap, and the lighting of fires at the wealthier homes. Chinthimani lay sleeping on the mat, the shadowy outline of her bones quietened by the medicinal herbs and the whisky she had insisted on imbibing through the afternoon. Shurika filled her nostrils, stretched up on to the tips of her toes and peered out of the window. Perhaps she could step outside for a little while. Her mistress was asleep and would not wake for hours. Surely she would not be missed if she slipped away just long enough to watch the neighbourhood children shouting excitable insults at the burning figures and playing pranks on their parents?

Outside, beyond the deserted alleyways, the streets groaned under the strain of the revellers, hordes of them all heading in the same direction, moving slowly like one enormous cacophonous entity. Shurika followed for a while, anonymous in the crowd, soaking up their vivacity but too self-conscious to join in the chanting of Rakshoghna mantras to ward off evil spirits, or to dance along to the beating drums. All around her faces glowed with excitement at the symbolic slaying of evil, the assured triumph of goodness, the prospect of all that was corrupt and damnable being engulfed by the leaping flames of the raging fires. She drank it all in, her skin alive. It intoxi-cated her, igniting distant memories of happiness and plenty, as though the child she once was had somehow emerged from a distant, secret place, insisting on resurfacing and tasting life again, if only for this fleeting moment.

An hour later, having taken her modest fill, it was with a heavy heart that Shurika finally tore herself away from the scene. She would have to satisfy herself with imagining the rest of the celebrations, suspended in that precious half-sleep when her stories filled her head and had life breathed into them. She prayed that tonight her dreams would be vivid, woven with rich detail, and that she would wake with every fragment still in place so that she might recount the tales over many days and nights to her beloved mistress. She would tell her how the fires had danced, erupting bright showers of glowing embers that flew right up to the stars. She would tell of the young lovers she had spied exchanging longing glances whenever their mothers' heads were turned. She would describe all the marvellous sights she had seen, and her mistress would listen contentedly while she rested, eyes closed.

Finding her passage blocked by the thronging crowds moving in their single, determined flow, Shurika turned away from the main thoroughfare, choosing to thread her way home through the warren of side streets and alleyways instead. Despite the darkness of the night, she felt no fear. The shadows would be safe enough this evening. No man would dare to offend the gods on such a holy day.

The commotion was upon her almost the moment she heard it rounding the corner. A deafening ruckus of shouting voices. The sickening, splintering crash of a door being ripped from its hinges. Metal pans clattering as they spilled violently to the ground. Then, to her horror, the terrible smell of burn-ing flesh. Shurika sucked in her breath and covered her nose.

Quickly, she turned to retrace her steps, back to the safety of the street. In the next instant, she was caught in the uproar. A mass of unintelligible shapes flooded the cramped space around her, thrashing out in the darkness. As she tried to untangle the images from the cover of blackness, a huge Brahmin bull, bucking and running amok, charged towards her, its panicked eyes glaring white, nostrils flaring. Its hindquarters were badly charred, the remains of its tail just a smouldering stump as it careered about the narrow alleyway, kicking great lumps out of the walls, grinding its hooves into the dirt. A thin group of barefooted men shouted after it, screeching hysterically, wielding sticks to no avail, the animal wild and unseeing.

The bull thundered down upon Shurika like an earthquake, the force of the impact sending her spinning. She howled and raised her hands to her head, shafts of bright colours splintering before her eyes.

Shurika had never known such a silence. There was no air. No air inside her. No air anywhere. Just the silence, and a bright white light that held the warmth of a thousand suns. She felt herself rise high into the air, floating from cloud to cloud, then down again, as though carried along above the heads of the crowds by eager upturned hands. She felt weightless, joyful, like a feather swept up by a dust devil and tossed around like a toy. Way off in the distance, a tiny crack appeared in the bright white light. Then came the noise, a terrifying roar, and a mighty, high-pitched scream from the depths of her own throat.

## 27

Father Lazarus presided over mass, Serafina perched dutifully in the corner at the pump organ, churning out the familiar chords to 'The Lord Is My Shepherd' without having to think about where to position her hands. She had played it a thousand times or more and the notes fell automatically from her fingers. The piece bored her, its simple structure giving her no satisfaction at all, unlike 'Jerusalem', which, at least, had a few passages where she might exert a little light and shade, should the notion take her. This spring, upon turning eighteen, Serafina had found herself accepting the honourable mantle of head girl during a special assembly set before the whole school, and finally permitted herself to feel some solace from the knowledge that her time here would soon be done. She watched Father Lazarus in the small mirror angled into the inlaid wood, from where she could take his cue without the need to turn around and strain her neck uncomfortably.

There was something out of place this morning, the atmosphere heavy with a strange, unspoken anticipation. They had all felt it, apparent in the nuns' glum expressions, in the absence of their usually cheery Sunday-morning exchanges. Sister Margaret and Sister Rosemary were nowhere to be seen. Both had been absent from the breakfast table, and neither of their strident voices was to be heard in the chapel. As Serafina closed down the last verse, she kept her eyes on the mirror. The chapel door opened, momentarily casting a slender shaft of sunlight across the narrow aisle and distracting the congregation. Sister Margaret kept her eyes on the floor, sweeping quickly to the back of the chapel and whispering to Sister Ann. The pair of them slipped out together, solemn-faced, without so much as a nod of apology to Father Lazarus. He noticed the immediate murmur running through the pews and called the girls to order with a swift, loud clearing of his throat and a purposeful 'Let us pray'.

All heads bowed in the chapel, hands clasped together in reverence as Father Lazarus offered blessings and prayers to the fractured world around them.

The note secretly passed down the line of elder girls during lunch was quickly detected by Sister Margaret, removed and destroyed. The pupil caught with it would be dealt with later and made to atone for her sin. There would be no Sunday walk this afternoon. Instead, the delighted pupils were told that they might do as they wished, although the offer came with a firm suggestion that their time should be usefully employed either by writing letters home or reading the Gospel of St Mark.

By the time everyone was washed and dressed for bed that night, a dreadful hush had descended upon the dormitory. Mary and Amelia sat on the end of Roley's bunk, the three of them pulling their knitted shawls protectively around their shoulders, huddled together against the chill.

'They tried to kill it,' whispered Roley. 'One of the villagers brought it up to the cook's wife and she sat up with it all night. She sent one of the kitchen boys to the nunnery to fetch help.'

Amelia nodded, having heard the story relayed from mouth to mouth all afternoon, collecting snippets of information and piecing the fragmented tale together once more. 'Sister

Margaret called for the doctor, but he said that there was nothing they could do.'

'They fed it opium.'

Mary was unable to conceal her horror, this harrowing account simply incomprehensible to her.

Roley leaned forward, her voice barely there. 'It was a girl child.'

The three of them sat in silence and thought about how the cook's wife had sat up through the whole of the night while the tiny body shook and fevered in her arms. They had sent for the doctor. Then for the priest. There was nothing more to be done except to wait, watch, hope and pray.

'Such a beautiful child,' the cook's wife had said. 'Let her live and I will raise her as one of my own.'

But the cook did not share his wife's sentiments. There was no money to feed another mouth. The child, if it survived, would be sent to the big orphanage in Kalimpong, and what kind of life would that be? Better that it died, as he had seen so many times before. He voiced none of this to his wife, for he knew that the infant would not survive.

'Yes,' he had said, comforting his wife. 'Such a beautiful child. Pray that God will spare her, and we will raise her as one of our own.'

Mary lifted the mosquito net tucked around Roley's bunk and crept to the end of the dormitory, where Serafina lay reading quietly.

'Can I get in with you?'

Serafina sighed heavily, as though greatly inconvenienced.

'No. There's not enough room.'

'Please! I'll make myself very small,' Mary said. Reluctantly Serafina pulled the net aside to let her sister in and continued reading. 'Did you hear about the baby?'

'Yes.' Serafina did not take her eyes from the book.

'Who would do such a terrible thing? How could anyone want to kill a baby?'

'It happens all the time. We were two of the lucky ones. That's all. I don't know why they didn't feed us opium too.' Serafina's voice was flat. Matter-of-fact.

Mary sat upright and stared down at her. 'What do you mean?'

'God, you're so stupid.'

'No I'm not!' Mary snapped indignantly. 'You have no right to talk to me like that.'

'They kill girls all the time,' Serafina said. 'They throw them into wells or leave them outside to die of exposure. Can you imagine how many female babies are born every night? Nobody wants them. At least the Indians are honest about it.' Mary stared at her. 'What are you looking at me like that for? I'm only telling you the truth.' Serafina glared back at her, her voice adjusted to sound like dispassionate boredom. 'You don't think for a moment that we were actually wanted, do you?' She laughed a little. 'That's why we ended up here. It's only one step down from the orphanage, and I suppose we are expected to feel grateful for that.'

'That's not true.' Mary's voice wavered. 'You know very well it's not true.'

'Whatever suits you.' Serafina returned to her book. 'You can think what you like. I really don't care any more.'

Mary lay down beside her and cowered into the sheets. 'Will you read to me for a while?'

'Here.' Serafina closed the book and handed it to her. 'Read it yourself.'

Mary took it, looked at the cover but didn't open it. Serafina began to talk to the ceiling, her voice a mere shadow.

'I can't wait to get away from this place. I'm sick to death of being kept in a birdcage, hidden from the whole world like

I don't exist. Just a few more days, then I swear I shall never look back. Not for a single moment.'

'I don't want you to go.'

'Don't be such a baby.'

Mary started to cry. 'I'm not a baby. I'm sixteen. I just don't want you to leave me here on my own, that's all.'

Serafina ignored Mary's small sobs, her own thoughts now thoroughly consumed by speculation about the endless possibilities that lay ahead of her.

'I'm going to leave everything behind and start again as though none of this ever happened,' she breathed. 'I'm going to find myself a wealthy husband and have the most wonderful life. You just see if I don't.' She moved her head to face her sister across the pillow and whispered sternly, 'You must never tell anyone where we came from. You must never mention the tea plantation or our mother and father. And never talk about this place. You are not to say a single word about any of it. Not for as long as we both shall live.'

'Why not?' Mary turned the book over in her hands, uncomfortable with the sinister undercurrent travelling the invisible cord that bonded the two of them together.

'Oh, for heaven's sake, Mary. Don't you understand anything? A halfling is a nobody. No one will ever want you. You'll never be accepted anywhere if people know what you are. Why do you think we were sent here? Why do you think we've been left to rot like this on a hillside in the middle of nowhere? You must never breathe a word to anybody once you leave here, or we shall both be ruined.'

'Shiva said always to be proud of who you are.'

'Shiva? A *servant*?' Serafina spat the word, grasping her sister's wrist. 'And what does he know? What do any of them know? You must promise me you will never speak so much as a single word of it to anyone. Never.'

Mary's wrist started to hurt, the skin burning under Serafina's vice-like grip.

'All right.'

'Say promise.'

'I promise.'

Serafina let go of Mary's arm. They lay there together in silence for a while, both staring up at the ceiling. Mary could sense her sister's anger, her frustration. Where it came from she didn't know, this unreachable place, this grim detachment from everything and everyone around her. How she longed to feel her sister's embrace, her sister's love. The Williamson girls had been inseparable, their devotion to one another unquestionable. Everybody knew that it was because they were sisters. Sisters of the heart. Sisters of the blood. Even when they were sent off to Kalimpong, that terrible night years ago when the dormitory had shuddered beneath the whispers, everyone had held a shred of hope, believing that they would be all right, that they would somehow manage to survive because they had each other. That was how sisters should be. There should be something between them. Love. Warmth. Anything but this deathly void. If Mary reached out a hand to touch her, Serafina would move away. If she told her that she loved her, Serafina would scoff at her sentiment. If she whispered to her that she was afraid, Serafina would snap at her to toughen up. Mary lay there quietly, keeping herself small, willing herself not to intrude so much on her sister's bed that she would eject her and send her back to her own bunk. She hoped, in some small way, that her presence might give Serafina a little comfort. She knew her sister well enough to be able to feel those long, dark silences and to recognise that there was nothing to be said.

Serafina took the book from Mary's hands, opened it and began to read to her.

*

The constant humidity and abundant rains blessed the convent gardens with a heavenly landscape that rose to frame the views of the distant blue hills beyond. It was a fair place for contemplation. Mary ambled through the orchard, red-eyed, having ignored the calls for her all morning. She wished she could hide away and never be found, never see the uncertainties of the future, never face the inevitable wrench of today's goodbye. She stood weakly, leaning against the gnarled bark of the old mango tree that reached over the far white wall, offering its fruit each year to anyone who cared to walk that way on the other side. Perhaps if she stayed still for long enough, she would become a part of it, absorbed into the tree and preserved there for ever. She closed her eyes tight shut and wished.

'Mary!' Roley ran towards her, huffing her exhaustion. 'Where on earth have you been? We've been looking everywhere for you! Everybody's waiting to say goodbye.' She grabbed Mary's arm and pulled her from the tree, dragging her in the direction of the big gates where a small group of the eldest girls waited impatiently to leave, their luggage loaded, their chatter all excitement.

'There you are!' Sister Margaret welcomed Mary to the leaving party. 'Another ten minutes and you would have missed the send-off. Half the school has been looking for you!'

'I'm sorry,' Mary said, trying not to cry.

'Ah, come on now, Mary.' Sister Margaret put an arm around her in a brief, reassuring hug. 'It won't be long before we're sending you out of these gates yourself, so pull yourself together and don't let your sister see your tears.' She smiled and offered Mary a handkerchief. 'Go on.' She urged her towards Serafina. 'This is an important day for her. You make sure you send her off with your love, otherwise you'll only leave her worrying about you, and that wouldn't be fair at all now, would it?'

Mary approached her sister awkwardly. Serafina's dress, pale mustard yellow with a neat matching jacket resting just above her slender waist, erased the last vestiges of childhood from her womanly form. Mary stole small glances at her, unable to connect this elegance with the pinafored girl she had seen yesterday, as if needing to reacclimatise gradually to the sight of her own flesh and blood. Father Lazarus stood beside Serafina, hands folded in front of his cassock, his towering height like a guardian angel before her.

'May God go with you, Serafina.' He smiled down at her. 'Your gifts are many. Take care to use them well.'

'I will, Father.' Serafina could smell the faint earthiness of stale tobacco on his clothes.

'Keep up with your playing,' he told her. 'What we will do without you in the chapel I really don't know.' Serafina nodded, knowing she would never lift a finger to play again. She would cut out anything and everything that reminded her of this place, including every note that had ever been drummed into her. 'You will always be in my thoughts and prayers.'

'Thank you, Father,' Serafina answered graciously. 'Thank you for everything.' Father Lazarus turned away and blew his nose.

Mary readied a smile for Serafina, as best she could.

'I like your dress,' she said self-consciously. 'You look so grown up.'

Serafina refused to acknowledge Mary's tear-stained face and swollen eyes, and spoke to her as if she were merely running an errand to the dak bungalow instead of leaving for good. 'I'll write to you as soon as I get to Bangalore.' Mary looked at the ground, still uncomfortable with Serafina's sudden air of maturity. 'Well? Aren't you going to wish me luck and kiss me goodbye?'

Mary snivelled loudly and tried to put her arms around her

sister. 'What am I going to do without you here?'

'Be careful of my clothes!' Serafina backed away quickly. 'You'll be fine. It will all be over before you know it.' In a moment of contrition, she hugged Mary back, softened her voice and whispered in her sister's ear. 'Always remember your promise.' Mary nodded silently into her shoulder. 'My life is just starting. I've been dead until now. So have you. Maybe one day you'll understand.' She kissed Mary on the cheek, a small, slight kiss that barely touched her skin. 'Take care of yourself.'

And with that, Serafina climbed into the waiting cart and was gone.

That night, Mary dreamed of the elephants working on the plantation alongside their shouting mahouts. The tea pickers rustling their way along the terraces, heads protected by brightly coloured cotton saris, their tiny hands plucking quickly at the delicate, shooting tips. She saw her father striding along in his khakis, pointing at where there was work to be done, speaking to his men in the voice she had not heard for so long that she could barely remember its melody. She felt the nudge of a velvet muzzle on her neck and turned to find Titan beside her. She found a big red apple in her pocket and gave it to him. He took it gladly, then lifted her on to his gleaming back. She grasped his mane in her tiny fingers and felt the wind in her hair as he carried her home.

## 28

The first suggestions of dawn washed through the hazy sky above the surrounding mist-bound forests, the horizon beyond the ghostly outlines of the temples glowing a pale burnt orange as the world began to waken. The morning commenced its ritual overture, monkeys howling, the plaintive cry of a distant peacock, the cacophony of a thousand birds rising to greet the day. Shurika stirred, half opened her eyes and listened for the ragged sound of her mistress's breathing. Her head felt thick, as though it were gripped within a tight metal band. She tried to sit up, then felt a hand upon her forearm.

'Do not move,' came a disembodied voice. It was soft, like butter melting on the warmth of her skin. Shurika tried to speak, but no sound came. 'Shhh. Do not try to talk,' the woman's voice said. 'You must rest.'

Shurika thought that she must be dreaming still, her motionless body refusing her, her senses dulled by the strange removal of her consciousness. Her feet ached, as though set with burning stones. She had walked through the paddies for hours, searching for the children, but they were nowhere to be found. Cook had made sweets for them and they would spoil if they were left too long. She had called their names until her voice was hoarse, and now she had no voice left at all, just a dry, rasping groan that barely lifted from her throat. Oh, how her feet ached. She must rest them awhile. She felt herself sliding into the cool waters of the river, slipping beneath the unbroken surface, where she could hear the fishes whispering to each other, their scales shimmering in the sunlight that bounced through the shallows. Yes, she thought. The fishes will know where the children are. I will become one of them, then they will tell me their secrets. The water welcomed her, caressing her exhausted body. Shurika smiled to herself and felt content.

The ghostly presence left her side and moved away, the voice now distanced. 'Pramod! Come quickly! She has awoken!'

A gentle hand came behind her head. The fishes dispersed, their silver tails disappearing into the depths. Shurika opened her eyes and saw the faint outline of a woman peering at her closely. The woman smelled sweet, like cloves and jasmine, her sari awash with every colour of the rainbow.

'You are awake.' She smiled. The figure of a man appeared behind her in the doorway, his features blurred. Shurika blinked at them both, her mind a mire of confusion. 'Do not be alarmed,' said the woman. 'You were involved in an accident. My son was passing and saw what happened. At first everyone thought you were dead.'

Although Shurika heard the words, they made no sense. She had been working the threshing machine. Tending the vegetable patch. Tying red rags to keep the crows from the strawberries.

'Perhaps we should try to sit her up.'

'My son, Pramod. He is a fisherman but thinks he is a poet,' she clucked. 'I told him, we cannot eat your poems.'

Shurika felt strong arms lift her, very slowly, some cushions eased behind her.

'Here,' said Pramod, offering a cup of water to her lips. 'You must drink. Take small sips.' Shurika felt powerless to resist, the few droplets of water moistening her parched mouth, freeing her tongue. 'Good,' he encouraged her. 'A little more. Then we will see about some food.'

When the cup was empty, Shurika finally managed a thin, cracked 'Thank you.' Pramod knelt on the floor and looked at her.

'Do you remember what you were dreaming about?'

'No,' Shurika said, her thoughts empty.

'Your children.'

'I have no children,' Shurika said. Suddenly something began to stir. 'Oh!' she cried, pain splitting her head, the cup falling from her hands.

'Hush!' The woman came to her quickly, reaching for Shurika's outstretched hand. 'Be calm!'

'But my mistress!' The mother and son looked at each other. 'Please! I must go to her! She needs me!' Shurika sank back, a sour taste coming to her mouth, the room swimming around her.

'Who is your mistress?' Pramod asked.

Shurika felt herself unable to breathe, as though a great weight had descended upon her. A fragment of something dark and terrible began to pull at her struggling memory. That night. The smell of bonfires. A pair of lovers exchanging glances while their mothers' heads were turned. Children, everywhere, but not hers. She had been in the street when she should have been home. And then, suddenly, pandemonium everywhere, a raging animal stampeding towards her, nostrils flaring, eyes white. The sickening odour of burning flesh. And then ... Oh, merciful gods, please do not let it be so. She clutched at her chest, a suffocating pain coming upon her.

'How long have I been here?' she wailed.

'Three days,' said the mother. 'Three days and four nights.'

'Help me!' Shurika raised a feeble arm. 'Please! I must return to her at once! She is sick!'

'You cannot go anywhere,' Pramod said urgently, kneeling beside her. 'You are not well enough.'

'But I …' Shurika's head began to spin. 'I …'

'She must lie down!' insisted the mother, taking hold of Shurika's trembling hand.

'Tell me where she lives,' Pramod whispered, lowering Shurika to the bed. 'I promise I will find her myself and tell her what has happened.'

Chinthimani fevered through unfathomable hours, the demons coming upon her repeatedly, tormenting her spirit, forcing pitiful pleas from her that disturbed the darkness of the nights, eliciting sharp-tongued calls of *be quiet!* from her neighbours. And then, after the seemingly endless hours, feeling the warmth of the eternal light, she cast herself adrift, as though floating through the air, a tiny seed attached to a gossamer umbrella caught on the skyward breeze. It had come to her at last, the release she had yearned for. She had dreamed of it so many times, imagining how it would be to leave her body far behind, to detach from this life and to have her atman, her very essence, set free into the endless heavens, yielding to the cycle of rebirth. At last, Shurika had left her to die in peace, but it had taken so long. Each time she had closed her eyes, she had wished it upon herself, pleading with the gods, only to wake again, the coppery taste of blood upon her lips, and face the sufferings of the body she no longer had any use for. She had felt it wane, the final embers of life's fire in her heart cooling from yellow to red, from red to rust, a peacefulness coming upon her like a mother's embrace, lifting her weightless *jiva*, carrying her to the subtle plain. She reached for death's mercy and asked it to hurry, for she could wait no longer.

*

Outside the peeling, decaying walls, the searing white sun arched through a hazy sky, tainted dull pink from the airborne dust, throwing its ruthless glare into every crack and crevice. The heat rained down without compassion, beating against the parched, cracked earth, testing every creature that dared to dwell in its wake.

'By whose charity does she live?' demanded the neighbour, crouched on her haunches, irritably picking stones from the rice, an infant clinging to her breast. 'Widows are not permitted to inherit money nor possessions, so what is she still doing here?'

'I heard from the landlord that she has a wealthy brother in the east.'

'Then why does she not go and spread her curse there?'

'Why should he take her in?' another woman said. 'Who wants a white shadow living under their roof, bringing their misery upon the whole family?'

'Perhaps she will die soon. I hear her through the walls, spluttering her sickness into the air for us all to catch our deaths. She should have poisoned herself years ago.'

'I'll bet that's what killed her poor husband. She is infected with disease.'

'And no children, either.' They all tutted and nodded their agreement.

'Some women serve no purpose at all. She should have burned with her husband's body. Where is her honour?'

'I would not wish to be a burden on my family, so I pray that both my husband and I will stop breathing at the same time!'

'Perhaps you will be one of the fortunate ones who dies first!'

'It is unlucky for us to have a widow living so near to us. My children have nightmares. What if one of them should meet her and accidentally step into her shadow? He would be cursed.'

'She should be begging in the streets or living in a widows' ashram, where she belongs, but the landlord refuses to throw her out.'

The unexpected sight of the stranger silenced them. Saris were reached over heads protectively, and the women hunched over their rice pans, disappearing into the silence of their daily chore.

Seeing he had come to a dead end, Pramod glanced around the motley clutch of tightly packed houses, each one no bigger than one room, perhaps two.

'*Namaste.*' He greeted the women with a small nod of deference. 'Forgive me for disturbing your work, but I am looking for the woman called Chinthimani.' They ignored him. 'I would be most grateful if you could tell me where she lives.'

Children's faces appeared at doorways, peering out curiously.

'There is no one here by that name,' one of the women said.

'You have come to the wrong place.'

Pramod stood and thought for a moment, running through in his mind the landmarks he had passed, the knotted trees at the mouth of the alleyway, the small shrine on the corner, the pink, crumbling wall with the garish painting of Krishna. All was as Shurika had told him, including the coven of unfriendly women who pored over their rice with sullen hands.

'No.' He shook his head decidedly. 'I am certain that this is right.'

'You are mistaken,' said the eldest woman, adjusting her weight pointedly. 'I have lived here all my life and I have never heard that name.'

'Please.' Pramod frowned his frustration. 'It is very important that I find this woman. She is sick and needs to be cared for. Are you certain that there is no one else living in these houses?'

'You have eyes in your head?' the old woman snapped. 'Then you can see for yourself that there are no other women here except us.' The others lowered their gazes and went back to picking through the rice grains, mumbling to each other.

'Perhaps he means the widow,' whispered the youngest of the women, her swollen belly heavy with child. 'The woman who looks after her has gone. I am sure of it.'

'She has run away,' murmured another knowingly. 'I saw her sneaking out on the night of the bonfires. She crept out like a cat, thinking that no one was watching her, but I saw everything. I always knew she was going to try to escape. That is why she would never look us in the eye.'

The youngest one snuck a glimpse at the stranger.

'Perhaps this is the brother you talked of.'

'He doesn't look very rich!' A brief flurry of laughter passed between them.

'Who is this person you whisper about?' Pramod asked.

The women did not look up, bunching tightly together around their pans, turning their backs on him. Pramod paused and looked around again. Every aperture in the hovels had been left wide open in the hope of dispelling some of the sweltering heat from the tiny living spaces. Lizards stuck to the walls, leaching the sun into their dark, succulent bodies. Sparrows squabbled noisily over a tiny, fast-diminishing patch of stagnant water. Children with dried, crusty faces hung back in the shadows of their grim homes, watching his every move with suspicious caution. Pramod took in each detail of his surroundings. The blistered paint on the rotting tethering post beside him. The irregular angles of the mismatched roof tiles. The wandering gaze of the young pregnant woman who snatched glimpses of him from beneath lowered lashes.

As though guided by some all-knowing instinct, his eyes came to rest on the furthest house, its door sealed. There could be no mistaking it. It was an odd size, regular in height but disproportionately wide, with a small, square viewing hatch set behind a fretworked panel. The aged wood, solid as cast iron, had been stained Vishnu blue, and bore the scars of the arid landscape, the thin layer of paint mapped by rivers of superficial cracks where the sun had sucked it dry. He glanced at the pregnant woman, seeing that she had followed his gaze. She covered her head and looked quickly away.

'Who lives in this house?' he demanded. They refused to acknowledge him, picking up their pots and disappearing behind closed doors.

'Hello?' Pramod stepped forward and knocked on the door. There was no answer. He knocked again, harder this time. 'Do not be afraid!' he called. 'I have been sent to deliver a message to you.' He tried the door and found it stuck fast. 'Please open the door,' he shouted, running his hands around the edge, searching for a latch of some kind. 'My name is Pramod. It is very important that I speak to you. There has been an accident.' He peered up at the window. It was not so high that he could not reach it with the tips of his fingers. He stepped back and jumped up, grasping the rough sill and hauling himself up, just able to peer inside.

There was little light in the room, and it took a moment for his eyes to adjust to the gloom. There on the floor lay a woman, unmoving, the jagged outline of her pelvis thinly veiled beneath the worn cotton of a white sari. Pramod dropped down from the window and rushed at the door, ramming it with his shoulder. It held tight, so he backed up and ran at it again and again until the wood splintered and the door gave way. The stench that flew out to greet him tore the breath from his body.

## 29

Mary knelt in the confessional, quite content to remain in silent contemplation while the world went on without her. She had seen Father Lazarus in his garden that morning, wandering barefoot among his plants, smoking his pipe, and had slipped past unnoticed. The confessional, like a tiny pair of cupboards set into the chapel wall, provided a perfect hiding place. She didn't have to speak to anyone, nor smile politely at a passing nun, nor pretend that she was happy when she was feeling sad. She had no idea how long she had been cocooned in there, only that it was long enough for her to have heard several sets of footsteps come and go, pausing to pray for a while. She began to worry that she might have inadvertently missed the bell she had so diligently listened out for, and that she would be in trouble for being absent at the start of afternoon lessons. The longer she stayed inside, the more stuck she felt. Another set of footsteps entered the chapel, then the door to the priest's side opened. Mary heard him settle himself on his seat beyond the fine mesh screen, and took a deep breath as the small curtain went back. Her head bowed to her hands automatically.

'Bless me, Father, for I have sinned,' she said. 'It has been two weeks since my last confession.'

'Me too,' whispered Sister Margaret. 'And Lord knows I shouldn't be in Father Lazarus's seat, so I suppose I shall have to add that to my list next time.'

Mary lifted her head and tried to peer through the modesty screen. 'Sister Margaret?'

'I've been looking all over for you, Mary. Are you all right, child? I know it's a big thing to get used to, but it's been months since your sister left and I really think it's high time you stopped moping around.'

'I can't help it.'

'Now yes you can.' Sister Margaret's voice was firm, but kind. 'We all have to get used to things. How do you think I felt when I first came here all the way from Ireland?' She didn't wait for an answer. 'I felt like an alien with two heads, child. Sick for home I was, so sick that I barely knew what to do with myself. Had it not been for the good Lord watching over me, I doubt I'd have survived.'

'At least you had a home to be sick for.'

'Oh, cheer up, Mary girl. Is there anything I can do to make you feel a bit better?'

'No.'

'Do you want me to see if I can sneak you a big piece of cake from the cookhouse?'

'No thank you.' Mary smiled a little.

'Are you sure now? I'd pass you a jelly baby but I don't think we'd be able to squash it through the screen.' A small flurry of laughter burst from them both, then Mary's tears came again.

'I miss my parents.'

'Ah,' sighed Sister Margaret. 'And isn't that just the hardest thing of all?' She saw Mary nod a little, unable to speak, and sat with her quietly, waiting for her to recover. 'The Lord knows what he's doing, Mary. You will find comfort in prayer, so try to pray as much as you can, and you will feel less troubled. That much I can promise you.'

And so Mary prayed. She prayed every morning, even before

her eyes were open, squeezing her hands together beneath the sheets and reciting the Hail Mary in her head, over and over again, imagining the jet beads of her rosary running through her fingers. She prayed while she washed and cleaned her teeth before breakfast, she prayed while she walked lethargically from one place to another during the day, she prayed when she readied herself for bed at night. Four months later, her prayers were answered.

The mother superior sat at her oak desk talking amiably with the well-dressed couple seated before her, the difficult business of the day now sealed in the envelopes she set aside, face down, in the drawer of the cabinet beside her. After the briefest of knocks, the door to her office opened.

'I have a little something here for you.' Sister Margaret stepped aside gladly, allowing Mary full view of the comfortable room. Her eyes widened, her mouth opening in surprise.

'Papa!' Mary rushed in.

James rose from his chair immediately, opening his arms to the youthful woman who ran to him, his expression visibly shocked by the sudden evidence of his long absence. Mary's pounding heart flew into her mouth, choking her like a thick welter of vines around her throat. It had been so long that she could scarcely remember when she last saw him. She threw her arms around his middle, squeezing the life from him, never wanting to let go.

'My goodness!' James swallowed hard, forcing himself to look at her, shaken by the strong, spectral echo she carried of her mother. The pretty heart-shaped face. The rosebud lips. The delicate structure of her slight body. 'Who is this strange young lady in front of me?' Mary twisted with embarrassment and flapped him away, suddenly conscious of her shape beneath her pinafore.

'Do you have one of those for me?' Dorothy asked.

'Aunty Dorothy!' Mary found her voice and hugged her too.

'I can't believe how much you have changed!' Dorothy took Mary by the shoulders, stood back and admired her. 'We knew you'd have grown, but this?' She laughed.

'When did you come?' Mary was all at sixes and sevens, suddenly overcome with confusion and a thousand unanswered questions. 'Why didn't you tell me? How long are you staying for? Am I coming home with you?'

The mother superior smiled sympathetically and brought Mary to order.

'Now, Mary,' she said. 'All in good time.'

Mary stood and stared at her father, uncertain if this was real or just another of her waking dreams. His face seemed different, deep lines etched into his brow, creasing the skin around his eyes. His hair, once raven black, showed flecks of grey at the temples. There were other differences too, in some small way that Mary could not pinpoint no matter how hard she looked. She wanted to reach out and touch him, to put her hands on his face and prove that he was not an apparition, to anoint her fingers with the perfume of his hair. The mother superior's voice floated into her reeling head.

'You may go out and have lunch with your father and aunt, but then he has a long trip to make, so you must save your questions and not be a nuisance.'

Mary smiled so hard she felt as though her face might split in two.

'Oh, Papa!' She held on to him again and pressed her head into his chest, filling her lungs with his scent. 'I don't care what anyone else says, I always knew you wouldn't leave me here. I have prayed every day that you would come for me.'

James caught Dorothy's eye, her grim expression speaking for them all.

The dining room of the little hotel in Haflong was remarkably busy for such a remote place. Most tables were occupied, some men in uniform in one corner, a group of Westerners of varying ages dining together, a young couple, probably passing through on their way elsewhere. Mary's initial exuberance at the sight of her father soon waned as the conversation turned to her future. James tried to jolly her along.

'Oh, come on! It won't be so bad, and it's not until next autumn anyway, so you'll have plenty of time to get used to the idea. We all have to finish school sometime and then take our place in the world, don't we? It will be a very exciting time for you. Just you wait and see.'

Mary sulked into her plate. James looked to Dorothy for support. She smiled softly and raised her eyes to the ceiling.

'Serafina says it's completely revolting. All blood and guts and—'

'Mary, we're eating.' Her father's attempt to be stern was short-lived.

'Who said I wanted to be a nurse? All those sick people everywhere.' Mary grimaced. 'I'll probably catch leprosy in the first week. Why can't I choose for myself?'

'And do what?' her father said. 'This is the next part of your education, Mary. It has all been planned and arranged, just as it was for your sister, and that's that. It might seem like a long way away right now, but you will have to earn your living one day. Stand on your own two feet and make a life for yourself. That means that you have to be properly qualified.'

'I know, Papa, but there must be something else—'

'Mary, listen to me.' James reached out suddenly and grasped her hand. 'What would happen to you if I were no longer around?' Mary's face dropped. 'I don't mean to frighten you, but every parent knows that they cannot look after their child for ever. What if something were to happen to me?'

'But nothing's going to happen to you, Papa,' Mary insisted, rejecting his words.

'I'm sorry, Mary, but the decision has already been made and we'll hear no more about it. Do you want to end up a common shop girl?' The sudden stress in James's voice silenced any further argument. 'I can't think of anything worse.'

'Your father's right, dear.' Dorothy leaned across the table and patted Mary's hand. 'Before you know it you'll be all grown up. You need a proper profession behind you. Something that you can always fall back on. That's why I became a doctor, so that I could make my own way and look after myself if ever I had to. You're a young woman, with your whole life ahead of you. The decisions you make now will affect you for the rest of your life.' She looked at James for approval, but his gaze was otherwise occupied, fixed on the sugar spoon as though in a daydream. 'And Serafina will be there. At least for your first year of training. You'll have a lovely time together. Just you wait and see.'

Mary managed a small, defeated smile. 'I suppose so.'

'That's my girl,' said James with some relief. 'Now eat all of that up and we'll see about some pudding, skinny legs.' He slid his hand under the table and tweaked her knee gently. At last, Mary laughed. They all did.

Outside the convent gates, Sister Margaret stood beside the mother superior, the pair of them keeping a respectful distance from the waiting car while James and Dorothy spent a last few minutes with Mary.

'I can hardly bear to watch.' Sister Margaret spoke quietly.

'Don't,' said the mother superior. 'Who knows what torture they're going through?'

'I didn't mean them,' Sister Margaret said crossly. 'I meant Mary.'

'Try not to be too harsh in your judgement, Sister. They are good people by any standards. At least he's taken the trouble to put his affairs in order and to make the proper arrangements for those poor girls of his.'

'When is he leaving?'

'I expect he'll be putting his uniform back on and heading up to the north-east frontier before the week is out. If the Japanese keep pushing through Burma at this rate, we're going to need every man we can get.'

'Dear heavens.' Sister Margaret shook her head. 'I can't even begin to imagine what hell awaits those men there.'

The threat hung over them like a dark, sombre cloud, and they watched as James ushered Dorothy into the back seat of the car, then put his arm around Mary and took her aside.

'Do well in your studies, Mary.'

'I will, Papa.'

'I want you to know that I shall always be thinking of you, no matter where I am.' James fought to control the slight tremor in his voice. 'You are very dear to me.'

'And I am always thinking of you too, Papa,' Mary said, her tone becoming urgent, trying to convey more than the small words that sounded so empty. 'There is not a single day goes by when I don't, but school will be finished soon and then I will be able to come and visit you in your new house. Is it as beautiful as the big house? Is Mother there with you? Aunty Dorothy didn't say in her letters.'

'Times change, my darling,' James said, unable to find the words to explain to her in those few fleeting moments that remained between them. There was no house. There was no plantation. There was no mother. The only hope he had for restoring his sense of honour would come in the guise of a

243

uniform, in which he would take up arms and stand side by side with his fellow men, facing whatever came their way. That he had resigned his position within the company as a direct consequence he regarded merely as a bonus, the milk and honey of his years of dedication now so bitterly soured.

James took something from his pocket, small and wrapped in a piece of homespun cotton, and gave it to Mary. She glanced down, untied the tiny bundle and took out the object inside, a carved wooden elephant, trunk pointing upwards for luck, fashioned from a piece of precious sandalwood. Its rich perfume filled her hands.

'It is from Shiva,' James told her softly. 'He made it for you a long time ago and asked me to keep it until I saw you again. It is to remind you of how you used to run and hide when the elephants came, and how the hairs used to scratch your skinny legs.' He leaned down and kissed her on the cheek. 'Goodbye, my darling.' He turned to leave.

Mary grabbed him and held on tightly, her eyes welling with tears. He squeezed her back, just briefly, then pulled himself free of her arms and got into the car. His command to the driver to move along was immediate, the car pulling away before Mary could shout her farewell. She ran for a few steps, grit flying into her face and hair, then stood and stared in disbelief at the disappearing car shrouded in red dust, waving furiously yet unable to see for her tears.

Sister Margaret held her serene position just long enough for the car to take the corner, before rushing to Mary's side. She would never see her father again.

## 30

*Dearest Mary,*

*Your father received your lovely letter. He is so very proud of you. Sister Margaret wrote to him just two weeks ago to say how well you are doing in your studies. I hope that you and Serafina are writing to each other often. She has settled into her training well but finds it all rather gruesome still. She will soon get used to it.*

Mary sat cross-legged on the dry grass. She had carried the letter in the pocket of her pinafore for three weeks, savouring it each time she read it, looking for something deeper, some hidden meaning.

*Your father has been posted to Imphal. His train will go through Haflong but will not be able to stop. He said that he will ask the train driver to blow his whistle when he passes the nearest point to school. Listen out for it.*

He was not to know that the whistle always blew, and how her heart now ached each time Mr de Souza's engine rose over the hill.

The fruit on the mango tree was almost ripe, but not quite. The cook used the green ones for making bitter pickles that fizzed on the tongue and tempered the hot sweetness of his summer chutneys. Mary was not supposed to be in the garden today. A leopard had been coming into the grounds lately, bold as brass, making itself quite at home. One of the younger girls had seen it sunning itself on the pantry house stoop two days before. It had glanced at her with boredom in its eyes, then closed them again and taken no further notice. The poor girl had nearly died of fright. The leopard hadn't caused any trouble, either here on in the surrounding area. They didn't usually bother with people. There was plenty of other food to eat that was a lot less awkward to prepare. Nevertheless, the mother superior had said not to wander too far from the buildings just in case it should change its mind and decide to make a tasty snack of a dim-witted girl. Mary didn't mind the thought of that, and believed that if she sat very quietly just reading and minding her own business, she would be perfectly safe.

*If there is anything else you need, you must ask the mother superior and she will send word or place an order with the big department store in Calcutta.*

Mary heard a rustle from the pathway behind her and looked around with an immediate sense of alarm before waving in relief at the reassuring sight of Sister Margaret's approach.

*Do your best. Your father sends you all his love and will write to you as soon as he can.*
*With fondest love, Aunty D.*

Sister Margaret reached Mary's side, made a quick check of her surroundings, then hitched up her habit, flashing a glimpse of sturdy grey-stockinged leg, and sat heavily on the grass next to her.

'I'm not disturbing you, am I?' Sister Margaret asked, without needing to.

'Of course not.' Mary folded the letter and tucked it away in the front pocket of her pinafore. 'It's an old letter anyway.'

'From your sister?'

'No,' Mary replied. Serafina's letters were few and far between, and rarely more than a few nebulous sentences. 'It's from my Aunty Dorothy. My father has been posted to Imphal.'

'Ah.' Sister Margaret nodded. 'It takes a very brave man to do what your father has done. He could quite easily have stepped aside and remained comfortably out of the way.'

'Why did he have to go?'

'War is a terrible thing, Mary. What would happen if our men refused to fight? Those are the kind of men we call cowards.' Her sigh weighed heavily. 'You would have thought that the world had seen enough bloodshed, but it seems that man has yet to learn his lesson.'

'Will he have to fight?'

'Who knows, child. Let's hope not.'

'Aunty Dorothy always sounds so cheerful in her letters, it's hard to tell what's going on.'

'There are censors, Mary. People who read all our letters and cross out anything we're not supposed to know. She couldn't write you more anyway. It would only arrive looking like a child had taken to it with a thick black crayon.' Sister Margaret stole a glance over her shoulder, then pulled a letter from the pocket hidden beneath the white apron she generally wore over her habit. 'Here.' She opened it. 'Look at this.'

Mary took the thin blue paper from Sister Margaret's hand. Apart from the salutation, not a single sentence remained intact, words obliterated, sometimes whole lines scored out with a vicious black stroke. She stared at it for a few moments, but before she could begin to decipher the remaining text, Sister

Margaret took it gently from her fingers and returned it to her pocket. 'We must be brave, like our soldiers, and pray that they come to no harm.'

The pair of them sat together for a while, quite comfortably, without exchanging a word. Mary leaned back, stretched out on the grass, and stared up at the cloudless sky.

'Why is the sky so blue?' she wondered aloud.

'I don't know, child.' Sister Margaret's lilting voice had lost none of the thickness of her soft Irish brogue. Her eyes quickly skimmed the perimeter, checking for any sign of her sisters. Seeing none, she flattened herself on the grass and gazed up at the heavens too. 'There is something about the deep blue of the sky against the green hills here that reminds me of home. You know, it's still set as sharply in my mind as it was almost forty years ago. My dear old mam used to tell me that it was made that way to match the colour of my eyes.' She sighed, picking a long blade of grass from the ground beside her and putting it in her mouth, then reached up to rest her broad hands behind her veiled head. 'But I doubt that's true, of course. The sky's been here a lot longer than I have.' Sister Margaret tutted a little, chewing on the blade. 'She did used to tell me some terrible whoppers, and you know, I believed her for the longest time. I was a very daft child, Mary. Thought the moon was made out of cheese too, I did.'

They lay there together, contemplating the endless lapis above.

All at once the peace was broken by a strangled gurgling noise. Flossie, the deaf and dumb girl, ran wildly through the gardens, flailing her arms and howling unintelligible noises. Sister Margaret sat up, watched her fly by, then gave Mary a knowing glance. 'Leopard,' they said.

*

Term had barely started when news of the evacuation spread through the convent like wildfire. The initial reports and warnings sent down to the mother superior from the governor escalated quickly, leaving no time for protracted arrangements. The Japanese had come right up and were now sitting on their very doorstep. The only certainty was that they would breach the Indian border any day. Telegrams were dispatched at once. All those girls who could be sent home left immediately under the escort of chaperones. Parents were sent for and came as quickly as they could from their scattered positions. This time the packing was done hastily and in silence, the trunks fetched quickly without ceremony or celebration. Soon, all had departed except the handful of pupils with nowhere else to go.

'Isn't this exciting, girls?' Sister Margaret's grey habit sailed behind her as she strode in front of the dozen or so evacuees, leading them to the crowded, idling train.

Mary whispered to Roley, 'I think poor Sister Rosemary is going to have a heart attack. Did you see her hands shaking at breakfast this morning? She looks awfully ill.'

Roley glanced over her shoulder at the weeping Sister Rosemary being urged to hurry along by the mother superior and two white-veiled novices. 'Looks like she's having a touch of the vapours,' she diagnosed. 'Everybody knows she's terrified of everything in the whole world. I expect she'll be praying like mad all the way to Shillong and worrying at her rosary until the cross falls off again.'

'Do you think we're all going to be killed by the Japanese?'

'That depends. They might want to capture us and use us as slaves.'

'Really?'

'Oh yes. They have slaves for everything, and when they can't work any more, they chop them up and feed them to their dogs.'

'I don't believe you.' Mary's heart thundered.

'It's true. Every word of it. That's what Amelia says, anyway.'

Amelia slowed beside them, watching a small group of Britishers with mountainous piles of luggage gathered on the station platform, regarding the convent party with pity as they passed by. One of the women nodded sympathetically to her companion.

'Orphans,' she whispered behind a gloved hand. 'The poor dears were left behind at the convent, you know. I suppose they'll be shipped off now to heaven only knows where.'

The other woman clucked and looked the menagerie up and down with a mixture of sympathy and disapproval. 'Poor little mites. What a terrible shame.'

'We're not orphans!' Amelia's sense of outrage brought the small party to an abrupt halt as she shouted indignantly at the strangers, her slight body rigid with fury. 'I'll have you know that we're all first-class boarders and that our fathers are busy fighting the war.' She turned away from the dumbfounded strangers and marched off, determined to conceal her upset. Under any other circumstances, Amelia would have been severely reprimanded for such an indecorous outburst. But not today. Sister Margaret witnessed the whole incident, stood tall and proud beside her girls, and issued the Westerners with an unholy withering glare.

The girls clambered into the carriage, along with the six nuns and novices who had remained at St Agnes's until the last possible moment, and settled in for the journey to the safe convent house at Shillong in neighbouring Meghalaya. Sister Margaret wore her most courageous expression today, and had a cheerful smile and a soft Irish lullaby at the ready for any girl who should need it. She kept the youngest of the waifs close to her skirts and encouraged the others to admire the scenery that passed the windows of the train. Travelling through the beauty of Meghalaya, where waterfalls tumbled from the high plateaus into virgin forests and crystal-clear rivers emptied into mirror lakes, the notion of war seemed unimaginable.

'Keep your eyes open, girls. You might be lucky enough to spot a tiger in the trees.'

'Do the tigers know whose side they're on?' Roley asked.

'Now there's an interesting question,' Sister Margaret replied with a playful smile. 'Even if they did, I think it would take an awful lot of tigers to eat us out of trouble this time.'

'What shall we see when we get there?' asked the little girl beside her, the one they called Lucy Laces because she couldn't tie her shoes, and whose small voice was so seldom heard. Sister Margaret wrapped a protective arm around her.

'Pineapples,' she said confidently, hugging her charge with a great sense of reassurance. 'We shall see lots and lots of pineapples.'

'How long will we be gone?' Lucy Laces looked up into Sister Margaret's bravely smiling face.

'That, my child, is entirely in God's hands.'

## 31

The sweet perfume of jasmine and cloves did little to relieve the oppressive heat, the temperature still steadily climbing with a full two months to go until it reached its stifling peak before the rains came in June. The windows, their painted frames laced and creviced by the sun, had been left open to encourage the spindly breeze, the door leading out to the narrow, shaded balcony affording some small defence against the suffocating heat. The house was cooler than most, being close to the brown, muddied river, set in an elevated position at the quieter end of the row where the buildings petered out and the trees began. Pramod and his mother occupied the first floor, the relatively spacious luxury of its three airy rooms having passed from father to son for four generations.

Pramod's mother sat passively on her mat, tolerating the heat, teasing raw cotton with experienced fingers, feeding it patiently to her spinning wheel. Not that she particularly needed the twine. On days like this, when rivulets of perspiration crawled around under her sari like ants on the skin, she found that the act of spinning soothed her querulous temperament. The heat of the high season did not suit her at all. It disturbed her sleep at night, the temperature barely dipping, making her irritable, tempting her to vent her usually silent frustrations.

'How are we supposed to survive when the British government is commandeering so much food for the war effort?' she said crossly. 'Prices are so high that people are dying in the streets because they cannot afford to eat.'

'You exaggerate, Mother.'

Pramod stood by the open door, looking out into the deserted, sun-baked street, half-listening to his mother's grumblings, his mind on another matter, as always.

'I do not exaggerate at all. And it is not just our food they are taking. What about our sons? Why should they give their lives for a ruler who takes the bread from their children's mouths? Every day, another mother mourns. I hear them all over. Their terrible wailing, tearing out their hair, drawing blood from their own skin. You can barely get to the shrines for all the flames burning. I don't know why we don't all just lie down and let them cut our throats. What is a community to do without its sons? I thank the gods that you have been spared.'

'I would rather have fought,' Pramod said, watching the street below.

'You are not a fighter, you are a fisherman. It is your job to charm the fish from the river and to keep our bodies fed. You should see the rice that came back from the market yesterday,' she complained. 'All dust and stones, hidden in the bag.' She shook her head. 'Those crooks in the bazaar are worse thieves than the street rats who rob from your pockets. They must think me stupid.'

Pramod allowed himself a small smile. Of the many things that his mother might be, stupid was not one of them. As a child, she had been taught to read and write by an educated father of modest means who thought himself scholarly and did not believe in the subjugation of women. As far as he was concerned, every man, woman and child in this noble country had already been enslaved by the British, and until such time as they understood the value of liberty, no matter what their gender, India would have no hope of regaining its autonomy. Pramod's mother liked to describe her father as *a visionary*, and reminisced to her son endlessly about the lessons he had taught her, telling each story like an ancient fable, delivering its moral with a satisfied smacking of her lips. Knowledge was power, her father had said, and no subject was considered out of bounds, even for a young woman. She was bright, quick to learn, and cunning in her application. Pramod looked at her affectionately.

'You, stupid? Only a fool would think such a thing.'

'We have all been fools,' she said tetchily, rolling the cotton through her fingers. 'This is not a war. This will go down in history as the lawless murder of millions of Indians who were too blind to see a hand in front of their own face. What do they think they are fighting for? For the British?' She gave a distasteful cluck. 'They treat us as though we are nothing, as though they have the right to send us to our deaths, like feeding worms to a hungry bird.'

'There have always been wars,' Pramod said. 'At least this time we are fighting together like brothers, and not pitted against each other.'

'Your heart is blinded by romance, my fine son.' Pramod's mother set the wheel in motion again, easing the line of spun thread to the spindle. 'When blood is spilled on the battleground, who is to know the colour of the body from which it came? Is Indian blood not as red as British blood? Do our wounds not run as deeply?' She flicked a hand in the air dismissively. 'Had your father lived, he would have been out there with Gandhiji, fighting for the freedom of his country, not for the jailers who stole it from under our noses.'

'Had my father lived,' Pramod said soothingly, 'you would have had sufficient sons to start an army of your own.'

'True.' She smiled. 'But still, you would always have been our firstborn and our most precious.'

Pramod leaned against the frame of the open door, looking outwards, his back to his mother. She did not need to ask to know that he was watching out for Shurika's return. Meek and subservient, she had been with them for almost a year now, becoming part of their daily landscape. She had not spoken for three months after the death of her mistress, the shock of the news having sent her into a grief so profound that it might have consumed her whole had it not been for their patience and perseverance. It was as though she had become an empty husk, devoid of all feeling. You could stick a pin into her flesh and she would not react, nor would she shy away from the burning heat of a naked flame. Pramod's mother had never seen her son so deeply moved by the plight of another. 'What is it about this woman that fascinates you?' she had asked him, to which he had replied, 'She is like a poem filled with sadness.'

Pramod's mother halted the spinning wheel.

'She is not for you, my son.'

'So you have told me many times, Mother.'

'She is damaged. I can see it in her eyes. And she is too old to be taught new ways.' Pramod said nothing. 'You are a man of great sensibilities, my son. When you are ready to take a wife, I will find the perfect girl for you. Someone who will lift that sombre heart of yours and make you happy. Someone who will bear you strong, healthy children. Preferably sons,' she added with a gently teasing smile. 'Although you would no doubt be as doting a father to a girl child as my own father was to me.'

'I never asked you to find me a wife,' Pramod murmured.

'You do not have to. A mother knows when her son is ready. He becomes restless, like a tiger in a cage.'

Pramod moved to the window and peered out, across the shallow veranda, to the view across the sprawling town, shimmering in the hot pink haze. 'I don't understand why any woman would have put herself through such misery,' he said.

255

'Why pretend to be a poor widow when you know it will bring nothing but shame and sorrow?'

'That is surely a great mystery,' his mother agreed sagely. Her son spoke of this often, so astounded was he at the thought of someone doing such a thing.

'You should have seen her.' Pramod took his breath slowly, the horror of it all still as vivid in his memory as the day he had found her shrivelled body, shrouded beneath a white sari as though it were nothing more than a thin white cloth laid over a meagre scattering of firewood. 'It seems impossible that she could have been alive just a few days before. She looked as though she had been dead for ever.'

'It is criminal that her neighbours should have left her like that.' Pramod's mother shook her head in despair. 'How are women to survive when they themselves are such ignorant creatures? Perhaps in another hundred years we will learn to be more civilised to each other.'

'It is not their fault,' Pramod said. 'It is written in the holy scriptures.'

'Holy scriptures?' She clicked her tongue. 'What is holy about the choices a woman is given? To burn in the flames with her husband, to marry his younger brother, or to live in filth and penury for the rest of her life? And what if every widow in the land were to be subjected to that supposedly holy law until the ends of time?' She bucked her head in irritation and dared to question the divine doctrine. 'The scriptures were written by men who were fearful of losing their servants. Your grandfather saw to it that no woman in his family would suffer such indignity. He witnessed with his own eyes what it did to his mother, his aunts, and what did he receive in return?' She shook her head at the way he had been ridiculed for offering assistance to those widows who lined the streets abandoned, hands outstretched for alms while they waited, longing for their own deaths.

Pramod came to her side, crouched down and took the spindle from her hand. 'He was a visionary.' He smiled. 'A trait he passed on to his daughter.'

'Still. I am not sure that I believe her story,' Pramod's mother said, taking the spindle back and unravelling the twine, testing its strength here and there before twisting the end on to her finger, wrapping it round and round, starting it into a tight ball. 'She told us nothing of how they came to be here or where they had come from.'

'She does not remember,' Pramod said.

'Maybe.' His mother wound the twine around her fingers thoughtfully. 'Or maybe she chooses not to remember. Perhaps that was more convenient for her.'

Although she tried to be charitable – after all, Shurika was a hard worker with a gentle heart who cooked and cleaned and mended for them tirelessly, despite their initial protestation that she owed them nothing – she could not bear to see her son's anguish, and secretly blamed Shurika for having stolen his silent attentions. Of course, she had always known that the day would come when her son would want to take a wife, but she had expected that wife to be a woman of her choosing. A woman who would be malleable, to some degree at least, so that she could shape her to the household in which she and her son had lived so contentedly since her husband's death. But to her dismay, she knew that Pramod's affections had been caught, despite her warnings. As Shurika recovered, he had sat for hours just watching her, reciting poems for her while she slept to calm her fitful dreams, praying that her mind might be released from its unknown afflictions.

Pramod's mother had watched her son closely through the passing seasons, hoping that it was just a short phase of fascination brought about merely by enforced proximity. Yet as the months slid by, she knew in her heart of hearts that he was truly lost, and that there was nothing she could do except to sit back and watch while she spun more thread that she did not need.

'A long time ago, you taught me how to tell when a person is lying.' Pramod went back to the open door, watching the street again. 'You told me that you would always know if I told you a lie because my eyes would not meet yours. They would flick around in search of something solid and unfeeling to pin them to. If I told a lie, I might touch my ear, or my nose, but never my heart or my chest. I would turn away quickly, and be grateful when the subject was changed.' His mother nodded her remembrance of the lesson. 'You cannot know how it frightened me as a child, believing that you would be able to detect the smallest lie. I was so afraid, I sometimes doubted my own truths. But then, as I grew older, I realised that to lie is to invite poison into your veins, and through my own honesty I learned to recognise with absolute certainty truth in others.' He turned his face briefly to his mother. 'She is not lying. Her heart is pure, and I doubt that she has ever told a lie in her life.'

'Be careful, my son. Do not lose your heart to an unworthy woman.'

'Unworthy.' Pramod laughed gently to himself. 'Oh, Mother,' he said fondly. 'I don't think any woman would ever be worthy of your precious son.'

'That is not true,' she snapped at him crossly, although the truth of it was real enough to cause her to turn on him defensively. 'I am only thinking of your future happiness.'

'And what if I have already found its source? What then? Must I deny it, just because it has come from an unexpected quarter?'

Pramod's mother bowed her head slightly, shamed by the sight of her son's daily torment. This was not what she had wanted for him, to see him torn apart each time Shurika entered the room to serve their food or wash their feet. He longed for her. She could tell from the way his spirit seeped from his pores, reaching out across the room like a vaporous silver thread, touching her lightly then shrinking away, back into the heart that he had closed to all others, bringing her essence with it.

'I have seen the way you look at her,' she said to him softly. 'The way that you wait for her when she goes to the shrine to pray. Why do you want to waste your life away like this? Her heart is already spent, my son. She cares nothing for you. Not in the way you want her to.'

'You cannot know that.'

'You must stop thinking of her,' she pleaded.

'I cannot,' he said, leaning his head wearily against the door frame. 'I am always thinking of her. When I throw my nets into the water, I think of her. When I go down to the ghats to bathe myself, I think of her. When I pray to the memory of my father, I think of her. I think of her all the time.'

Pramod's mother felt her son's pain and cursed herself inwardly. It was no use. She had tried her best but she had failed him. Failed her own son. Perhaps those people who had criticised her father had been right. That to educate a woman was to interfere with the very nature of all things. Perhaps it would have been better if she, too, had remained ignorant. Perhaps then she would have betrothed her beloved son while he was still in his infancy, rather than shunning the ancient traditions and allowing him to grow up in his own time. She had always imagined that he would one day come to her, a fine and sensitive man, to tell her that he was ready, to ask her to find him a match. But now she saw that she had been misguided, and she would have to pay the price for her folly. She put down the ball of twine and nodded to herself in defeat.

'Then you must tell her, my son,' she conceded. 'And I will give you my blessing.'

*

Shurika lit two sticks of incense, dipping their tips into one of the flames left to burn there, and placed them carefully before the carved figure of Krishna, alongside many others. The incense spilled thin, aromatic ribbons of white smoke that curled and lifted away in the still heat that felt as though it would bake her dry. She knelt before the shrine, bowing her head to the floor, sweeping her hand around her face, chanting her prayer to the gods, thanking them for restoring her, as she did every day, and begging for their forgiveness. Her bones had healed well enough, her foot now just as it was before, except for the way it ached when the rains came. She had been skilfully nursed, her scars now no more than a few faint traces that would be gone completely in another season or two. She had wished that they would not fade, that they would stay with her always as a constant reminder of her iniquity.

From the folds of her sari, Shurika took the piece of cloth in which she had wrapped the sweet laddu she had saved, given to her this morning as a secret treat, left beside her while she was sleeping. She had gone to Pramod and thanked him for it, bowing her head in deference, staring at his feet before sliding silently away. He had seemed a little disappointed, as though he had wanted to witness her consume it, to watch her succumb to its sweetness, closing her eyes as it coated her mouth. But she could not eat it. She did not deserve the pleasure of such a delicacy. She did not deserve any pleasures at all. For her, it was sin enough that she allowed herself sufficient roti and vegetables to sustain her body, that she allowed herself to drink water when she was thirsty, that she allowed herself to breathe in and out, for she had committed a terrible wrong. Had it not been for her selfishness, her thoughtlessness, her mistress would not have died. Had she not run off into the night like a

260

spoiled child looking for a moment's thrill, her mistress would have recovered and lived long.

Her terrible wrongdoing followed her around like a crow's black shadow, swooping low, whispering its condemnation.

She knew that others could hear it too.

She had often seen Pramod looking at her covertly when he thought himself concealed. Sometimes it seemed as though he wanted to speak to her on a matter of great importance, his mouth all but forming the words, but then he would change his mind and slope away, despondent. Shurika knew that he had heard the spirit voices whispering her guilt, but that his heart was too kind to tell her. It pained her deeply, for he was a good man, sensitive to the needs of others, and he had a natural gift for songs, although he spoke them, rather than singing, which she had found a little strange at first. In the weeks that she had lain and grieved, eyes closed against the dereliction of her own survival, his voice had soothed her wounds like a magical healing balm. He painted with his words, great epic pictures that flowed and swirled like the monsoon skies. His songs seemed subtly different every time she heard them, even when the words were the same, new meanings revealing themselves like layers in ancient stones. As time passed, she had wanted him to think well of her, although she now knew this to be impossible. And then there was his mother, without whom she would surely have perished. Shurika had never encountered a woman like Pramod's mother. She knew so much and spoke so wisely, but only in the confines of her own house. She could read and write – something that Shurika had never imagined possible – and she was a widow, who refused the teachings of the ancient scriptures. At first, she had treated Shurika like a daughter, with a touch so tender that it made Shurika's heart ache for the mother she had once known, the memory of her now so faint, like the furthest-flung stars in the cold night sky. But then, gradually, she had begun to change, distancing herself from Shurika's gratitude, whispering to her son when she thought Shurika asleep. Perhaps she too had heard the voices, and knew that Shurika's heart was filled with darkness. But they had taken her in anyway, Pramod insisting that she could not return to the grim hovel hidden down the alleyway on the other side of the town, persecuted by the accusing eyes of those evil neighbours. Shurika had wept with gratitude and, although they had not asked her to, had taken it upon herself to serve them. After all, it was the only life she knew.

She placed the sweet laddu before the shrine, bowed her head to the floor, and recited her mantras once more. Bringing herself to her feet, she offered her final devotions and moved away, another woman taking her place immediately, pouring out her grief, begging the gods to hear her suffering.

The streets were virtually empty, the heat of the high sun too much to bear. Shurika held her sari in a wide canopy above her head, its light cotton catching what little air it could as she walked along, face tilted to the ground. The rains would be here soon, she thought. A few weeks perhaps, then they would all be able to breathe again. She hoped that the monsoon would sweep away the tension that had built up in the house. Pramod's mother did not like the heat. It made her tetchy. Shurika made sure to bring her plenty of water laced with fresh lime juice and a little sugar syrup. On the worst days, she hung dampened cottons at the windows to cool the flimsy air as it passed through them. Pramod would tell her not to fret so much, not to work so hard, but Shurika could not rest while his mother was in discomfort. The woman had saved her life and been good to her when she should have been left to die in the street to pay for her unforgivable disloyalty.

Shurika moved quickly, regardless of the heat, keen to get back and return to her chores. As soon as she arrived, she would pick through the bags of rice and lentils she had bought in the bazaar yesterday. Stones and grit had been mixed in with both, but the street trader had made such a fuss when she complained that she had finally given in, too hot to argue with him. Besides, it was not as though she had been singled out for his cheating treatment. Every woman in the bazaar was grumbling about the high prices and the poor quality of the provisions on offer. There were many who blamed the war raging in the north, but Shurika suspected that the traders were merely touting that as a convenient excuse to profiteer from the whole sorry situation.

As she neared the house, Shurika saw Pramod standing on the narrow veranda, watching out for her as he always did. Upon seeing her, he lifted his hand in a wave and smiled. Shurika nodded briefly and looked away, unworthy of his kindness. She slipped in through the doorway and up the stairs, her bare feet pressing silently against the old wooden boards. At the rear of the house, in the room in which they kept the provisions and prepared food, the room in which Shurika also lived and slept, she swept the floor, although it was already clean, then made Pramod's mother a sweet *nimbu pani* and took it to her. Upon entering the room where she sat with her spinning wheel, Shurika felt their eyes upon her. She bowed and placed the cup gently on the floor beside the mother's mat.

'Shurika,' Pramod's mother said, her voice as soft as it had been when Shurika had first opened her eyes and seen her, sari awash with colour, the sweet scent of cloves and jasmine in her hair.

'Yes, *mataji*.' Shurika kept her eyes respectfully downcast.

'My son and I wish to speak with you.'

For a moment, Shurika was filled with dread. She dared to lift her head and steal a glance at their faces, her heart in her mouth. What she saw left her confused. Pramod was smiling as though every trouble in the world had come to an end, and his mother had tears in her eyes. She reached a hand out to Shurika and caressed her face, murmuring at the softness of her skin, the delicate trustfulness of her sad brown eyes.

'Shurika, do you love my son?'

Shurika's eyes darted to Pramod. He was gazing back at her, his smile now more than just the simplicity of happiness. It told her of a thousand things she could never explain, filling her senses like the poems he had recited to her in her darkest hours, engulfing her like a fast-flowing river, dense with shimmering golden fishes and a rare magic that few could understand. Inside, her spirit stirred, then began to sing the songs that she had banished from her heart long ago. And then, suddenly, a new awareness came over her that she did not know. She felt herself burning, her skin ablaze, and dropped her face to the floor in shame.

'Yes, *mataji.*'

Pramod's mother placed her hand upon Shurika's head and said, 'Then it is settled.'

She took a sweet laddu from the dish beside her and offered it to Shurika's lips.

## 32

The population of the safe convent house in Shillong swelled to bursting point as it opened its doors to offer shelter to those who had journeyed from the nearby states to escape the perils of the far north. They were crammed in like sardines, every inch of the living quarters put to best use to accommodate the sudden deluge of pupils, sisters and priests who had come upon them. Among the local population, beneficent well-wishers moved in with their neighbours, giving up their homes and insisting that the convent's overspill take up residence in their humble abodes. All offers were gratefully accepted, and morning prayers, held outside to spare the crush of the tiny chapel, were commonly filled with thanks and blessings for the generous provisions of all those who had made sacrifices in order to come to their assistance.

'I don't think I can live like this for much longer,' Amelia complained tearfully, desperately searching the small allocated space beside her temporary bunk for the third time, looking for the one and only possession she had been permitted to bring with her. 'Oh, where is it?'

'Don't upset yourself.' Mary consoled Amelia from her squatting position on the floor, where she had tried to find a small space between the stacked cases forced into every conceivable nook and cranny. 'It's a wonder that any of us manage to find anything in among all this clutter.'

'They promised us we'd only be here for a few weeks. Yet it's been almost three months and we don't even have proper beds to sleep in, and now I've gone and lost my book.' Amelia began to weep.

'Please don't cry.' Mary tried to put her arm around Amelia's shoulders, but Amelia shrugged her off and threw herself on to the tiny bunk, burying her face in the pillow. Mary lifted her head to the sound of a slight knocking from the open door.

Sister Margaret raised her finger to her lips silently and motioned with a small tilt of her head that Mary should leave Amelia alone. Reluctantly, Mary got up and followed her to the crowded grounds where far too many children gathered to play in the sunshine, colliding with each other at every turn, their voices raised into a constant, chattering mass. Sister Margaret steered her through the mêlée towards the one quiet corner, a tiny copse of jacaranda trees set behind the chapel, their deep mauve blossoms falling in gentle showers, carpeting the ground beneath their feet.

'She's lost her book,' Mary explained as they walked. 'It's the only thing she brought with her and—'

Sister Margaret placed a solemn hand on Mary's arm.

'It's not about the book, Mary,' she said, slowing to a halt by the wooden bench under the shade of the trees, taking a seat amid the soft petals. 'We received several wires this morning. They had been sent to Haflong, so heaven only knows how long it took for them to be relayed to us here.' Mary sat beside her. 'I have never seen so much terrible news in one day.' Sister Margaret bowed her head, allowing herself a brief moment. 'I don't even know how to say this. Amelia's father has been taken prisoner. We knew there must be something wrong because it's been so long since we've heard from him, but with all that's been going on I suppose we just assumed he was lying low somewhere. He was one of the men who volunteered to

266

stay behind in Burma and help destroy the oil wells when the Japs invaded.' Mary pressed her hand to her mouth, her heart turning over. 'I know you girls heard about it. Heaven only knows why we didn't think to start removing the newspaper packing from your parcels much earlier, although you would have thought that their senders might have shown a little more sense. We've gone to great lengths to protect you girls from the awful truth of what's going on.' She shook her head painfully. 'Poor Amelia. Father Lazarus spoke to her this morning. At least we know he's alive.'

'Oh, Amelia,' said Mary, almost to herself. 'Why didn't she say anything?'

'There are some things that are just too terrible to contemplate. You girls must stick together and offer each other whatever comfort you can. We came here as a family, however odd we may appear. And now we must stand upright as a family, because we are the only people we have right now.'

'Yes,' said Mary. 'Of course we will.'

'There is something else I have to tell you, Mary,' Sister Margaret said, pausing for a while to gird herself. 'There have been a number of reports coming out of Imphal.'

'Imphal?' Mary shouted. 'That's where my father is!'

'Yes, child, I know.' Sister Margaret found herself unable to smile. 'It would seem that the city has been surrounded by the Japanese.'

'What?' Mary's face became ashen. Sister Margaret prevented her from leaping up from her seat, grasping her arm.

'Now don't you panic,' she said sternly. 'Just because your father is in among it all doesn't mean to say that anything bad is going to happen to him. I'm telling you this because it is better that you hear it from me before word spreads around the others and gets exaggerated out of all proportion. God looks after his own, Mary.' Tears cascaded from Mary's eyes, her nostrils flaring. Sister Margaret pressed a handkerchief into her hands, its familiar monogram the same delicate hue as the jacaranda blossom. 'Now stop that crying. There are plenty of other people receiving far worse news than this today.' She swallowed hard and paused a while, her heart already unbearably burdened. 'Father Lazarus has two fine nephews back in Germany, you know. They have disappeared, along with his only brother. He received word directly from the Cardinal of Berlin yesterday. Heaven only knows where they are or what has become of them. All we can do is hope and pray.'

With the passing of a small breeze, a brief flurry of pastel blossoms flew about them, circling in a cloud of soft confetti.

'It is hard to imagine why man has to create such ugliness in this world. I shall never pretend to understand it.' Sister Margaret seemed to slump in her seat. 'I'm so sorry, Mary, but I have no doubt that God will keep your father safe and well while he's doing his bit. And as for those Japs,' she tightened her jaw in anger, 'I wouldn't fancy their chances against our troops. We're not giving an inch, you know, and I'd bet you our boys will take down every last one of them.' Sister Margaret's hands balled into hard fists. 'Everyone is suffering, one way or another. You and I need to pray harder than ever, because your father will need your prayers, as will Amelia's.'

Mary nodded, sobbing into the handkerchief for a moment longer, then with an effort pulled herself together.

'Come on, now.' Sister Margaret hugged Mary hard, then stood up. 'There are others to think of. We have things to do. Important things.'

'Like what?' Mary swallowed her tears and took a deep breath of determination, standing ready for Sister Margaret's instructions.

'Like finding your friend's book, for a start.'

*

The ferocious fighting stretched on for three more weeks, then at last the news came that the worst of the bloodshed was over, the broken Japanese forces, every gun and tank lost, beaten back from the Burma front and forced to retreat across the Chindwin river as the Allies pushed on towards Mandalay. Stories soon began to filter from mouth to mouth of Japanese soldiers chained to trees by their commanding officers, bound to fight on to the death despite the hopelessness of their situation, many of them without so much as a single bullet.

The girls received the announcement placidly, unable to bring themselves to show any sense of celebration, the price of victory already far too great.

Although the region remained perilous, the decision was taken that they should return to Haflong as soon as possible, to try to restore some sense of normality to their war-torn lives. Their temporary bunks were dismantled, cases fetched and filled, and the Haflong party prepared to go back to their abandoned convent, sending a cable ahead to the staff, in the assumption that at least some of them had stayed on. The relief of leaving the overcrowded safe house was clouded by a sense of trepidation over what they might find waiting for them. As they made their way to the station on foot, a small convoy of open trucks passed by, heading in the opposite direction, their benches filled with uniformed men, some with obvious injuries, heavily bandaged or bearing crutches, others seemingly unscathed but for their catatonic state.

'Wave to the soldiers!' Sister Margaret commanded as the trucks rolled past. 'And give them a nice big smile.'

'Where are they going?' asked Amelia.

'Wards Lake, I expect,' Sister Rosemary said, referring to the grand body of water basking in the middle of the city, surrounded by parkland and favoured by honeymooners before the war came. 'The army has taken over one of the hotels and turned it into a respite home for the officers. I expect most of them have been sent down from Imphal and Kohima. The Japs have inflicted terrible casualties there.'

'Sister!' Sister Margaret shot her a sharp shake of her head. 'Hasn't there been enough trouble already without adding to it with idle speculation?'

'Sorry, Sister.' Sister Rosemary was duly corrected and looked at the girls apologetically. 'Don't take any notice of me. It was a silly comment.'

Mary stopped and stared at the weary faces of the exhausted officers, searching for a glimmer of recognition. Among the convoy, few had the energy to wave back, although some did lift a hand and manage a smile. As the last of the trucks rumbled past and the rest of the girls picked up pace towards the station, Mary found herself beset with the urge to turn and run towards the disappearing soldiers, to ask if they had indeed come from Imphal and whether they could give her any news of her father. She felt certain that at least one of them would be bound to know of his whereabouts and condition. Her feet refused to move.

'Mary?' Sister Margaret urged her along. 'Come along now. We don't want to miss our train, do we? Heaven only knows when there'll be another one.'

Mary did not hear her. She stood, shrouded in grief, her abandonment all at once separating her from the street and everything in it. She could not think how she came to be here, her life passing before her in a rapid succession of disparate snapshots. A courtyard. A song. A bright, jagged blossom from a flame tree. The sound of tiny bells, like shards of glass falling. Glimpses of places she could no longer remember.

'Mary?' A shadow of Sister Margaret seemed to move towards her, floating, a figure in slow motion, then star-bright flecks danced before her eyes as a black curtain came down and her legs gave way beneath her.

They found the convent just as they had left it, peaceful and undisturbed, the gardens a little overgrown perhaps, the school-rooms and dormitory slightly musty, in need of a few days' fresh air. No enemy had laid a footstep here, the dusty lock on the gate untried, the supplies in the cookhouse untouched. If any trouble had passed this way, it had not stopped to defile this consecrated place. They were silently grateful, all of them, to find their home spared the shame of an invading army of plundering men. Yet everything had changed and nobody felt the same, the fragility of life having been so clearly demonstrated to them all through the indiscriminate vagaries of war.

Soon after their return to Haflong, the extent of the human tragedy infiltrated the sanctuary of the convent's whitewashed walls. Those wretches who had had no choice other than to walk through Burma and cross the border into India began to emerge from the jungle. They had waded through leech-infested swamps. Fallen victim to malaria and become riddled with tuberculosis. Many had tried to bring their possessions with them, only to abandon them by the wayside as the merci-less trek through dense, hostile territory became harder and harder to bear. The bodies of all but the strongest soon joined the discarded heirlooms surrendered to the ground. Mothers died. Infants were born and perished before the sun set.

But some made it. Like the girl who emerged all alone, half naked, with rags on her feet, barely alive and having somehow survived despite losing everyone who had started out with her. She just walked and walked, and one day her unimaginable journey ended on the steps of the convent. The newspapers came to interview her. Her picture was everywhere, perhaps in the hope that she would be recognised, that someone would claim her. But nobody came, so she stayed with the handful of children who had nowhere else to call home and became one of them. There was no question that the nuns would dispatch her to Kalimpong. She had suffered enough.

## 33

James sat on the veranda, the late morning sun shimmering over the wide horizon, and warmed his weary face. Gone were the valleys and the hills with their high, whispering trees. There were no tea gardens here. No slender women picking their way along the high terraces, black eyes hidden beneath the wide canopies of their bright saris. Just the open African plains and more heat than most men could imagine. James rarely permitted himself the indulgence of his memories. They always began well enough, spurred by the glimpse of a flower, the call of a bird. Yet he did not linger, for the ache was never far away.

There had been much talk among the officers as the war came to an end. With the sun setting on the Empire's finest jewel, most were preparing to reacclimatise to the distant shores of Britain or to seek out new fortunes elsewhere. Once it became no longer a matter of choice, there were many who found themselves reluctant to leave their self-made princedoms. James knew very well that he would rather do almost anything than find himself tending an English garden and living a colourless life behind a clipped privet hedge. Yet there were plenty of others who couldn't wait to get out.

'If they think things were bad in Delhi, they should have seen the chaos here in Calcutta!' James had found himself stuck with the talkative brigadier while awaiting news of transportation.

'All this bloody Quit India business. Nobody wants out of this hellhole more than the British Tommy, eh?' James had nodded politely from his chair at the next table in the officers' mess. 'We were going past one of those damned demonstrations in Chowringee. All these bloody wogs chanting *Quit India! Quit India!* So of course the chaps fell in behind them and started chanting along with them! The whole bloody regiment was falling about laughing!' The brigadier had taken a large swig of his whisky and demanded another with a wave of his glass at the orderly. 'And what about you, old chap? What dump have you been stuck in, eh?'

'Burma,' James had replied.

'Oh! Oh, right. Yes. Bloody rum.' The brigadier shook his head ruefully. 'Filthy state. Alive with germs and bugs that do their damnedest to get their teeth into you or burrow under your skin. There's always some ruddy piece of flesh on show no matter what you do to cover up, eh? You'd be bloody lucky not to get a dose of malaria up there. One chap I ran into said one of theirs had contracted smallpox. He got over it all right, but his face was a bloody mess. They sent him home but his fiancée wouldn't have anything to do with him. Poor bugger.' James had nodded in sympathy but remained quiet. 'Can I get you another one of those, old boy? Burma, eh? Bloody awful show over Singapore. I saw some of those poor buggers who escaped and came over the border on foot. Laid up in the same hospital, we were. I took one in the shoulder.' He had gently slapped the pips on his uniform to indicate the whereabouts of his injury before returning to his tale. 'It was a sorry sight, I can tell you. They were so full of disease that all anyone could offer them was a clean bed to die in. There were headhunters too, you know. Bloody savages would just cut off your head and keep it as a trophy! God only knows how many of our men were left to rot in the jungle and get eaten by wild animals. It's a bad business. What were you doing up there?'

'Engineer.'

'Jolly good, jolly good.' The brigadier had rolled the whisky around in his glass, wondering whether to continue pressing this man for a bit of conversation. Perhaps he was one of the tricky ones whose nerves had been shot and were best left alone.

Then James had noticed the tremor in the man's hand, had taken pity on the stranger and engaged him despite his own overwhelming fatigue. 'Are you waiting for transport?'

'What? Oh, yes. We were supposed to fly out of Dum Dum yesterday but got caught up in that bloody sandstorm. Couldn't take off so I'm stuck here until tomorrow. Still, I hear some of the navy lads will have to hang on for months before they can get shipment back. Not that they're complaining. Most of the chaps are billeted in one of those awful seafront hotels, but they seem to be making the most of it. Nothing much else to do except wait until your number comes up, is there?'

'I suppose not.'

'They'd get through them a whole lot quicker if the war office hadn't put a stop to demobbing out here. Apparently they were getting all sorts of complaints from the womenfolk that their men weren't returning! You know what I say?' The brigadier winked at James. 'What man in his right mind would want to go back to a hard-boiled English wife after tasting the exotic delights of the East? It's no wonder so many of them have demobbed and disappeared! If anybody wants to stay abroad now, they'll have to make their way back under their own steam and at their own expense. I don't really see the point of it myself. If a chap wants to stay here, then why not? Seems daft to make everyone go home if they don't want to.'

'Making your way back to England?'

The brigadier had looked surprised. 'Good God, no.

Whatever for, man? An old chum of mine says that now this place has gone up the Swanee, it's time to move on to a younger colony where the natives don't make so much ruddy trouble!' He had touched his nose at James confidentially, as if disclosing a great secret. 'Southern Rhodesia, old boy. He's growing the big cash crops and hauling in a tidy fortune by the sounds of it. That's where I'll be heading. You mark my words. It's the next big thing.'

Somehow the brigadier's words had stuck.

But first, before he could leave India, an invisible thread had drawn James back to the hills of Assam, breaking open the fresh wounds of everything that he had loved when he was a more youthful man. The flash of a sunbird, the smell of the rain on the thick, shiny leaves, the call of the mahouts and the sounds of his children at play. This life once lived.

He and Dorothy had been welcomed at the big house like old friends and generously entertained. Yet James had felt displaced and ill at ease from the moment he arrived, despite Shiva's obvious joy at seeing him. He had noticed that the new master had the staff wear the uniforms he had dispensed with long ago. Felix seemed to approve of the changes and had come to share one last *burra-peg* with his friend.

'Best of luck, James.'

'Thank you, Felix.'

Dorothy had leaned forward and kissed Felix on his ruddy cheek, his whiskers getting in the way. 'We'll miss you,' she'd said. Felix enlarged his cheerfulness at the sight of her watery eyes, uncomfortable with the formality of this final parting. He was glad to see his old friend well settled with a suitable woman, and relieved that he had seen sense and moved on.

Shiva had waited patiently beside the car and opened the doors for the master he had once known so well. To his surprised delight, James ignored his bowed head and clasped palms and insisted that they shake hands. Shiva's arm had moved awkwardly, unused to the gesture, and he had smiled like a boy.

'Thank you, Shiva,' James had said. 'You have been a loyal servant and a good friend. I shall always remember you.'

'Thank you, Sahib. You have been very good to me. I shall always remember you too.'

When James had left the estate a handful of years before, he had fulfilled a long-held tradition, even though Shiva still had many years left to work. A devoted servant knew that the small wage he received throughout his service would be handsomely supplemented at the end of his working life with the gift of a pension. This amount, decided upon by his employer, was intended to keep him through his old age. If his employer was generous, he might look forward to a comfortable retirement. Without it, he could expect only years of hand-to-mouth living and the prospect of working long into the future until his ageing body gave out and submitted to the endless cycle of rebirth. James had been generous indeed, in case the new master was not.

Shiva had continued to shake James's hand hard, his smile beginning to waver. 'I will call my first son after you, Sahib.'

'Still no boys?'

'No, Sahib.'

'I wish you would change your mind and come with us.'

Shiva had lifted his hand to his breast and shaken his head. 'This is my home, Sahib. And besides, our elephants are much prettier.'

James and Dorothy had then slipped into the car. Shiva closed the door on them and moved aside for Felix. James wound the window full down.

'And don't you stand any nonsense from those bloody Africans.'

'Don't worry, Felix.' Dorothy had smiled back. 'He won't!'

Felix had slapped his hand on the roof of the car as the driver pulled away, Dorothy looking over her shoulder, leaning on the back of the seat and waving. James remained facing front. She noticed his poignant expression. 'Not wanting to take one last long look, darling?'

'No,' he said, unable to voice the subtle torment of the ghosts that plagued him still, following him day and night, shaking him awake during the darkest hours of war while shells had exploded relentlessly overhead. He yearned to find peace, to be able to rest his troubled mind. Dorothy took his hand and squeezed it.

Suddenly James leaned forward and spoke to the driver. 'Take the western estate road.'

At the point where the ground roughened to become impassable, he halted the driver and left Dorothy in the car, walking the rest of the distance alone to the small enclave set among the tall trees. The moment he entered the rusting gates, he realised that he should not have come back.

Chinthimani's quarters lay empty and neglected, the courtyard overgrown with towering weeds and the creeping tendrils of untended plants. The silver oak by the far wall stood choked with thick coils of wild pepper, its lower boughs overwhelmed by the parasitic vines. A lone, scrawny chicken pecked around in the dust outside what was once the busy cookhouse. So quiet all around. James wandered bleakly among the ramshackle buildings. The threshing machine had gone, along with everything else that could be carried, the entire fabric of the cowshed dismantled and spirited away. As he passed across the foundations for the building of a new storeroom that had never been finished, he noticed two small handprints set into the concrete at an awkward angle. He bent down and swept the loose leaves aside, slowly tracing their image with the tip of his finger, caressing the indelible marks of the child who had left them there, before covering one with his own palm, holding its hand.

The bitter smell of smoke from the supper fires burning in the distance coloured his view, pricking his eyes and drying his throat. Whatever life had lived here had long since flown.

James's enquiries in the village as they passed through had been met with suspicion and silence. If anyone had any notion as to what had become of the woman and her companion, they kept it to themselves. There was no word to be extracted from any of them, not even for the price of a sack of grain. It was as though she had simply vanished.

At that precise moment, James knew that there was nothing left for him there.


And so began the exodus as the British planters pulled out. There had once been more than a hundred of them across the region, often descended from the pioneering families who had come here a century before, growing indigo, then sugar cane and rice before the tea gardens arrived. Yet as India's tide turned, they feared that freedom would prejudice all against them, and that once the British officials were gone, there would be no one around to prevent them all being murdered in their beds.

James had the big old Riley motor car, a parting gift from Felix, shipped to Africa, and they ran it into the ground searching for the new lands on which they would establish a farm to raise tobacco. With the help of a hundred reluctant, slow-working men, a new house was built, the land cleared and irrigated, and a curing barn constructed of burnt brick. A lesser man might have been defeated by such an ambitious plan, beginning from nothing in an unknown land, yet James was a man of exceptional abilities. To carve a new life into a foreign landscape was not beyond him, no matter how trying the conditions. He knew how things worked, how to build machines that would stand the test of time, and the structures in which to house them. Dorothy stood by his side and devoted herself to the country that they would now call home. Like the India she had met all those years earlier, she could never have imagined how different this place would be.

James rose slowly from his chair and moved to the veranda, leaning on the brick-built balustrade in the full glare of the Rhodesian sunshine, staring out across the veld. Faint columns of smoke rose towards the horizon, lifting from the distant compound where the workers lived in a rambling hotchpotch of rough mud-built houses. How his memories haunted him. He tried not to think of them, and cast his eyes across the arid land-scape. It seemed desolate to him, this difficult place. Colourless, despite the dull green of the few flat-topped trees that remained and the changing hues of the light skimming against the kopjes, the rough, jumbled outlines of rocky outcrops standing proud of the high grasses, immovable. In the bush, the cicadas buzzed their curtain of sound. James had learned to tune them out, the strident humming a constant backdrop to the heat. The rains had failed again. It was almost certain that they would lose this harvest too, no matter what vain efforts were made to rescue the wilting crops.

James folded the letter from the mother superior telling formally of Mary's progress and the passing of her exams, and slid it back into his shirt pocket. It was old news now, of course. It could take a long time for a letter to cross the ocean and reach the farm. Dorothy appeared from the house and noticed how much he seemed to have aged these last few years. She walked to his side and put her arm through his.

'Penny for your thoughts?'

He smiled down at her and patted her hand. 'I wish it would rain.'

## 34

The pupils sat at the long trestle tables in the refectory reciting grace, the four rows of respectfully bowed heads descending in size down to the handful who were still permitted to eat with a spoon. Mother Superior presided over the prayer, her crackling voice bearing testimony to the persistent ill health she had suffered of late. The girls said amen and crossed themselves before reaching hungrily for the serving dishes to be handed around amid the clatter of cutlery. Mary, perched at the far end along with the rest of the eldest girls, looked at the meat on her plate and waited for Sister Ann to pass by before stabbing it with her fork and slipping it under the table to Roley.

'You must promise to write to me always. Until we both die. I just can't bear the thought of you going.'

Mary grimaced at her plate. 'At least I'll never be forced to eat anything this awful again.'

'I have to wait a whole extra fortnight before I can leave. My arrangements couldn't be made any earlier.' Roley sighed heavily and leaned a forbidden elbow on the table, sulkily dropping her chin to her hand, rumpling her rosy cheek. 'I'll be so bored that I'll probably explode like one of those enormous bombs they dropped on the Japs.'

'It'll pass in no time. You'll be in England before you know it.'

Roley pursed her lips. 'But what if my aunt doesn't like me?

That would be just my luck. I hope she's not a complete witch.'

Mary pushed the boiled potatoes around her plate. She had no interest in eating today at all, her only hunger now for the promise of freedom that lay ahead. 'Oh, don't start all that again. Your father would never have arranged to send you there if she was. You know how much he adores you. She'll probably turn out to be very nice indeed and all your worrying will have been over nothing.'

'As long as she doesn't try to mother me.' Roley folded the stowaway slice of meat in her fingers and popped it into her mouth, talking as she chewed. 'I do wish that Mama hadn't gone and died like that.' Mary smiled tenderly, nodding her sympathy. 'I'd much prefer to go back to Father, but he's been moved to another temporary post in Delhi and is adamant that I can't stay here because of all the trouble that's going on. He said that if they thought the war was bad, they haven't seen anything yet.' Roley cleared her mouth with a gulp of water and set about her lunch. 'He said there's going to be a blood-bath.'

'I wish I could come with you. You'll get to sail on a big ship and see half the world before you get there.' Mary sighed. 'Just think how exciting it will be.'

'Exciting? I can't think of anything worse. I'm going to train as a school teacher, then I intend to come straight back to India before my aunt can marry me off to some distant cousin she's earmarked for me. That's why my father's sending me there. I just know it is. He wants me out of the way and off his hands.'

'Don't be so silly.'

'I'm not. I can always tell when people are scheming about me.'

'What if he's telling the truth about the trouble?'

'He is. The penguins missed a bit of newspaper in my last parcel. There was one page with a picture of the viceroy saying that we had all better put our tin hats on, but I had it confiscated.' Roley stopped eating and lowered her voice. 'It said that it's only a matter of time before they all start killing each other, but better that than they start killing us.'

'Really?' Mary said, trying not to sound as scared as she felt. Roley nodded solemnly.

'It's all Gandhi's fault. He's got the whole country complaining about one thing and another and the viceroy doesn't know what to do with him. My father says he has no idea how much it costs the British to keep him in the poverty he is accustomed to. He travels all over the place and makes a complete nuisance of himself, bringing half the population with him each time and refusing to sleep in a proper bed or to eat anything other than dhal.'

'Why would anyone want to do that?'

'I have no idea,' said Roley, loading her fork again. 'All I know is that all the governors are run ragged trying to put up hundreds of tents and emptying trains so that he can travel up and down the country with his followers making mischief for everyone. He says that the British are nothing more than common thieves and that they should all go home of their own accord before they're thrown out.'

Mary forced herself to manage a piece of cold potato, the two girls mulling over the great politics of the day with little or no understanding of their meaning. They were not permitted to see the newspapers. A few stories were shared with the pupils after breakfast on a Saturday, just so that they might have some basic acquaintance with current events, usually to do with the king's travels overseas. Mary's appetite deserted her as she began to worry about what might happen to her in the outside world, the knot tightening in her empty stomach. She changed the subject.

'I saved you my birthday cake.'

'Really?' Roley paused her cutlery and stared at her friend. 'Is it one of the big fruit cakes with the sugar crystals on top?'

Mary nodded. Roley rubbed her ample tummy, eyes bulging, and made licking noises, knowing how it made Mary laugh.

A nun's arm suddenly appeared between them, the big palm landing heavily on the dining table. 'Quiet!' a voice snapped sternly, the girls jolted rudely into silence. Sister Margaret removed her hand, leaving two jelly babies sitting on the table. Mary glanced up at her with a smile. Sister Margaret winked down solemnly and glided on.

Mary felt strangely out of place, sitting in the office with the mother superior and Sister Margaret, eyes gritty through lack of sleep. Last night she had tossed and turned for hours, staring into the darkness until the dawn lifted its soft light to the small windows. Poised neatly on the edge of her seat, she was unsure of what to do with the hands that fiddled with the handker-chief she held in her fingers. The mother superior seemed so fragile a figure today, frail even, the wisps of hair beneath her wimple thin and silver white, tucked in by bony hands. Mary remembered how she had once quaked in the presence of this strong, stern woman with the brass-rimmed half-moon spec-tacles perched high on a pinched nose. She returned the mother superior's kind smile, her piercing blue eyes still twinkling yet missing the fire that had once frightened her so.

Feeling awkward in her skin, Mary did her best to ignore her self-consciousness and determined not to fidget. Her pinafores, along with almost everything else familiar to her, had been discarded yesterday evening, taken away by one of the sisters with the breezy comment that she wouldn't be needing them any more. She sat instead in a cotton dress of blue and white seersucker, the sleeves cut just above the elbows and trimmed with a pretty border of broderie anglaise, and tried not to stare at her shoes – soft leather courts with a neat heel and a stylish bow at the front. Her black steamer trunk, secured and waiting beside the gates, lay packed with the things that had appeared as if by magic, like a simple trousseau sent to replace her childhood. She had taken everything out to look at it, choosing the clothes she wanted for the morning, then had packed it all away again. As she closed the trunk, hearing the final thud of the latch, she had suddenly found herself overcome, the years colliding and passing before her in a flash, the memories of her tiny self, the seemingly endless days she had walked within these walls.

The mother superior poured tea into painted china, needing both hands to steady the steaming silver pot, stubbornly refusing Sister Margaret's immediate offer of assistance.

'Well, Mary.' She passed her a dainty cup and saucer, one chattering against the other with the effort of her unsteady hand. 'It is always a sad day when we see one of our special girls leave.' This was the term she attached to her permanent wards. 'And I dare say that to some of us, you have been more special than most.' She lifted her eyes momentarily to Sister Margaret, who conceded her open affection by reaching for the handkerchief tucked into her sleeve.

'Thank you, Mother Superior.' Mary held the teacup in her lap, glad that her hands were at last occupied.

'I hope that we have taught you well, Mary. It is not easy to prepare a child for life. There is so much that you will have to learn for yourself, but it will come, in time. Is there anything that you want to ask of us before you go?'

Mary had not been expecting the question and faltered, suddenly feeling desperately unprepared for the imminent enforced separation from her protectors. In that moment, she could not recall a single instance when she had been expected to think for herself, to make a decision of any importance. Every hour of every day had been planned and presented to her – the food she ate, the clothes she wore, the hours she slept. She stared into her teacup, her insides churning, then heard herself say, 'I would like to go and visit my mother.'

The mother superior sat motionless, a moment of awkwardness passing between her and Sister Margaret. She acknowledged Mary's request with a small shake of her head.

'I am afraid that that is perhaps the only thing that we cannot help you with, Mary. It was your father who placed you here with us, and because of your mother's – circumstances,' she spoke more slowly, choosing her words carefully, 'we were not actually informed of her whereabouts.'

'I know where she lives,' Mary said. 'Her house is near to my father's old plantation. If I went there, I am sure I would be able to remember the way.'

'I am not so certain that she is still there, Mary. Your father moved away many years ago now, and so much has changed since then. We couldn't possibly send you on a journey of such folly. As much as I understand your wishes, we have a duty to fulfil to your father, so I'm afraid that it really is out of the question.'

Mary's head dipped. Sister Margaret put her cup and saucer down on the mother superior's desk. 'You mustn't dwell on the past, Mary. It will do you no good, no good at all.'

'And that is the truth of it,' the mother superior said, her voice returning to its regular level, as if to bring the subject to a close. 'Now let's all cheer up and look to the future with bright eyes and open hearts.'

'All your arrangements have been made,' Sister Margaret said. 'Your father has left provision for your further education and said that you are to write to us if there is anything else you need.'

The mother superior nodded. 'We'll miss you, Mary

Macdonald. You're quite the silliest girl ever to have passed through these walls.' She exchanged a subtle glance with Sister Margaret, then stood. 'I'm going to leave you two here for a little while to talk between yourselves. Eat some of this delicious cake.' She motioned towards the towering sponge on the china stand, filled with generous layers of jam and buttercream. 'You know, Cook made it for you specially.' She wagged her finger and remembered the countless times the child had been sent up to her office to take her punishment for sticking her fingers in the sugar. 'I expect he will miss you most of all.' With a small smile, she slipped out of the office and quietly closed the door.

With the boundary between adult and child imperceptibly lifted, Sister Margaret and Mary sat together in the window seat overlooking the gardens, pondering the places that Mary would soon see and the homes they had each left behind. Sister Margaret licked jam from her fingers, considering for a while before speaking.

'You know, Mary, you have led a very sheltered life here. We keep ourselves locked away from the outside world for good reason. Even though the war is over, there is still much trouble to come.' She set her plate aside. 'There are some things that you should know, for your own safety.'

'Like what?'

'Well, for one thing, the British are pulling out of India.' Mary felt her insides turn over. So the rumours were true. 'India is to be restored to her own people, but it won't be easy. The battles have already started.' She sighed. 'You'll read all about it in the newspapers once you are out of here. Try not to let the reports frighten you. It's just the same old story of men squabbling over power, which is usually where all the trouble starts. They are going to split India in half.'

Mary stared at her incredulously. 'How can you possibly split a country in half?'

'Ah.' Sister Margaret sucked her teeth. 'And therein lies the question that nobody wants to answer. You must promise me that you will be very careful, Mary. Watch what is going on around you and stay well away from trouble.'

'I will,' Mary said.

Sister Margaret noted the shadow of apprehension that had settled upon Mary's face and sought to lighten the mood. She gave her a gentle shove. 'Would you like to hear a little secret of mine?' Mary recognised the mischief in the nun's voice. 'You know, many years ago, when I was even younger than you are, I was once madly in love with a boy.'

'Really?' Mary's eyes widened at the unlikely picture.

'His name was Monaghan, Patrick Monaghan.' She tutted softly. 'Flaming red hair and a quick temper to go along with it, mind you. Quite what I saw in him I really couldn't tell you. He lived in a house above Killala Bay back home in County Sligo. The wind would rip right through you if you didn't put a good thick jumper on, so I froze myself half to death trying to get him to notice me. A whole year I spent mooning after that ridiculous boy, until my mother cottoned on and beat some sense into me.' Sister Margaret shook her head. 'My, what a grand waste of time that was. He never even looked at me once. Broke my heart he did and never gave it a second thought.' She brushed the crumbs from her lap.

'You were meant for higher things,' Mary said.

'Ah, Mary child. You're a sweet girl. I will surely miss our little chats.' She nudged Mary affectionately. 'I hope you find a nice boy one day. Somebody who will take care of that silly nature of yours and love you with all his heart.' Mary blushed a little. 'What's all this? There's no need to be embarrassed now!' Sister Margaret feigned surprise. 'It's what the good Lord put you here for! To fall in love with a fine man, to get married and raise a family together! Oh yes, you may think it's all very daft now, but just wait and see.' She tapped her nose. 'It'll happen to you one day, you mark my words, and that's a promise made.' Her smile faded. 'I only hope he'll be worthy of you, Mary. You're a precious child. I don't mind telling you that.' She turned away, lifting her sleeve to her eyes for the briefest of moments.

The two of them sat in quiet affection, looking out of the open window towards the gardens in which they had strolled so often side by side, the special place in the corner beneath the old mango tree where they had lain on the grass and talked of many things. They were all quiet now. Pensive. It was almost time. Sister Margaret took Mary's hand and clasped it hard, staring at Mary's soft brown fingers sandwiched between her own pale palms.

'Mary, child.' She hesitated for a moment, then drew a deep breath and started again. 'Mary, child. Do you know who your Aunty Dorothy is?'

Mary smiled directly at Sister Margaret and appeared somewhat baffled.

'Why yes, of course I do! She's my father's sister!'

Sister Margaret's sigh hung heavily on the flower-scented air. She met Mary's puzzled gaze with a small, sympathetic smile. 'No, child. She is not your father's sister. She is your father's wife.'

Mary got into the carriage with a smartly dressed woman she had never met before. The chaperone would escort her on the long and arduous journey to Calcutta, from where they would cross the bedlam of the city, making their way to the big station at Haora to catch the onward train that would transport them all the way down to Bangalore in the south.

Mary had promised herself that she would not cry, despite the waves of fear tearing at her insides. It was as though the world had turned upside down, leaving her unable to get a fix on what was real and what was not. There were no answers, just endless questions that seemed to make no sense. Serafina must have known, but had said nothing. The sense of betrayal filled Mary with a terrible uncertainty, that she could have been so gullible, so trusting, while all around her nothing was as it seemed, her whole life little more than a paper-thin veneer. Her hands trembled, her throat clenched and unclenched, impairing her speech in a slow asphyxiation. The few tiny bites of cake she had managed turned over and over in her stomach, like gravel tumbling down a shallow river bed.

A burst of steam rose from beneath the carriages, the shouts and whistles indicating the imminent roll of the big engine. Sister Margaret perched precariously on the step, pressed halfway through the window, leaning her bulk in towards Mary, handkerchief in hand, calling her love and good luck. A passing porter tried to encourage her away, but she shooed him aside crossly, reached in and grasped Mary's hand.

'You be careful now, you hear me?' she shouted, afraid that her warnings would be lost amid the noise from the strain of the engine and the whistle that blew. The train groaned with effort. 'And mind that you write to me as soon as you get there to let me know you're safe. And every week after that to tell me how well you're doing!' Sister Margaret dropped down to the platform, her hands still entangled with Mary's, forcing her to stand and lean out with her. 'God be with you, Mary! God speed, child!'

The train began to pull, but Sister Margaret refused to let go, first walking with it, then forced to break into a faster, uncomfortable pace. Within moments, her hefty frame was unable to keep up with the movement of the carriage. She finally wrenched herself from Mary's grip, her handkerchief coming free in Mary's hands, and pressed her empty arms to her bosom as she stood and watched the train slide away through the whorls of steam.

Mary waved madly out of the window until the station curved out of sight, taking Sister Margaret's hazy figure with it. As the heat rushed to her cheeks, she recognised at once the sharp pain gnawing at her flesh. She felt utterly abandoned, bereft as the day she and her sister had been left at the convent, wailing as their father walked away. A huge, involuntary sob rose from her body as she crumpled into the seat beside her chaperone. Bringing Sister Margaret's handkerchief to her eyes, the sweet smell of sugar touched her nostrils, a jelly baby dropping silently into her lap.

*Part Three*

# BOMBAY
## 1953

## 35

Dorothy's prediction turned out to be right. Mary eventually became used to the grim realities of her prescribed profession, the memory of her dispatch from the convent having gradually ceased to cause the sickening anguish she carried with her for so long afterwards. Crossing the mighty Brahmaputra on a ferryboat, she had remained locked away safely in a cabin with her chaperone while all around the decks groaned, crammed with the miserable bodies of the poor fleeing the horrors of the new India as it formed itself around them. She had never seen such wretchedness, nor had she expected to find herself travelling among the hordes of refugees, traversing miles of watery wilderness stretching further than the eye could see. The drone of the boat's dirty engine had fuelled the rocking anxiety of being taken to a place she did not know in preparation for a future that she could not imagine. Endless hours in train compartments trickling slowly southwards revealed her first glimpse of the scale of her country. It had taken her breath away.

By the time she arrived in Bangalore, exhausted, disorientated and impossibly unprepared, the only thought that had kept her from falling apart was the certain knowledge that her sister would be waiting for her.

Only it was not like that at all.

During the preceding two years, Serafina had diligently

made her own mark, choosing her acquaintances carefully, and was nearing the end of her training. If Mary had hoped that she would find protection and companionship with her sister, she was soon to be disappointed. Serafina had plans of her own. She would be leaving Bangalore the moment she qualified to take up a post at the King Edward Memorial Hospital in Bombay, a burgeoning, cosmopolitan city with a great deal more to offer than Bangalore's fabled greenery and glorious gardens. She told Mary in no uncertain terms that she would have to settle in with the rest of the new intake and fend for herself just as she had done. Any onlooker would have thought that Mary's arrival was nothing but an irritation and that Serafina might have preferred to sever all connections with her. But Mary knew better. It was just her way. Instead, Mary had found herself roomed with two other newcomers, Florence and Ruby, both of whom seemed to be just as at sea. They quickly realised that all three of them must have been born of similar circumstances, and that none of them had had much of a say in the matter of their onward paths. Not that it was ever discussed. The subject never raised its shameful head and remained conspicuous by its absence, but everyone understood, such was the nature of these things. Serafina made no pretence of her disapproval of Mary's friends, to the extent that Ruby and Florence were quite glad to see the back of her when she finally left a few months later.

Mary's new life had begun at the Lady Curzon hospital in Bangalore, a sprawling low-slung building with pretty blue latticed porches, occupying a generous plot not far from Blackpully, an old, congested suburb somehow graced by the incongruous presence of the medieval gothic Roman Catholic church of St Mary with its ornate, soaring spire. After just two weeks spent in a constant state of distress, enduring the most menial of tasks meted out by unsmiling matrons and their ill-tempered sisters, Mary had begun to wonder what on earth she had done to deserve such cruel punishment. The routine, untouchable duties of her lowly status made her stomach churn and her lungs ache for the fresh air of the hills. She had considered running away, but could think of nowhere to go.

And so it continued for three long years.

There were times when Mary believed that she simply wouldn't last the course. That she would never be able to survive the constant pain of her complaining feet and the daily assault of gore. The turning point had come on her first day as a student in the operating theatre. Upon the surgeon's incision, the colour had drained from Mary's face, her knees buckling beneath her. She had some vague recollection of a nurse shouting at her to fall backwards, not forwards across the patient, which she duly did. She had come round in the sluice room with a bucket between her knees, and had received no sympathy at all from the bloodied theatre nurse who had been sent out to deal with her. It took Mary a full hour to recover from the trauma, after which she had been given a stark ultimatum: she was to pull her socks up and get on with it or go elsewhere. It was the first time that she had been forced to think about the practical realities of her future. The worry of it kept her awake half the night, and when she did eventually fall asleep, she dreamed that she was a shop girl behind the counter at Anderson & Hall in Calcutta. She was dusting the glass cabinet when a customer approached her and asked to see some white lace handkerchiefs for his daughters. It was her father, but he did not recognise her. She found herself unable to speak except to serve him, then woke up to a dark room, lying in a cold sweat, still filled with the crushing feelings of desperation and shame that had washed over her in the dream. In that moment, she had accepted her fate, and worked like a slave towards the shining clover-leafed pin that now sat proudly above the breast pocket of her uniform.

Terrible events had come to pass over the last six years. No sooner had Mary left Haflong than the troubles had begun to escalate, as the inevitable power struggles gathered momentum and India tore itself apart while pressing to reinstate its identity after years of subjugation. True to his word, the last viceroy had brokered an impossible deal with India's politicians to displace twenty million people, causing untold misery and setting in motion the wheels of catastrophe. In the absence of an agreement for a single, united land, everything was divided in a tragedy of epic proportions. Bitter, divisive fighting gripped Bengal. The Punjab was ripped in half, sending a deluge of refugees flooding into Delhi. Sikhs rampaged. Muslims retaliated. To the east and west there were massacres on the bloodiest scale. Hospitals were overrun with the sick and injured. Hundreds of thousands took to the roads searching for safety, Muslims travelling one way, Sikhs and Hindus the other. Caravans of wretched humanity, stretching for more than a hundred miles in each direction, walked themselves to exhaustion, searching for borders that nobody could find. Whole armies were divided, regiments lined up at the side of the road and told there and then to choose where they wanted to go, India or the Pakistani states. Those wishing to go to Pakistan were sent on their way at once, with no thought to the brotherhood within their ranks or the war they had just fought together, side by side. Two million people died, slaughtered merely because they were in the wrong place. Trains were ambushed and arrived at their destinations filled with nothing but dead bodies. Only the drivers were spared, so that they might bring the train back to tell the tale of their triumphant assailants. Each night, when darkness fell, the horizon filled with the terrible glow of the fires of destruction. Order collapsed. Police deserted their posts and fled. There was rioting everywhere. As is so often the way, it was the women who suffered the most. So that the men might be freed to fight and kill for the glory of their beliefs, and to avoid the shame of rape, their womenfolk were burned. They would be herded into rooms, babes in arms, soaked with kerosene and set ablaze in the name of honour.

## 36

Mary's soft white shoes moved noiselessly along the polished hardwood corridor, the occasional ceiling fans moving sluggishly overhead, their wide propellers lazily sloughing at the thick Bombay air to little or no effect. Her starched uniform had long since become a daily familiarity, its angular handkerchief veil no longer the nuisance it once was during the early days, when she could never get it to stay.

'Nurse!' Mary heard the sharp-tongued bark perfectly well but walked smartly on, head bowed as though too busy to have noticed. '*Nurse!*' This time much louder, followed by striding footsteps. Unable to duck out of the way, Mary slowed to a reluctant halt and turned to take her medicine. 'Did I or did I not tell you to see to Mr Johnson's ablutions this morning?'

'Yes, Matron.'

'So where do you think you're going?'

Mary looked down at the cloth-covered bedpan in her hands. 'To empty this, Matron.'

'Well? What are you standing around here for? Get on with it! And I expect you to be back here to deal with Mr Johnson in less than two minutes. Do I make myself clear?' Matron Kemp removed her spectacles and checked their clarity, flicking her eyes up and down Mary's slender form disapprovingly before placing them back on her nose.

'Yes, Matron.'

Matron Kemp turned abruptly and marched away, leaving Mary smarting as she returned to the duty at hand. Before she could take another step, a faint whisper came from a side room, its door left ajar, inviting the small breeze that wound its way slowly through the corridors, laced with the constant smell of yellow disinfectant.

'Hey! Psst! Nurse!'

The hushed tones belonged to the young ex-army officer still in traction after two torturous months. Mary took a step backwards, craning her head to peer into the room. 'Sounds like the old dragon's got it in for you again today.' He tried to pull himself up a little, grasping the metal handle that hung down from the heavy cord bolted into the ceiling. Mary returned his smile and rolled her eyes. 'Don't take any notice,' he said. 'And if she keeps giving you trouble, you just let me know.'

'Thank you, Colonel Spencer.' Mary couldn't help but flirt a little. Despite the scar that ran the length of his right cheek, still an ugly red welt not yet healed to a less shocking hue, Colonel Spencer was a fine-looking man with more than his fair share of charisma. Mary paused at his door. 'But I can assure you that I'm well used to it.'

'For the hundredth time, it's Eddie,' he said with a wink.

'We like calling you Colonel,' Mary confided. 'It's romantic.'

'What's a nice young girl like you doing in a place like this anyway?'

'I'm not so young.'

'Twenty? Twenty-one?'

'Now, Colonel, you know better than to ask a lady's age. I'm twenty-five.'

'And not yet married off by your family?'

'No fear.'

'Really? Well, that's done it.'

301

'What?'

'If a girl isn't married by the age of twenty-five, she is official-ly on the shelf, which means that you have no choice other than to accept the next proposal that comes along.'

'I'm far too busy looking after the likes of you.' Mary laughed a little.

'And emptying bedpans.' He grimaced at the vessel in her hands.

'It's my profession,' Mary said. 'I can take perfectly good care of myself. What on earth do I need a husband for?'

Mary's cheerful smile belied the brief flurry that stirred her insides. Her innocent childhood pact with Serafina had taken on a certain grim malevolence over the years as she had come to see for herself just how deeply most people's social prejudices ran. She had heard what people said, usually beginning, *girls like those*. That they, and their corrupted parents, were disgraced. That few had a family who would defend their honour. That as a consequence, many were open to easy seduction in the des-perate hope of snaring a doltish man. Behind her uniform Mary could hide herself away, one nurse among many, preserving at least some small sense of self-worth in an unforgiving world that placed such high stock in matters of birth and rank.

'What time do you get off today?'

'And what business is that of yours?'

'I'm bored senseless. Thought you and I might go out and paint the town red tonight. Then I'll ask you to marry me. What do you say?'

'In that case,' Mary said, 'seven o'clock on the dot.'

It was good to see the colonel in cheery spirits today, and she saw no harm in playing along with him. So long as he was still thinking about getting up and out, they were all in with a fighting chance of a successful recovery. It was the ones who lay back and surrendered to their injuries who worried her.

'Good. I'll come and pick you up for dinner at eight, then we'll go dancing and stay out until dawn. Put on your raciest frock.' A sudden surge of pain jolted his face into a tense grimace. Mary's smile disappeared.

'Pain again?' she asked. He was barely able to say yes, and began to lower himself back on to the bed, grappling awkwardly with the support handle. Mary deposited the bedpan on the floor and quickly came to his aid, carefully holding his head, turning and moving the pillows to receive him. 'In your legs?' He nodded sharply. 'How about the lower back?'

The colonel sighed angrily in response. 'This damned thing. I didn't survive a war only to be half killed by a bloody horse.' He stopped, shook his head in despair and leaned back gratefully on the rearranged pillows, thoroughly exhausted by his small efforts.

'You mustn't think like that,' Mary said softly, smoothing his sheets and checking the traction lines. 'Just rest yourself and concentrate on getting well.' Beads of perspiration had appeared on his brow, placed there either through heat or pain, and Mary reached for a cloth to dab them gently from his face. 'Better?'

He closed his eyes and smiled a bitter half-smile.

'All this for the sake of a chukka I was too drunk to play,' he said wearily. 'You should have seen me when I was younger. I used to run cross-country for my college. Fast little bugger I was. There wasn't a single chap who could catch me once that pistol went off. Set a new record and broke it twice myself. I had more cups and medals than you could—' He stopped midsentence and turned away.

Mary looked down at him, watching his face closely, trying to assess the extent of his discomfort. Picking up the charts hooked over the bottom of his bed, she glanced at her watch, calculating, then frowned.

'Has nobody brought you a shot?'

'I told them I didn't want any more.'

'Are you sure?'

'Yes.' He grimaced. 'I was getting to like it too much.'

'All right.' Mary sighed her understanding, took a pen from her breast pocket and wrote a prominent note on his chart, *patient has refused further morphine*, tutting to herself at the previous nurse's oversight. Every dose was supposed to be witnessed and accounted for, whether it was administered or not, in an attempt to frustrate those medical staff who had fallen into the habit of slipping the needle into their own flesh, or indeed pocketing the whole ampoule after injecting the patient with an innocuous saline solution instead. Addiction was rife. Guilty nurses were usually discovered quickly and dismissed, but everybody knew more than a handful of doctors who had been feeding their own cravings for years. The rules, no matter how lax, were rarely applied to them, so long as they didn't go killing their patients or stumbling around the hospital in an opiate-induced stupor.

'Is it easing off a little?' Mary asked, returning to the colonel's side, checking his pulse. He nodded, eyes still closed, refusing to turn towards her. 'Do you want me to send for the doctor?' He shook his head, then reached out a hand. She took it immediately and felt his fingers squeeze hers hard, perhaps to help him endure the pain, perhaps to reassure himself that there were still such things in this world as kindness, love, beauty. The wave took hold of him again, urging him away from consciousness. Mary leaned down and whispered to him softly, 'Try to rest now. I'll come back in a little while to check on you.' She tenderly returned his hand to the cool sheet beside his broken body before taking up the bedpan and quietly leaving the room.

She had not gone more than three paces when the matron appeared in front of her.

'Nurse!' She pointed furiously at the cloth-covered pan. 'Are you still standing around here with that same bedpan?'

Mary looked at the evidence in her hands, and sighed.

Mary slumped miserably on the edge of her bed in the nurses' quarters, soaking her aching feet in a basin of hot water scattered with black mustard seeds.

'You should have tipped the contents of the bedpan over her head,' said Ruby, admiring herself in the mirror. 'That would really have given her something to moan about.'

'Instant dismissal,' Florence declared. 'Thankfully Mary isn't as hot-headed as you.'

'It would have been no less than she deserves. It's a wonder that nobody's done it to her already. I dared to answer her back one day and she put me on the graveyard shift for a whole week.'

'I knew we should never have left Bangalore,' said Florence. 'Now we're having to work twice as hard and live in a space half the size.'

'You didn't have to come,' Mary said. 'And I do wish you'd stop going on as though this is all my fault. You were just as fed up as I was.'

'No I wasn't,' said Florence.

'I was,' Ruby said. 'Bombay is much more exciting than Bangalore and the men here are so much more ...' she thought for a moment, '... cosmopolitan. I shall find myself a rich husband in no time at all. Just you wait and see.'

'A husband? Dressed like that?' Florence looked her up and down. 'The only thing you'll get yourself is a bad name.'

'Oh, here we go again,' Mary sighed. 'Can't you two stop arguing for five minutes? My head is pounding.'

'It was your idea that we should all share,' Ruby said.

'But who is it that makes all the mess?' Florence flicked her hand at the clutter. 'I'm beginning to wonder if the economy was worth it.'

'Then why don't you apply for a single room?' Ruby mumbled. 'You can turn it into your own personal little cloister and live like a nun with nothing on show except a Bible by the bed. The extra cost won't be a problem because you never spend any money anyway, and Mary and I will be free to make as much mess as we like.'

Mary closed her eyes to blot out the bickering. It had seemed like such an exciting plan last summer, that she would up sticks and follow in her sister's footsteps, just as she had always done. She had pined for Serafina awfully, feeling deep down as though a part of her was missing, the only part that felt that it had ever really belonged. Yet before she knew it, her plan had escalated to include all of them, a seemingly natural progression between three friends who had become inseparable with no one else to cling to. Mary had thought that she might share with Serafina, at least until she had learned the lie of the land, but Serafina had rejected the suggestion immediately and said that it was high time Mary learned to stand on her own two feet.

'Had we known there'd barely be enough room to swing a cat we might all have thought twice about it,' Florence said to Ruby pointedly. 'But for now I suggest we make the best of it, and that includes you picking up after yourself.'

Mary looked down at her crumpled toes and wiggled them in the steaming water. 'Just look at the size of my feet,' she moaned. 'I doubt I shall ever be able to get my shoes back on. Maybe I'll pretend to be sick tomorrow. Kemp's on duty again and I don't think I could stand another of her roastings this week.'

'Don't take it personally.' Ruby handed Mary a small towel. 'We're no better than a pack of mongrels as far as she's concerned. Anyway, she despises everyone, except her precious Mr Browning.' Patting the sides of her hair, Ruby gave a small impersonation of Matron Kemp's simpering manner whenever Mr Browning passed on his rounds.

'Ruby!' snapped Florence. 'What have I told you about spreading malicious rumours?'

'Everybody knows it's true!' Ruby said. 'Just because he's married doesn't mean to say they're not—'

'Don't say it!' Florence clapped her hands to her ears. 'I won't hear such vulgarity.'

Ruby threw her arms open and sang aloud, 'They're having a torrid love affair! They tear off each other's uniforms in the sluice room and do it right there among the bedpans, grunting like a pair of old water buffaloes!'

'Stop that this instant!' said Florence. 'That's precisely the kind of talk that starts trouble. We are not to forget ourselves nor our circumstances. There are plenty of unscrupulous men out there eager to prey on a young woman who seems free of the usual family constraints. What on earth would a man think if he were to hear you using such language?'

'You're such a prude,' Ruby said.

'Just because we must work for our living does not mean to say that we are not of good stock.' Florence stamped her foot. 'Were it not for me, I have no doubt that the two of you would have fallen by the wayside long ago.'

## 37

'Do you have any idea what this could do to your reputation? To *my* reputation?' Seated in the far corner of the cheap, clattering restaurant, Serafina seemed to tower over Mary, her astonishing beauty drowning her sister out with its constant, immutable presence. Mary continued to stare into her lime water, refusing to look up. 'You can't just go gallivanting around with any Tom, Dick or Harry, you know. For goodness sake, Mary. Heaven only knows how far things have gone with Ruby. Everybody knows that she likes to go out and have a good time.' Serafina took a deep breath and paused for a few moments, curbing her rising fury. Why Mary had insisted on adopting such undesirables as friends was completely beyond her. 'Don't you realise that by hanging around with these women, women of no pedigree at all, you risk being tarred with the same brush?' It was just too much.

Right from the beginning, Serafina had resolutely refused to share a room in the nurses' quarters, preferring instead to keep her own company and preserve her privacy despite the additional strain on her modest income. This existence was nothing more than a stepping stone. A barely tolerable way to hold body and soul together while she waited for the life she believed she was due. She despised the whole set-up, having to deal with the sick and the injured regardless of how they made her recoil. Being lumped in with these working women. She was not like them, and nor would she have anyone make such a comparison.

'All we did was go to the beach,' said Mary quietly.

'And who exactly was that man you were with?'

'He's a friend of Ruby's.'

'Friend? Huh. What is his name?'

'Clive.'

'Clive what? Where does he live? What does he do?'

'I don't know.'

'I can't believe you'd be so naïve.'

'Ruby said he was a gentleman.'

'Give me strength,' Serafina muttered. 'If Ruby wants to associate herself with men like that, that's her business. What on earth does she think she's doing wearing a bikini, for heaven's sake? Goodness knows how many people saw her. And you! Out with her like that for all and sundry to see!'

'I did tell her it wasn't suitable.' Mary tried hopelessly to defend herself.

'And what is a man supposed to think if a woman goes out on a date with him half naked?' Mary hung her head. 'Men have expectations, Mary. Especially from women who behave like Ruby. You have to stop fraternising with people like that. I won't stand for it, do you hear me?'

Upon her arrival in Bangalore nine years earlier, Serafina had realised immediately that she was not the only one who had been forced into a life of degradation and servitude. It was easy to spot those who had been sent away, out of sight, out of mind. She could tell just by looking at them. These half-breeds. She would have nothing to do with them. She settled a reprimanding glare upon her sister.

'It's bad enough that we ...' She choked on her words, unable to finish the sentence.

'That we what?' Mary finally raised her head, tiring of the

constant criticism. 'Bad enough that we what, Sera?' Serafina remained tight-lipped. 'What is it that you're so ashamed of? Or have you told so many lies that you're having trouble keeping up with yourself? I don't know why you bother to speak to me at all sometimes. All I ever seem to do is annoy you.'

'You know exactly what I'm talking about,' Serafina whispered furiously. 'You have to stop making a spectacle of yourself. And I suppose everybody knows your business?'

'What is that supposed to mean?'

'I doubt that any of your friends would even know the meaning of the word discretion.' The disdain in Serafina's voice scorched Mary's delicate skin. 'For heaven's sake, Mary. How could you be so careless? I swear I just don't know what to do with you sometimes. You had absolutely no business coming to Bombay in the first place, following me around like a stray dog. Why couldn't you have stayed in Bangalore if you wanted to carry on like that? I had everything set up here just nicely, then you had to come bowling along with your ridiculous friends, determined to wreck my life when all I want is to get settled. How dare you draw such attention to yourself? To *us*. If you refuse to behave in a sensible manner for your own sake, then you should at least consider the effect it will have on me. You should be thoroughly ashamed of yourself.'

How heavily these reproaches weighed on Mary's heart. On the rare occasions they met up like this, usually as a direct result of a summons by her sister, it seemed that their talk was always of impropriety and the harsh consequences of Mary's misdeeds. She gave in and answered the question that her sister refused to ask directly, lowering her eyes in submission.

'You don't need to worry about my saying anything. I don't have anyone to tell anyway.' She hoped that this would bring the matter to an end, that they would be able to make up and talk instead of more pleasant things, but Serafina had not yet finished with her.

'Are you deliberately refusing to hear my concerns? Don't you understand that I am the only person who will look out for you? It's not just my future that I'm concerned about. It's yours too. If you don't find a suitable man and settle soon, what do you think will happen? You'll be ruined. Then we'll both be unstuck.'

'I refuse to pretend to be something that I'm not.'

'Don't be an idiot.' Serafina struggled to remove the strain from her voice. 'You remember your promise?' Mary nodded. 'Do you understand why it is so important?' Serafina sighed. 'I'm not going to suffer for the rest of my life as a punishment for a crime I never committed. I have plans for my life. Big plans. And you're not going to spoil them for me.' She wrung her napkin unthinkingly. 'No one is.'

Together they sat in frustrated silence, staring blankly at the table, Mary's face flushed with humiliation, her loyalties torn this way and that. She examined her conscience and reached for Serafina's hand.

'I'm sorry,' she said.

The wind dropped from Serafina's sails. Instead of giving Mary a final telling-off before ordering their lunch, she remained quiet, her eyes still fixed on the same spot.

'Sera?' Mary gave her hand a little shake. 'Is something the matter?'

Serafina slipped her hand from beneath Mary's and reached for her handbag, settling it into her lap and taking out a small enamelled compact to check her reflection. She snapped it quickly shut, returned it to her bag and emerged composed.

'No,' she said. 'There's nothing the matter.'

Mary knew instantly.

'You've met someone.'

'Perhaps I have,' Serafina said coyly.

'Oh, Sera!'

'Shhh!' Serafina cast her eyes around the room.

'I'm sorry,' Mary whispered. 'What's his name?'

'Joseph Carlisle.' Serafina flushed at the very mention of it. 'We met two months ago. It was one of those drinks gatherings to welcome a new arrival from England.'

'Really?' Mary knew none of Serafina's acquaintances outside the hospital, but she engaged with her enthusiastically anyway, imagining her sister's smart set of undisclosed friends.

'It was the usual thing.' Serafina played with her fork. 'Quite boring really, but then I noticed a man looking at me. He was terribly handsome.' Mary began to giggle, having lost none of the silliness that had hallmarked her childhood. 'He couldn't take his eyes off me all evening.'

'So what did you do?'

'I pretended not to notice him, of course, and left early, just as the party was getting into full swing.'

Mary gasped in admiration. 'No!'

'Well what did you expect me to do? Fawn around him like every other woman in the room?' Serafina took a cool sip of her drink. 'I made a few discreet enquiries while I was there, and it would appear that I had caught the eye of one of the most eligible bachelors in Bombay.'

'Oh my goodness!' Mary's eyes widened. 'Why didn't you tell me before?'

'Shhh.' Serafina placed a finger to her lips. 'It would have been inappropriate. I hardly think he would have been very pleased had I started broadcasting his attentions. All in good time.'

Mary's tummy rumbled loudly. 'Can we please hurry up and order some lunch? I didn't have any breakfast this morning and I'm famished.'

They ordered the plate of the day, curried fish with lentils and plain boiled rice.

'He sent me flowers and asked me to have dinner with him.'

'Gosh.' Mary's stomach turned somersaults. 'Where did he take you?'

'Don't be silly! I didn't accept, you ninny. Whatever do you take me for? I sent a note back declining his kind invitation, saying that perhaps we would run into one another again at a future social engagement. So he sent me more flowers, this time with an apology.' She lifted her eyes to Mary in amusement. 'It was quite funny really, and terribly sweet.'

Their lunch arrived in an instant, spooned from the enormous cooking pots bubbling away on the open stove sited in full view of the hungry passing traffic. Mary suppressed her raging appetite while waiting for Serafina to settle her napkin. 'I really mustn't get any marks on this dress,' she said absently. 'I've already gone and accidentally ruined one this week.'

'It's lovely.' Mary admired the flower-print cotton. 'I just don't understand how you manage to dress the way you do on our meagre wages.'

'Good housekeeping,' Serafina replied. 'And a matter of priorities. You like to squander your money on silly holidays and going to the pictures; I prefer to spend mine on clothes.'

'Well just you make sure that you pay your bills.' This time it was Mary's turn to admonish her sister. 'The last time I went to visit Mr Chagdar, he almost threw me out of the shop because of your unpaid account.'

'Do you expect me to walk around in rags?'

'Of course not.' Mary smiled at the notion of Serafina, always immaculate, in rags. 'And stop trying to change the subject. I want to hear more about your Joseph.'

'He's not mine yet, and I would thank you to please keep

this conversation to yourself. I don't expect you or your friends to go gossiping about me behind my back.'

'Cross my heart.'

'I know what they think of me, but I don't care.'

'And whose fault is that? Perhaps if you weren't so judgemental ...' Mary stopped herself before they descended into another fight. 'Oh, don't take any notice. So tell me,' she tapped on the table, 'what happened next?'

'I kept putting him off until he practically begged me to put him out of his misery, so I finally agreed to have lunch with him.'

'Where did he take you?'

'The Taj Mahal Palace.' Serafina smiled proudly.

'Really? Golly. I've always wanted to go there. What was it like?'

'Wonderful.' Serafina sighed. 'In fact, it was a perfect day. You know, his family has very long connections with India. I would imagine he's on just about every wealthy family's list of prospective husbands.'

Mary's movements slowed as she listened. 'I'm assuming he's—'

'British,' Serafina said without looking up from her plate. 'Of course he is.'

'And does he know about ...'

Serafina shot Mary one of her looks. 'I thought we had already discussed my position on that before lunch,' she snapped, her irascible temperament piqued once again.

'But you must have told him something? How can you have been seeing this man without him asking you a single question about your own circumstances?'

'I told him the truth. That our father left India after the war ...' She faltered for a moment. 'And that our mother is dead.'

'What?' Mary gasped. 'She's not dead! How could you say such a terrible thing?'

'Then where is she? And what good has she ever been to us?'

Mary sat in silence, her upset profound, her appetite evaporating as the food in her mouth turned to sand. She could not bear to think of any of it. She lay awake at night sometimes, trying desperately to remember every detail about her mother. A white sari. Always a white sari. But what else? There were times when she could no longer conjure a clear picture of her mother's face, just a brief, hazy vision that clouded and dispersed before she could bring it into focus. She tried to piece it back together, the fragments scattering further apart each time. The more she concentrated, the dimmer the image became, forcing her to dig deeper for the memories before they were lost to her for ever. Sometimes they would come out of nowhere, a small sound, way off in the distance, evocative of a woman's tears. Yes, she would cry so very much. The jingle of tiny silver bells tinkling as she moved in that slow-paced way of hers. The scent of the oil she massaged into her hair. The fragrant spices carried on the air from the cookhouse. Then, the other, darker moments. Pitiful howls of anguish during the long nights. Shouting. Clay pots being hurled and smashed. A broken woman, crouching to her knees, tearing at her hair while she wept.

'Don't you ever wonder what happened to her?' Mary's posture drooped, her sudden sadness all-consuming.

'No,' Serafina said resolutely. 'I don't. And nor do I want to.'

## 38

The sun shone tirelessly in Bombay at this time of year, bringing with it endless excuses for outings and picnics. Mary, Ruby and Florence attended an earlier mass than usual, leaving plenty of time to cross the city and reach the hanging gardens, perched on the rise of Malabar Hill, before the Sunday afternoon crowds arrived and spoiled the tranquillity. The greenery of the park stretched out like a free-breathing lung amid the fog of humanity, the lawns cleverly terraced to cope with the heady incline. Together they climbed the steep paths through the topiaried trees and lush borders, coming to rest at their favourite spot with its far-reaching views across the city to the south, and sat on the close-clipped grass to enjoy the hastily assembled picnic stuffed into Florence's bag – hard-boiled eggs, cold chicken, and a flask of lukewarm tea.

'You can say what you like about the British,' said Mary, picking half-heartedly at a tough piece of chicken, 'but I expect we wouldn't have parks like this had they not come along and taken the place in hand.'

'I'd be careful who hears you say that,' Florence replied. 'The last thing I want is to be lynched by an angry mob while peeling an egg.'

Way off in the distance, white smudges moved slowly on the glittering sea. Mary squinted towards the horizon, thinking about the big ships on their way to harbour, wondering who their passengers were and what they might think of their first glimpse of the Gateway of India. She had always thought it to be something of a white elephant – a monumental archway leading nowhere, serving no purpose at all, built just for show. There was supposed to be a grand, ceremonial road leading from it to the heart of the city, but it had never been built, for lack of money.

'Have you ever thought about leaving India?' she asked.

'Whatever for?' Ruby frowned at the wrinkled drumstick in her hand.

'I don't know.' Mary licked her fingers and searched around for something to wipe them on. 'Don't you ever wonder about what lies over the ocean?' Ruby rolled her eyes at Florence, suspecting that Mary was about to go off into another of her wild daydreams. 'All those Britishers who came over here. It makes me wonder what they were running away from.'

'They weren't running away from anything,' Florence corrected her. 'They flocked to India to fill their pockets and turn us into a nation of slaves.'

'Oh don't start all that again,' said Ruby. 'If I have to listen to one more of your political lectures, I swear I'll choke myself on that egg.'

'Still,' Mary said, 'I can't help but wonder what it's like there. I'd like to go to England and see it for myself some day. You know, just pack my things into a trunk and get on one of those big steamers down at the docks.'

'And what would you do when you got there?' Florence said, the small hint of sarcasm in her voice ready to ridicule Mary's romantic notions. Mary kept her eyes on the distance.

'I have an aunt there,' she said in a small voice. 'Her name is Edith, Edith Macdonald, and I was told that if ever I found myself in England, I was to contact her and let her know of my whereabouts.' Florence's arm halted the chicken midway to her mouth. Ruby flashed her sable eyes at Florence, stunned by Mary's revelation. They never spoke of such things, and had no precedent for the breaking of this cardinal rule. Mary continued to stare out to sea. 'I realise that she may well not wish to have anything to do with me, of course, but there you are. A real, living relative, tied to me by my father's blood. I wonder what she would do if I were to turn up on her doorstep one day?'

Neither Florence nor Ruby attempted to answer.

'I swore never to speak of any of this.' Mary felt something give inside, like the tiny snapping of a dry twig underfoot. Ruby reached for her hand. 'Do you know, the woman I thought to be my aunt turned out to be my father's wife?' Mary's mouth rose into a painful smile. 'Can you imagine that? I was told on the day I left school, and I hadn't had the faintest idea.' The smudges on the horizon softened as her eyes misted. 'I don't even know what happened to my mother. Nobody would tell us anything. She could be dead for all I know, or out there somewhere, lost among countless millions of people.'

The three of them gazed seaward, contemplating their own concealed thoughts for a little while, secrets disturbed by this pebble thrown so casually into their silent millpond. Mary's head bowed, and she stretched her arms around her shoulders as if to hug herself away from an unexpected chill.

Unable to think of anything to say to her, Ruby suddenly sat bolt upright.

'Who wants to go to the pictures?'

'But we're having a picnic!' Florence held up her chicken.

'The chicken's horrible, Florence.' Ruby took the drumstick from Florence's hand and slapped it on to the grease-stained brown paper. 'And the park is for old people and children.' She jumped to her feet. 'Come on! We'll have to hurry or we won't get a seat!'

They held hands and took the downward hill at a giddy pace, finally arriving back in the hustle and bustle where the gardens ended and the busy street surged back into view. Waiting patiently to cross the road, they stood clear of the unpredictable traffic, making way for a big car honking discourteously, impatient to reach its destination, hindered by a pale, wandering cow. There was no mistaking the figure seated in the back. Mary immediately began to shout and wave.

'Look! There's Sera!'

Serafina stared unblinkingly out of the window as the car found a gap in the chaos and moved on.

Ruby sniffed her distaste. 'Hmph. I don't know who she thinks she is. The Maharani of Cooch Behar? She crossed the road to avoid me last Sunday.'

Mary sprang to Serafina's defence. 'Ruby! How could you suggest such a thing? Serafina would never do that.'

'She'll deny it if you ask her, of course, but I know she did. I could tell.'

'She can't have seen you. It's as simple as that.'

'Oh she saw me all right. I think she was worried that I might dare to say hello to her. Heaven forbid that she should be seen passing the time of day with the likes of us.'

'It's a mighty grand car,' said Florence. 'I wonder where she's going?'

Mary wondered too, but kept quiet.


Serafina endured the discomfort of the soaring temperature inside the car and refused the driver's request to remove his hat after her insistence that the windows remain firmly closed for the duration of the short journey. It had taken almost an hour to get her hair just right, even though the girl at the hairdresser's barely seemed to know what she was doing and had to be told, several times over, just how her curl should be set.

To open the window would bring nothing but dust and insects, and Serafina, wearing a dress of the palest cornflower blue, was determined that it must remain spotless despite its impractical- ities. The car slowed to a halt, pulling up to the kerb.

'Not here,' Serafina said firmly. 'Wait until the vehicle in front has moved off, then take the free space directly outside the entrance.'

She waited for the driver to open her door before gracefully stepping out on to the pavement in full view of the hotel's ter- race. Seeing his car arrive, Joseph sprang to his feet, waving at her the moment she alighted, her sudden, dazzling smile directed only at him, despite the attention she drew from all quarters. Joseph took the steps in easy strides, greeting her proudly before guiding her inside. Every head she passed turned to stare. Joseph dismissed the boy standing by to seat them and settled Serafina into the chair himself.

'Hungry, darling?' He placed a small kiss on her cheek before taking his seat.

'Famished,' she breathed, having eaten nothing since lunch- time the previous day, the discipline demanded by her slender waistline far more important to her than her body's need for breakfast or supper.

Joseph motioned to the waiter. 'Two gin slings, and bring us the lunch menu, will you?'

The boy bowed and left. Serafina barely gave him a glance. She never made eye contact with a servant. They were not to be trusted. Joseph took a flat gold case from his inside pocket, flipped it open and offered her a cigarette, waiting patiently while she searched her handbag for the tortoiseshell holder he had given her as a token of his affection shortly after they had first met. She would never dream of putting a cigarette to her lips without one.

'Did you manage to convince the sourpuss about Saturday evening?'

'I'm afraid not,' she said. 'Although I haven't quite given up hope just yet. Perhaps I can find someone to take my shift.' She found what she was looking for and leaned forward to accept the flame he offered her. 'I'm sure that she deliberately puts us on the weekend rota when she knows very well that we'd rather be at the pictures.'

'We're not going to the pictures.' Joseph began to peruse the menu casually, adding nothing more and encouraging a sense of mystery into his playful air. He knew very well that Serafina's curiosity would be burning, but that she would not permit herself to ask. It was a game he never tired of.

'Oh?' Serafina masked her intrigue, picking up her menu and making some pretence of examining each description. 'I wonder what the soup is today?'

'Would you like me to ask the boy?'

'No,' she said. 'I don't think I want it anyway. It's far too hot for soup.'

'The fish looks rather good,' Joseph suggested. 'They brought out a tray of silver pomfret to show the couple over there. Would you like to share one with me?'

'If you like.'

'And perhaps a little asparagus to go with it?'

'Yes. That would be perfect.'

'Good. That's settled, then.'

Joseph waved his menu at the boy, relayed their order, then sat back and relaxed with his cocktail. He hummed a vague tune and allowed his eyes to roam the room as though having forgotten the conversation he had begun with her. Serafina fidgeted slightly, her hand wandering to the napkin folded on the table.

'You're looking particularly lovely today, I must say. That's a very pretty colour.'

'Thank you.' Serafina glanced down at her dress, then looked up at him questioningly. He sipped at his drink a little, then gave in. It would be cruel to keep her waiting too long. She was not a woman to be toyed with.

'I'm taking you to the company dance on Saturday evening.' The immediate drop in Serafina's expression betrayed her alarm instantly. Joseph feigned normality, but allowed a small smile to pass across his handsome face. 'It will probably be dreadfully stuffy, you know how these things are, but I thought you might like to come along and meet a few of the chaps and their wives.' Serafina's insides began to churn. 'And if it's too awful, we can skip off and have a late dinner here instead. Richard Patterson will be there. He's a good chap. It's about time the two of you got acquainted.' He winked at her. 'Wear something wonderful.'

Clothes lay everywhere, draped across every available surface in the cramped single room in the nurses' quarters, hanging from the spartan furniture, strewn across the bed amid piles of mess and the occasional odd shoe. A small mound of shawls gathered on the floor where they had been tried and tossed aside. Serafina stood, breath drawn, clutching on to the back of the chair, utterly panic-stricken.

'Hold still, will you!' Mary struggled to fasten the fiddly row of hooks and eyes.

'I am! Pull it harder or you'll never get them done.'

'I'll be surprised if you're still able to breathe. Shouldn't you wear the blue one instead? What if you go and faint?'

'Don't be so ridiculous.'

'I don't know why you have to have your things made so

tight on the waist. You'll be impossibly uncomfortable and you won't be able to eat a thing.'

'I have absolutely no intention of eating, and it's perfectly comfortable. You just have to set it right once it's on.'

'Lift your arm a little more, I can't get to it.'

'Ouch!'

'I'm sorry.'

'Watch what you're doing!'

As the last of the fastenings were pulled into place, Mary huffed her exhaustion and collapsed dramatically to the bed. Serafina regarded her own reflection in the inadequate mirror, turning side on, approving of the effect that such unforgiving tailoring had on a figure of her splendour. She was uncommonly tall, with the graceful elegance of her father, her tiny middle rising to a full and luscious bosom, her legs, long and athletic, tapering to fine ankles and pretty feet. She raised a perfectly arched eyebrow and seemed satisfied with what she saw.

'This is the one,' she said, twisting this way and that, examining her image. 'I have been saving it for a special occasion.'

'Thank goodness for that. I don't think my fingers could stand any more.'

'What do you think?' Serafina swayed gently from side to side, her many-layered skirts rustling like autumn leaves.

'It's beautiful. Really it is.' Mary marvelled at the raw silk gown with the intricate embroidery curling around its bodice, the honey-cream skin of her sister's bare shoulders accenting the sculptured line of her collarbones, lengthening her neck.

Serafina had spent most of the afternoon at the beauty parlour attached to the big hotel favoured by rich tourists and Westerners. While having her hair dressed in the new style and her nails painted deepest scarlet, she had met an American woman who declared herself to be the wife of an ambassador. She was to attend some grand event at Governor's House that evening and was keen to tell the whole world her business. Striking up a conversation with Serafina, she had asked where she was from, to which Serafina replied that she was merely visiting and had an important engagement of her own to prepare for. This contrived response had the effect of triggering a barrage of questions from the American. Serafina had been evasive, which the lady clearly found rather vexing, but she introduced herself anyway and insisted that Serafina should call upon her should she ever find herself in New York.

If the beauticians had held any suspicions about Serafina, they had not shown it, the natural wave in her hair and faint smattering of freckles across her nose quietly masking any real sense of identity. They would never have guessed that she hailed from the remote hills of the far north, nor that she spent her days walking endless corridors in a white uniform, perfumed with disinfectant.

Serafina leaned towards the mirror and fastened her earrings.

'All these clothes.' Mary gasped at the mess in the room. 'I don't understand how you can have the gall to overspend the way you do, and don't deny it. Mr Chagdar told me to remind you that you still owe him for five new summer dresses. Five! He was very cross. I didn't know quite where to put myself.'

'So? He should be grateful for my custom. He'll be paid eventually, just like he always is.'

'And what am I supposed to do in the meantime? I nearly died of embarrassment.'

'He can wait.' Serafina continued to appreciate herself in the mirror, holding up a succession of shawls to see which one suited best. 'The man's a thief anyway.'

'That's all very well for you to say. You should pay your dues and not expect me to put up with getting a telling-off on your behalf. Don't wear that one. It doesn't look right.'

'Which, then?' Serafina flung the shawl back to the floor and sighed her confusion.

'The green and gold one.' Mary got up from the bed and found it for her, then began to arrange the gilded shawl while Serafina watched on. 'Here. Drape it around your shoulders and let it fall naturally.' She placed the fine silk organza around her sister, just so, and kissed her powdered cheek before answering the gentle tap at the door to find Florence, hovering self-consciously in full uniform, holding a white enamel tray covered with a muslin cloth.

'Drink this,' she said, quickly lifting the cloth aside to reveal two china cups. 'For your nerves.'

Serafina, still fussing with her lipstick, looked at the pair of them in the mirror's reflection.

'What is it?'

'Gin and soda. At least, I think it's soda. We couldn't find any tonic water.' Florence stared down at the cups, the guilt of their contents creeping up on her. 'Not that I condone the drinking of alcohol. And for goodness sake do hurry up! I've been gone from the ward for nearly twenty minutes and Matron's bound to be on the war path.'

Mary took the cups and thrust one at Serafina, who took an uncharacteristically enormous gulp, shuddered at the bitter taste and sat heavily on the edge of the bed. Florence couldn't help but stare at her.

'What a heavenly dress,' she whispered. 'And your hair! You look like a film star.'

Serafina glanced up at her and smiled anxiously. 'Thank you, Florence. And for taking my shift.' In a rare move, she reached out and took Mary's hand. 'Thank you, both of you. I would have been stuck without you.'

'Not a bit of it,' said Florence. 'The more hours I can do, the better. We're all saving up for a holiday. Mary keeps telling us that we should go and see Kashmir before they open up the new tunnel, but I still say it's too dangerous.' She trailed off, seeing that she had lost Serafina's attention almost the moment she had opened her mouth, and dipped back out of the door.

'Thanks, Florence,' Mary began, but Florence had already fled, her fading footsteps dashing along the corridor.

Serafina rose from the bed and stood by the window. The swelling orange sun lowered itself in the hazy sky, hailing the start of another long, balmy evening where the heat of the day refused to give way as darkness fell. Staring out at the evening closing in, Serafina settled herself with a few deep breaths of the city's thick air.

'You do look wonderful,' Mary said quietly.

'Thank you.'

'Is it terribly important, this evening?'

'Yes.'

'Do you ...' Mary wondered if she was prying. 'I mean, are you in love with him?'

At this, Serafina smiled. 'He's the man I'm going to marry.'

'Are you sure? Oh my goodness.' Mary knotted her brow and chewed on her lip. So this was what all the fuss was about. 'Won't that cause difficulties? I mean, does he—'

'Mary, please.' Serafina returned to the mirror and began pulling at the bones in her dress, setting it correctly on her waist. 'Can't you see that I'm in quite enough of a state as it is?'

'I'm sorry. Of course, you must be.'

Mary hushed herself, having already sensed her sister's dark mood. Serafina was withdrawn, pensive, as if plagued by a constant uneasiness. Mary watched her nervous reflection in the mirror and couldn't think of anything to say to make her feel better. She glanced down into the second cup sitting on the tiny side table, picked it up, and quickly swallowed its vile contents in one go.

The company's clubhouse echoed the grand colonial style introduced by the Empire more than a century before, its low-slung gables draping generously from the roof with a wide veranda passing all the way around the outer wall, edged by a shining teak handrail on carved balustrades. A chattering menagerie of women in shimmering dresses and men with starched white collars wandered with drinks in hand among the drifting music that hung on the heavy, perfumed air. They met and greeted each other with confident handshakes and wide smiles, exchanging well-worn pleasantries among themselves, consummately at ease with the luxury of their positions. The sweet scent of evening jasmine blossom clung to every corner of the night, while droves of staff, dressed in formal uniform with golden cockades terribly unsuited to the overbearing heat, aided the spectacle of a dying splendour. A small army of valets rushed around, attending to the steady line of cars waiting to deposit their passengers at the alighting point of the scrubbed pathway set with whitewashed stones, whisking the vehicles out of sight to stand and wait with their drivers until the early hours. There was a certain amount of nudging as a shining American car slid up to the marker posts – a Chrysler, gleaming red, quite clearly recently shipped, that drew admiring glances and whispers of approval. Two valets reached eagerly to open its doors, grinning from ear to ear. From the back seat, Serafina emerged beneath a cloud of emerald silk and gazed up at the sprawling building.

Without warning, she froze, her legs seeming to dissolve from under her as she found herself suddenly caught up in a fleeting memory that hollowed her insides. This aspect. This sprawling elevation. It reminded her of a place she no longer thought of for it tore her heart in two. A big house she once knew so well, with green-tiled gables that spread their shade far beyond the veranda, and two neatly clipped hibiscus hedges guarding either side of the wide steps, and more than a dozen servants who would smile and call her *missybubba*, and, sometimes, music, just like this, from a brass-horned gramophone that sat on top of a polished mahogany stand in a drawing room laid with an enormous tiger-skin rug. It came upon her all at once, a vivid picture of such rich detail that it engulfed her completely. She stood and stared, paralysed by the sleeping memories that stirred within, mesmerised by the sight that glittered before her aching eyes. The voices around her faded into the distance. In that moment she heard only the sound of the whispering wind through the tall silver oaks.

Joseph was by her side, offering his arm. 'Serafina? Are you all right?' The concern in his voice was apparent as he searched her wounded face.

The vision in her head disappeared as quickly as it had come.

'Yes. I'm fine. Really.' She accepted his gesture and allowed him to walk her along the flower-flanked pathway, up the whitewashed steps to the wide entrance, past the low, sweeping bows of the doormen, through the hallway and into an opulent room hung with sparkling chandeliers and filled with glassy chatter. Guests halted and gazed at her as she passed by. Men forgot what they were saying mid-sentence, much to the consternation of their female companions. Sensing her nerves, Joseph murmured soft words of encouragement into her ear.

'Didn't I tell you that you would be the most beautiful woman here? Just be yourself. And for heaven's sake try to relax!' He felt some of her stiffness disappear through the lessened grip on his arm. She nodded and smiled at him.

From the far corner of the room, the company chairman noticed Joseph making his way through the crowd, and prepared his small entourage for the dreadful embarrassment they were about to endure.

'Oh dear,' he breathed indiscreetly. 'I've just spotted Carlisle. I suppose this is where we all have to save our colleague's blushes while he makes a complete fool of himself. I told him outright, "You can do what you bloody well like in your private life, but we don't bring junglies to the clubhouse."' A warm patter of laughter rose from the women, the chairman's wife craning her neck to steal a glimpse but frustrated by the obscured view.

'I'm surprised you agreed to it, Charles,' she said. 'Although from the whispers I've heard, nobody seems to have the slightest idea who she is or where she comes from. I expect she's one of those deluded sorts who tries to pass herself off as a European. I know several young ladies who will be mightily put out if he falls prey to such an unsuitable match. Whatever happened to the days when men like that kept their sordid little peccadilloes to themselves?'

'He didn't give me much choice about it,' the chairman mockingly confided to the group. 'Came marching into my office a week ago and virtually demanded that I break the sporting rules and allow him to bring his floozy with him this evening. Why he can't manage to observe the usual discretion, I really don't know.' Heads nodded their agreement around him. 'When I turned him down, the bloody idiot threatened to resign on the spot! I couldn't quite believe what I was hearing.'

'So I heard.' Richard Patterson rolled the drink in his glass. 'Sounds to me like he's thinking with his trousers.'

'Well he wouldn't be the first, Patterson, would he now? I seem to recall that you've had one or two colourful liaisons yourself, if my memory serves correctly.'

Richard Patterson smiled defiantly through the ripple of laughter. 'Maybe I have. I don't see anything wrong with a man availing himself of a little local culture, but I wouldn't go bragging about it,' he added slyly.

'I'm surprised you don't already know this creature he's taken up with. I thought you and Carlisle were quite the pair around town.'

'We were,' Richard said. 'Then the poor chap suddenly took leave of his senses and refused to play any more. I did try to warn him off as soon as I got wind of it. She's a bit of a difficult character apparently, and something of an ice queen, though quite a looker if the rumours are to be believed. In fact I might have been tempted to have a go there myself had he not gone and pipped me to the post.' He took a long swig of his drink.

'Really, Richard!' said the chairman's wife. 'You men are just too awful!'

The chairman cleared his throat and stood upright, warning his company of Joseph's approach.

'Charles.' Joseph stepped into the gathering and shook the chairman's hand. 'May I present Miss Serafina Macdonald?'

Serafina stood valiant, her eyes locked on the chairman, holding the breath that now felt leaden in her body. Her gaze refused to give way despite what she saw in the stupefied eyes of the man before her. She did not falter, not for one second, and in that moment remembered what it was to feel taller than the trees and braver than a lion. With every shred of her fear well hidden, her indestructible beauty rendered the group all but speechless. Richard Patterson, high colour in his cheeks, offered her his outstretched hand. She lifted hers in graceful acceptance, perfect smile on ruby lips.

'We were just saying,' he placed a kiss on the back of her hand, unable to tear his eyes from her, 'it's about time Joseph stopped keeping you all to himself. Everyone's been dying to meet his mystery woman. Now I understand what all the

fuss was about. Richard Patterson, at your service.' He flashed
Joseph a manly smile while the chairman struggled to contain
his shock and the women just stood and gawped.

## 39

It seemed as though every nurse had deserted her post, as a dozen or more white uniforms crammed into the small office, huddled around the crackling wireless. An intrepid New Zealander, assisted by a single Sherpa, had set foot on the point on earth closest to heaven. The newscaster, quite overcome with the sense of occasion, repeated the report several times over, word for word, his voice occasionally becoming unintelligible in the unreliable pitch and whistle of the tatty radio set. The nurse charged with trying to keep it tuned banged the side sharply each time it lost hold of the signal.

'Can you imagine what it would have been like up there?' one nurse said.

'Cold,' replied another. 'If you've ever seen the high Himalayas, you'd know that a man would have to be out of his mind to even attempt it.'

'What makes someone want to do something so ridiculous?'

'Fame,' said one.

'And typical that the British had to send a team to do it when it's not even their mountain.'

'So that's that,' said Mary. 'There's nothing left in the world to be discovered. Every desert, every ocean, every mountain, done and dusted.'

'Quick!' hissed the nurse on lookout. 'It's Kemp!'

The wireless was silenced in an instant, the light flicked off, and the nurses scattered on silent shoes back to the quiet of their night wards. Mary paused at the door of the colonel's room, listening for his breathing, hoping that she would find it deep and regular, filled with sleep. Instead she saw him lying there, staring restlessly towards the window, where the smile of a new moon split a bright white crescent into the blackened sky.

'Still awake?' she whispered. He looked at her and nodded. She slipped into the room and pulled the door closed behind her. 'Why don't I go and find you a sleeping pill? You need your rest.'

'No thanks,' he said. 'But I'd kill my own mother for a cigarette.'

'Shhh! You're not supposed to smoke in here. Kemp's on duty this evening and you know what she's like with her precious rules.'

'What's she going to do about it, string me up?' He pulled softly at his traction lines with a smile. 'Come on, Nurse Mary. Where's your sense of adventure? Open the window and pass me a smoke. She'll never know it was you. Promise. I won't say a word.'

Mary went back to the door to check the empty corridor before pulling it properly closed. Quietly sliding open the window nearest to his bed, she stuck her head out. 'The stars are shining,' she said, stretching herself out up to her waist, taking a few deep breaths. 'Can you hear that?' In the pools of light that fell from the hospital windows, clouds of insects whirled and fluttered like thick soup. She watched for a while, listening to the song of the night-time, forgetting herself. 'I love the sound of the insects. In the place where I am from, you could hardly get to sleep sometimes for all the noises coming out of the jungle. And the stars were so much brighter than they are here. There were no lights there to interfere with them, of course, and no pollution either. You should go to the north one day, Eddie, if only to see the stars at night. Such a beautiful sight.' She tutted to herself. 'Just dazzling.'

The colonel gazed longingly at Mary, his eyes free to stare for as long as she chose to lean out of his window admiring the moon and stars. Her uniform glowed in the half-light, its white cotton skimming the slight curve of her slender hips, the gentle round of her behind, her hem pulled up by her stretched position just enough to expose the fragility of her legs. She looked as though she would waft up and flutter away if he blew just one breath hard enough.

'Yes,' he said. 'A beautiful sight indeed.'

Mary bobbed her head back into the room. 'In here?' she asked, opening the drawer of his bedside locker. She found him a cigarette and lit it with a match, puffing incompetently and trying not to cough and splutter before handing it to him.

'Thanks.' He smiled, amused by the face she pulled at the bitter taste of the tobacco. 'Will you have one yourself?'

'No thank you.'

'Don't smoke?'

'Of course I do,' Mary said indignantly, making a mental note to buy some and practise while Florence wasn't looking. 'But I'm on duty, so I'm not allowed.'

She took the small kidney bowl from the shelf by the wash-basin and perched herself on the edge of his bed, holding it for him as an ashtray. 'Did you hear the news about the Everest party?'

'Ain't that something?' He drew long and hard, then blew out a plume of smoke and let out a sigh of gratification.

'The things we mere mortals do,' Mary murmured. 'It never ceases to amaze me.' She felt his hand upon her own, and sensed his concern. 'You mustn't worry, Eddie. Mr Browning is the finest of surgeons and his team know exactly what they're doing. They'll have you out of this lot in no time.' She glanced around at the tangle of weights and pulleys. 'I know it's going to be strange and you'll have all the physio to come, but you'll be all right. I just know you will.'

He patted her hand and took another long drag on his cigarette.

'I won't hold you to that,' he said.

'Well you jolly well ought to. You'll be on your way back to England before you can say Jack Robinson.'

'Not if I have anything to do with it.' He flicked his ash into the bowl. 'I have a very cushy number set up with one of the big petrochem firms once I'm out of here. An ex-officer with two dialects tucked under his belt? They almost bit my hand off.' He allowed himself a congratulatory smile. 'I have absolutely no intention of going back to that bloody awful life. Think of England like the food it dishes up – boiled beef with carrots and puddings made out of suet. Trust me, you can't possibly imagine how stodgy the place is.' He puffed away for a while, eyes on the ceiling, thoughts elsewhere. 'Have you ever been?'

'No,' Mary said. 'But I'd like to.'

'Don't bother. It's a miserable, grey country full of miserable, grey people. Take my word for it. You'd hate it. It's no place for an exotic little bird of paradise like you. As for me,' he took another drag, 'wild horses wouldn't get me back there.'

'Well, thank you for that insight, Colonel. Now I'm even more curious than ever.' Mary took the cigarette from his fingers and extinguished it in the kidney bowl before throwing the butt out of the window. She moved around the darkened room, flapping her arms ridiculously in a hopeless attempt to disperse the smoke and get rid of the pungent smell. 'I'll have to leave this open for a while, but I want you to close your eyes now and try to get some rest. And if you're not asleep in half an hour, I'm going to bring you that pill whether you want it or not.'

'Yes, sir.' He gave her a small salute as she crept out and closed the door.

Mary rinsed out the kidney bowl in the sluice room, then washed her hands, humming to herself as the cold water ran over her wrists, cooling her blood. It was hard not to worry about the colonel. Heaven knows she had learned her lesson long ago about becoming emotionally entangled in the uncertainty of her patients' outcomes. His complications had been great, and she had seen far too many unexpected deaths and surprise recoveries to trust her own predictions. She soaped her hands for a second time.

'So this is where you've been hiding.' The door was open in a second. Matron Kemp snatched the towel from her hands. 'And don't think that I don't know what you've been doing. Sneaking off and smoking like a common streetwalker.' Mary reddened, her mouth opening in silent outrage. 'I can smell it on you. Filthy and disgusting. Well you won't get away with it. This time I'm going to report you to the director of nursing. It's a disgrace. That's what it is. Now get back to your ward.'

'Make it a little tighter on the waist.' Serafina scrutinised her reflection as Mr Chagdar pinched the surplus sliver of fabric from the small of her back and pinned it tight.

'I should refuse to do this until you pay your account,' he grumbled.

'I'll pay you some today if you promise me you'll have this one finished by tomorrow.'

'You have the cheek of the devil, Miss Macdonald.'

'And you have more customers than you know what to do with. Everybody asks me who my dressmaker is. Perhaps it is you who should be paying me?' She laughed lightly.

'Is that tight enough?' Mr Chagdar stood back and watched the dress. Serafina moved slightly, breathing deeply.

'Yes,' she said. 'That's much better.'

'All right.' Mr Chagdar shrugged his charmed defeat. 'I'll have it ready for you by twelve o'clock tomorrow, but you must bring me proper payment this time, not an empty promise and a bold smile.'

Outside on the blazing street, behind the dark-green lenses of her sunglasses, Serafina's eyes shone. It was only a matter of time before Joseph offered her a marriage proposal. She was sure of it. He had taken on a more sober manner this last week or so, kissing her hand solemnly while gazing into her eyes, leaving certain sentences unfinished. Content to bide her time, Serafina kept herself to herself and spoke not a word of her suspicions to anyone. It would do no good to tempt fate. She had waited this long, she could wait a little longer. There was only one thing that mattered to her – that when his proposal came, she would be ready for it.

'Miss Macdonald?' Serafina turned towards the voice, the man's outline silhouetted against the bright sun. For a moment she did not recognise him. 'It's me.' He pointed at his chest. 'Richard Patterson. Remember?'

'Of course!' Serafina relaxed. 'With the sun behind you like that ...'

'I know. It's a blinder today, isn't it?'

'Yes.'

'Have you been to see your tailor?'

'How on earth would you ...'

'Spotted you coming out of the shop.' Richard thumbed casually over his shoulder with a warm smile. 'Can I offer you a lift somewhere?'

'Oh! Thank you.' They began to walk together. 'What a coincidence, us running into each other like this. What were you doing here? It's rather out of the way from your neck of the woods, isn't it?'

'I was looking for a bookshop somebody told me about.'

'A bookshop?' Serafina frowned. 'I've never noticed a bookshop around here before. Did you write down the address?'

'Never mind.' He shrugged it off. 'I no doubt misheard and came to the wrong place. Still, look what I stumbled across instead!' His smile broadened. 'In fact, why don't we go and have tea somewhere? Now that the bookshop sortie is off, I suppose I find myself at something of a loose end.' They reached the car, Richard opening the door for her.

'Well,' Serafina said hesitantly as she got in, her careful sense of etiquette ruffled by this unexpected turn. The last thing she wanted was to offend him, yet his wolfish grin had made the suggestion of tea feel somehow improper. Uncomfortable with the idea of accepting his invitation, even though she was free, she said, 'I'm afraid I already have plans for the afternoon. Perhaps I should . . .'

'Nonsense!' Richard insisted, shutting the door on her before getting in himself. 'We may not be running the country any more, but teatime is sacrosanct to the British way of life and I simply won't take no for an answer.' He turned the engine over. 'I'll have you back in an hour. Scout's honour.'

'All right.' Serafina submitted to her seat.

'So,' Richard said after a while, 'it looks like you have the great Joseph Carlisle utterly smitten.' Serafina smiled demurely. 'Can't say I blame him. Tell you what, why don't we take a little detour since we're out and about? They're finishing some new houses for the company not far from Malabar Hill. We could go and have a look if you like. I expect the company wives will be fighting each other over them tooth and nail.'

'Well I don't . . .'

'Oh come on!' he chided her. 'Aren't you even a little bit curious to see?'

'All right.' Serafina smiled. 'Why not?'

During their leisurely drives around the manicured neighbourhoods of the rich, Joseph had frequently pointed out the grace-and-favour houses, occupying generous plots, immaculately presented with well-kept lawns, that served to sweeten the high company positions. Serafina couldn't wait for the day she became mistress of such a household, taking her rightful place beside a husband of high regard. She would be the envy of all her neighbours. The wife every other woman wanted to be.

The car soon found its way to a quiet residential district, the new houses cordoned off behind high walls, Serafina barely noticing as they drove through open gates, the car pulling to a halt beside a seemingly deserted house.

'Want to take a look inside?' Richard switched the engine off and got out of the car, Serafina following as he strolled casually to the door.

'Is it open?'

'Don't worry.' He produced a key from his pocket and gave her a conspiratorial smile before unlocking the door and pushing it wide.

'Are you sure it's all right for us to be here?' Serafina stepped in tentatively, a small gasp escaping her lips as her eyes came to rest on the grand interior, not quite finished.

'Of course!' Richard encouraged her. 'In fact, I should come right out and confess that I'm tempted to nab this one for myself. Quite a place, isn't it?'

'Where are the workmen?'

'Finished for the afternoon,' he said. 'They'll be back later this evening once it's cooled down.'

'Gosh.' Serafina wandered into the main salon, noting the

floor-to-ceiling cream silk damask curtains, some furniture still in packing cases.

'I expect Joseph would have been earmarked for one of these, especially if he was about to take a wife.'

Serafina felt herself seduced by the splendour of her surroundings, a smile rising on her lips. This was what she had been waiting for her whole life. She ran the tip of her finger along the deep shine of a cherrywood table and wondered if its glaringly bright finish wasn't just a little too showy for a woman of her taste.

'It's a shame about his career, though. I say that a man should be able to follow his heart and marry whomever he likes, don't you?'

'I'm sorry?' Serafina turned sharply.

'The company.' Richard lit a cigarette. 'They can get a bit sniffy about their senior men taking up with, shall we say, unsuitable wives.'

Serafina felt herself stiffen.

'I beg your pardon?'

'If a man like Joseph expects to marry a girl like you, he will have to take it up with the board and get their permission, otherwise there'll be all hell to pay.' Serafina's eyes widened at this surprise humiliation. 'Now, now,' Richard said softly. 'You're a big girl. There's no need to take offence. Let's not pretend, shall we? After all, we're all friends. There are a thousand men like that who used to be thought of as having great potential, yet ended up pushing pieces of paper around in windowless offices. Still. Who needs a place like this? Love conquers all, eh?' Serafina felt a sudden hotness in her cheeks. 'I'm sorry, has he not discussed any of this with you?'

'I . . .' Serafina floundered. 'No.'

'Mmm,' Richard said thoughtfully. 'So he hasn't proposed to you, then?'

'That's really none of your business.'

'I see.' He paused. 'Perhaps they headed him off at the pass and he's changed his mind. Looks like I've gone and let the cat out of the bag, doesn't it?'

'I'd like to go back now.' Serafina fought to calm herself.

'He's a stickler for rules, our chairman. Likes to do things the old-fashioned way.' Richard moved towards her, coming close, reaching for the ashtray on the table. 'Mind you, under the right circumstances, I've known him to be persuaded once or twice. I suppose that's one of the benefits of being related.' Serafina held her breath. 'Without his blessing, Joseph wouldn't have a hope in hell of progressing the way he ought to. Pity. He's a valuable man.'

'Richard, I really don't think you should be speaking to me like this. I'm not comfortable with ...'

He stubbed out his cigarette.

'What if I were to tell you that I could straighten all this out for you with a few choice words to the right people?' He smiled, touching her arm. 'Assuming, of course, that I get a little something in exchange?'

'I'm leaving.' Serafina turned away and headed smartly for the door. Richard was fast on his feet, catching her by the hand, wrenching her back.

'What's your hurry?'

'Get away from me!' She snatched her hand away, breaking into a run, just for the second until he caught up with her, his arm around her waist, hand clamped to her mouth.

'There's nobody here,' he whispered in her ear. 'Nobody here except you and me.' Serafina crushed her eyes closed and fought to free herself, kicking out wildly, her delicate shoes flying from her feet as he picked her up and hauled her into the ghostly, sun-drenched parlour. 'There's no point in fighting. Besides, it's not as though I'm asking you to give up anything you haven't already passed around, is it?' She felt his clammy breath on her neck, his lips, his tongue. She squirmed her head away, her skin shrinking as she heard him inhale her perfumed hair. At last he took his hand from her mouth, fumbling his clothes, releasing her screams. 'Shhh!' He grasped at her breasts, pushing her against the table, pressing her face to its shining surface, bearing his weight down upon her. 'Careful now.' She felt her skirts lifted, her thighs exposed. 'We wouldn't want to spoil this dress now, would we?'

Mirrored in the expensive, polished wood, Serafina saw the grotesque reflection of his face, and shut her eyes.

## 40

Serafina squatted in a basin of hot water, yellowed with sting-ing disinfectant, head resting on her knees, the trickle running from the tap spattering loudly against the wet bathroom floor. She held the jug under the leaky tap until it overflowed, lifted it over her head and poured, the water slicking down her skin.

She shivered, deep, groaning convulsions that made her hairs stand on end, tightening her scalp, releasing their grip only when she clenched her fists and breathed hard until she was light-headed.

*It didn't happen.*

*It couldn't have happened.*

She filled the jug again. Dipped her head. Poured the water over, her hair sheeting a black veil across her face.

*I got in the car with him.*

*I got in the car with him and let him take me to a house, alone, in the middle of an ordinary afternoon.*

The shiver took hold, Serafina's shining nakedness shud-dering hard. She tightened her grip on her knees. Pulled in her breath, fast and deep.

*Nobody knew where I was.*

*Nobody knew where I was or who I was with.*

*And I went with him in his car to a house and nobody was there except us. And he ... And he ...*

*And he ...*

She retched again, her empty stomach wrung out, the soap she had swallowed burning inside. The tap juddered, water sputtering in angry, intermittent bursts. She struck the tap hard with her fist, bruising her hand, the warmth of her silent tears dissipating into the cold water on her face.

*There is nothing I can do.*

*If I speak, I will be ruined.*

She curled herself into a tight ball, gripping her hands to her shivering sides, oblivious to the ambient heat, then strained downwards as hard as she could, purging him from her depths.

*I could kill him.*

*I could take a knife and cut his throat and watch him bleed to death like a goat slaughtered on the roadside.*

*How could he? How dare he?*

Serafina stood, the water cascading down her mute, unmarked body, pooling around her perfect feet. She reached for a towel and pressed it to her face.

*There is nothing I can do.*

She wept into the towel, pushing it into her mouth to stifle her cries of lament.

*It didn't happen.*

## 41

Dorothy clutched the truck's jolting steering wheel, bracing herself as the vehicle pitched and rolled. The Ford Pilot had been thrust upon them some while ago by a distant neighbour who had disconsolately sold up and gone back to Australia before he lost his shirt. Although solidly made by British hands and equipped with a monstrous American engine, the body of the stunted pick-up was scarcely more than four feet long and ridiculously low-slung, rendering it totally unusable for bush work. Dorothy ground down a gear, navigating a deep pothole that seemed to have doubled in size in the last fortnight. The previous season's rains had made a mess of the three miles of gravel road that linked Nalla Farm with the Tarmac highway, and they had all but given up with the soul-destroying annual ritual of trying to repair it. The scant labour they managed to retain was hard pushed enough trying to maintain the fragile crops and coaxing the thin livestock through the harsh, drought-ridden summers.

Dorothy slowed as she neared the house, pulling up on the wide, cracked patch of ground she had once tried to cultivate in an attempt to create something resembling a garden. It was no wonder the native workers had looked at her as though she were mad. She brought the truck to a shuddering halt in the shelter of the one partially shady spot beneath the two thorn trees, wrenching on the handbrake, releasing a cloud of dust into the dry air. She jumped out, slapping the dirt from her trousers, her boots hitting the ground with a soft, deadened crunch, and took a moment to shield her eyes and look up at the sky through the scant branches. It was going to be another hot one, the heat haze already bleaching the horizon to a shimmering mirage. Dorothy walked around the vehicle, opened the passenger door and pulled the box from the seat, casually checking the contents over as she called hello and swung the door shut. Instead of the usual barrage of barking, her greeting was met with silence.

Balancing the box under one arm, she grappled with the tall gate set into the high chicken-wire fence. The catch was prone to be temperamental, but it gave her no trouble today. Although undeniably ugly, the fence had been relatively successful in barring the smaller scavengers from the house, but wouldn't have been much use if something bigger came along and decided to take a look around. So long as it kept the dogs in and the impalas out, Dorothy was satisfied.

'James!' she called again. 'I picked up our mail from the station!' His seat on the veranda was empty, the dogs gone. Dorothy wandered into the house, the insect screen clattering sharply behind her. 'James?'

'He no here, missus,' Kapo said without looking up, bending past her, sweeping the dust messily out of the door on to the veranda.

'Oh.' Dorothy deposited the box on the table and stretched the stiffness of the road from her back. 'Did he say where he was going?'

'The farmers' meeting, missus.'

'Has he gone already?' Dorothy clucked at her forgetfulness. She had meant to be back in time, but then she had stopped in on the nearby kraal to check on the worker who had burned himself badly while tackling one of the bush fires that had broken out a week ago. Of course, a string of villagers had appeared out of nowhere, as though they had known she was coming, bringing their ailments with them, most of which were made up just for the excuse of seeing the white woman doctor, while the children gathered round, laughing and staring at her, touching her clothes then running away. She had become used to working under the close scrutiny of an audience, and had once ended up spending several hours waiting patiently while everyone took turns listening to their own heartbeats with her stethoscope, eyes wide with amazement.

There were those on the neighbouring farms who were speechless when they heard about Dorothy's close contact with the native workers and her misplaced concern for their welfare. For a white woman to touch black skin was, as far as they were concerned, about as shocking a thing as they could imagine. Western medicine was for the whites, and the natives should be left to their own ways and nostrums, regardless of how ineffectual they were. Not that Dorothy cared for her neighbours particularly. She had found little to draw her to the company of the other farmers' wives, all of whom had either been born here or had lived here long enough to have adopted a sense of rightful superiority over the natives, speaking of them with open distaste. It made Dorothy's skin crawl to hear some of their comments, although she had seen with her own eyes just how difficult the native workers could be. It was no wonder, she thought, if this was the way they had always been treated. Still, it was not her concern. She had sworn, when she was still a young woman, to practise her art to the best of her ability. There had been nothing in the Hippocratic oath about the colour of a person's skin. And if her neighbours didn't like it, well that was too bad. It didn't stop them from calling on her services when it suited them.

Dorothy glanced at her wristwatch and wished that she had

been more vigilant. She should have made sure to be home in good time and gone with James. He hadn't asked her to, but she felt she should have done all the same, given the general state of things.

'There's been trouble on the Jannsen farm, missus,' Kapo said. 'Elephants been raiding them crops and take all the mealies.' Dorothy closed her eyes in exasperation and suppressed a sigh. 'Nashe say they make big mess.'

'I'll bet,' she muttered, and started unpacking the box – a newspaper, various medical supplies she had sent for which had taken an age to arrive, a few provisions, a scant handful of mail. She looked at the blue aerogramme, neatly glued at the edges, postmarked from Bombay.

'You want coffee, missus?' Dorothy stared at the letter. 'Missus?'

'What?'

'You want coffee?'

'No thank you, Kapo.' She put it down with the rest of the things. 'I'll have some tea in a little while, once I've cleaned up a bit.'

'The road is bad, missus.'

'Yes. It is rather.'

Kapo hung around, his broom idle.

'Boss teach Kapo to drive, missus. Then Kapo go to station for you.'

'We'll manage,' Dorothy said diplomatically. If he ever learned to drive a car, she had no doubt that Kapo would help himself to the keys and disappear as soon as look at her. She had been tempted to get rid of him more than once, but knew that the next boy would be no improvement, and might well turn out to be a whole lot worse. Better the devil you know, she had remarked to James when they discovered Kapo had been pilfering from the pantry again. James had said ruefully that he would gladly have given half the farm to have Shiva by his side.

'You bring things from the store?' Kapo tried to peer at the supplies laid out on the table.

'Nothing of any interest to you, Kapo,' Dorothy said lightly. 'Did boss say when he would be back?'

'No, missus.'

'All right, Kapo. And don't clean the rug like that. Take it outside and give it a good beating, only please make sure that you take it properly outside this time, and close the doors and windows first.'

'Yes, missus.'

Dorothy hung her shirt on the back of the bathroom door, filled the sink and drenched the flannel. Leaning forward, she pressed it to her face for a while, the water running down her arms, dripping from the points of her sharp elbows to the slats of wood on the floor. She passed the cloth around her neck, her skin breathing with relief as the parched dust came away. She rinsed it through again and rubbed it over her face, standing as she did so, tilting the shaving mirror to catch her reflection, pausing as she wiped away the last of the dirt, leaning in to inspect her unruly eyebrows. She frowned at herself closely and wondered where her tweezers were. She had used them the other day to remove a couple of stitches from a patient, then promptly mislaid them. Never mind. They would probably turn up eventually, although things like that did have a habit of going missing if she turned her back for one moment.

She peered again at the face in the mirror and, instead of reaching for the towel, found herself tracing the faint lines that had settled on her darkened complexion in recent years. Her whole body was much slighter than it had been in her youth, her waistline having shed the evidence of her previous privileged life within months of their arrival in Africa. She didn't mind. It wouldn't do to attend to the sick and malnourished looking like a fattened calf. Any curves that had once been hers had long gone, not that she had noticed at the time. That was the way of gradual changes. They crept along like silent shadows and before you knew it, everything had altered, and nobody seemed to realise. It was only when she had taken the scissors to her hair and James had commented that she looked like a boy, that she had realised the full extent of her accidental transformation. She regretted the haircut for a while after that and let it grow back, but not so much that it flew into her face as it used to when she was driving the truck. It was turning grey anyway.

Dorothy leaned towards the mirror, following the creases in her skin that ran from her nose to the corners of her mouth. The crow's feet around her eyes, highlighted white where she squinted against the sun, seemed more prominent than ever. Perhaps they would diminish in the winter, she thought, although she knew better. Towelling her hands dry, she slipped a fresh shirt on and considered for a moment whether she shouldn't go back to wearing a little make-up, if only to preserve the illusion of a once fair face for a little longer. A sigh rose on her lips, and lifted silently away.

James let himself in through the gate, the dogs an excitable tangle around his legs. He banished them to their kennel with a commanding word and a click of his fingers, then made his way to the house, his heavy gait slowed by the devouring heat. By the time he reached the door, Dorothy had it open for him. She kissed him hello, then, unable to wait a moment longer, 'Serafina's getting married,' she said. 'There was a letter waiting for us at the post office. I'm so sorry I missed you. I really wanted to come to the meeting with you.'

James sat down, pulling off his hat. 'What does she say?'

'It was from Mary,' Dorothy said. James nodded. Of course it was from Mary. 'His name's Joseph Carlisle. Mary writes very highly of him. Says he's a lovely man and that Serafina is very happy.'

'That's good.'

'The wedding has been set for the twenty-fourth of next month.' James seemed to glaze over. 'In Bombay. Here.' Dorothy offered him the letter. James took it from her, glancing over Mary's familiar writing, then stood up and went to the sideboard where the drinks were kept locked up, the letter limp in his hand. He reached for the whisky and poured himself a short measure, sipping a while, staring out of the window to where the dogs lay napping in the yard, the three of them curled up on the scrubby ground in what few patches of shade they could find.

'I think Jess might be going blind,' said James. 'She's been bumping into things.'

'I know,' Dorothy said. 'She's old. She'll be all right so long as we don't go moving too many things around.'

'Maybe we should have her put to sleep.'

Dorothy looked at him, surprised.

'I don't think she's in any pain,' she said. 'I had a good look at her yesterday and gave her a bit of cod liver oil for her joints.'

'She's been a good dog,' said James with bleak resignation. 'She was like my shadow for years. Remember how she used to follow me around?'

'Yes.' Dorothy got up and came to the window, standing beside him, just close enough. 'We could go if you wanted to.' She touched the hand in which he held the letter still.

'We can't leave this place,' he said. 'Not now. There's too much at stake.'

'Just for a visit,' Dorothy said. 'We could find a way. Ask one of our neighbours to keep an eye on the farm for us, just for a few weeks.' He silenced her with the merest touch of his hand. 'I know,' Dorothy conceded. 'I just thought you might want to . . .' She trailed off.

'Like it or not, we belong here now,' James said. 'Although why I chose to pick here of all places is beyond me sometimes. It's a fool's game. You would have thought I might have learned my lesson after watching what happened in India.' He drank some more of the whisky. 'Maybe it won't be so bad.'

'Was there much talk at the farmers' meeting?'

'Of course.' James threw back the rest of his drink and put the glass down heavily. One of the dogs stirred, then got up, shaking the dust from its coat, stretching its front legs, bowing to the ground. 'It's the same old thing.' He opened the door to the veranda and let out a whistle. The dogs jerked towards his voice, the younger two ripping themselves out of the dirt and bounding to the house, while Jess creaked to her feet and ambled after them. James went outside and dropped to his haunches on the porch, fussing them roughly as they ran into him.

'The Fitzpatricks are hauling out,' he called over his shoulder. 'Old Johannes Rademeyer made him an offer for the land and the man fair bit his hand off. I was thinking, we might pick up a few of his cattle.' A rare curl of breeze through the open door flipped the letter up from the surface where it had been left. Dorothy caught it, folded it in two and watched James's unease. 'All right, boys,' he grumbled in a low voice, pushing the dogs away, making room for the unsteady Labrador loping to his side. 'Come on, old girl,' he said, brushing the dust from her yellow coat. 'Who's a good girl?' He rubbed her ears affectionately, Jess panting heavily, as though the weight of her own head had become too much for her in the heat. 'You going blind?' He knelt down and hugged the animal, rubbing his face in her fur. 'Are you?' He pulled back and held her head. 'Let's have a look at you, eh?' He peered into the milky eyes, then shouted, 'Don't you have anything you can give her?'

'James?'

'What?' he said, scrutinising Jess's face.

'Didn't you want to read Mary's letter?'

'Later.' He kissed his dog's head. 'I'll read it later.'

Dorothy hunched close to the paper, writing by the fey, flickering light of a single storm lamp. The electricity was out again and nobody had fixed the generator. James had promised to see to it first thing this morning, but he must have forgotten about it, so now he was out there with two of the men, doing the best they could in the dark. Dorothy removed her spectacles and pinched the bridge of her nose, rubbing gently with her fingers, feeling the indentations pressed into her skin. Her eyes were tired, dried out by the landscape. She pulled the short shawl up around her shoulders against the chill of the evening, put her glasses down and leaned back on the wooden chair, stretching her neck, her reflection thrown back at her from the black window. Jess moved at her feet, just a small spasm, as if dreaming. Careful not to disturb her, Dorothy got up and tiptoed away, letting herself out on to the veranda, closing the door softly behind her. In the near distance, she could hear the men working, the steady drone of voices, the soft, faint glow of the storm lamps seeping from the small wooden hut that housed the generator.

'Africa,' she murmured to herself, flicking the word open with her tongue. For all its beauty, what a desolate place this could be, like a self-imposed isolation, the distances from one place to another far too great to allow her to cling to any sense of civilisation as she had once defined it. At night, it felt like a vast expanse of nothingness, the outline of the veld sinking into a blackness so dense that it defied comprehension, like infinity itself. A noise came from the darkness beyond the chicken-wire fence, the deep-throated groan of a distant animal. Dorothy lifted her face to the sky above, thick with stars, the night air layered with the rare essences of this vast continent. She breathed deeply for a while, insects picking at her sweet, unprotected skin. All at once, a stiff judder came from the generator hut, a triumphant cry sailing into the darkness as the engine thumped into action and the lights in the house glowed back to life. Dorothy smiled to herself, returned to the room they laughingly referred to as the parlour, and sat at the writing bureau, running through the letter she had somehow penned in the dark before signing herself off.

'Better?' The door clattered closed.

'Thank goodness at least one of us knows what they're doing.'

'We really ought to get a new one,' James said. 'Or at least a decent selection of working parts. I'll go into Buluwayo and have a word with Tinker to see what he can rustle up.'

'Darling?' Dorothy held up the aerogramme apologetically. 'I left the last two folds blank for you to write something.'

'Oh.' He nodded, then held up his oily hands by way of explanation. 'Bit of a mess,' he said. 'It'll take me days to get this lot off.'

'Just a few words,' Dorothy urged him gently. 'It would mean a great deal.'

'Next time.' James wiped his hands on the rag hanging from his pocket and turned to leave. 'You finish it for me. You'll know what to say.'

## 42

'A transfer?' Joseph held the flame steady for Serafina's cigarette. 'Whatever for?'

'Aren't you a little tired of Bombay?' Serafina sighed, lifting her cigarette away with a casual puff.

'I hadn't really thought about it,' Joseph said.

'Don't you think it might be nice to have a change? For us to start off as a married couple somewhere new?'

'Ah.' Joseph smiled. 'Worried about running into jealous old girlfriends, are you?'

'Not at all,' Serafina said, circling the diamond around her finger.

'Or wanting to dismantle my bachelor lifestyle now that you've decided to make an honest man of me? I hear that some men are never seen or heard of again,' he joked with her. 'Are you drawing up a list of my most undesirable friends?'

'Perhaps.' Serafina's insides tightened, the parasite of that man eating into her flesh. She could feel it, taste it, smell it, like a bitter river of poison coursing through her veins. The sickness stirred within her again. She made certain to smile. 'Can you blame me for wanting to keep you all to myself once we're married? We'll make wonderful new friends together. Married friends,' she added with a deliberate hint of mischief, although the brightness she attempted felt brittle. It was all she could do to look him in the eye, the fear of what he might see setting her into a panic so deep that it shredded her insides.

The waiter came with fresh drinks and cleared their glasses away.

'Darling?' Joseph said. 'Are you feeling quite all right? You've hardly touched your drink.'

'Don't take too much notice of me,' Serafina replied, casting off the wave of nausea and employing her most charming smile. 'Every woman is allowed to feel a little nervous before her big day. It's perfectly natural.'

'Shall we order something to eat?' Joseph suggested. 'I know these slim waists are all the rage, but you seem to be disappearing before my very eyes! It's no wonder you're feeling skittish. Here.' He pushed her glass towards her. 'This will make you feel better.'

'Thank you,' Serafina said, her stomach turning at the very thought of it. She picked it up and took a good long sip under his watchful eye, murmuring her appreciation. 'So, you'll think about the move?' she persisted.

'I suppose I could have a little word.' Joseph picked up his gin and tonic. 'They've been crying out to get some new blood up in the Chittagong office, from what I hear, but I'm not sure how you'd feel about it, though. The climate's rather unpredictable and there's still a bit of uproar going on with the Pakistani states. These things take a while to bed in, I suppose.'

'There, you see?' Serafina said, decisively. 'You're exactly the kind of person they would need. The very best of their crop. They would fall at your feet with gratitude if you so much as mentioned your interest.'

'Perhaps you're right.' Joseph considered it for a while. 'And I have no doubt that they'd be very generous.'

'I think it would be a wonderful opportunity for you.'

'Well, well.' Joseph raised a thick, curious eyebrow. 'You're full of surprises today. What about Mary?'

'What about her?'

'Wouldn't you miss her if we were all that way away?'

'Don't be silly! We're well used to being apart. She can't go clinging to my apron strings for ever, can she? Besides, I want you and I to build a life of our own together, just the way we planned.' Her hand slid to his, playing with his fingers.

'If that's what you really want, darling.'

'Yes,' she said. 'It is.'

Mary returned from her night shift, eyes gritty with fatigue, to find Serafina waiting for her outside her quarters, pacing the path, smoking a cigarette. She looked tired and drawn, thinned out already by the heat of the morning sun.

'Where have you been?' Serafina threw the cigarette to the ground. 'I've been waiting here for an eternity.' With her faculties dulled by exhaustion, Mary just stared at her, wondering what she had done wrong this time, bracing herself for the rebuke. 'You have to come with me right now.'

Yearning for her bed, Mary obediently followed Serafina to her room.

'Can't this wait?' She flagged on the chair and stifled a yawn. 'I've been run off my feet all night.'

'No.' Serafina closed the door quietly and leaned against it, her palms damp against the metal handle. Now that the moment was upon her, she felt herself numbed, her body no longer her own, her voice drifting in from elsewhere, hollow and unfamiliar. 'Mary,' she said. 'I'm pregnant.'

Mary flew up from the chair, sending it crashing to the floor. '*What?*' Serafina peeled herself from the door and slumped to the bed, dropping her head into her hands. 'I mean, are you sure?' Mary pressed her palms to her cheeks. It was impossible. Unthinkable. Serafina would never be that stupid.

'Yes. I'm sure.'

'And is it—'

'Mary, please. I can't think straight.'

'Oh, Sera!' Mary sat beside her, her thoughts charging at a hundred miles an hour. 'Does Joseph know?'

'No.'

'Why ever not?' Mary leaped up. 'You have to tell him! You have to get married straight away!'

'I can't.'

'What do you mean, you can't? Don't be so ridiculous! You must tell him at once, before you start to show.'

'Mary!' Serafina shouted, tears springing to her eyes. 'I can't! Don't you understand?' She screwed up her face. 'I have to get rid of it!'

Mary froze, Serafina's expression unlike any she had seen before, halting her breath. 'Oh my God.' Her hand came slowly to her mouth. 'Oh my God, Sera. What have you done?'

## 43

'Bangalore?' Florence looked up from her newspaper. 'Why on earth would you want to go back to Bangalore? I seem to recall that you couldn't wait to leave the place.'

'It was Serafina's suggestion. She thought it would be nice for us to take a little break together.'

Mary was not a natural liar. It didn't come easily to her and she felt certain that her face would give her away. She occupied her guilty hands, rearranging the clean uniform pinned over the wardrobe door, her stomach lurching beneath the unease that had gnawed at her bones for three torturous days.

'Really?' Florence said, quite perplexed. 'I thought she was far too busy playing all high and mighty to bother with you.' Mary battled with her conscience, desperate to unburden herself of this terrible weight. 'I never wanted to leave Bangalore in the first place,' Florence sighed, setting the newspaper down on the bed. 'It was you who wanted to go running off to Bombay. I could quite happily have stayed on for ever. It's so beautiful there. All the gardens and the flowers everywhere. Sometimes I yearn to go back. It's so noisy and dirty here. Too many people by far. Do you remember that tiny house we used to share?' Mary nodded. 'And the little shoe man on the corner?'

'Yes! My goodness, I had forgotten all about him.'

'Was there nothing that he couldn't fix?'

Mary smiled fondly at the memory of the tiny man who

would sit cross-legged with his tools laid out neatly on a coir mat set beneath his makeshift shelter on the corner of their tree-lined street, mending all manner of things with worn straps and loose buckles while they were struggling along on their student allowances. 'And if he wasn't happy with the repair, he would make you a new one!'

'I have a wonderful idea!' Florence suddenly announced. 'Why don't I come along with you? We can go and see who's still working at the nursing home. I wonder if Father Ignatius is still chaplain there? Can you imagine how surprised everyone would be to see us?' Overwhelmed by her own enthusiasm, Florence bounced excitedly on her bed.

'Oh!' Mary had been rather more convincing than she had intended. 'I'm not sure that Serafina wanted us to turn it into a group visit.'

'A group visit? The three of us? Don't be so silly.'

'I really think it would be better if you and I were to go another time. You know how Serafina can be when her plans are interfered with.'

'I see.' The offence in Florence's voice was not easily hidden. 'So it's nothing to do with my company not being good enough for her, I suppose?'

Mary sat beside her and searched for a plausible reason to keep her in Bombay. 'Not at all. I know that she can be a bit stand-offish, but she really doesn't mean anything by it. It's just her way. Besides, don't you see that somebody has to stay behind and make sure that Ruby keeps out of trouble? Can you imagine what might happen if she were left to her own devices?'

'Goodness me,' Florence said. 'I hadn't thought of that.'

That evening, threading their way nervously through the busy streets, passing the musty, humid smell from the crowded bazaar, Mary drank in the seedy surroundings while Serafina kept her eyes straight ahead. They were unlikely to be recognised in this district, teeming as it was with the kind of street life that grew on a burgeoning city like mould in an unwashed jar. Serafina reached in her handbag for a handkerchief and put it to her nose against the dank smell that hung on the air. Had they walked a little further, they would have found themselves rubbing against the darker side of Bombay, where women with garishly painted faces lurked in doorways, beckoning any man who looked as though he might have money in his pocket to exchange for a few moments of pleasure.

'This way,' Serafina said, turning into a crammed alleyway. A few yards along, she ducked into a shoddy open-fronted tea room, Mary following her to a corner table where a woman sat waiting for them. They were barely able to hear themselves speak for the cacophony spilling in – brash music from distorted radios, the shouts of tradesmen, a distant, songful call from the minaret of a nearby mosque.

Faded film posters had been pasted loosely over the peeling plasterwork on the walls in a vain attempt to disguise their decay, the stained table at which they sat rocking on uneven feet. Cries of discomfort rose from the makeshift dentist's surgery in the open stall next door, half drowned out by the sea of commotion. Serafina bore the grim surroundings with a stiff courtesy, as though none of it could be helped, and what could not be helped must be endured. She ignored her tea in its chipped cup and sat with her hands in her lap, constantly scanning the steam-damp room, checking that there was no one who might show an interest in eavesdropping on their unutterable, snatched sentences.

'Take the train to Bangalore tomorrow morning,' the woman said. 'You must go straight to the address in Marathahalli.

Here.' She took a piece of paper from her *choli* and gave it to Serafina. 'This woman has a good reputation.'

Serafina, pale as a ghost, didn't even glance at the note before stuffing it into her bag. The piece of syrup cake sitting in front of her remained untouched. Mary put two spoonfuls of sugar in her tea instead.

'Try to eat something,' she urged. 'Even if you don't want it, you have to eat or you'll make yourself ill.'

'I am already ill,' Serafina said. 'I heard of an old woman in Andheri who makes what they refer to as remedies. She gave me a concoction and charged me the earth for it. It made me sick as a dog, vomiting all night like I was turning inside out.'

Mary leaned towards Serafina and quietened her voice to a whisper. 'Are you sure she is to be trusted?' The woman smiled at them pityingly, got up from the table and left.

Mary had known that there were doctors who would do these things, but only for certain people, and always at a price. That Serafina should know where to find them had come as a shock. Serafina refused to speak a word of how she had come to discover the whereabouts of these doctors, or, as was more usual, their complicit nurses. Mary didn't press the matter. Some things were better left unsaid.

'It seems I have no choice,' Serafina said. The jangling music blaring from the street grated on her nerves, pushing her temper to its limits. 'And if we are caught ...' She stopped short of finishing the sentence. People had been sent to prison for far less.

'You don't have to do this.' Mary reached for her hand. 'We'll find some way to manage.'

'Manage?' Serafina forced a bitter laugh. 'I don't want to manage. I want this thing over and done with so that I can get on with my life.'

Mary fiddled with her teacup. 'Do you want to talk about—'

'No,' Serafina snapped. 'And you are never to ask me again, understand?' Mary nodded. 'If you ever say anything to anyone, I shall say that you are a liar.'

'Of course I won't.'

By the time they left the café it was dark, yet the constant throng of street life went on regardless. Filthy children slept in doorways under the watchful eyes of crouching, unsmiling mothers, hands held out towards any stranger passing by, hoping for a coin or a piece of bread. Shopkeepers stayed open to haggle with late customers over their pots and pans. Men sat around talking in lazy groups, smoking hand-rolled beedies and drinking cheap liquor from shared bottles.

'Don't look at them.' Serafina kept her eyes dead ahead and walked at a quickened pace.

Mary did as she was told, reluctantly tearing her gaze from the colours of the underworld that so intoxicated her. When she finally got back to her room, the scent of the streets was still clinging to her clothes. She took off her blouse and held it to her face, breathing deeply, before throwing it in with the rest of her laundry.

The journey to Bangalore and the appointment that awaited them took three interminable days. Travelling long avenues of blossoming trees as they headed away from the bustling station crammed into the back of the rickshaw, Mary was reminded of just how happy she had once been here. If only they had all stayed, perhaps this would never have happened, this unthinkable, unbearable thing.

The house in Marathahalli came as a terrible shock. Rusted gates creaked on broken hinges. Faded blue paint peeled in great swathes from the tatty outside walls. Untended plants overhung the pathway to a dirty front door with a single, fractured window. The woman who came to answer their tentative knock was plainly interested only in their money and demanded that payment be passed through the broken pane before letting them in. She stood, counting the notes in her hand, while the two of them stared incredulously at their surroundings, the awfulness of the household surpassing their worst fears by a thousand miles.

Everything was unclean, the back yard overrun with dogs, the smell of stale food and body odour clinging to the thread-bare curtains. Every instinct told them to turn and walk out of there as quickly as they could and not to look back, but there was nowhere else to go. Serafina began to tremble. The woman poked her finger towards Mary, then Serafina, asking in jagged Kannada which one of them it was before noticing Serafina's indignation and smiling to herself.

'You, go,' she said to Mary coldly. 'She stay.' She pointed at Serafina. 'She stay here. You go now. Leave her. Doctor come tomorrow.'

Serafina, shocked into silence, seemed unable to speak, stunned by the grotesqueness of it all.

'No.' Mary spoke up. 'We will both come back tomorrow morning, and I must be present when she undergoes the procedure.' The woman shook her head violently and waved them away, shouting, *impossible! impossible!* but Mary stood her ground, arguing with her sister's ferocity until the woman reluctantly agreed to admit them again the following morning.

They spent the long night in an unassuming guest house they had found along the way, about half a mile from the decrepit building. Despite their exhaustion, neither slept, the pair of them tossing and turning uncomfortably on the pair of worn charpoys in the tiny kerosene-tainted back room.

'We shouldn't go tomorrow,' Mary whispered. 'It's asking for trouble. We should have gone straight to the railway station this evening and got on the first train back to Bombay.' Serafina felt the rope circling her neck, knowing that Mary spoke the truth. 'For heaven's sake, Sera, you could *die*.'

'Do you think I don't know that?' she said bitterly. 'This is what happens when women get stupid ideas about love and romance. It's not a game. It's a tragedy.' Her caustic words reverberated around the thin walls. 'Men aren't interested in love. They want sex, ownership, possession. To be able to take what they want when they want it. Any woman who doesn't realise that is an idiot. Men want gratification. Women want security. That's what marriage is about. It's no more complicated than any other business transaction.' The lump in Mary's throat grew. She swallowed and swallowed, but still it would not go. 'Are you listening to me?'

'Yes,' Mary responded, as hard as it was. None of it made any sense, her sister's apparent destruction of her own happiness simply beyond her comprehension.

The pair of them lay on their bunks in silence, devoid of the energy to argue any further, the atmosphere between them thickened once more. Mary's insides churned. Her sister's altered state was unfathomable to her, the rosy pinkness in her cheeks gone, her constant expression almost brutal in its anxiety. She no longer blushed and smiled at the mention of Joseph's name. Instead she looked away, as if ashamed of it, her breath coming sharply. Mary turned it over and over in her head, then, beneath her thin sheet, a terrible, all-pervading sense of dread shivered over her skin, shrouding her in a cold film of damp perspiration as the realisation crept upon her. Serafina would never have compromised herself. Of that much Mary was certain. There could be only one explanation.

The thought of it cut her open and tore out her insides. For a moment she could not catch her breath, her lungs burning as though filled with acid that rose into her throat. She pressed her hands to her knowing heart.

'Serafina,' she whispered. 'Did something happen?'

'No.'

Mary turned on to her side and tried to make out her sister's features in the gloom. 'Sera,' she said, her voice shaking. 'Who did this to you?'

'I told you,' Serafina said coldly. 'This is none of your business.'

'Of course it's my business!' Mary sat up. 'You're my sister! You have to tell me!'

'Just leave it alone, will you?' Serafina snapped. 'And don't you ever ask me again.'

Mary lay back grimly, heat surging into her face, her eyes suddenly awash with tears. She pushed the sheet into her mouth until she felt she would choke.

'These men,' Serafina said to the darkness, her trembling voice thick with fury. 'They should be castrated.'

Mary stared into the blackness, afraid to speak for fear of igniting the rage that smouldered in Serafina's darkest recesses, afraid to disturb the very seat of her fury, this woman, born of a man's lust. She turned away, her tears spilling in silent torrents, willing her sister's agony to enter her instead.

They arrived at the house the next day to find a doctor in attendance, the sickly odour of alcohol on his breath, eyes stained ochre yellow. Under the light of a single lamp, Mary watched on helplessly as the woman who had taken their money held the mask to Serafina's face while the doctor worked, gas leaking into the room all around them, its sickening, dizzying effects reaching her in a matter of minutes. Despite his shockingly unkempt appearance, the doctor carried out the task quickly, his hands working with the skill of someone who had done it many hundreds of times before. Serafina moaned from beneath the curtain of anaesthesia, turned her head and vomited on the floor. The doctor ignored her, wiped his instruments and threw a cloth over the bloody contents of the bucket. After briefly washing his hands in the cracked basin, he began to throw his things into his bag, perspiration running down his face.

'I must go now,' he said.

'No,' Mary said sternly. 'Not until I have seen her properly awake and recovered.'

The doctor stared at her. 'I don't think you understand me,' he said. 'I must go. *Now*. So should you. The woman will stay here with your friend. She will be fine.'

'I think I should inform you that we are both nurses,' Mary said. 'I can see for myself what a mess she is in.'

'You expected this to be tidy?' The doctor looked up, his eyes widening with indignation before settling on her coolly. 'You knew what the risks were before you came here. Women like you, with your fancy Chutney Mary clothes and loose morals. You think this is how decent women behave?' He jerked his head at Serafina, still groaning beneath the anaesthesia, now fast wearing off. 'She was lucky. It was straightforward this time. Maybe next time she won't be so fortunate.' He picked up his bag distastefully. 'Women like you should learn to keep your legs closed.'

They returned to Bombay the next day in near silence, the pair of them deeply shaken and sick to the pits of their stomachs. After seeing to her sister's needs, Mary left her to rest in her darkened room then slipped away, taking herself to a church she had never visited before, as though anyone who knew her face would be able to tell, just by looking at her, that she had committed a mortal sin. Kneeling down on the furthest pew from the altar, hidden in the semi-darkness, a penitent Mary ran through her rosary twice, rolling each of the black glass beads between her fingers and thumb with every passing prayer, trying to free her mind from the sins that plagued her. From the church, she began to walk, heading into the breeze, moving slowly until the land came to an end. She found an empty bench and rested awhile, inhaling the damp salted air, watching the growing numbers of people coming out to stroll the wide sandy beach as the day soothed into evening. She stared emptily across the vast body of water and sighed with the weight of the world. The ocean was a forgiving body on which to cast one's troubles. It spoke in eternal whispers, carrying secrets out to sea with every seventh wave. Mary sat quietly in contemplation, her sari pulled anonymously over her head, and watched as the sun lowered and sank into the watery horizon, gloriously igniting the sky.

## 44

Mary was unable to settle herself. She remained wakeful throughout her nights, tormented by bloodstained visions of twisted, dead infants, and the screams of the desperate women from whose bodies they had been torn. The change in her demeanour did not go unnoticed.

'I knew you should have let me come with you.' Florence fussed around and felt Mary's forehead again. 'What did I tell you about taking care of yourself while you were away? You've probably gone and eaten something poisonous.'

'I'm fine. Really I am.' Mary tried not to cry.

'Well you certainly don't look fine to me. Did you buy food from any of the wallahs on the station platforms? How many times have I told you that you must take your own picnic when travelling? These hawkers are not to be trusted. They'd feed you the meat off a dead donkey as soon as look at you.'

'Please, Florence. Stop fussing. I just need to get some rest.'

'Rest? You've hardly left your bed since you got back. If there's nothing wrong with you, you should go out and take some fresh air and exercise, otherwise I shall send for the doctor and have him take a look at you.'

There came a knock on the door, quickly followed by Ruby's head. 'Are we ready to go?'

'No,' Florence replied matter-of-factly. 'Mary still isn't feeling well, so I think we should all stay in.'

'What?' Ruby closed the door with a bang. 'But I've been looking forward to this all week!'

'I told you I'm fine.' Mary sat up and attempted a smile. 'I'll be perfectly all right here on my own. I was thinking of going to church later.'

'Oh!' Caught off-guard by Mary's dedication, Florence reassessed her plans for the afternoon. 'What a nice idea. I think I'll come along with you.'

'That's not what I meant,' Mary said. 'I just need a little quiet time, and if church is the only place I can find it, then that's where I'll go.'

'See?' Ruby attended to her reflection in the mirror. 'Now hurry up or we'll be last in the queue.'

'I'm not going anywhere with you looking like that.' Florence pointed at Ruby's cleavage. 'Do those buttons up before somebody sees you.' Before Ruby could protest, Florence had hold of her sweater.

'What are you doing? Will you please stop pulling at my clothes!' Ruby swiped at Florence's hands. 'It's only the pictures, for heaven's sake!'

'So you won't need to be putting everything on show, will you?'

'Do your buttons up, Ruby.' Mary turned away, po-faced. 'What do you want people to think of you?'

'And since when did you become all holier-than-thou? I don't know what went on between you and that sister of yours while you were away, but I'm not sure that I like it one little bit.' Ruby leaned towards the small mirror, checking her lipstick and pinching colour into her cheeks. 'You've been no fun at all lately. The Saturday matinee is bound to be brimming with handsome young men, and I have every intention of attracting at least one of them.'

'Don't be so ...' Serafina's word dropped spontaneously from Mary's mouth, '... *obtuse.*'

'Obtuse, am I? Well that's a mighty big word to come out of a mouse's mouth.'

'For heaven's sake!' Mary burst into tears and shouted at her friend. 'Just do them up!'

'I hope you realise that no doctor's letter means ten days without pay?' Mary couldn't bring herself to answer. 'And what time do you have on your watch, Staff Nurse?'

Mary seemed to sag under the burden of the constant bullying. 'I'm sorry, Matron,' she said. 'I know I'm a little late.'

'A little late? There's no such thing as a little late, Staff Nurse. Late is late.'

'Two minutes!' Mary pleaded. 'Just two minutes! I said I'm sorry.'

'Well now that you've decided to honour us with your company, you can go and see to Mr Johnson. He's been asking for the commode, so I'd hurry up about it if I were you. We don't want him having another one of his accidents, do we?'

Mary took a deep breath and went about her duties, her footsteps slow and laboured.

Attending to Mr Johnson, she steadfastly refused to smile.

'Where the bloody hell have you been?' he snapped at her, his face pulled into its customary surliness. 'I've been subjected to the humiliation of half a dozen totally incompetent nurses while you were gone. Hopeless, all of them. Weeping and complaining about me like a bunch of snivelling children.' Mary ignored him. 'What's the matter with you today?'

'Nothing,' Mary replied, not wishing to speak to him at all. 'Lean this way for me, please.'

'Rubbish.' He moved grudgingly. 'You can't come in here with a face as long as a canoe and say nothing's the matter.'

Mary concentrated on her work, towelling then covering his one exposed leg before moving on to the other, soaping the wet flannel again. 'I see,' he said. 'I try to make a little polite conversation, just to pass the time in this godforsaken dump, and you can't even be bothered to be civil to me. Well that's not what nursing's about, young lady. You should watch your manners.' Mary braced herself. She hated washing his feet most of all, the sight of his thick, cloudy toenails leaving her feeling quite nauseous. Quickly running the damp cloth over the cracked skin, she did what had to be done and looked away. 'I know I can be a bit bad-tempered now and again,' he conceded. 'But you try lying around all day bored out of your skull while a bunch of inept, bungling doctors pretend that you're getting better. They must think I'm some kind of idiot. It would be enough to drive a saint to drink, not that there's much chance of that in here. God, what I wouldn't give for a flask of malt whisky.'

'Turn over, please.' Mary helped him roll on to his side. She pulled his ageing, flaccid arm free of the loose pyjama sleeve and rinsed the flannel again.

'So, if you're not going to tell me what you're looking so gloomy about, I suppose I shall just have to guess for myself, now won't I?' Mary refused to humour him. She'd fallen foul of his buttering-up once before and the next thing had felt his hand on her behind. She rubbed harder with the flannel until he frowned and flinched. 'So, let me see now.' He tried to face her, but Mary lifted his arm to such an extent that he winced and turned his head back to the pillow. 'Boyfriend trouble?'

'Mr Johnson,' Mary said. 'Will you please keep still and let me finish what I'm doing? I do have other patients to attend to, you know. And my private life is none of your blasted business.'

'Ah!' he said, with great satisfaction. 'Just as I suspected.'

'Sit up.' Mary helped him into a clean pyjama shirt. 'You can do the buttons up yourself.'

'That bad, eh?'

'Really, Mr Johnson. If you carry on like this, I might well be sorely tempted to say something I shouldn't.'

'I should have guessed.' He fastened his buttons with slow fingers. 'I may be old, but I'm not deaf. There's nothing to do here except watch and listen, and I've heard you canoodling with the colonel next door.'

'Canoodling?' Mary bristled. 'What a ridiculous assumption. You certainly do have a vivid imagination.' She took the basin and tipped the soapy water into the sink. 'Colonel Spencer is a perfect gentleman, unlike some people around here I could mention. He's been a model patient and has gone through more pain and suffering than I care to imagine without a word of complaint. You should try it some time. It would certainly make my life a lot easier.'

'So you're going to deny it, are you? How very tiresome. I've seen you hanging around his door watching him when you're on nights. You don't do that for me, now do you?'

'I hardly need to. It's you that keeps half the hospital awake with your snoring.'

'I don't snore.'

'Yes you do, and that's quite enough from you for one morning.' Mary put the basin back on its hook beside the sink, hung the towel on the rail and made to leave.

'I expect you're missing him, so I'll excuse your discourteous manner today.' He flicked his hand at her in dismissal. 'And where's my ruddy newspaper?'

'What?' Mary felt herself blush.

'My newspaper,' Mr Johnson repeated, frowning at her as though she were stupid. Mary passed him his newspaper

373

without receiving a word of thanks then took her leave and crept into the neighbouring room.

The windows had been left wide open to let in the fresh air and the inward breeze rushed at her the moment she stepped in. Inside, the colonel's bed lay cold and empty, new sheets turned back, pillows piled uniformly one on top of the other.

## 45

A thousand flickering candles illuminated the cavernous interior of the Cathedral of the Holy Name, its high vaulted ceilings bathed in a soft golden radiance. The coolness of the air inside gave way the moment the party spilled out into the glorious sunshine on this fine morning, bride and groom flinching briefly with wide smiles under the sudden scattered shower of rice and orange blossom.

Serafina stood proudly on Joseph's arm, allowing Mary to fuss with her gown and adjust her veil in anticipation of the photographer's portrait. The dress, layer after layer of translucent white silk, had been chosen from the pages of a glossy magazine and sent for all the way from Europe. It could not have been more perfect. Mary had cried when she first saw it, overcome by the heavenly scent of a life in clover as they lifted it from the box. Her own dress, also of white silk, had been made by Mr Chagdar. Although simple in its design, the cut was flawless, the needlework sublime. Determined not to be outshone, Mr Chagdar had gone to great trouble, working the delicate fabric with his own experienced hands rather than giving the job to his apprentice as he usually did. He had cheerfully given Mary his best attentions without mentioning a word of her sister's bill. It had been cleared in full two weeks earlier by a gentleman caller, who had also left a generous allowance in anticipation of the bridesmaid's dress for Mary.

Attending to Serafina's gown, adjusting the folds just so, Mary cut a vision of loveliness haloed in the blazing sunshine, the soft waves of her shoulder-length dark hair pinned back and held in place by a fragrant curve of wax-white flowers.

'There.' She stepped back, happy with her final touches to Serafina's whispering veil. 'Perfect.'

Serafina seemed not to hear her, carried away by the sight of the world slowing around her. Passers-by dawdled, taking time to gaze upwards. People on bicycles and packed into rickshaws waved and smiled their congratulations. Standing at the top of the cathedral steps with Joseph by her side, Serafina found herself smiling back at them, glad that they should have happened to be there to share in her joy, feeling herself as if in a dream, grateful for the noise of the street. It was over, her tortured life. She would have nothing to fear now, her future safely entombed in the tiny weight of the golden ring on her finger. She caught her breath, held it there, and squeezed Joseph's arm.

'Happy, darling?' He placed his hand over hers.

'Yes,' she said, without taking her eyes from the scene. 'Happier than you could possibly imagine.'

The crowd took quite some organising, with much laughter and changing of positions on the steps until everyone could be seen by the camera.

'Isn't this exciting?' Ruby jostled alongside Florence.

'It was so nice of Serafina to invite us.' Florence peered out from the low brim of her borrowed hat. 'I wouldn't have missed this for the world. Wasn't it a beautiful service?'

'Of course she invited us,' Ruby said curtly. 'And everyone else she ever met by the looks of it. She wanted to make sure the whole world knows she's done so well for herself. I expect there's been an announcement in every newspaper from here to Timbuktu.'

'Do I detect a note of jealousy?' Florence shuffled along a few inches in compliance with the photographer's wave. 'I wonder what our weddings will be like?'

'I don't care.' Ruby sighed and waved back at a group of smiling pedestrians. 'So long as he's filthy rich and able to keep me in the style in which I intend to become accustomed.'

The photographer held one hand high in the air, his head buried beneath the black cloth draped behind the camera. At his command, the gathering on the steps smiled and cheered. The shutter clicked, freeze-framing the moment.

Richard Patterson offered Joseph a hearty congratulatory handshake. Serafina forced herself to look at him, turning herself to stone so that he might see nothing in her eyes except the loathing that burned inside. He acted as though nothing had happened, smiling like a snake, tapping his cigarette lightly on the gold case before flipping it casually to his mouth and taking a match from his pocket. To look at him, anyone would think that he was an ordinary man, unremarkable, undistinguished. He breathed easily, filling his lungs and blowing his smoke carelessly into the air. Serafina suppressed the savage ferocity that threatened to erupt from within and send her clawing into his face, tearing at his flesh with her fingernails until there was nothing left of it except bloodied tatters hanging from bare bone. She swallowed, her mouth dry, and willed herself to get through this one last, torturous encounter. After this day, she would see to it that they never saw him again.

He spoke through his snake-like smile.

'May I kiss the bride?'

'No,' Serafina said coolly, stepping back.

'But darling!' Joseph smiled. 'It's traditional!'

'Am I being snubbed?' Richard said with a small, convivial laugh.

'I said no,' Serafina repeated to Joseph. 'My kiss is for you, and nobody else.'

'Well,' Joseph said sheepishly, taken aback by her sudden bellicose manner. 'You heard my wife.' He offered Richard an apologetic shrug. 'Looks like you missed your chance.'

'Women, eh?' Richard rolled his eyes before taking up his mantle as best man once more and urging the party to move along to the wedding breakfast.

'Anybody with a car,' he shouted, 'would you please grab as many passengers as you can! We're rather short on transport by the looks of it, so a friendly game of sardines would be much appreciated! Anyone who doesn't know where the Wayside is, just keep up with the person in front. If you get lost, ask for directions and head for the Army and Navy. It's right opposite. Just follow the noise!' Nobody seemed to be listening as the guests crammed in, squeezing up to make room.

'Do you want us to wait for you?' Ruby called to Mary while Florence dithered on the pavement, unsure of how to handle the offer of a strange gentleman's lap inside the already overcrowded vehicle.

'No.' She waved them on. 'We're getting a lift with Richard.'

'Is there room for me too?' Florence asked.

'Just get in, will you!' Ruby reached out and yanked Florence into the car, her face glowing puce as she landed on a man she had never met before, who cheerfully clasped his arms around her waist. 'See you there!' Ruby called as they pulled into the frenzied traffic.

Mary, still giddy with excitement, took the steps quickly, the skirt of her dress bouncing with her girlish movements.

'Feeling all right, Colonel?' she said, a little breathless.

'Yes.' Eddie smiled, his eyes adoring her. 'Although I'm not sure I would have got very far trying to cram in with that lot.'

Mary accepted the offer of his arm and slid her hand neatly

into the crook of his elbow, glad to have his company. Upon finding his room empty on that awful day two months ago, she had felt her heart leap into her mouth, chilled by the thought of what might have happened to him. Quietly she had returned to Mr Johnson's room to find out if he knew anything.

'Don't ask me,' he had replied crossly, barely bothering to lift his head from the newspaper. 'I'm just the grumpy old bugger who no one wants to nurse. Nobody tells me anything around here anyway.' Mary had stood defeated, unable to muster the energy to press him further. 'But I did hear his doctor talking to Sergeant Kemp. What's his name? Browning? The one with the ridiculous moustache.' Mr Johnson had remained buried in his paper, speaking as though none of it were of any interest or consequence to him at all. 'They got him out of that spaghetti contraption without too much trouble and everything seemed to be fixed up quite nicely by the sounds of it. They thought he'd be better off somewhere quieter with a bit of garden to exercise in. He's been moved to a private nursing home somewhere. Now what was the name of the place?' At that moment, he had stolen a glance at her over the top of the page and smiled, before offering her a scrap of notepaper, jotted in a hazy hand.

Mary squeezed Eddie's arm lightly. 'Any discomfort?'

'For the tenth time, no,' he said. 'In fact I might even risk a turn on the dance floor a little later.'

'Good man!' Richard slapped him bluntly on the back. 'We'll kill the pain with a few whiskies and throw your sticks out of the window, eh?'

'Any day now,' Eddie said with a rueful smile.

Mary was pleased that he and Richard had hit it off so well. When she had asked Serafina if she might bring a friend to the wedding, Serafina had reminded her stiffly that she had already sent an invitation to Ruby and Florence, much against her better judgement, and that it wasn't a free-for-all. Mary had blushed and said that it was an old patient of hers who could do with getting out and kicking his heels up, at which Serafina had twitched her eyebrows and assumed that a love affair was coyly taking root where she had been too busy to notice. A few probing questions later, covering the usual matters of background and propriety, and Serafina was sufficiently satisfied to offer her a breezy 'Bring him along, by all means.'

Eddie clambered awkwardly into the front seat, refusing any assistance, his method of swinging in the stiff leg while holding himself half-seated having been much rehearsed and well perfected in recent weeks. Richard tried not to watch and adjusted the rear-view mirror while Mary clambered into the back.

'Seems to me you're going to be rid of those things in no time.' He knocked one of Eddie's sticks with a curious knuckle. 'How long before you're shipshape again?'

'Oh.' Eddie shrugged. 'About a month, I suppose. Maybe more, maybe less. It depends on who you ask. One doctor says one thing, then another comes along and gives me a completely different opinion. To be frank, I stopped taking any notice of them a long time ago, didn't I, Mary?'

'I always said you'd be fine,' Mary reminded him. 'Just keep up with your physio and do as the nurses tell you.' The two men exchanged a mildly salacious glance, and laughed.

A pleasant hubbub rose from the guests, who, at the tinkling of a glass, burst into a warm round of applause as the happy couple arrived and began to circulate among the gathering, Serafina's smile never altering as she moved from one acquaintance to the next. Mary watched her, mesmerised by her confidence, and felt a deep yearning within for all the things that she was not.

'Gosh.' Eddie struggled to her side. 'Quite a squash in here, isn't it?'

'Yes.' Mary nodded. 'It was one of Joseph's favourite haunts in his bachelor days, from what I hear. Richard set this up for them as a little send-off gift. Good idea, don't you think? Everyone seems to be having a lovely time.'

'I've enjoyed a little rowdy male company here myself once or twice,' Eddie admitted. 'The old place hasn't changed a bit, I'm very happy to say.'

'Hello, Colonel!' Ruby thrust herself through the tangle of bodies, Florence following cautiously behind, apologising for her every step. 'Don't you think Mary looks wonderful in her dress? I was just saying to Florence, they should have made it a double wedding, seeing as she looked the part so well.'

'Ruby!' Mary felt herself flush, a cold rush of guilt creeping over her, her fondness for Eddie having remained little more than that despite his unmasked affection.

'Quite right.' Eddie stood to attention. 'But she's already refused me three times, so I'm assuming it's these things that are putting her off.' He waved a stick a little, unable to give it sufficient room for further drama. 'We shall have to wait a while longer then see if she comes round to the idea. Either that or I shall have to knock her out with a handful of painkillers and drag her up the aisle before she wakes up.'

Ruby helped herself to another glass of wine from the passing waiter.

'I think you've had quite enough of that.' Florence glared at her. 'You're already talking far too loudly. It's most unladylike.'

'Nonsense,' Ruby said. 'It's a wedding! We're supposed to be celebrating, remember?' Florence sipped at her fruit juice and despaired of Ruby's behaviour as she shamelessly started making eyes at a nearby man. 'Besides, I have a distinct feeling that this would be a perfect place for me to meet a husband of my own.'

*

Under the watchful eye of a deceptive moon, Joseph stood behind his bride and smoothed the hair from her neck, barely touching her perfect skin, exposing her nape, placing his kiss upon it. Serafina shivered involuntarily as his lips brushed against her shoulder, his hands caressing her softness, his fingers tracing slowly to the fastenings of her dress. She swallowed hard, the panic streaming through her almost unbearable, willing him to do what he needed to do and get it over with, hoping that he would not look at her face or read her guilty body.

A subtle heaviness settled in Joseph's sigh as he murmured his love, the terrible heat of his passion burning right through them. Serafina fought to stay calm as she felt the delicate hooks on her dress give way, one after the other, a tiny chill lacing its way down her spine as the layers of translucent silk fell from her, finally slipping to the floor. She heard his sudden intake of breath, his thickened swallow, then felt his body against hers, the ardour beneath his clothes unrestrained.

'Serafina,' he whispered, over and over. 'How I have longed for you.'

Serafina held her breath, an icy chill coming upon her like a deathly curtain of blackness, paralysing her limbs, leaving her numb. She fought to push it aside, to resurrect the feelings that had once kept her awake at night, filling her dreams with unknown desires, causing her to blush through the day whenever she thought of him. Joseph's hands slid around her waist, resting on the soft curve of her stomach for a moment. Serafina stiffened, her body rigid in its response.

'Shhh,' he murmured in her ear, his lips touching her velvet lobe. 'It's all right,' he said. 'Just relax and let yourself go.'

Serafina's eyes began to burn. She closed them tight shut.

'Turn out the lights,' she whispered.

## 46

The shutters kept out the worst of the fierce midday sun, casting blinding slats across the desk in Joseph's study. Through the shafts of sunlight, smoke from Serafina's cigarette festooned upwards. She sat in the leather armchair, legs crossed, her free foot tapping in irritation while Joseph paced the floor, awash with grief for his wife's actions.

'But why did you have to fire him, for God's sake? Have you any idea what you've gone and done?'

'He was disrespectful. You should have seen the way he looked down his nose at me.'

'It was his son's wedding! In God's name, I told him myself that he could take as much time as he needed.'

'Well that can't be helped. He should have made proper provision for the work while he was away.'

'But why couldn't you have seen to it yourself?'

'Me? Deal with the kitchen boys? And what on earth do you think that would look like? It's his job, and if he can't manage to organise things to allow for his absences, then he has no business being here at all.' Beneath her cool exterior, Serafina's anger simmered unchecked. Despite her legitimised status as a British wife, the undercurrent of suspicion and ridicule had followed her, whispering in corners, tugging at her insecurities. She puffed at her cigarette, refusing to be moved by her husband's anguish.

'There must be some way this mess can be undone.' Joseph was at a loss, but knew there was nothing to be gained by causing a scene. He had not so much as raised his voice at her. He never did, no matter how strong the temptation. 'You really shouldn't have done it, darling. He's been in good and loyal service to my household since long before you and I were married. Of course he might be a little set in his ways, but you can't just go around sacking the staff whenever the mood takes you.'

'They need to learn some respect.'

'Go and tell Davindra to fetch him in here now. Although what I shall say to him I really don't know. You do realise that I can't just go and reinstate him, after what you've done?'

Above everything, the British household had to appear unshakeable, rock solid as the Empire itself once was. With the smallest crack, the rot would set in, the rumours begin, and the carefully constructed veneer peel away. A man must rule with a strong arm here. His superiority must never be called into question, and certainly never tested by a mere woman. And woven into the layer beneath this, the wife must never be undermined in the eyes of the staff.

'Why didn't you come and speak to me first?' he implored her. 'Now I will have to stand by your decision, otherwise we'll both look ridiculous. You'd better send for him quickly.'

'It's too late,' Serafina replied. 'I told him this morning to pack his things immediately and be gone in an hour.'

'You did what?' Joseph paled.

The cook was just three months away from his pension gift.

Serafina supervised the last of the packing while Mary stood aside uneasily, taking in the emptiness as Serafina issued curt instructions to her servants. She placed her teacup on the mantelpiece, the clack of the porcelain saucer on the cold marble echoing around the room.

'I can't believe that you would deliberately set out to deceive him.' Mary sat precariously on one of the packing cases and shook her head. Serafina met her incredulity with a sigh of impatience.

'I've told you, Mary. That's the end of the matter, and you are never to discuss it with Joseph, no matter what he asks. Do you understand? What do you think would have happened if I had gone around broadcasting that I was the product of a tea planter's fling with a peasant? Joseph wouldn't have given me a second glance.'

'Don't speak about our parents like that.'

'What parents? In case it has escaped your notice, Mary, we don't have any.'

'And what about Papa?'

'What about him? You talk about him as though he matters. The last time I saw him, I was a child.' She laughed thinly. 'I doubt if he even remembers.'

'Of course he does,' Mary said. 'It must have half killed him.'

'Huh! So he left us here and went to the one country he could be sure we would never follow him to?' Serafina scoffed. 'How very convenient. He never had any intention of seeing either of us again, and you're a fool if you think otherwise.'

'That's not true!'

'Of course it is.' Serafina took a sip of tea. 'Why else go to Africa?'

'You must write to him once you arrive and let him know where you are.'

'Why? So that he and Dorothy can keep their conscience clear with an occasional letter about their dogs?' Mary bowed her head. 'They talk about those blasted animals as though they're the most important things on earth.'

'Will you send him a photograph of the wedding?'

'For him to display proudly on his mantelpiece?' Serafina

put down her cup. 'Yes. Why not?' she scoffed sarcastically.

'And what am I to say if Joseph asks me?'

'He won't. Joseph is aware that our father is from a well-to-do family and that he is a farmer in Rhodesia. That's all he needs to know.'

'Oh, Sera.' Mary sighed. 'How can you begin your life as a married woman on nothing but a pack of lies?'

Serafina turned on her. 'And what exactly would you have me say? It is the truth. My truth. I'll decide what people should know about me, and you would do well to keep the whole messy business to yourself, unless you want to spend the rest of your life having people look down their noses at you. I'm married now. Joseph is the only family I have that matters.'

Mary drew a sharp breath.

'So where does that leave me?'

'You know what you have to do, Mary. Life is unfair. We both know that. It's up to you to do something about it. As for me, I'm finished with all that.' She pressed her cigarette out on her saucer. 'I shall never set foot in this city again, nor in any place that reminds me of it. Now it's my turn to live.' She snapped open the clasp on the small vanity case set down by the door, leaned down and took out her passport. 'I'm British,' she declared, holding the deep blue cover firmly in front of Mary's injured face. 'And from now on, woe betide anyone who dares to suggest otherwise.'

The delicate edge of Mary's sari, woven from the soft silk of mulberry worms and printed with a bold black and purple design, fluttered around her feet, bright colours melting into the crowds teeming through the gargantuan Gothic structure of Bombay's Victoria Terminus. Mary strained her neck upwards towards the ornate gargoyles glaring down from the towering arches.

'You take great care of yourself, Mary,' said Joseph. 'And if there is anything you need, just call the number on the card. I've asked Richard to keep an eye out for you and told him that if you get into any difficulties now that we're gone, I shall hold him personally accountable.'

'Thank you, but that won't be necessary.'

'Well, let's just say that it's for my peace of mind rather than yours. It doesn't do for a young woman to be without a champion in a place like this, although if he asks you to have dinner with him, run a mile!' He winked. Mary knew Richard's dangerous reputation well enough, and Serafina had made no secret of the fact that she couldn't stand the sight of the man. 'Seriously, Mary. You be careful now that you're on your own.'

'I will,' she said, warming under Joseph's kind smile and gentle voice. Her sister had chosen well, a good man with a tender heart, generous of spirit, charming of nature, capable of offering Serafina everything she had ever wished for. And he loved her. Oh, how he loved her. Mary could see it in his eyes whenever her sister came into view, his silent sigh of ecstasy as he surveyed the beauty of his prize. She yearned for a love like that, a love of her own to cherish her above all others. Nothing else would matter.

'I expect we'll be staying in Chittagong for a good long time if things work out,' Joseph said. Mary looked down at the card he had given her and ran her thumb over its smart raised lettering. 'If you lose it,' Joseph smiled, 'the Bombay office will always know where we can be contacted.'

'You're a good man, Joseph. Sera is lucky to have found you.'

'Nonsense. It's me who's the lucky fellow.' He touched her arm. 'I think she and I were hoping to see you at least somewhere near the altar before we left.'

'Not much chance of that.' Mary self-consciously adjusted the shoulder of her sari.

'Are you sure?' His voice teased her slightly then sobered. 'Your colonel friend appears to be quite taken with you. You could do a lot worse. He seems like a decent fellow with a good background. There's a lot to be said for that, you know. It goes a long way these days.'

'What's the big rush?' Mary looked away, pretending to be distracted by something in the distance. 'I've only known the man for six months and already everybody's trying to marry me off to him.'

The thought of accepting Eddie's proposal had left her stone cold and she didn't know why. Perhaps Serafina had been right, that to desire the burning ache of a passionate, undisciplined love, over and above the need for shelter, status and security, was nothing short of foolhardy.

'It's not such a difficult decision.' Joseph poked fun at her befuddled expression. 'All you have to do is say yes and hope for the best. You should think about it. I promised your sister that I would speak to you before we left, and that's all I'm saying.'

'Thank you, Joseph.' She accepted the sweet kiss he placed on her cheek and brushed his concerns aside, silencing the disquiet in her heart with a trite response. 'But I'm far too busy enjoying myself.'

'Be careful not to enjoy yourself too much, Mary. Serafina worries about you, and I think she's right. If you spend too much time with your head in the clouds, it can be hard to see where you're putting your feet. Think about your future, and try not to take too long about it.'

The stationmaster shouted and blew his whistle long and hard, sending a cold wind of bereavement through Mary's thin shadow.

'Do hurry, Joseph.' Serafina returned from the platform kiosk and busied herself arranging the stack of magazines in her bag. 'You know what these people are like. They'll pull out and leave us behind without a second thought.'

As Serafina fussed with her bag and brushed a stray hair from her husband's shoulder, Mary felt herself sliding away, pulled back to a great distance, as though looking at the world through the wrong end of a telescope. The familiar spectre of emptiness opened its cloak to her as she prepared to separate from the one constant presence she had relied upon throughout a lifetime of uncertainty.

'I'll miss you.' Mary kissed her sister, determined in her cheerfulness. 'Write to me as soon as you arrive.'

'Of course.' Serafina glanced disapprovingly at Mary's clothes, whispering quietly, 'Couldn't you have worn something else?'

## 47

The clear waters of Nagin Lake ran deep and blue. Here lay a paradise, a Garden of Eden, set like a shining jewel, a lake within a lake. The *Rowallan*, carved from rich, dark teakwood, rocked gently on its moorings beneath the tall green chinars leaning in from the tree-lined shores. Delicate, fretworked wooden shutters patterned remnants of the low afternoon sun across the luxurious cabins that once housed an Englishman and his wife before the last spate of trouble drove them away. It was a serene isolation after the chaos of the city. Mary sat on the sun deck watching dragonflies dart above the lotus blossoms on the lake, brilliant blue kingfishers dive for fish, and a hoopie bird rustling his crown of feathers.

They had been ferried to the *Rowallan* two days before in a pair of shikaras, the gondolas of Kashmir, reclining on seats scattered with plump pillows decorated with heavy embroidery. Children ran along the bank shouting '*Salaam! Salaam!*' until they were far from the shore. The boatmen's steady strokes with heart-shaped paddles barely broke the water's glassy surface. Beneath the smile of a rising moon, the passengers covered their legs with soft cashmere blankets, a small charcoal brazier tucked at their feet, listening to the boatmen's gentle voices sing a love song. Mary had offered a handsome price for the mouse-brown blanket, explaining that she wanted to keep it as a souvenir. The boatman had thought her quite mad and happily took her money.

News of their arrival spread quickly. The next morning, the houseboat was visited by a steady stream of anxious tradesmen, their shikaras piled high with wares that they hauled into the salon or up on to the sun deck to spread out and display. An old man, his dyed red beard proclaiming his recent pilgrimage to Mecca, smoothed a white cloth over the carpet and laid upon it a display of uncut jewels and Tibetan jade. None was very good, and he nodded understandingly when no sale was made. Another trader arrived to show his collections of embroidered shawls and rare shahtooshes, but his mind was not on business. He wished to talk of politics, whispering his confidence that Kashmir really wanted to join Pakistan, not India, and negligently accepted a derisory price from Ruby for an antique paisley before paddling away furiously to attend a town meeting. A sunset-reddened range of noble peaks rose to the distance above the plains behind the furthest shores. As the light began to fade, so the dimming sky filled with hundreds of birds returning to roost.

'I miss the mountains,' Mary sighed, although she was not speaking loudly enough to address the rest of the party. She looked out over the silver lake instead. The shikaras were returning home now, some of them with lanterns lit already, having finished their slow-paced daily business of fetching and carrying between the houseboats. She heard Eddie's footsteps slowing to her side, the trace of his once prominent limp now less noticeable.

'What did you say?'

The scar across his cheek had long given up most of its redness and faded into a pale pink crescent that pulled gently at the side of his mouth, cocking it into a permanent half-smile that lent the terrain of his features a certain charm.

'Oh, nothing of any importance. But I do wish the cook would hurry up. I'm half starved to death.'

'I'm not surprised. You look as though you haven't eaten a square meal in a decade.' He took advantage of the legitimate reason to openly assess her elfin figure. 'There's nothing of you.'

Ruby overheard his remarks and called out from the salon, 'She has the skinniest ankles I've ever seen!'

'Better that than to have legs like an elephant!' Eddie called back.

'It is a beautiful country, this India.' Mary returned her gaze to the outline of the mountains fading into the darkening sky. 'I've always wanted to see Kashmir. We'd been planning this holiday for such a long time, but Florence kept putting us off, three women travelling alone.'

'You were right to be sensible. I wouldn't have let you risk it either, although I do wish you'd told me first instead of Richard.'

'Why?'

'Because then I could have had the three of you all to myself!' He leaned in and whispered to her, 'And frankly, the man's a bit of a boor.'

'Joseph made me promise that I'd tell Richard if I was planning on doing anything even remotely dangerous.' Her eyes skipped to the sky for a moment. 'I hardly expected him to insist that he come along and play chaperon.'

'Of course he did.' Eddie sighed at her naïveté. 'And if you think he did it for your benefit, you're even more daft than you look. Do you really think I'd let you out of my sight with him around?' He pulled at her arm playfully. 'Although I think I'm quite safe in assuming that he has enough distractions on his mind for now.'

'I know,' Mary whispered under a sharp intake of breath. 'I do wish that he would leave poor Ruby alone.'

'Oh, I wouldn't worry too much about Ruby. She seems to be enjoying herself well enough. I'd say she's positively glowing with all the attention.'

'That's what concerns me,' Mary said. A sudden flash of blue flew across the water, the kingfisher's iridescent wings catching the last of the sun's rays. 'Did you see that?' She pointed towards the tiny splash rippling out from a drifting patch of water hyacinths. 'I could happily stand here all day long just watching.'

Eddie slipped his arm around her waist. 'I could get a posting here if you wanted, then you need never leave. Once the Banihal Tunnel opens up, there'll be rich pickings for whoever gets here first. It wasn't so long ago that the only way to transport anything in or out of this place was to drag it on a bullock cart.' He came closer, Mary's skin sensing the heat of his breath. 'I have a feeling it could be a very comfortable life indeed. What do you think?'

'It's just wonderful.' Mary broke away from him. 'I shall never forget it.'

'Mary?' She compelled herself to look at him. 'I mean every word I say. Here, there, another country. I would take you anywhere you wanted to go, and I mean anywhere, if it would make you happy.'

'What is all this whispering?' Ruby crept out to see what she could hear. Eddie released Mary from his gaze and excused himself to find another drink. Ruby smiled sweetly as he disappeared into the salon.

'He's crazy about you.'

'I know.'

'So what's the problem?'

'Keep your nose out of my business.' Mary's scornful manner was only half serious. Her heart had already made up her

393

mind, and there was nothing that could be done about it. 'We are here for a holiday, Ruby, nothing more.'

Ruby flicked her eyes beyond the curlicued shutters towards Richard. 'He's wonderful, isn't he?' she enthused. 'And terribly clever.'

'Ruby,' Mary warned her. 'I hope you know what you're doing.'

'Of course I do,' Ruby replied. 'I fully intend to see to it that by the time we get back to Bombay, Richard is as mad about me as the colonel is about you.' She sidled up to Mary, leaning against the teak rail, sharing her view of the placid lake. 'What better place to melt a man's heart and get him to promise his undying love?'

'Just be careful,' Mary said. 'That's all I'm saying.'

Ruby brushed an early night insect from Mary's shawl. 'You're a fine one to talk. I've never known anyone so fickle.'

'I'm not fickle. I'm just waiting to fall head over heels in love.'

'You're going to turn him down again, aren't you?' Ruby allowed her head to drop and ran her hand along the dark timber rail. 'Have you told him yet?'

'Not in so many words, but he knows. I'm sure of it. I just wish it were easier.'

Ruby played with her necklace uncomfortably.

'Don't feel that you have to stop talking on my account.' Eddie reappeared, carrying a drink in each hand. 'Ruby, my dear. Would you care for one of these?'

'No thank you. I still have mine on the table inside.' She cast Mary a sympathetic smile and retired to the salon, leaving the two of them alone again.

'Did you like your gift?'

He was talking of the exquisite oyster silk dressing gown he had presented to her when they first reached the *Rowallan*,

394

embroidered with chrysanthemums in green and red and lilac on a silver background with thousands of tiny silken rows laid in by hand over many hundreds of hours. Mary had been reluctant to accept it, torn by his generosity, but was soon persuaded when he explained to her that it contained the magical Forbidden Stitch, sharing with her the tale of how he had smuggled it over the border and carried it all the way back from China, just for her.

'Yes. It really is quite beautiful. But you shouldn't have.'

She looked up into his face and knew what was on his mind. Heaven knows, he had shown the patience of a saint. The kiss he thought of placing on her mouth was shattered by the dinner gong.

'At last,' Mary said. 'I thought I was about to faint.'

The dining room, beyond the salon, was at once quaint and grand, with a polished oval table and a long sideboard complete with neatly arrayed glass and silverware. Dishes of dense, sticky-grained rice, fragrant with saffron, were brought to the table, illuminated by the enormous orange silk lamp that hung above their heads. Florence had asked for fish and lotus root, the men preferring the rich mutton curry that ran red with Kashmiri chillies.

'I'll bet the cook's not made any sweets,' Mary whispered. 'I heard him complaining to the cabin boy when I asked him. He was saying that he had quite enough to do without pandering to our whims. I think he assumed I couldn't understand.'

'We must visit the gardens of Shalimar while we are here,' Florence said.

'The ones at Nishat Bagh are even more impressive,' added Richard, flexing his superior knowledge of the region, his eyes wandering to Ruby's breasts. 'The marble arches and formal lawns are perfectly symmetrical. It really is quite something.

We should take a picnic and go tomorrow.'

Eddie watched Mary from across the table. He drained his wine glass for a second time, put it down heavily and openly declared himself to her.

'Mary? I must insist that you marry me. There's not a single person at this table who doesn't approve, and I think you've kept me waiting for long enough. I love you. You've always known that I love you. And I want to marry you.'

The room became still, silent like a painting, all eyes upon Mary as she sat, open-mouthed, staring back at him. In her embarrassment, she answered hastily, before considering his feelings.

'Don't be so silly, Eddie!' She looked around the table for support, but found only discomfort.

'I'm not being silly. It's a perfectly reasonable offer.'

At Richard's guffaw, everyone laughed good-naturedly, except Eddie.

'I told you three months ago, there's only so many times a man can stand to be turned down. You could certainly do a lot worse. I'm not a bad-looking chap, despite this awkward decoration.' He indicated vaguely the welt on his cheek. 'In fact, I think I would make a rather good catch.' He straightened himself and adjusted his jacket. 'I have excellent prospects, you know.'

'I know you do, Eddie.' Then, before she could stop herself, it was out. 'But I'm not in love with you.'

The table quietened, the nature of the man's passion so painfully laid bare in front of them all.

'So? There's a lot more to marriage than being besotted, you know. You could learn to love me over the years, and I promise I will take great care of you. You will want for nothing.'

'But what do I want for now? I have everything I could

possibly need and the freedom to do whatever I choose.' Eddie concentrated on his glass, his frustration turning it round and around. Mary did not care to dampen the mood of the evening on such a special night and softened her judgement. 'I'll tell you what, why don't you ask me again in another three months?'

'I don't think I want to wait that long.'

Richard raised his glass towards Eddie, a wry smile on his face. 'I told you she'd turn you down flat.'

Eddie permitted himself a heavy sigh and shook his head at Mary in weary defeat. Florence didn't know whether to laugh or cry. She would have given her eye teeth for such an offer and had been praying hard ever since they arrived that Mary would come to her senses and finally see what was standing so plainly right in front of her.

'You could always ask me instead,' she said shyly. Eddie looked at her in surprise and seemed cheered.

'Really? Why thank you, Florence. One can always count on you. I like that in a woman. It's a very fine quality. Very fine indeed.'

Mary lay awake in her bed, the shame of her insensitivity devouring her, pulling her this way and that as she tried to justify her actions, hopelessly denying her undoubted collusion in his misgivings. His plea, so impassioned, so impotent. Her rebuff, so callous, so unthinking. She bled inwardly for the wrongs she had done this good man. Florence had given her such a look as she readied herself for bed and had told her in no uncertain terms that she was a fool of the very worst kind. Mary pressed her hands to her chest, as though trying to reach in and drag out the part of her that could not belong, the part of her that would remain unworthy until the day she died. She would go to him tomorrow, explain herself in the hope that he could find some way to forgive her and preserve their friendship. It would never be anything else. She had nothing more to offer him.

In the dark of the night, a powerful shape moved stealthily along the open deck. Florence slept peacefully, her hair in neat plaits tied with rags, one arm slung out of the bed, the other curled protectively around her shoulder. Mary stared up at the wood-panelled ceiling, listening intently to the small telltale sounds. She slipped out of her bed and reached for the silk dressing gown, pulling the soft fabric closed and tying the belt around her middle before creeping to the door in her bare feet. Tiptoeing to the salon, its open panels now hung with rush matting like night curtains, Mary waited, silently alert, before reaching a tentative finger to pull the coir aside and peer out. A dark form passed momentarily across the trees, its shadow cast by the lamp-bright moon. She froze, but continued to watch, motionless. The big cat inspected the deck then took the steps up to the roof in two easy bounds, its sudden weight tilting the bulk of the houseboat into gentle undulation. Mary rushed to the two-room cook boat tethered to the stern, where the staff lay snoring, and pulled at the rope, reaching for the craft as it neared her. She picked up two large pans and turned back. Before she could take another step, Eddie appeared in front of her.

'I couldn't sleep for thinking about you,' he said, his breath strained. 'Don't you know that's the only reason I came here, to convince you to be my wife?' he implored her. 'Say yes, Mary. Don't even think about it. Just say yes.'

Forgetting herself, Mary brushed past him, concentrating only on the noise of the unmistakable intruder. 'Be quiet, Eddie!' She stopped and stood, stock-still, listening. His mis-understanding was instant, his arms suddenly around her as he leaned down to kiss her. Mary jerked her head away. 'What on earth do you think you're doing?'

Their awkward embrace was wrenched apart by Ruby's terrified screams.

Mary wrested herself from Eddie's arms and rushed to the salon, tearing back the coir screens and making an almighty noise, shouting at the top of her voice, banging the pans together. A loud, soft thud rocked the houseboat as the leopard took fright and dropped to the deck before leaping off and disappearing into the shadows. In a moment, everyone was up. Florence in her floor-to-neck nightdress, the cook with the cleaving knife from the kitchen, the cabin boy with sleepy eyes.

Ruby flew down the steps leading down from the two bedrooms on the upper deck, pulling her dressing gown about herself, sobbing with fright, hair thoroughly dishevelled.

'What in the name of God is going on?' Richard appeared behind her in a moment, his face glowing red with the perspiration of his recent efforts. Florence looked Ruby up and down critically.

'Well,' she said tightly. 'I can see that we needn't ask you the same question.'

'You should be thoroughly ashamed of yourself,' Florence said the next evening, refilling Mary's teacup.

'Oh, do give it a rest, Florence,' Mary sighed.

'Don't go on at her.' Ruby struggled to fasten her bulging case. 'Of course we all assumed that he would lick his wounds for a day then brighten up and forget the whole thing. It's not as though it's the first time she's turned him down.'

'So?' Florence barked. 'Does that give her the right to humiliate him and destroy his feelings in front of everyone?'

'It's not Mary's fault. Nobody expected him to duck out like that.'

Eddie had packed his bag and left the houseboat at first light, making his silent departure before anyone else had woken. It was only when he missed breakfast, then lunch, that Richard went looking for him and found his cabin empty. After assuaging Ruby's initial hysteria, convinced as she was that he had been taken by the leopard in the night, they had turned to the staff, who casually disclosed that the colonel had asked for a shikara to collect him at dawn, slipping away in the stillness, the boatman's paddle cutting silently through the water without disturbing a soul. It was mid-afternoon before Mary discovered the note that had been slipped under her door, the envelope inadvertently pushed partially beneath the rug. It had said that he could not bear to stay, but that he would fulfil his promise of safe escort and would wait for them to send word to him when they were ready to leave. He had then given the name of another houseboat, *Morning Glory*, moored across the lake on the opposite shore. Mary's heart had sunk, and she had hidden the note away, wishing that he had just gone back to Bombay and been done with it. It would be impossible for her to avoid her conscience now, knowing that he was little more than a stone's throw away. As the day wore on, her mood had slumped to such depths that she was unable to raise a smile for anyone, and moped around until her friends reluctantly agreed to cut the trip short. She couldn't face Eddie. She would write him a note and arrange to have it delivered in the morning a few hours after they left.

'I hope you're pleased with yourself,' Florence said, unleashing her frustration. 'This holiday has been an unmitigated disaster.'

Mary stood up, upsetting her teacup, and threw her hands into the air. 'That's enough!' she said. 'I'm sick and tired of your bickering at me! Just leave me alone!' She stamped out of the cabin, slamming the door behind her.

*

400

Mary stood forlornly on the deck and gathered her thoughts from the darkness. The storm lamps had been extinguished early, as nobody was in the mood to socialise that evening, and the lights would serve only to attract swarms of night insects to the houseboat. She pulled the shawl around her shoulders and shuddered against the chill.

There was barely a ripple on the water's surface. For a moment the clouds parted, the moon catching its reflection and holding itself in the lake's black surface amid a sea of floating stars, giving the impression of being suspended in space with no sense of the land.

'Not thinking of throwing yourself overboard, are you?' came Richard's hidden voice. Mary startled and turned to find him almost upon her, his shape barely visible in the darkness as the clouds shrouded the moon once more.

'Richard!' She grasped at her shawl in fright. 'How long have you been standing there?'

'About an hour before you came up. Trouble down below?'

The sudden flare of a match lit up the deck, Richard's face glowing orange as he put the flame to his cigarette and drew on it. Sucking the smoke deep into his lungs, he flipped the match over the side, the tip of it hitting the lake with a hiss. Darkness fell around them again, punctuated only by the burning end of his cigarette.

'Quite a show you gave us last night,' he said. Mary dropped her head and sighed, wishing that she had picked somewhere else to sit out the flak, tired of the constant persecution. The glowing orange dot moved closer. She could taste the cigarette smoke as it drifted into her face. 'Poor bastard. Not that I blame you, mind. No woman wants to find herself saddled with a cripple. What you need is a real man, who knows how to treat a woman.'

'I beg your pardon?' Mary gasped. 'Don't be so rude!'

'You should let me take you out some time,' Richard said coolly.

'I don't think so.' Mary felt a sudden uneasy sense of claustrophobia and tried to move away, stumbling around in the darkness. Richard gave out a little laugh and took hold of her elbow for a moment to steady her.

'Are you sure about that? Or are you just pretending to be coy, like your little friend downstairs?' He drew on his cigarette again. 'I've seen you twisting that miserable sap Spencer around your fingers whenever it suits you, leaving him hanging on a thread like the weakling he is. He's been quite a pushover for you, hasn't he?' Mary stared at his shadowy outline, dumbfounded. 'A stronger man wouldn't let you get away with it.' She felt his hand upon her shawl, pulling her towards him. 'I could teach you a thing or two about love.'

'Leave me alone!' Mary wrenched herself away, the shawl unravelling from her shoulders, but stopped short before she could tumble over the side.

'You girls are all the same,' Richard said sourly, stepping away from her just a fraction. 'Acting like butter wouldn't melt in your mouths.'

'Give me your matches!' Mary demanded, stranded in the dark, scarcely able to believe this sudden, grotesque behaviour.

'You don't know what you're missing,' he said, shaking the matchbox lightly, taunting her with it. 'Just ask that prissy sister of yours.'

'What?'

'Oh yes.' The tip of Richard's cigarette glowed as he dragged on it hard, momentarily illuminating his face, which Mary now saw had set into an ugly sneer. 'She gave it up all right, after a little friendly persuasion, just like I knew she would.' Mary caught her breath sharply, her insides turning to liquid, her mouth hanging agape. She felt as though a train had slammed into her. Her head began to spin, her legs trembled, and she cursed herself for her ignorance before realising with a terrible sense of foreboding the unspeakable danger that she had so unwittingly exposed herself and her friends to. And now there was no one here to protect them. Her stomach began to rise to her throat. She brought her hand to her mouth, swallowing hard.

'So she told you, did she?' Richard tipped his head back and released a cloud of smoke into the night air, mocking her with a small self-satisfied sigh. 'That Joseph Carlisle's a lucky, lucky man.'

'You!' Mary reeled away from him in horror, then began to shout. '*Koi hai! Koi hai!*' A sudden shaft of light from the far end of the houseboat cast a bright reflection across the surface of the lake. '*Koi hai!*' she shouted again. 'Bring a light to the deck! *Jaldi karo!*'

She gripped the railing, too shocked to do anything else while she waited for her rescue. The pool of light travelled along the gunwale, exposing the deck as the cabin boy scurried towards them, a storm lamp swaying in each hand, confusion on his face. She snatched one of the lamps from him and held it high above her head, swinging it from side to side, signalling to the distant flickering lanterns on the lake. 'Call for a boat-man!' she commanded the boy. In the next instant, Florence appeared, clutching the neck of her dressing gown.

'What in heavens?' She took one look at Mary's ashen face.

'Get our bags!' Mary shouted at her. 'Now!' Florence glanced at Richard's thunderous expression before turning and running for the stairs.

The shikara slipped noiselessly through the water, dispersing the stars floating in its soft wake, melting them away, leaving the *Rowallan* far behind and, on its deck, Richard.

Florence and Ruby exchanged apprehensive glances, holding hands beneath the blanket set across their laps, while Mary sat away from them, her own hands folded into her chest, her eyes fixed on the distant shore. Barely a word had passed between them other than Mary's frantic calls for them to hurry as they boarded the boat. She refused to say where they were going, telling the boatman to paddle hard, waiting until they were at a safe distance before asking him if he knew a houseboat called *Morning Glory* moored on the opposite bank. He had nodded his response, then, at her request, had extinguished the lanterns so their destination might not be traced by a curious eye.

'Mary?' Florence leaned forward, offering her a blanket. 'Put this around your shoulders. You'll freeze.' Mary looked at it absently. She had lost her shawl somewhere in the ruckus and sat shivering, even though she felt no cold. On Florence's insistence, she took the blanket and wrapped it about herself silently. It seemed that they had been on the lake for hours, stuck right out there in the middle of the water, the shore ever distant, refusing to be coaxed closer despite the boatman's rhythmic strokes. Her eyes became heavy, settling upon the far-off lights, her weariness almost too much to bear, seeping into her bones. She felt empty inside, and foolish beyond measure. She willed the boat to make speed, counting each slither of the heart-shaped paddle, breathing along with its steady movements.

After a thousand breaths or more, the boatman relit his lanterns and hung them up, then slipped his paddle deep into the water, sliding the shikara towards a row of houseboats moored closely together on the treeless bank.

'*Salaam, Morning Glory!*' he called softly. '*Salaam!*'

A stick-thin man quickly appeared on the small deck at the stern, holding a lantern aloft, rubbing his eyes before peering into the darkness. '*Salaam,*' he replied suspiciously, his face a picture of puzzlement as the shikara slowed, floating towards him, revealing its cargo. Without waiting to be invited, the boatman tied off and hauled the first of the bags on to the narrow landing platform. The thin man started to protest, demanding to know what the boatman thought he was doing, waving his hands in refusal, at which the boatman just shrugged his shoulders before unloading the next bag. The man shook his head in umbrage and scurried away through the salon.

'*Morning Glory*,' the boatman said to Mary, helping her out of the shikara. Mary felt her legs unsteady, her head giddy with the motion of the water, and held on tightly to the carved newel post. Ruby and Florence followed, Florence looking around nervously as Ruby paid the boatman.

'Mary?' she said. 'What are we doing here?' Before Mary could answer, light flooded the salon, confused voices coming towards them, bearing more lanterns.

'*Kiya aap mujhay bata saktay haiu kay*—' Eddie stopped the moment he saw them and stood, unmoving, in the salon's open doorway. 'Mary?' He stared at her in disbelief. For a moment he made to step towards her, then halted, as though unsure of himself, mistrustful of her. Mary tried to speak, but nothing came. Instead, her face contorted, a huge sob rising from her chest, releasing a deluge of tears as she folded in two. Eddie rushed forward and gathered her up in his arms. This time, she did not protest.

## 48

The blinds were drawn in Mr Johnson's room, diluting the worst of the afternoon heat, diffusing the searing light. He lay back in his bed, a sickly, colourless shape, his breathing irregular, ragged gulps, occasional low moans of discomfort. The cancer had spread quickly, creeping insidiously from one organ to another until it could no longer be denied. Everybody knew that it was now only a matter of time, and a respectful distance had opened up between the eerie quiet of Mr Johnson's room and the hustle-bustle of the hospital corridors. It was a small courtesy shown to a dying man, that he should be spared unnecessary disturbance and released from the rigours of the usual matronly routines of the day.

All Mary could do now was to keep him comfortable, to feed him when he wanted food, to keep him clean, and to sit with him kindly when he was lucid enough to need a little compassionate company, holding his hand while he spoke earnestly of his life, reading him snippets from the daily newspaper he could no longer see, although such occasions had become fewer and further between, before petering out altogether a few days ago. Mary had nursed him assiduously through his final weeks, biding her time as he faded from this life. Mr Johnson had become her primary patient, partially because nobody else felt inclined to do it, on account of his difficult reputation, but mainly because she had readily volunteered, which had cheered him up no end. As the cancer took hold, so the doctors gave up and lost interest, dropping by now and then just for the sake of appearances, their faces set with the same fixed, blank expression, designed to mask their impotence while writing him up for generous palliatives so that his pain might at least be kept at bay without further need for his nurse to refer to them.

Mary crept to Mr Johnson's side, threading the thermometer carefully into his pyjamas and under his armpit, and left it there while she examined his charts, although the papers blurred nonsensically, her determined mind unable to fix itself upon anything other than the terrible compulsion that had gripped her continuously for weeks, to the exclusion of all other thought. Her meticulous planning had finally come to fruition. Today was the day. And tomorrow, everything would change.

All her life, Mary had been uncertain, dithering at every turn, unable to make up her mind about anything of any importance. Not that it mattered to her. Every decision had been made for her anyway, one way or another. Her upbringing. Her schooling. Her profession. And she had followed those paths benignly, as though she had no say, tossed around like a leaf on the breeze, never landing to ground herself for more than a moment. Yet all that had altered in the blink of an eye a month ago, on the deck of a houseboat under a lamp-bright moon when a man she barely knew cut out her heart and threw it aside. It was as though a cold hand had reached through her flesh and torn out her very soul, leaving a barren wasteland in its place where nothing could exist except emptiness. This was what death must feel like, she had thought to herself.

When the night-times drew in, Mary's dreams would take hold, the same visions, over and over. Serafina, reading stories to her in a chilly, narrow bunk while she clutched at her hand for comfort. Serafina, luminous in the beauty of the love she had finally found. Serafina, bathed in blood, the image burning itself so indelibly that it would not leave her all day, pressing itself into her mind's eye like a grisly talisman. At first, Mary had felt powerless, as useless to her sister as she had always been, a superfluous, pointlessly conceived child who had served no purpose other than to burden another human being with her existence. She had done nothing for Serafina, except to unthinkingly cause her unnecessary anguish at every turn. Serafina was the one who had borne the brunt, the one who had had to deal with the unspeakable burden of responsibility with no one to turn to, not even in her darkest hour. Mary had torn herself to shreds after her encounter with Richard, weeping herself to sleep night after night, waking to a pallid reflection in the mirror, until her conscience had spoken to her in a voice so clear that it had taken her aback. With a sense of divine clarity, she had known then what she must do. Her sacrifice would be small compared to those her sister had suffered.

Mr Johnson moaned again, his sleeping face twisted with the tenacious pain. Mary checked his pulse, one eye on her fob watch, then removed the thermometer and noted down the vitals that nobody would read, going through the motions automatically, before bringing the enamel tray from the table and lifting the cloth aside. Using the small, serrated blade she kept in her pocket for that purpose, she filed the neck of the glass ampoule before snapping off the slender tip and drawing the full ten milligrams up into the syringe. Still sleeping, Mr Johnson wouldn't feel a thing, yet Mary was as gentle as she had always been, her touch tender and warm. In better days, Mr Johnson had once told her that the shots she administered to him were as light as a butterfly, and he was not the first of her patients to have said so. Carefully, she slid his pyjamas down, exposing the top of his rump, and gave him the injection before depositing the syringe back on the tray and sliding the second ampoule into her pocket. It was all she needed. She already had the other nine.

*

'Well, well,' Richard said, running his eyes down Mary's figure without inhibition. She was wearing the dress she had ordered specially from Mr Chagdar, a bold red flower-print design on a sky-blue background, cut daringly to reveal a glimpse of her modest cleavage and set wide on the shoulder, baring as much flesh as she could tolerate. She had felt self-conscious when she had tried it on in the tiny dressing room, and had forced herself to bear in mind that this was the kind of thing that Ruby would wear every day, given half an excuse.

Mary smiled at Richard and accepted the kiss he placed on the back of her hand before taking her seat and allowing him to order her a drink. Richard regarded her with a knowing smile.

'Had a little change of heart, have we?'

'I owe you an apology,' Mary said meekly. 'I acted like an idiot on the houseboat and ruined the holiday for everyone. Whatever must you think of me?'

'Women,' he laughed to himself, eyeing her up with interest.

'I know,' said Mary.

'Spencer's been like a dog with two tails since you went scurrying back to him. What did you say to the poor man?'

'You've seen him?' A small rush of anxiety shivered over her. Although Mary had alluded to some ungentlemanly conduct that night in Kashmir, she had kept the details of Richard's abomination to herself, begging Eddie to let it lie when he threatened to break the man's neck.

'No, but there are some very interesting rumours passing around the Wayside. I hear he's thrown in his job and is planning to move on. It's all very intriguing.'

'Oh.' Mary feigned ignorance.

'Want to know the funniest thing I heard? He actually thinks that you're in love with him!' Richard picked up his drink and tipped it towards her. 'I wonder what he would say if he knew

409

you were sitting here with me, playing him for a fool?'

'That is funny.' Mary smiled. 'But still, you didn't mention any of this to anyone, did you?' she added demurely, although she knew very well that his word counted for nothing. She had been as careful with Richard as she could be, refusing to leave messages, speaking to him directly on the telephone and pleading for his confidence. Although the risk was out of her control, she considered that he was unlikely to go boasting about a conquest as yet unmade, but she sought the reassurance anyway, if only to calm her agitation. 'Only I wouldn't want him to know that you and I were ...' She picked up her drink, clinking her glass gently against his. 'You know.'

'Mum's the word. It'll be our little secret.' Richard tapped his nose. 'And this place is about as out-of-the-way as you can get.'

'So I was thinking,' Mary said coyly. 'Perhaps we could have a few drinks here and then go somewhere private?'

'Oh yes?' He raised a lewd eyebrow at her. 'And why is that?'

'I've never been with a man before.' She raised her eyes to his, a flush of colour coming to her cheeks. 'And seeing as you so kindly offered to instruct me in the ways of love, I thought we might ...' She effected an embarrassed cough. Richard sat back in his chair, regarded his whisky thoughtfully and rattled the ice in his glass, enjoying Mary's blushes.

He leaned towards her, resting his hand on her leg.

'What say we leave these and go to my place right now? I've got drinks there.'

'No rush.' Mary sipped her gin and tonic, her hand wandering to the sheath of folded paper she had slipped into the tiny pocket Mr Chagdar had sewn specially into the side seam of her dress at her request, checking it was still there. 'I have all the time in the world. Do you have a cigarette?'

'Of course.' Richard took a slim gold case from his pocket, flipped it open and offered her one.

'Thank you.' Mary searched in her handbag, a frown of frustration settling on her face. 'Oh, blast.' She looked around. 'I've gone and dropped my cigarette holder somewhere. Perhaps it fell out in the car. Would you mind?'

Richard was already on his feet.

'Back in a jiffy,' he said, leaving her at the table alone.

Mary took the paper sheath from her pocket and opened it, tipping its contents into his drink.

Mary had often wondered what these houses might be like on the inside. She had seen them being built, passing the district as she did when they went for picnics on Malabar Hill. She and Ruby had even made a special detour one day to take a peek above the high walls, Ruby sighing her determination to find herself sitting pretty one day in a home not too dissimilar.

Running her hand along the shining surface of an expensive cherrywood dining table, Mary cast her eyes around the room, taking in the luxurious surroundings, marvelling at the way some people lived without conscience.

'Drink?' Richard said from the cabinet in the corner of the room.

'Gin, please,' said Mary. She watched him carefully, mindful of the time that had lapsed.

'Here you go.' He came to the table and pressed the cold glass into her hands.

'Shall we sit?' Mary wandered to the settee and arranged herself prettily at one end.

'If you like,' Richard said impassively, beginning to show his impatience, his smile all but gone as he came to join her. Then, as he sat, the drink slipped from his hand, the full glass exploding with a loud pop against the marble floor. 'Damn!' he said, then looked at it as though suddenly confused. He closed his eyes for a moment and took a deep breath. 'I ...' he said. 'I'm sorry. Just let me ...' He shook his head slightly, then put his hands to his temples, leaning his elbows to his knees. 'Too much whisky,' he mumbled.

'Are you feeling all right?' Mary asked softly, her voice gently lilting, hypnotic.

'Mmm?' He took a deep breath, looked up and tried to smile at her. 'Yes. Yes, I'm ...' A small giggle escaped from him. 'I think I'm drunk!' he said.

'There, there.' Mary moved along the settee and touched his hand. 'Lean back and close your eyes for a while. You'll feel fine in a minute.'

His eyes opened again and settled on her, his mouth curving into a smile. 'Come here,' he said, crooking an unsteady finger at her. Mary moved closer, steeling herself. Slowly, slowly she reached towards him, undoing the top buttons of his shirt, loosening it at the neck. His head fell back against the cushions and he murmured to himself, 'Hot in here.'

'Would you like me to open a window?'

'Mmm,' he mumbled.

Mary did not move. Instead, she stroked his chest, soothing him with hushed words of comfort. His eyes closed again, his mouth cocked into a smile. 'Take off your dress.' His speech became slurred, his breath thick.

'Yes,' Mary whispered, reaching slowly for her handbag, sliding her hand within, feeling for her sister's vengeance. His head moved slightly, one eye half opening.

'Kiss me.'

'Yes.' She smiled back at him.

Leaning gently to his face, Mary placed her soft, rosebud lips upon his, and pressed the needle into his thigh, waiting for his body to slacken.

## 49

'Is that everything?' Ruby asked quietly.

'Yes. I think so.' Mary arranged the last of her clothes in the trunk and brought the lid down, fastening the thick straps, her palms damp, heart pounding through her chest with every footstep she heard in the corridor. Florence watched mutely.

Mary had gone out alone that morning, as she often did, and they had thought nothing of it, assuming that she was merely running an unremarkable errand, to buy stamps or the suchlike. It was only when she returned with a posy in her hand and a pensive smile that she disclosed to them the quietly momentous event that had taken place an hour ago in a small chapel on the edge of Chaupati district, where she had stood beside Eddie as they exchanged their wedding vows. Shocked into silence, Ruby and Florence had been scarcely able to believe their ears, before accepting her apology for keeping them in the dark and helping her to gather up her things. Mary could not have borne for them to have been there. It had been hard enough as it was, to stand in the company of strangers and promise her life away, all the while thinking of the dead man she had left last night, wondering how long it would be before his body was discovered.

'But why go running off to England?' Florence sat heavily on Mary's bed, shaking her head. 'I've heard the stories. They treat foreigners like dirt. You'll just be another unwelcome immigrant. That's what they call us over there.'

Mary felt her stomach flip over and forced a smile. Although their passage had been booked two weeks ago, she had steadfastly refused to ponder the prospect of the unknown life that awaited her in that far-off place. All she knew was that she could not stay here, and that with every moment that passed, the danger grew.

'They say it rains all the time in England,' sighed Ruby.

'I am accustomed to the rain,' Mary said. 'It used to come down in buckets at home. You could barely hear yourself think for the hammering on the roof. The heavens would open and let out a great deluge that went on for ever.' She sat back on her haunches and sighed. 'We had hailstorms, too. They pelted the ground like golf balls once. Like this.' She lifted her arm and stretched her fingers into a wide roundel, then closed her eyes for a moment and conjured the feel of them melting in her hands. 'My father dashed out into the storm with a big black umbrella. He ran around and gathered them up for me. I wanted one, you see, to see what it was like, so out he went into that hammering downpour.' Mary stopped speaking and succumbed to a small shiver, as though it would do no good.

In all the time she had lived in Bombay, Mary had never once been down to the docks. Until now, they had been nothing more than a constant vague animation way off in the distance, viewed from the hanging gardens at Malabar Hill on a Sunday, ripening the air as she rummaged in the bazaars on Thursday afternoons. She had never considered just how big an ocean liner might be, but standing there on the quayside, new passport in hand, staring up at the gargantuan white steel structure, she felt a weakening surge of insignificance in the presence of the enormous ship towering above them.

Four wide gangplanks stretched upwards from the quay, busy with traffic, two designated for the passengers, the other

414

two bowing under the weight of the porters and their sack barrows laden with steamer trunks and parcels. To the stern of the vessel, a dozen or so crew shouted orders to each other, attending to the weighty bundles and boxes swaying overhead, craned in from the dockside, ropes swinging wildly as they pulled at each load, guiding it into the freight hatch.

'It's vast.' Mary gazed up in awe, steadying herself against Eddie's arm. 'I had no idea it would be so big.'

She stepped aside for a moment, allowing a pair of nurses to weave through with two wheelchairs, one carrying an old gentleman in a dark-blue quilted jacket, the other filled with oxygen cylinders and a tangle of dismantled apparatus. A smiling boy appeared at Mary's side and tried to press upon her a book of badly printed postcards, shouting, 'Souvenir! Souvenir! Ten rupees!' Mary took no notice of him and he soon gave up, rushing along to the next group.

'Tickets! Tickets!' A man in a peaked cap thronged his way through the sea of people, waving a handful of checked tickets in the air and searching the crowds, his experienced eye picking out the passengers from the bystanders. 'Tickets this way! This way!' Recognising Florence and Ruby's lost expressions, he addressed them directly with a flourish of his hand. 'Passengers only! Passengers only!'

'You had better go.' Ruby pulled her shawl closer around her shoulders and tried to smile, she and Florence loitering impotently, clinging to those final moments.

The ship's air horn gave out a mighty choral blast, one long, sonorous flare, then another, filling the docks with its deep resonance. Then Mary saw something she had never witnessed before. Florence started to cry. Tiny, soft shrugs that barely moved her at all, and rivers of tears. Mary shivered at the sight, her resolve deserting her as she realised what she had done, and what she was about to do. In that moment, it was unthinkable, and she couldn't for the life of her remember how she had come to be standing here, moments away from boarding a ship that would take her to the other side of the world. Her heart began to pound, a rush of fear swirling up to engulf her. She could shout out now, confess to her madness and say that she hadn't known what she was doing and she wanted to go home. Home. The word flew around her head like a panicked bird trapped in a tiny cage. Home. A place where she could finally belong without looking back. A place where a soul could settle and live a life without shame, finding its peace. The ship's horn called again.

'That's you,' said Ruby, her voice tight with the strain of the day. 'Now hurry up, because I don't think I can stand here like this for a moment longer.'

Mary's bag fell to the ground as she threw her arms around her.

'Ruby,' she murmured into the softness of her neck.

Ruby pulled away, wiped her eyes with the back of her hand, sniffing away the tears and adopting a brave smile for Eddie.

'You take good care of her,' she said to him.

'I will.' Eddie kissed them both, one last time, before turning tenderly to his wife. 'Ready, Mrs Spencer?' Mary nodded, pushing her sodden handkerchief into her sleeve.

She held on to her husband's arm tightly as they walked up the gangplank, leaning on him for support. Making their way to their allocated deck, pressing through the excitable huddles, colourful paper streamers flew by, thrown by the first-class passengers on the highest decks, fluttering downwards in cheerful spirals while the band on the quayside played its farewell.

Finding a tight space against the railings, Mary looked down on the dock, searching the crowds on the quayside, desperate to catch one last glimpse of her friends. She scanned the diminutive figures for Ruby's distinctive shawl, bright red, chosen specially for the occasion. Only it seemed that everyone had done the same thing, and a thousand splashes of scarlet fluttered in the sea breeze. A fleet of tugs began to haul the mighty vessel from its moorings, its gargantuan bulk sliding slowly from the dock, huge whirlpools rushing into the gaping chasm that opened up so quickly between it and the cumbersome shore.

'I love you,' Eddie whispered to her.

'I know,' she said.

'Everything's going to be all right.' He tucked her hand firmly into his arm. 'I promise.'

Mary looked up at him, and felt as though her heart would break. She breathed deeply, closing her eyes and snatching what last remnants she could of the thick, scented air, her spirit reaching out and stretching away from her, clinging to India's burning soil. She leaned her head on his shoulder and, like a passing cloud, they floated away with the tide, gliding towards the swelling sun as the ship moved towards the horizon, the smoke from its funnels threading a silver-grey ribbon in the sky.

# *Epilogue*

*England, 2006*

Serafina's daughter searched her dog-eared address book, picked up the telephone and dialled the number of her only aunt two hundred miles away, tucked in a tiny white cottage called The Limit.

'If you want to see her, come now,' she said.

Mary held strong for her sister's child, fighting the stone suddenly lodged in her throat. 'Is she very bad?'

Caitlin, unable to answer, clutched the telephone. There were no words to describe the shadow of life that remained. Mary's heart began to bleed.

'Hush, now,' she sang softly. 'Try not to upset yourself. You have to preserve your strength. You will need it.'

'She's going to die and I don't even know her.' Caitlin's voice crackled.

Outside the cottage window, the morning sleet had turned to snow, floating lightly downwards, coming to rest amid the nodding daffodils. Mary pulled her shawl about her shoulders, lifting its frayed edge to mop her face, her thoughts hauled relentlessly towards her sister's plight and the damage she had done. People mistook her fearful silence for elegance. Her coolness for decorum. If only she had told her family, freed herself from the no-man's-land where nothing belonged. Mary felt herself shredded, her loyalties scattered to the four winds as she listened to her niece's jagged breaths.

'The decisions we make.' Mary tutted softly. 'Sometimes so young. Too young to understand anything at all. That is one of life's great lessons, Caitlin, that we should learn by our mistakes, even though by the time we are old enough to realise them, it's often too late to do anything about it.' She sighed to herself. 'The things that frighten us most lose something of their terrible lustre as the years pass by.' She stood from her old, worn armchair and went to the window, pulling back the lace curtain, watching the snow cascading in slow circles. She ached for Serafina's child, and she thought of that solemn promise: *Not for as long as we both shall live.*

Caitlin's tears ran dry. 'There's nothing of her. I'm so sorry, Aunty.'

Mary had to end the call quickly, before she broke into a thousand pieces. She pictured her beloved sister, the spent slip that lay waiting for death's release, and could hold back the tidal wave no longer.

'I'll call you soon,' she managed, then hung up.

Taking a deep breath against the stale, imprisoned air, Mary followed the auxiliary, recognising the surly countenances of the occasional nurses who had long since desensitised themselves to the grim conveyor of this forgotten place for bygone people. Halfway along the bleak corridor, the auxiliary left Mary at an open door, motioning her loosely towards the bed, before taking her leave without expression. Nobody smiles in death's waiting room.

Mary entered the flowerless room and pulled a grey plastic chair up next to the bed. Seating herself quietly, she leaned in close to her sister, watching her faded, vacant eyes, searching for some glimmer of recognition amid the merciless disease that had taken her mind apart, piece by piece. Mary had sometimes wondered if this terrible illness had not been a small mercy sent by the gods, that her sister should be stripped of the memories that had tormented her so, that she might live out her final years in peace.

Mary had seen little of her since leaving India. Serafina had stayed on in Chittagong for many years, living the high life well beyond Joseph's planned career. Such was his value that irresistible offers had been laid at his feet as his hair greyed, enticing him to postpone his retirement for one more year, then another. They had finally said their goodbyes amid a splendid send-off before boarding the Boeing to begin a new life in a house set beside the River Thames in Oxfordshire. Compared to the grand perquisite residence in Chittagong, with its dozen servants and endless social engagements, the Henley house was undeniably modest in size, and ghostly quiet. Serafina had borne her immediate loss of status tolerably, busying herself with a headful of plans for a long and peaceful descent into old age with her husband, only to discover that his health would not support him for much longer. Joseph ailed within months of their arrival, his once handsome frame shrinking to nothing while she watched on helplessly. He was laid to rest before the dawn of his sixty-third birthday. And when he died, it was as though something inside her died too. Then the Alzheimer's took hold.

'Serafina, do you remember the river?' Mary whispered. 'The rustle of the high grass around our legs? The chattering houseboys, sent ahead to search for snakes? The coolness of the water when we dangled our feet from the bank?'

Serafina stared blankly into space. Mary extended her hand, her once fine fingers now deeply wrinkled, joints twisted with arthritis. Desperate not to let her sister down with an outward rush of grief, her eyes ached with the effort of stifling the tears that burned behind them, her face blushing vermilion beneath her soft brown skin.

'Do you remember the fresh concrete that was laid down once at our mother's house? Something was being built next to the cowshed. Papa's coolies went away for the afternoon and we were told that we mustn't go anywhere near it until it was completely dry. Do you remember?' Mary urged her. 'We waited until they were gone then stuck our palms in it, right up to our wrists, and when we stood up, there were two perfect imprints.' She took up Serafina's limp hand. 'So you see, my darling, we have left our mark there.'

Mary stroked her sister's unkempt hair, thin and white, like a ghostly halo circling her unrecognisable head.


Serafina died at ten minutes past five on the morning of Thursday the twenty-third of March in a small nursing home in Sussex, with nobody at her side. When the end came, it came quietly, like the turning of a page.

Mary sat with her grief, cross-legged on the carpet before her old packing trunk. Wiping the dust from its surface, she opened the lid on what remained of her keepsakes. There on top, tied with a white ribbon, were the few letters from distant friends that had survived her many moves. Among them, held separately by a loose, half-perished rubber band, was the brief, intermittent correspondence she had received from Dorothy over the years, the once confident hand having become increasingly shaky before being replaced entirely by the neat, rounded lettering of the secretary at the nursing trust in Marondera where she had spent her remaining months, driving the staff around the bend with her determined efforts at independence, refusing to have a maid by her side despite being well over ninety and rather absent-minded.

Mary forgot her task for a while, permitting herself the indulgence of looking at a life from long ago.

Sifting deeper, she began searching for the two journals she had kept up as a younger woman, and the envelope of old photographs and onion-skin aerogrammes she knew to be tucked between them somewhere. Finding the envelope concealed beneath a blue sari of Benares silk, she tipped out the contents. Among the papers lay a faded black and white picture of a group of student nurses, barely out of their teens, beaming at the Box Brownie camera, arms slung carelessly around each other's shoulders. She and Serafina were barely recognisable, faces still carrying remnants of childhood, their attempts at modern hairstyles protruding stiffly from beneath their uniform white veils. Mary touched the picture tenderly before putting it with the others and setting them aside.

Retiring to her room, she sat at her dressing table and began to write a letter, starting at the beginning when the world was a different place, and ending in the small hours of the morning when she had nothing more to say. She placed the letter in an old stationery box with the photographs and journals, and wrote her niece's name on the outside.

The cold, persistent drizzle of the early English summer seemed fitting for such a tiny cloud of mourners. Mary walked solemnly alongside her niece, a nurse like her mother before her. They came to rest at a lone bench beneath an ancient yew and sat together beneath its spreading branches. Caitlin, face spent with grief, struggled to speak, interrupted by the deep, involuntary sobs that rose from her chest.

'As I grow older, I feel such a yearning to know who my mother was. She said that her life was none of anyone else's business. I was never to speak to you about it. She said that we had no right to delve into the past. And now she's gone.'

'You poor child.' Mary reached up and stroked Caitlin's hair. 'Always be proud of who you are. Proud of where you came from. Without that, what do you have?'

'Will you tell me about her?'

Mary didn't reply, but instead dropped her soft leather hand-bag from her shoulder, unzipped it on her lap and rummaged for a while before taking out an old handkerchief, wound protectively around something small. She handled it carefully, cupping it lovingly in her palms for a moment, then passed it to Caitlin.

'Open it,' she said. Caitlin unfurled the tiny bundle, reveal-ing a carved wooden elephant, trunk pointing upwards for luck, its back darkened with the waxy patina of a thousand caresses from Mary's fingers over many, many years. Mary pressed Caitlin's hands around it closely. 'This,' she whispered. 'This little elephant was made for me by our father's manservant. His name was Shiva.' Caitlin lifted it to her nose, the faint scent of sandalwood anointing her hands. 'Come,' said Mary, indicat-ing with a small movement of her frail arm that she wished to stand. 'Let us go and say goodbye to your mother. Then I will tell you all about him.'

Mary watched as her beloved sister was laid to rest on this verdant hillside so far away from home. A lone crow swooped down, its melancholy caw piercing the sky, and landed beside the freshly dug grave. Mary closed her eyes in silent prayer and was transported to a life that once was. The hills that rise beneath the mountain mists. The elephants that weep above the emerald terraces. The silver bells that graced her mother's footsteps. And the world continued to turn.

# The Secret Children

## Reading Group Notes

# The Story Behind *The Secret Children*

EVERYONE wants to know who they are, but for me the question was never simple. My mother, Mary, was born in India in 1928. I was born in London in 1964, when mixed marriages were still a rarity. My father was orphaned so I could only turn my mother for answers. I used to ask about where she was born, to which she would say Assam, but nothing else. I knew I had a grandfather who lived on a farm in Africa and I had seen one lone photograph of him in an Indian army officer's uniform. She never mentioned anything about her mother, *ever*, and I knew not to ask.

Occasionally I was allowed to look through her old photo album and my mother told me a little of the people and places in them – Bangalore, Kashmir, the Himalayas. There was a picture of my Aunty Joan (who now lived on an estate in White City) on the beach in Bombay, wearing a starlet's bathing costume. In the photograph, she was utterly beautiful, as was my mother and my mother's sister (my only *real* aunty, although we rarely saw her). I didn't understand how these beautiful young women could have come from those achingly scenic landscapes to the grey skies of Britain. My questions drove my mother half mad. I had no idea at that point that she and her sister were the illegitimate daughters of a British tea planter to his Indian concubine. The shame

*My mother (lying down in the bathing suit), and friends (also 'secret children' nursing students). Just off Bombay beach, circa 1953, picnicking.*

of it had followed her like a shadow. Even now, in her eighties, she is not completely comfortable either here or in India, knowing that she belongs to neither place entirely.

It has been like a compulsion, to write *The Secret Children*, to give those fragments of memory a complete story of their own. There came a point when I knew I would have to tell my mother what I was writing. At first, she wasn't happy about it. But then she began to talk, unburdening herself of every memory, good or bad. Together, we pored over maps, trawled through old keepsakes and trudged around India. She told me things that she had never told to anyone else. All my aunties are now dead, my

*My mother trekking in the Himalayas, around 1958.*

Rowallan, *the houseboat in Kashmir.*

mother the only survivor. Nobody talked about these things. They still don't.

I have finally come to know who my mother is and why things had to be the way they were. We don't fight any more. Instead, we talk for hours. Any sense of shame has long since fallen away. She has learned to be proud of who she is and where she came from. *The Secret Children* was written with her blessing, and is dedicated to her with my love.

Alison McQueen, 2012

*My mother in a shikara.*

*My mother taking a tea break, KEM Hospital, Bombay, 1949.*

# For Discussion

- 'A girl could not remain so for ever. Once she had crossed that divide into motherhood, she could never return to her former self, and no man would ever look at her again with the same eyes.' Do you agree with Shurika, or is this view solely a product of time and place?

- 'Nothing is what it used to be. And I have a feeling that this is just the beginning.' How has the author set about capturing the sense of impending change in *The Secret Children*?

- 'You mustn't dwell on the past, Mary. It will do you no good, no good at all.' Is Sister Margaret right?

- 'Any onlooker would have thought that Mary's arrival was nothing but an irritation and that Serafina might have preferred to sever all connections with her. But Mary knew better.' How would you characterise the relationship between the sisters?

- 'I'm not going to suffer for the rest of my life as a punishment for a crime I never committed.' What does this say about Serafina?

- 'That was the way of gradual changes. They crept along like silent shadows and before you knew it, everything had altered, and nobody seemed to realise.' How does this chime with your experience?

- How does the author illustrate the differences between India and Africa?

- 'Men want gratification. Women want security.' Do you agree with Serafina?

- 'Life is unfair.' Is this always Serafina's starting point? Was that always the case? And if Mary is different, why is she?

- How has the author dealt with the themes of shame and guilt?

- 'We should learn from our mistakes.' Do the characters in *The Secret Children* learn from theirs?

- 'The things that frighten us most lose something of their terrible lustre as the years pass by.' Is that your experience?

- 'Always be proud of who you are. Proud of where you came from. Without that, what do you have?' Is this is the strongest message of the novel?

# In Conversation with Alison McQueen

*How did your convent education influence your depiction of St Agnes's?*

I have clear memories of what it was like to be educated in a convent environment. The nuns were a very mixed batch of women, dedicated to their calling, some of them kind and friendly, others not so much. They chose to live a life removed from the outside world, and stuck rigidly to the old-fashioned ways passed down through the order. Routine and discipline shaped everything, and anything to do with 'becoming a woman' simply did not exist.

●

*How important do you think historical accuracy is to a novel set in the past?*

*The Secret Children* is set against a vast backdrop – the closing scenes of what came to be known as the British Raj, the advent of World War II, and the partition of the new independent India. Historical accuracy was essential to give the story its sense of time and place. These events changed the whole landscape of the British Empire, and sealed the sub-continent's fate as a nation divided.

*How did you physically write* The Secret Children *and why?*

I wrote the opening dedication on my mother's seventieth birthday, fourteen years ago. That sole paragraph sat in a notebook for seven years before I felt ready to begin writing the story. I was totally unprepared for the emotional impact it would have on me, creating the grandparents I never knew, writing of lives and places I could only imagine, trying to piece it all together. It was an exhausting process, but it taught me a great deal.

*Which character in the novel are you most like?*

I'm not sure that I am particularly like any of the characters in the novel, as much as I would like to be. I admire Dorothy greatly, and I envy Mary the kind purity of her nature which remains to this day. If pushed on that question, I think I would say that I am most like Shiva, watching quietly from corners without saying much.

*Dorothy.*

*Have you always written?*

Yes. I kept a dossier on one of my teachers when I was in primary school. She drank sherry behind the book cupboard, and she wore *Je Reviens* by Worth, a grotesquely pungent perfume, no doubt to cover the smell. My mother kept the dossier, a red Silverline exercise book, so I expect it is still around somewhere.

•

*What authors do you admire and why?*

Oscar Wilde, Stephen King, Daphne du Maurier, Annie Proulx . . . my list of favourite writers is endless, and they all have one thing in common – great storytelling, and the ability to move me.

•

*Are big secrets always a bad thing?*

That's an interesting question, and the only answer I can think of is yes, and no. It depends on who you ask, and what the secret is.

•

*Silence or music while you write? If music – who do you listen to?*

Absolute silence when I write. I can't bear any sort of noise or intrusion, so it was particularly bad news when the next door neighbour decided to get the builders in for four years. There is also a man nearby who likes to get his chainsaw out whenever the sun is shining.

●

*What's your most treasured possession?*

Aside from my daughters? I'm not particularly interested in possessions. Things have a habit of tying you down and cluttering your life. I am looking forward to the day when everything I want or need fits neatly into a bag that I can sling over my shoulder and clamber onto an Indian train with. In it will be the small carved wooden elephant my mother gave to me, alongside a toothbrush and some simple cotton clothes, and a notepad of course.

●

*Do you think that the strong threads of reality in* The Secret Children *give it more truth as a novel?*

Truth is everything in writing. It has to come from a place that gives something of yourself, or what's the point? There must have been thousands of children born under similar circumstances during an era when such things were considered beyond the pale. Yet where was their voice? I was privileged enough to know some of these secret children, and it was my honour to write a story for them.

●

*What single thing about you would surprise us the most?*

I am horribly accident-prone.

•

*What's your most vivid memory?*

All my memories are vivid. Perhaps it is a trait that many writers share, the storing of pin-sharp details, no matter how small. I have a tendency to remember feelings in particular – fear, joy, grief – and I try to hold on to those memories in the belief that they will serve me well, both in life and as a writer.

*My mother telling me off while on a visit to London Zoo. 1968.*

*My father.*

# Suggested Further Reading

*The Kashmir Shawl*
by Rosie Thomas

•

*The Vanishing Act of Esme Lennox*
by Maggie O'Farrell

•

*Jubilee*
by Shelley Harris

•

*The Glass Palace*
by Amitav Ghosh

•

*The Far Pavilions*
by Mary Margaret Kaye

•

*Tiger Hills*
by Sarita Mandanna